The World of Ancients

Into the Mythical Realm

LAKSHMANAVARADHAN_VICKY

INDIA • SINGAPORE • MALAYSIA

ISBN 979-8-88805-423-9

Contents

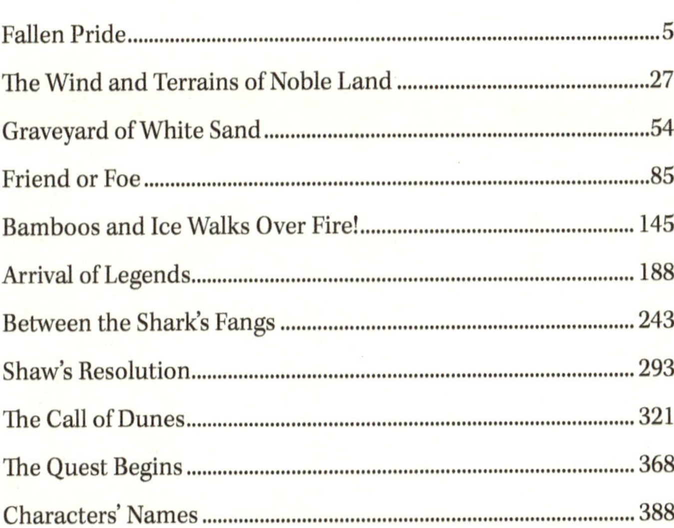

Fallen Pride....................5
The Wind and Terrains of Noble Land....................27
Graveyard of White Sand....................54
Friend or Foe....................85
Bamboos and Ice Walks Over Fire!....................145
Arrival of Legends....................188
Between the Shark's Fangs....................243
Shaw's Resolution....................293
The Call of Dunes....................321
The Quest Begins....................368
Characters' Names....................388

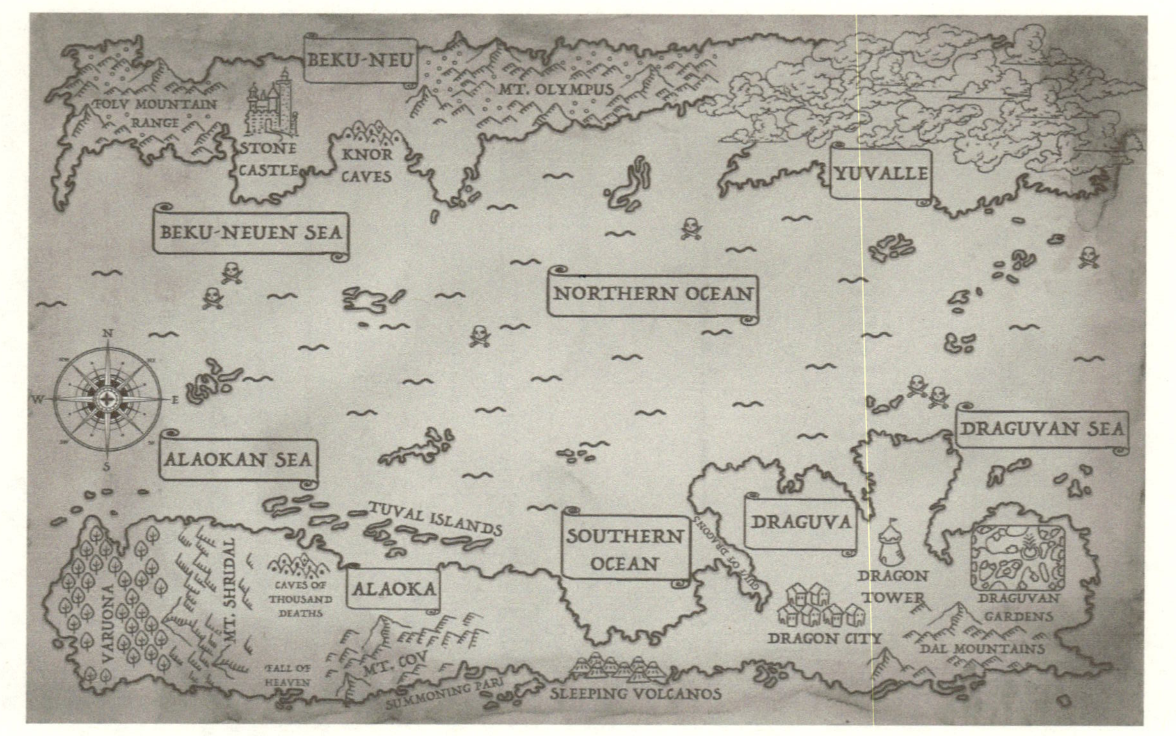
BEKU-NEU
FOLV MOUNTAIN RANGE
STONE CASTLE
KNOR CAVES
MT. OLYMPUS
YUVALLE
BEKU-NEUEN SEA
NORTHERN OCEAN
N
W
E
S
ALAOKAN SEA
DRAGUVAN SEA
TUVAL ISLANDS
SOUTHERN OCEAN
GULF OF DRAGONS
DRAGUVA
DRAGON TOWER
VARUONA
MT. SHRIDAL
CAVES OF THOUSAND DEATHS
ALAOKA
DRAGUVAN GARDENS
DRAGON CITY
DAL MOUNTAINS
FALL OF HEAVEN
MT. COV
SUMMONING PARI
SLEEPING VOLCANOS

Chapter 1

Fallen Pride

The early sun started to shower its yellow light over the horizon. Golden rays glorified the ocean and dolphins visited the surface to feel the energy. Dolphin pods start their morning routines by dancing through the waves. To welcome the sun, the big mammals of the sea arrived at the sun party with spouts. The mist created by their blowholes got the fragrance of the yellow light; it was a feast to the vision and the lazy break of the seagull was pleasant to the ears. The first light brightened the ocean and started to explore the coastlines of Alaoka. The coastlines of Alaoka made the sun close its eyes. Wrecked ships and the fallen corpses of the Alaokans spread all over the coast. Naval troops of Alaoka under commander Tibor took severe damage in last night's battle; it was hard to beat the shark in the ocean, but fallen black sails and fleeing leaderless black vessels conveyed that commander Tibor and his comrades smashed away the pirates out of their coastlines. The deadly pirates crashed most of the fleets in the Alaokan army. Tibor has a routine of welcoming the sun with the wish of "having a pleasant day," 30 years of Tibor's routine made the red giant search for him. The yellow light started wiping the shadows of the night with agility. Red blood changed the color of the Alaokan beach. Buzzing flies rounded the corpses and the odor of blood cursed the Alaoka. Finally, the sun found the commander's lifeless corpse with 12 deadly cuts. For sure, it's another bad day for the sun and a bad day has just begun. Dark clouds hug the sun to comfort him. Still, yellow light escapes the clouds. Like Tibor, the sun has another friend named Zaka, and he decided to check for him.

All the island villages of Alaokans were burning on fire. The cries of the wounded, the smoky odor and the souls of the fallen flooded the cluster islands of Alaoka. The sound of clashing swords from the small island rang in the ears. A tall young man with messy hair was jarring his sword against the beefy pirate. The fat pirate was bridging all the attacks with his heavy club, but the agility and strong reflexes of the young man didn't allow time for the pirate to charge his weapon against him. At one point, the beefy pirate parried the attack and delivered an unexpected kick on the chest of the young man. The powerful kick of the beefy pirate pushed him to a decent distance, but he managed to land on his knees and the grip of his sword wasn't lost.

"*Akello, are you okay?*"

Phase scratched the ears of the young brat. His coal-black eyes rolled to check the surroundings. The huts burning in the east released dark smoke. In the west, he noticed his comrade and friend Figo charging his spear against two eagles flocking wings above him. The eagles were friendly beasts of the pirate, and they were good war machines for them. An experienced beefy pirate was laughing at brats, and his three pirate comrades were entertained by the kick. Figo and Akello were just 18 and rookies of the Alaokan army. Both were self-signed into the mission of exterminating the pirates. Challenging the skilled pirates was like handling the falling rocks but rookies ran out of options. All experienced heroes of the village got their tickets to the afterlife on the edges of the swords and spears of black troops. So, young brats decided to put their life on the line to save the leftovers. After the fall of the pirate leader, black flag troops decided to retreat from Alaoka, but the 10 experienced captains and his men decided to play as a decoy, to buy some time for ships to flee. In the tradition of pirates, if the situation is odd, elder captains volunteer to sacrifice their heads to save the ships. For pirates, their ships are more precious than the headcount of the crew. These four pirates were leftovers from one squad.

Akello replied to Figo with an attitude smile, "*Stay on your guard! Eagles are aiming for your eyes. I can handle the beefy beast.*" Figo knew very well that they were in need of backup. Words of Akello increased the rage of the beefy pirate. With an angry face and gritted teeth, he stomped on the floor and shouted, "*Rat, you will be finished today!*" The powerful stomp of fatso pirate raised the dust above ground level. He charged at Akello with his three-foot-long club. Akello's hand was equipped with a long sword, and he also unsealed the dagger from a sheath. With two sharp weapons, he is ready for the hunt. Akello's agility has an advantage over the beefy pirate. He put all his trust on his knees and rushed toward the pirate. He evaded the club attack with his speed. Swinging heavily, the club missed the target and reached the ground every single time. Akello waited for the moment when the pirate bent down to lift up his heavy club. In a flash of a second, Akello rounded beefy beef and jumped on his back and thrust his dagger. Blood was rushing out; the dagger punctured the gullet of the beefy man. The next moment, Akello rolled down on his shoulder and moved a few meters away from him. In the meantime, Figo strapped the two eagles with his sharp spear and threw one of them at the feet of the black-teeth pirates. The final scream of the pet eagles and the blood shower of a beefy pirate converted the laughter of other pirates into an angry roar. Their red eyes marked our young heroes. Courage and bloodlust in the beefy pirate did not eliminate him easily. When other black troops decided to run back, these volunteers knew very well that today at some point in time, they have to feel the pain of death. Moreover, they were never afraid of death.

Fatso erected his overweight body with his mouth leaking red, and his eyes were angry. When he pulled out the eagle pommel dagger of Akello from the side of the neck, blood splashed out. The beefy pirate put all his last energy into the dagger and aimed it at Akello. The reflex of Figo released the spear to stop the breath of the beefy pirate. As he targeted, a sharp spear pierced the cold heart and escaped out through the back, but the moment before his death, the pirate released the dagger at Akello. Figo thought, *"He was late!"*

Luck favored the messy-haired brat. The beefy pirate's target was missed. With the loud scream, he collapsed down, which created a vibration underneath.

With speed, Akello and Figo reunited near the corpse of the fallen pirate while Figo pulled his spear from the corpse. The remaining pirates surrounded them. It was three vs two. Akello and Figo guarded each other back, and they prepared for their glory. It was an unlucky day. Brats' debut war was against the strong-willed pirates. Figo knows very well that they have no chance of standing against them. Two brats are not even a match for these exceptional pirates. All of a sudden, from the west, the wild scream of the eagle, "*Krrrr...*" disturbed the pirate's ears. For a moment, everyone's eyes were focused on the sky. It's a griffin.

After seeing it, a smile and hope developed on the faces of Akello and Figo. In the lightning seconds, Black griffin's claws punctured the chest of a pirate and stood confidently between the brats and pirates. A savior has arrived. An angry scream of a griffin on pirates created an impact. It temporarily disabled the hearing ability. The name of the fine black griffin was Rudo, and Figo was its rider. Griffin is a magnificent beast with the head of an eagle and the body of a lion with a pair of wide wings that help to glide in the sky. The forelegs of the hybrid beast inherited the claws of an eagle. Hind legs and a muscular body hold the strength of the jungle king. Alaokan shares a special bond with griffins. Griffins owe their loyalty to a single master, until the very end. Another surprise from the west stunned the pirates; it was an unexpected airstrike. Riders on the griffin's back triggered the arrows at the pirates. Arrows drilled the life of the black troopers and drained their souls to the underworld.

Backup has arrived. Three griffins and five human companions came to save their ally, but only two of them were in good shape. The rest of them swooned. Two black griffins and one olive-green griffin lowered their wings to touch the ground. Their claws and paws made their way toward the duo's team. On the back of the black griffin, there was a girl with an apple face bent her butter hands to put back the arrows into the quiver. She is neither milk nor chocolate, her skin tone was the color of a newborn leaf, her silky ponytail even made the pony feel jealous and her friends call her "*Amara*." Akello was happy to see his friends! After a deep breath, Figo was loud, "*I appreciate it! At least, today, you guys were on time!*" and walked to check his griffin. Amara's green lens adjusted her vision to Akello. After finding Akello in good shape, she wanted to hug him tight and stick to him like glue, but she couldn't do it. Amara's feelings for Akello made her shed tears. Akello's welfare is enough for her. His wellness relaxed Amara's uneasy mind. Akello has the same happiness to see her, but the tough guy was poor at expressing himself. He nods his head at her and runs to treat his swooned comrades. Figo concealed the sadness on his face and removed the blood strain from Rudo's beak. While Akello was checking on his swooned friend Kino, an olive-green griffin gently rubbed his head on his rider's shoulders. Akello gave a hug to his beast and applauded, "*Well done, Neo.*" The eyes of his beast were unique from the pack. When other griffins have green and blue eyes, Neo has bright yellow eyes and a radiant nature. Neo's angry eyes have the power to loosen the bladders of foes.

A coup of Varuonans against Alaoka caused terrible damage and too many heads were slaughtered down and bloodstains fixed on the soil. The alliance of Varuonans with nasty pirates set the attire of graveyards on Alaokan grounds. With a broken tone, Amara opened, "*Killers of the sea (pirates) fled, but Varuonans are not backed off! When Alaokans were helpless against Varuonans' cavalry, then Akello's Neo showed up with a wild scream, 'Krr...' and the rage in his eyes made the mustangs and mares withdraw from the battlefield, but they are not done yet. With long howls and whinings, their beasts entered and started to hunt us like mad dogs. Their fangs tore the wings of griffins. The arrows of bull-eyed Varuonans burst into the lung tanks and hearts of Alaokans. With all strength, we faced the Varuonans in the Tuval Islands. Kino and his beast gifted the dead as a price for more than dozens and made them regret trespassing on the lands of Alaoka. But...*"

Amara's other companion, Zina, shouted, "*Enough Amara!*" and continued with hesitation, "*Akello! Figo! We ran out of numbers and we couldn't hold on much longer! To save Kino, without choice, we slipped away from Tuval island and Kino's griffin attained its glory! If we treat the wounds of Kino in time, we can save his dangling life."*

After hearing her, Akello's face was struck by lightning and questioned, "*You guys abandoned the battleground when you were most needed?*" Figo was speechless by their actions, but he has not lost his mind. In the moment of unexplained silence, the scream of falling Hibo broke the serenity, and the pain in her scream touched the hearts of the young griffin riders. Their eyes were fixed on the sky. Zina cried out, "*It is chief Ekon!*" Ekon, the commander-in-chief of the griffin unit, and his griffin Hibo are crashing toward the ground. She was trying to flap her wings up but still, it was hard for her to maintain the altitude; they both crashed down in the nearby woods. In a panicked tone, Figo commanded Zina and Amara to take Kino to the medical care and asked Akello to accompany him.

Amara's heart froze in fear of losing Akello; she gritted her teeth and tried to maintain calm. She is brave but love is a feeling where the unafraid are fragile. She wants to hold his arms tight and say please, "*Don't leave me.*" Rudo spreads his wings and starts to glide in the sky, and on Neo's back, Akello prepares to mount. Akello's coal-black lens locked at Amara's green eyeballs, she knew that Akello sent Neo to protect her. Akello's love is wild and deep. Behind his eyeballs, he pictured his hands around her waist and he was inhaling her fragrance to cure rushing blood pressure. While hugging her tight, he gently planted a kiss on her forehead, but in his physical existence, he vocalized, "*I will be back soon.*" Amara nods her head with a fake smile that reaches her dimples. She knows Akello more than anyone; his combat moves are agile and he speaks what strikes his mind. He is fearless and handsome; he never regrets his actions. For many, he is rude, but according to her, he has a brave heart. She also knows one more thing: when he comes back, he won't be the same. In the flash of an eyelid, Akello was following Figo in the wide sky. Amara's eyes dwelled in tears.

Neo and Rudo found the crash site of Hibo in the woods. Figo and Akello ran to help Ekon. Both Hibo and Ekon were badly injured with heavy bleeding. Wounds are bite marks of large canine families. Ekon gained consciousness to recognize the faces, and he was the mentor of Akello and Figo. Figo tightened the wounds to stop the bleeding, but Ekon's wounds were deep. In heavy pain, Ekon said, "*I and my best warriors stood against Kayon and his hyenas' army and we defeated them. Kayon is the next leader of Varuonans and the successor of Zaka. After the execution of the pirate leader in the west by Gamba (chief of Alaokan ground units) and company, we griffin riders were surrounded by Varuonans and their scavengers in the center of the eastern market. Kayon's master plan is to occupy griffin riders in the east so that ground units will never get the support of griffins on the mainland battlefield. We are forced to accept the fight against Varuonans in order to save the civilians on the eastern islands.*" Ekon confessed that he underestimated Kayon. Kayon became the Alpha of Hyenas and took away the lives of countless griffins and their riders, but in the end, he and his company managed to kill Kayon and his scavengers.

Ekon strongly doubted that another army of hyenas was hidden in the savanna of Varuonans. By now, the leaders of Alaoka and Gamba were heading toward the main lands of Varuonans, and a trap was waiting for them.

Ekon grieved, "*I had lost my limelight of dying next to leader Eric.*" He also ordered two rookies, "*Take all good-shaped griffin riders to support the Alaokan ground units and alert Eric about the hyena army.*" He entrusted his will to guard Eric with their lives on Akello and Figo. Ekon handovered the longsword of the air commander to Figo and made him a temporary commander. A sudden breeze chilled Figo; he is the first rookie in Alaoka to become the commander, and it was his dream. His dreams came true in an unexpected way, but with the commander's sword in his hands, his clear thoughts slipped a little. For a minute Figo can't differentiate reality and dream. His hands removed the blood-covered sheath. He was stunned at the workmanship of the sword as he gently rubbed the blades with his thumb. With star-struck eyes, Akello joined the sword show, forgetting seriousness, and commented, "*Super cool sword!*" The long, shining straight blade reflected the amber light of the sun. Sharp edges were perfect for slicing and dicing the limbs and muscles. The weight of the blade was less than expected and that was made purposefully for faster movements. The handle of the sword is made of ivory with a carved griffin head pommel and two red gems on the eyes of the giffin pommel.

After all, they are still brats. Ekon moved his hands to gain the interest of the brats but no use; their star-struck eyes were stuck in the sword. He gained his leftover energy and shouted at them, "*Rookies! Don't waste time; we are in the middle of the war.*" In eye-flashing seconds, both vanished with their griffins. Previously, before Rudo's engagement in the battle against pirates, Figo asked Rudo to bring his sister to his location. She is a highly skilled griffin rider. When Rudo returns alone, he understands that she is no more. He controls all his grief and is ready to serve Alaoka. Figo is a sensible person, but his lust for the commander's designation made him stuck. He forgot all his pain and mission for a minute when his eyes were locked on the sword.

Ekon was panting in pain; he questions himself, "*What I have done?*" He believed that leader Eric was right about him. Ekon blamed himself for being inexperienced and foolish even in the last minutes of his life. His own decisions set him on fire for entrusting his will and his duties to amateurs and sending them to the front of the battleground. Both physical and mental pain made him suffer. His brain failed to justify the action of his heart. To reach the borders of Varuona, Akello and Figo have to cross the Cov mountains. Alaokan and Varuonan lands were separated by long savanna lands. On the way to the border of Varuonans, Akello and Figo made their griffins screech in a unique high pitch. Screech is short but loud; it is an "SOS call of Alaokan air units." SOS of Rudo and Neo added 18 more riders from the Cove mountain villages. With the company of a dozen and a half, Akello and Figo reached the borders of Varuona. Eyes caught the corpse of Varuonan hyenas and Alaokans in the entire mixed wood-grassland ecosystem.

Meanwhile, the blazing sun has some good news. "*Zaka, the leader of Varuonans, is alive.*" Akello hit his palm forcefully on his forehead for being late. All riders waited for orders from the new commander to proceed further. The silence was all around the sky; Figo's mind was analyzing the situation before reacting. From the dead bodies in the savanna, he found that Varuonans had already unleashed the army of hyenas. All of a sudden, the loud painful howls of the wolf hit the ears of the griffin crew from the nearby villages of Varuonans. Immediately, Figo raised his commander's sword and directed his blackbird and other griffins in the direction of the sound. Within a couple of minutes, the griffin crew hovered over the villages of Varuonans, and they caught sight of wolf riders, Gamba and Eric, with 100s of Alaokans, who were involved in a duel against a huge bunch of Varuonans in their capital. All 18 griffins entered the battlegrounds to support ground units. Scissor teeth of giant wolves, the claws and beaks of the griffin along with sharp-edged weapons put an end to the life of the rest Varuonan warriors. Blood spilled all over the village! The dripping lineage of Varuonans mixed in the pond located in the center of the main village and made it unfit for drinking. The leader of Varuonans Zaka is now a lone wolf, and he was surrounded by hundreds of Alaokan warriors. Lone wolf Zaka was still ready to fight all alone to get a decent death, with a silver sword and dagger in his hand. A man with a muscular body in a bear skin outfit with a horse tattoo on his ripped shoulder entered the circle to duel with Zaka. He has a salty long beard and carries a unique sword with a black handle. Long and loud cheers among warriors made us understand that he is a leader of Alaokans, Eric. Gamba, the commander of the ground units, sends out his best men to eliminate the hidden Varuonans soldiers.

All the Alaokans howl in unison, "*Kill the bastard!*" The pain in their heart was expressed in their words. Eric raised his sword to stop the howl and started questioning Zaka.

"*I was afraid that this situation would never happen, but you brought us here to hunt you. Pirates and you bastard mindlessly killed our children and adults. We have shared everything with you: ships, fertile lands, and cattle. We supported you in floods and wars against other civilizations. You hunted our pride (griffins). We waited calmly instead of waging war against you. You made all your land liquor factories and hunting grounds. You suffered winter in hunger and pain. Even then, we saw you as our brothers and gave you enough red meat and greens to survive. Answer Zaka! After doing all this, where do we Alaokans create vengeance in your hearts? What is the fault we have done, to establish the alliance with dirty pirates and invited them to slaughter us like pigs and beef? In the name of Alaoka, I don't want to cut your throat and entrust vengeance in the hearts of the future of Varuonans. Run away to deep woods and never show yourself again in Alaoka.*" Again, a whisper began in the Alaokan ranks. Akello was scolding Zaka in a louder tone, but Figo was a silent listener. Even after seeing Zaka's crime, one pleaded to show mercy on Zaka; it was the fireball burning in the sky.

Zaka answered Eric, "*This vengeance is rooted in our blood and it has a 1,000 years long history. We don't want to share this land with you. Varuonan ancestors were founders of this civilization, and we are not slaves to you and don't want to depend on you and your pride. Remember Eric! The sword decorating the griffin throne did not belong to you. I am a failure, but we have killed many of you and soon the neighboring civilization will finish my mission to eliminate the Alaokan race before the next harvest season. Now, Alaokans are vulnerable and your prideful griffin number is reduced to half and below. Soon, Alaoka will fall."* Again, the furious howl, *"Kill! Kill!"* It touched heaven. The words of Zaka lighted the anger in Figo too. In the twinkling of eyes, Zaka executed himself with his dagger by cutting his gullet. When blood rushed from his throat, he panted in pain and said that he never wanted to be killed in the hands of Alaokans and reached the ground with a smile of fulfilling the vengeance. A deep silence halted in the Alaokan armies. The fear of future dreads occupied their facial expressions. The sun decided to set back. He was neither Alaokan nor Varuonan. The loss of both Tibor and Zaka made him upset.

The red giant allowed the dark clouds to cover him, gray shadows of clouds covered both Alaoka and Varuonan lands. Gamba has well-built tight muscles and his green lens read the situation and ordered his troopers to collect the corpses of fallen Varuonans and dump them all in the center of the village. Old man Eric reset his back near the pond and gazed at the misfortune of the blood-mixed pond. The Army of Alaokans raided the huts of Varuonans to check if anyone was hiding in the huts. All of a sudden, the cries of Alaokan warriors reached the ears of Eric; he stood up and rushed to address the sound. Women with butler knives broke the latches of their huts and wounded the Alaokans with great anger. In his 60 years of life, Eric has never witnessed such anger in household women's eyes and rising weapons against skilled warriors. Their act clarified one thing; they don't want to live anymore! Instead, they want to fight for a decent death. The army under Eric is highly respected for its good qualities. They never misbehave with hostage women and ill-treat the prisoners, but today to save their own lives troopers killed the women. Under the gray shadow of clouds in the capital of Varuonans, huge piles of dead bodies were stacked. Dumped corpses set the attire of a haunted village.

From an unknown location, arrows were released at the Alaokans, but many of them missed hitting the target. A few other arrows drank the lives of armed warriors. Based on the speed of the arrows and missed targets, Gamba understood the shooters of the arrows were amateurs. On the command of Gamba, the search party is scattered to find and eliminate the culprits. An arrow shot from the top of the hut pierced the shoulder of a horse-tattooed old man. It again missed the target. Eric's eyes caught the sight of the archer, but pierced arrows made him lose his balance. Gamba already had a scratch on his chest made by hyenas, and he was about to apply the leaf extract to his wound, but seeing a pierced arrow on the leader's shoulder made him rush to Eric. Along with a fast breath, blood was dripping. Eric pulled out the arrow and with a broken voice he beamed, "*I am alright!*"

Akello started chasing the shooter of the arrow and got him. Akello was paralyzed in fear after seeing the archer's face.

He flipped the bow from the archer's hand, tied his hands with bow thread, and dragged him to Gamba. When he came back along with an arrested archer, his eyes captured a bunch of archers who were arrested for what they had done and lined in. There were 15 bowmen in total and they were neither skilled nor old enough to lift the bow. After all, they are a bunch of tweens. A group of tweens were the owners of the shot arrows. After seeing the arrested faces, every Alaokan face was filled with misery. Akello stood behind the archer he captured. In the past, the sun has never witnessed such vengeance in his service to the earth. After seeing what Zaka has done to his people, the burning fireball cursed Zaka and rays of the sun escaped between the clouds to grace the light on Eric and he was waiting for Eric's response. The faces of the kids were in a state of high anger and vengeance filled in their vision. Their noses exhaled fire breath. Tormented, Eric graced the thundering clouds and then heaven started to weep for what Zaka had done. These tweens were soaked in the ocean of vengeance. Eric had no good reason to let them live. If Eric let them live, he was planting the roots for the fall of Alaoka.

All of a sudden, one of the tweens undone his hands and ran toward Eric to take him down. Escaped tween hands were empty, and he needed to beat Gamba to touch Eric. The roar of tween panicked the entire army and Akello was stunned to see the valor and vengeance in him. The tween jumped on Gamba, bit his shoulder, and ripped out the upper skin. Out of pain, Gamba kicked the young lion to save himself. The tween hit the walls of the hut and fainted with a bloodstain on his mouth. Unfortunately, the physical strength of the kid did not match the size of the vengeance in his heart. Gamba got the eyes of Eric. With a steel heart, Eric ordered execution. Akello and others were frozen by the words of Eric. Figo was also unhappy, but he was a clever brat to understand the situation. In the rainwater, blood dissolved and every inch of mud got the color of blood. Akello looked at the face of the tween and was not ready to execute the tween. An executor next to Akello, with a rug face, he pushed Akello away and took the sin in his name. He beamed at Akello, "*You're too young to carry this sin.*" With a confused face, Akello walked to Neo and stood silently in the cattle. He questioned himself about what had happened in this world. His heart is not ready to accept the execution of tweens.

The last-minute struggle of the tweens at the moment of execution blurred his vision. His mind recalled the conversation between Eric and Zaka; Eric spoke about pirates and Varuonans who slaughtered Alaokan children, women and old. Guilt in Akello's heart stirred anger in him and made him feel Eric and Zaka were both cold-hearted murderers. Now, Eric has committed the same mistake that Zaka has made. Killing women and kids was unacceptable. Even the so-called gods stood silent today. Do they really exist or are they just myths? If power and leadership are everything, then where the hell does justice go?

By staring at his strong palm, he blamed himself. "*These hands caught the tween, and I am responsible for the slaughter of the tween.*" For a minute, his eyes closed and his ears were disturbed by the tapping sound of the rain. From the corner of his eyes, pain escaped out. A picture of the dead tweens doomed his head. At the same time, Figo was having a conversation with Eric about the condition of commander Ekon. With bent knees, he handed over the commander's sword to Eric. Eric accepted the sword and asked Figo and his companion to meet him in the great Alaokan caves.

All of a sudden, a scream was made by the soldier. Everyone rushed to him. Akello too ran, and Neo followed him. Another young child was in the hands of an Alaokan soldier. The young child bit the wrist of the soldier and the blood wound was washed away by the force of rainfall. After seeing another child, Akello was stunned. A rush in his blood vessel released the sweat in the heavy rain. His eyes were locked on the red bloodstains on the kid's mouth. The kid's age made him cry in fear, but strong vengeance gave him bloodstains on his teeth. The captured kid got a bow tattoo on his shoulder. This tattoo was responsible for the elimination of the kid. He was the pinky finger of Zaka's legacy, and the elimination of this kid was mandatory. With a blood leak in his heart and a stubborn face, Eric decided to execute him on his own. He walked forward with a downed head out of shame and misery. Eric took the young child in his cruel hands and decided to slaughter him in the shadows. But Akello was new to the accepting ecosystem. In fear of sin and pure heart, he failed to control his mouth.

Akello raised his voice against Eric. "*Is the future of Alaokans dependent on the elimination of young children and caring women? I can't find any differences between Alaokans and*

Varuonans. Our bloodthirst and vengeance are all the same. They lack power; they invited pirates to take us down. After the triumph, we are no different. In my own eyes, our leader and Zaka are different in the sunlight, but in the shadows, both are the same."

Gamba was silent until the very moment Akello's complaints were against Alaoka, but the moment he compared the savior of Alaoka with Zaka, his rage busted out. Without notice, he stomped his foot in the liquid mud and rushed toward Akello with tightened knuckles. An adrenaline rush in Akello's nerves raised his arms to parry the blow, but in a fraction of a blinking second, "berserker of wolves" Gamba smacked Akello's face in great force. In no time, Akello's head touched the mud ground and his ears buzzed with the ringing sound. When everyone was silent, Figo ran to stop Gamba and aid Akello. A friend in need is a friend indeed. Figo was a good friend of Akello. Fallen Akello saw the majestic body of Gamba in his blurred vision. Gamba has a strong reflex and rippled body. All over his shape, scars looked like medals. Akello thought Gamba was a beast in human form. Akello realized his speed and power were not a match for the commander Gamba. In moments of thunderclaps, after seeing Akello reach the ground, the temper of his olive-green beast increased. Without delay, the loyal beast got into the action!

With the force of thrusting his hind legs, the griffin raised his upper shape and delivered a decent scratch on the chest of Gamba with his strong claws. Along with the old wound, a new wound created the X mark in Gamba's chest. The force of the attack pushed him down, but his eyes got locked into Neo's radium lens. To counter griffin and payback, the commander's blue-eyed dire wolf, Blu, ran fast and jumped into the assault with his scary teeth. Teeth and beak punctured the skin of both. All eyes were locked on the fight of wolf vs griffin. The sound of growling and screaming outran the metal music of thunderclaps. The thunderbolts from clouds hit the nearby rocks, but still, all eyes were stunned by the fight of beasts. The whistle of Gamba made Blu step down with growls and loud barks, and the anger in Blu's eyes was still burning. Both griffins and wolves were royal and loyal beasts, but griffins have a habit of functioning on their own and orders of the riders have no effect on their emotions, which makes them scarier than wolves and any other wild.

Akello was back on his feet to control and put a leash on Neo's anger. He stood up, but still, his vision was blurry and his ear was ringing. The loud, strong voice of the leader hit the ears of the Alaokan ranks. Eric ordered in his name that no one should lay a finger on the young griffin rider; he also mentioned that Akello is the grandson of honorable Davu. Whispers started in the armies, and he gave his answer to Akello. "*Yes, I am a brutal murderer and reaper of thousands of souls. I knew that my afterlife was going to be hell, but beyond all, I am a servant of the Alaokans. With the title of their leader, it's my responsibility to protect each of you!*" He turned his back and walked inside the hut to slaughter the young child in his own hands because he didn't want any fellow Alaokan to carry out this evil. The rumbling sound of thunder ruled Alaoka. When executing a young child, Eric controls his tears, but the moment the bloodstain of the kid wet his hands, tears rushed out of self-anger and pain. The army stood silent and waited for their leader. The tapping sound of rain and breaking thunder beats haunted the hearts. Dizziness and ringing ears black out Akello's vision. All of a sudden, he drowned and went unconscious.

In the afternoon heaven stopped weeping, but the sun was not in the mood to shower its shine. With the dry fire-woods in the Varuonans' huts, troops set fire to the corpses of Varuonans. Gamba and Eric carried out a huge raid party in the terrains and woods for several days in removing weeds of vengeance from Alaokan soil. With a stone heart, Eric put a stop to Varuonans' bloodline, and all sinful executions were done in his very own hands.

Chapter 2

The Wind and Terrains of Noble Land

In the wide blues above the Alaoka, cotton candies scattered all over the sky. The push of the wind influenced the clouds toward central Alaoka. Shadows of smoke balls changed the weather of green and brown lands. The gentle breeze created rustling music in the crop fields, which brought peace and eased the minds of hardworking farmers in the field. Alaokans believed that wet soil and yearly rainfall were the gifts of the sun as a sign of loyalty to kin. The sky full of playing griffins is their pride. The sound of their screams and the majestic attire of the eagle-headed beast have the ability to implant fear in human hearts, but the Alaokans learned the art of riding griffins from the goddess of the wind.

In Alaokan history, griffins can't be tamed inside cages or on a leash, but the majestic beast selects its rider only once in its lifetime. When it does, its furious long beak signs a blood contract with the rider. Bite scar of a griffin in the rider's forefinger gains respect among Alaokans. The screams of the griffin echo in the caves, woods, terrains, and smallholdings of Alaokans. 3,000 years old Alaokan civilization lived on its own code: "*Understanding the gesture of nature is an important part of wisdom.*"

Somewhere above Alaoka, two young riders were traveling to an unknown location on their olive-green and black griffins. Fresh air from the forest of Alaoka made their lives longer than usual. They cherish the life between nature and the average lifespan of Alaokans was 130 years; they live long up to 150 if luck favored. The teen on the olive-green griffin inhaled the freshness of the air with a narrow nose and his fine sizzling shape identified that he should be a trooper of the Alaokan army. He is dusky as a mountain and his attire was oval-faced with coal-black lens, messy black hair, and rippled shoulders portraying him as a strong man but a tough guy's sharp vision attracted to the gravity of a girl riding in the pitch black griffin. She is beautiful with limited curves; she has an apple face. In the force of the wind, her horsetail hair danced; her name was 'Amara.' The rider on the olive griffin was Akello and his eyes were stuck between her black eyes and dimple cheek. She is sharper and more sensible than Akello. Akello was on cloud nine because he was flying along with Amara. His vision dwelled in dreams that they were both seated under the tree and discussing their future. In his daydreams after a sweet talk, she fell asleep on his shoulder, but the reality is flat and just the opposite.

Akello was on his griffin's back and showing all teeth and staring at Amara. The spider-web smile was not welcomed by Amara's black beast, Aro; he screamed and ascended with great speed and vanished into the clouds. The fact is, Aro is not aware that Amara has already fallen in love with Akello. Reading a girl's heart is not only challenging for men but also for four-legged beasts. Akello's golden-eyed griffin is as fast as lightning and his name is Neo. Neo flapped his wings for the chase. An elbow-tall olive-green feather dropped from Neo. The feather danced in the flow of wind and gently touched the cave entrance of the Shrirdal mountain range. We can find elbow-tall griffin feathers in the wide pavement and crop fields of all Alaokan villages. Many Alaokan have the habit of collecting unique griffin feathers.

Nothing can escape from the eagle's vision. In the eyes of the griffin, the stronghold borders of Alaoka were visible. Shirdhal is a wide-legged, cranky mountain range in the north that had become the natural border for Alaoka. In the west, the southern ocean and its pushing wind made it hard to sail. In the northwest, clusters of green and brown islands became a barrier to entering central Alaoka. In the east, sleeping red volcanic mountains opened Alaoka's doors to raiders and enemies. The eastern red volcanic mountains are a common border for Alaoka and its neighboring civilization in the southeast. The old saying: "*The sun and rain bow their crown in front of the selfless leader.*" Eric, the leader of the Alaokans, decorated the griffin feather throne and rained the entire Alaoka from the Shirdhal caves. Shirdhal is a long and deep cave located in the Shirdhal mountain ranges, the cave gets enough sunlight, and small villages were located inside it and the flow of the river inside the caves made life possible. At the time of war, Shirdhal caves act as a bunker to save the lives of Alaoka. Wide savanna grounds behind the Shirdhal mountain ranges were ruled by Varuonans; they share the same bloodline as Alaokan, but they claim that the entire Alaoka was theirs. From the golden eye of Neo, the river Kogi is visible with its 32 twists and 38 cuts. Kogi is a non-perennial but nature never turned her back against Alaokans. The river flows first in Alaoka and later shares the same water with Varuonans before reaching the southern sea.

Alaoka is covered by 60% of the forest, rich in medicinal herbs and deep woods with sufficient resources for a tremendous number of four tuskers (ancient elephants). Neither big nor small, random ponds and waterfalls were found all over Alaoka. Neo used to take Akello to unexplored places in Alaoka. It took him to abandon a village of 15 huts, a pond of giant crocodiles and small no-man islands in northwest Alaoka. Other than combat training and helping his mom in the fields, Akello spends the rest of the time on Neo's back.

Neo's loud screams announced that it found Amara's Aro inside the white smoke. After seeing Akello, a small smile bloomed on Amara's lips. It created a dimple on her left cheek, but Akello didn't notice her smile. When Neo maintained the same speed as the black griffin, the speed of the wind favored Akello.

The wind lifted up Amara's cotton outfit, her curvy hip naked to Akello's eyes. Without a word, Akello's lusty eyes started to stare at her assets, but his lust didn't last for long. As usual, Neo starts to act on his own and descends toward the forest, looking like he found something interesting in the woods. The loud calling of Akello's name hit Akello's left ear; it was Amara. She directed Aro to follow the olive-green griffin. Descending speed made Akello wide open his lip, Neo smoothly grounded adjacent to the river and gulped some water. In a flash of seconds, Amara joined Akello. The place was all green, with small gravel on the sides of the river. Aro also walked to wet his throat. Amara confirmed Akello's welfare, and both nodded their heads as the wind blew between them.

The music of falling water was noticed by both of them. Amara's ears reacted to the sound, and she started chasing the sound of water hitting the rocks. Akello shouted, *"Amara stop...Amara stop."* But she neglected him and continued on her path. After a long run, Amara stopped and bent her upper body, panting heavily. Akello was running behind her and he was amazed to see the extraordinary beauty of nature with, "*Wooow...*" She found a waterfall in the woods and its water source started from "heaven" and their griffins joined with a never mind reaction. They rested their belly near the pampas. Amara raised her head to check the water source. Water was falling from the extreme height of the cliff and white clouds almost covered the origin of the waterfall. In the excitement, she smiled and her dimple was expelled. The cold breeze from the waterfalls stopped the rushing sweat of Amara. Akello gently touched her shoulder; she could feel the shake in his fingers and caught his eyes. He suggested giving a name for the falls that she found. With great excitement and lighting teeth, Amara named the waterfall as "falls of heaven," which was the perfect name.

In the beauty of nature, both were frozen, but the anxiety of touching her for the very first time made Akello's fingers vibrate. The screeching of bats and the chirping sound of birds flying near the falls hit the ears of young lovers. Both knew each other for a long time, but none of them had the guts to open up about their love. The water flow was seamless and the divine water was sweet like a watermelon. After spending quality time, both took their seats under the tree; the tree looked like one Akello saw in his daydream. The chill of the waterfall spread all over the grasslands. From the bottom of the tree, they can see nature's beauty and the music of falling water relaxed their minds until she rested her head on his rippled shoulder. It happened. Akello's dream changed into reality. There was no little space between his shoulders and her head. It was a forever cherishing moment for both young hearts. The pleasant environment, moist air, and the melody of nature erased the shyness and magnified the love she carried for him. That moment she rested her head on Akello, he became a bit nervous and she could feel the rasping heart of Akello. He looked at her with expanded pupils; birds in the tree stared at them. Something inside him crawled to speak out, but words failed to escape his gullet. The voice inside him advised him, "*Don't be a fool. Tell her now and make her yours.*"

He knows very well that he can't be alone with Amara like this again. He spilled a pickup line to Amara. "*Your left dimple is beautiful.*" She raised her head to listen more from his man with a smile on the corner of her lips, which is not explicit but more beautiful. Akello's nerves increased the blood flow; he is ready to express his feelings. "*You are so beautiful and brave. I wish to make every sunrise and nightfall meaningful by clutching your fingers tight.*" After a moment of silence, Akello could hear his heart tickling. Both of their eyes locked without a blink. All she waited for was for this day; she wanted him to confess his love first.

Amara's pupils expanded, and a smile bloomed with her cute dimple. The golden rays of the setting sun reflected in her eyes, and the wind caressed her long, black hair. She gently clutched his fingers tight and Akello felt the warmth. Before words, the tightness in between their fingers expressed her love. Words expressed her wish, *"I love spending every moment of my life with you! Today, tomorrow, and forever."* She also mocked him, saying she expected it would take another harvest season to express his feelings. In happiness, Akello's lips expanded and displayed all his pearls. He hugged her for the first time. The smell bud sensed her fragrance and registered it in his memory. She reciprocated the hug with her radiant smile and caring heart. Olive and black griffins watched them without moving their heads. The flow of feelings made him gently pinch her dimple and move his long finger to rub her small lips, but all of a sudden, her shyness made her step aside. Birds in the trees sang their best melody to wish the young lovers. A beam of the setting sun gave its light yellow shade to the falls, and it was an evening in paradise. Sweethearts decided not to reveal their love story to friends and family because of the customs and cultures of Alaoka. In Alaoka, the legal age for marriage is 21.

This moment was special. Amara recalled her first meeting with Akello. They met each other for the very first time in the woods; it happened between the huddles. Survival test was mandatory for every Alaokan soldier. After training, Alaokan soldier candidates have to survive in the deep woods for three months by using the resources available in the forest. Leaders of Alaokans believed this way a soldier learns nature in his own way and respects its value. Amara felt it all happened a few days back; it had been two years since Akello lost control of his own heart. Akello approached Figo's team to aid his fallen friend, Kino. Figo, Amara and Zina formed an alliance to survive the forest. At that moment, Akello's eyes were filled with fear of losing his friend; Amara sensed it very well. Amara stepped up to save Kino's life with all she got. Her father is a medic, and she is the first one selected by the griffin in her family history. In return, Akello and Kino saved Figo and his company twice in the dark forest from black mambas and wild spiders. Amara and Akello hunt together for food and scout together at night. They worked together on hunting for food, slept on the barks of the giant trees and small caves, and supported each other for two months. When they left the deep woods after three months, all five of them became troopers of the Alaokan army. In addition to that, Akello's marrow developed feelings for Amara. As the days passed, Amara loved spending time with Akello and Neo.

We all have heard that true love is stronger than gravity and even hurricanes can't separate true love, but two decades ago, a new problem arose in Alaoka. The young teens of Alaoka fell in love and got married in their late teenage, but their married life was not as smiles as expected. Time shaded the false colors and love emptied the hearts, resulting in family fights. After a certain extent, the unhappy couple started having illegal affairs. Cases of illegal affairs were flooded in the huts of Eric. The huts of Alaoka were on fire. It mentally affected the Alaokan kids. When Eric investigated these cases, he found these cases were common among the age group of 15 to 21 and he was afraid about the future of Alaokans. By consulting elders and advisors of the Alaoka, Eric put a full stop to the problem. He can't stop teens from falling in love, but he advised that without intimate relationships, the love is divine and strong. Years of love without intimate relationships help teens to identify whether they fell in love with the right person. Time reveals the real color which created the door for Alaokan teens to think twice before marriage. Eric imposed a new marriage law for Alaokans and declared 21 years as the legal age for marriage. Heavy penalties were charged to those who disobey the rules and their families. It's been 13 years. Everyone started following the law imposed by Eric. True love is eternal. Many young couples waited for years and finally got married to the right ones. Figo's elder sister and her husband waited for 9 years. They later clutched each other's hands on marriage, but the battle of pirates and Varonans gave them the limelight to show their valor along with death as a reward. She and her husband were one of the best warriors of Ekon and defeated Kayon's hyena army (commander of Varonans). Those who married at the age of 21 were mature and lived happily. The time they waited allowed their hearts to build the tangled roots of trust and love, which became a strong foundation for marriage life.

The traditions of the Alaokans were unique. They used to celebrate festivals on each seasonal change, and they worshipped nature as their god on auspicious days. One among them was "welcoming fallen." They believed after death pure souls would become stars and decorate the skies of Alaoka. There was an ancient Alaokan saying, "*The sky is full of ancestors!*" During the lunar eclipse, Alaokans believe their ancestors in the sky will come down to check the well-being of their legacy and falling stars from the sky denote the ancestors' arrival. Souls from the stars walk on the terrains, forests, and riversides of Alaoka and at last, the souls are summoned to the big graveyard with the help of wolf howl and the music of Udukku. Summoned souls use the body of the old ripe Alaokan to tell the prophecy for the upcoming year. The big harvest season of rice and wheat was considered the start of the Alaokan New Year. Usually, prophecy talks about yearly rainfall and harvest. Sometimes, very rarely, they prophesied about changes in leaders and wars, but this year was more about "war and evil."

"Under the luminous pearl, the pride will fall!

Fangs of sharks and scavengers hunt the clusters in the darkness.

Bloodstains stink the green, wheezing huts and debris all over Alaoka!

Out of pain, heaven weeps in the savanna!

Dead sails calm the white sea, but breathing carries evil!

Rookie confronts the superior! Stone heart and half will survive!

After the fall! Bamboos will walk on ice and fire!"

Many Alaokans failed to believe the prophecy, but as usual, the prophesied words came to reality and the war broke out in Alaoka.

After the triumph of Alaokan against Varuonans and pirates, every survior is weeping for the death of their kin. Akello's blackout vision lightened again at dawn. As he circulated his eyes to find where he was, the clay-painted hut and hanging griffin pommel dagger clarified that he was at his very own house. A song of chirping birds was pleasant and the early sun started to pop up in between the clouds. From the window of Akello's house, the sunrise was amazing. The mind of the young brat recalled the blood sin and strike of Gamba. While he recalled the powerful smack of Gamba, it made his ears ring again. He rubbed his ears with his forefinger and walked to find his little sister, mother, and grandfather. He couldn't find anyone in the hut, and his steps continued to find them in the crop field. While on his way out, on the doorstep, he found sleeping Neo. After seeing Neo, a small smile developed on his face; his hands gently rubbed the head of the dozed griffin.

Eyelashes of the eagle beast opened slowly, in the yellow lens of Neo Akello's face reflected with spark. After seeing Akello back on his feet, Neo got up on claws and started expressing his love by rubbing his head against Akello's chest. Akello caressed Neo to make him feel comfortable and better. After a few minutes of sharing love, Akello moved his foot outside the hut to check on others.

The morning breeze and wet soil underneath made Akello feel the freshness in the air. At the same time, bloodstains on crop fields, half-burned neighboring huts, and empty cattle sheds became a fear factor. Fear aroused in his heart that something terrible could have happened to his family. Out of an adrenaline rush, his body temperature increased. He felt shivering inside his body. Total silence was broken by the hooves of the horse; he focused his vision in the direction of the horse's hooves' sound. Akello's eyes caught sight of the piebald color horse that belonged to his cattle. The rider of the horse was his own grandpa Davu and the kid accompanying him was his little sister Moona. After seeing Awaken Akello, Moona expressed her happiness and shouted his big brother's name out loud, "Akello!!". Grandpa Davu was also happy to see his grandson with his griffin. Grandpa's eyes and cheeks expelled inner joy. The hooves of the horse stopped near Akello. In the horse's eyes, Akello sensed a track of tears. The tragedy was that the piebald horse was the only survivor of Akello's cattle; the rest were looted by pirates. The horse moved his large lips near Akello's face to show his love. He gently rubbed the horse and grabbed his little sister on his shoulders. By holding Akello's shoulder, grandpa Davu unmounted the horse. He gently patted the young man's shoulder and started to walk without a word.

Akello ran behind his grandpa and flooded him with questions, "*Where's mom? Is she ok? What has happened to cattle farms and neighboring huts?*" Without turning around, grandpa stood silent. His little sister started to give answers to the questions that their mom was well, but they lost their maternal grandma. Moona also added that their mother is on their way home with neighbor aunty. With silence, old Davu slowly walked into the hut. Before entering, he washed his hands and legs. Akello was shocked to hear about the tragedy that happened to his grandma and she told that this day is the third day after her death. We all walked to her grave for rituals. When she said that today is the third day, he was stunned. He paused her and asked, "*What! Today is the third day's ritual?*" She ignored his question and continued on her way. Moona was just seven and the only sister of Akello. He had to wait to get answers to his question. The hot sun started to fry. Their skin started to feel the heat. Moona said that their neighbor lost their children in the battle. In addition, their house was destroyed. She also felt bad for Akello's family cattle. The next moment, their horse made a pitiful face at Akello. Even without being bothered by the stinging smell from the horse, he patted it with love and care. Akello seated Moona on the horse's back and directed the horse to the cattle. Neo followed them with a small screech.

Akello questioned Moona gently, "*What has happened to me in the last three days?*" With gasps, she continued in her childish tone, but her watery nose interrupted her voice. She began in a kiddish tone, "*You were unconscious for the past two days. Medics expected that you would wake up after the passing five suns.*" She added that they also conveyed that the slap commander delivered on Akello's face created equivalent damage of being stuck under fallen rocks. After hearing her, his facial expression changed to a serious look. She also voiced that Neo screamed in fear of losing him. After listening to the words of big brother Figo, Neo decided to wait for Akello's recovery at the doorstep. She shouted at Akello with rage, "*You made grandfather and mother ashamed in front of others.*" She landed a punch with her cotton palms on Akello's chest for the tears, sleepless nights and sufferings that their family had spent because of him. Akello hugged her tightly and consoled her with his apology. It was the first time in her life that she saw tears in her grandpa Davu's eyes. Moona voiced, "*Brother Figo and sister Amara came to check your health thrice.*" She added that Figo asked her to convey Akello something once he was back on his feet. She felt bad because she forgot what Figo told her to convey. Moona's words about Amara were unexpected to Akello. She said that her big sister Amara came thrice a day for the last two days with her medic father to check his health. Moona also voiced Amara's worries about Akello's health and his actions against Eric. At last, Moona recalled what Figo told her to convey and expressed it like a repeating parrot, "*I have never seen such a foolish griffin like Neo and a mad rider like Akello.*" After hearing Moona, Akello's nose pumped out hot air and targeted his frowning eyes at her. Moona moved her eyes from him and added, "*I just repeated what big brother Figo told me.*"

After a few minutes, Akello stepped to his grandpa to seek apologies for what he had done. Davu was resting in his chamber; he was wise, and he was in his 100s. He has been the head archaeologist of Alaoka for the past 40 years. He has seen Eric from a closer distance. At first, Akello's words against Eric made him angry, but he knew his grandson very well, and that made him calm. Akello was straightforward and plump, but not sharp enough to think from political aspects. Davu knew that very well. Akello walked over and sat on the cot where his grandpa was lying. Davu asked Akello about his health, but he has not spilled a word or questioned about his action against Eric. Akello questioned his grandpa. "*We can't create resolutions for the problem with blood signatures. Am I wrong, grandpa?*" Davu smiled and erected himself to answer his grandson. With a smile, he started, "*Visions of the young and old are always different. We can't deny the fact. Your black lens captures the view of wet soil and a plant popping out of it, but the man beautifying the throne of Alaoka should be wise and strong enough to analyze the growth of the plant. Beyond all, a leader holds the responsibility of protecting every leaf of a plant from bug waves and from the horrible songs of hurricanes and rainfalls. Our enemies, Varuonans, are not bugs or hurricanes, but they are the decay in the roots of a plant. Rotten plants cannot survive long. The leaders of Alaoka knew that very well. Medications to prevent decaying have been taken over the past 200 years, but medication has failed to fructify. Rot spread to leaves and a small portion of the stem. The compassion of Alaokans and dead leaders has no power to cut their own blood. The time they delayed resulted in a new alliance of Varuonans with pirates. Finally, pirate waves invaded the green Alaoka.*

Today, souls that cross the holy river of Kogi (aftermath) are victims of the time we delayed. After all, the leader's path of rightness is to protect his land and his people. To save the Alaoka, even sins and blood rain are tolerated. When you grow a white beard and get bald like me, you will understand the events of this day. Until then, remember, Eric has done what our precious leaders and ancestors failed to do."

Anger in Akello's heart and the fire burning in his tongue escaped the heat waves. "*But grandpa, by the name of weeding out, slaughtering pregnant women, infants, and tweens is not justice and tolerated."*

Davu roared, "*To show mercy and live in the line of justice, first Alaoka has to live. Leaving a single rotten soul to live is a threat to the legacy of Alaoka. I am glad and happy to say that whatever Eric has done is correct and good for Alaoka. The prophecy was stone heart and half will survive! Rookie confronts the superior!"* As prophesied, the stone-hearted leader and half of the Alaokans survived. where the unexpected part is that rookie to be you.

Davu's words stirred the anger of the young man; he bashed the doors of the hut and walked to the cattle farm with Neo to spend some quality time. The rule of Alaoka was very clear; it doesn't matter whether it's a peasant or king, a mistake is a mistake and justice needs to be saved. But today the entire Alaoka and its population carry the evil, for the blood spilled from kids and pregnant women. Blood of Infants cursed the Alaoka. The red giant and wide blues knew very well that Alaoka would suffer for what they had done. Akello never expected such words from his grandpa. Akello's eyes dwelled on thoughts of his late father and all his sufferings. In his wavering thoughts, he missed the chucking sound of horse hooves approaching, and a woman in her 40s walking down from the white horse. She has light brown skin like Moona but not dark as Akello. Both Akello and Moona replicated her eyeballs. She wore an outfit that matched the color of Akello's crop field. She was hardworking and strong-willed. The shape of her body resembles it. Today her strength is trampled like straws scattered in the cattle. Her face was dull and her shortened eyes explained the pain she carried in her heart, which leaked from her eyes. In the battle, she lost her friends, mother and other distant family members. Beyond all, the reason for the heavy heart is the one she gave birth to. His name is Akello and her name is Ava. After Ava landed her foot down, her princess Moona ran toward her with excitement on her face and continued to speak with gasping. She conveyed to her mother that her swooned brother had woken up. Ava's eyes and lips glowed with happiness. She carried her child on her hip, and her foot increased the speed of seeing her son.

Ava walked to the cattle shed behind the hut to see her son. Ava's watery eyes got sight of her brat. Akello was lying down and rested his head on the back of sleeping Neo. The neigh of the loyal horse brought Akello back to reality. The moment he saw his mother, his eyes became gloomy, but he managed not to tear up. He stood up and hugged her tightly with love. Her cloudy eyes leaked tears on Akello's shoulders. That very moment, he felt the pain she carried; a stream of tears started to rush from Akello's eyes too. He asked for an apology from her and her family for the bother he caused. She showed her love for her son with a gentle kiss on the forehead and said, "*My precious, you are in good shape; that is enough for me.*" Grandpa's old legs walked to cattle and the lone survivor horse also joined the family, and sometime later his friends and love joined him at his house. The hot day became a happy day for Akello's friends and family to see him back on his feet. With angry eye movements, Amara conveyed to Akello, "*Idiot come to our paradise (falls of heaven).*" That night under the stars, Akello understood one thing: his confrontation against Eric made the whole Alaokans not only against him but also his family. But luckily, these people complained about Akello's age and his inexperienced nature for his act and forgave him. Akello was actually happy about those fools who complained about his age and did not turn against him and his family.

It has been a month, and everything is back to normal. Perfect smiling sun and hardworking Alaokans have started rebuilding their livelihood. However, Akello was unhappy with the justice of Alaoka, but Eric's decision brought peace to Alaoka. As Akello was dripping sweat on his farm, Figo visited Akello's residence in hooves. Figo suggested Akello to put on fine clothes and pushed him inside the hut. Akello's trust in Figo made him do as he mentioned without a word. When Akello came out, his eyes caught sight of his friend who was waiting on a mare and his hands were busy holding the leash of Akello's old mustang. Akello wore a white full-sleeve outfit weaved in cotton. Figo complimented in his way, "*Ah! Fine clothes have the ability to portray a fool to be smart.*" Akello's new short haircut and fine clothes applied to magic Akello's look. Akello replied with a smudged face and asked about the destination of the journey. Without leaking a breath, Figo galloped the mare. Out of no option, Akello followed him. Rushing pair of four legs stopped at the cave entrance of Shridal. Akello is happy to spend time in Shridal. Shridal was sacred. The villagers live inside caves and the ruler of Alaoka protects all secrets of Alaoka that are stored in the chambers of caves. Beyond all, it has the largest market of Alaoka to buy and sell in exchange for goods. Figo and Akello tied the horses near the cave entrance and stepped into the sacred caves.

Mount Shridal is a magnificent wonder standing tall in the large savanna of Alaoka. The scars on her body have a decent depth; they are homes for the wild in the forest. But those small caves are just camouflaged to the massive shallowness hidden under the ground level. The opening in the west of Shridal has a long throat that can swallow hundreds of heads at once. Long throat entrances open to the subterranean; a wide, three-storey tall underground city of Alaoka is located below. The history of Alaoka says that once Mt. Shridal was an active volcano. Its lava created the subterranean. Caves have enough sunlight, small and big chambers, air ventilation and drainage systems to lead a peaceful life. Falls inside the cave pushed water to the bottom. Water flowing in the caves has a unique taste; many believe the medicinal herbs at the top of the mountain are responsible for its taste and its pale pink water.

Akello followed Figo. While walking, he asked, "*Figo, what are you going to buy? Our hands are empty.*" Figo's foot paused for a moment and he continued his walk without a word. The long throat opens to five channels, and three of them lead to the market on the first lower floor. The rest leads to settlements inside the caves. Figo stepped into the one that directs to the village, Akello moving further with voice, "*But, why?*" Figo turned around and reversed the steps to his friend, then he clutched the hands of Akello and walked toward the village. The path was flooded by guards and officials of Alaoka. When they identified Akello, their eyes leaked poison and bad whispers echoed in the crooks of the tunnel. Akello's eyes expressed shame. With anger, he undid his hands from Figo's and continued walking toward the village. He looked at Figo with fire in his eyes. Figo was literally burned to ashes, but he had no other choice. It's been a month since Eric asked Figo to meet him in the cave, along with his companion.

Crooked tunnels ended at a vast underground village in the caves. The sides of the huts were made of stone. A small pink water pond created greens on her sides. God rays of sun escaped from the pointed and craggy roof of the caves. Figo avoided eye contact with Akello. He felt sorry for what he had done. Akello got a chance to meet some high-ranking men of the Alaoka again. The way they looked at Akello was like an owl, eagle, and snake. Akello's ears started to ring when he glimpsed the face of Gamba. Gamba's well-built chest added an X-shaped scar gifted by the canine family and Neo. Eric was busy with official duty, and as usual, Gamba was standing adjacent to him.

Eric's head caught sight of a brat who stood for justice and the law of Alaoka. He also noticed the restlessness in his shape. Eric excused himself from official work and walked near Figo and Akello. Alaokans have a tradition of bending on their knees before the leader as a sign of respect, especially in the warrior ranks. Figo bent on his knees when the leader moved next to him. The next moment, Akello downed his frame to show his respect. Akello's overthinking attitude was better than any fantasy. Akello's inner voice screamed, "*I am going to be executed for my crime!*" All of a sudden, the robust voice of the salt-bearded old man pronounced, "*RISE...COLTS...*" He congratulated Akello and Figo for their successful debut in the pirate war. He mentioned that reinforcement gathered by Akello, and the company changed the course of the war. Akello and Figo stood silent with their heads down, but everyone's eyes were targeted at Akello.

Eric asked their fellow Alaokans to appreciate the young brats for the valor they showed in the war, but still, the silence continued. A man with an X-shaped scar on his chest broke the silence with a stomp and his palms clapped to cheer the brats. Akello's down-facing eyes noticed claps from Gamba that made the tiny gravel stones dance. Once again, he was amazed by the physical strength of the commander. In no time, Akello and Figo felt the earth tremor underneath and thunder claps on their heads. Eric whispered a secret in the ears of Gamba and ordered the brats to follow him inside the cave. When Akello walked out of the cave, he was punched by sticks. Akello's shirt was partially covered by blood stains. Beyond all, once again Eric regained his legendary status in

Akello's heart and Akello's face glowed in pride, and he was glad that Figo had brought him to the caves.

Alaokans have a tradition of tattooing as a reward for their individual acts in critical situations and wars. The order of issuing tattoos needs to come from the almighty leader. Like a griffin bite scar on the forefinger, these tattoos are also highly respected in the Alaokan society. Most tattooed Alaokan warriors prefer outfits that tend to show their tattoos.

Alaokan has four tattoos of honor.

- Tattoo of self-possession: steel wings of griffin
- Tattoo of loyalty: head of the howling wolf
- Tattoo of bravery: claws of the tiger
- Tattoo of generalship (strategy): eye of a griffin

Akello was gifted with a tattoo of bravery for his actions against Eric. However, many consider him a cashew nut and blood-rushing teen. The brown lens of the wise leader found wild courage and free will in Akello's voice. When the sky was pouring, Akello's words were like fearless lightning arrows and the electric charge it carried was justice out of the free will. Sin carried out on Eric's name, making him feel that he was a failure.

"*YES! Eric is a failure. We can't deny the fact. Alaokans won the war by breaking their code of life, executing evil along with heavy casualties. Eric had nothing left with him to brace himself from the shock arrows of Akello, but he dodged them in the name of protecting Alaoka. Still, internally, he felt it was not fair justice.*"

Alaokans never show their back to their leaders, but the best strategist in the world was Eric. He knew his reign was a dark age for Alaoka. He recalled the last vocalization of his late father, Gorath, one who forecasted the end of Varuonans with his administration and analytical skills:

"*Good leaders and strong-willed people are the perfect combos for a better tomorrow!*

To be a good leader, you need to have brave people to question you!

You can't undo the mistakes, but you can find the resolution!"

Eric grieved, "*My doors passing to heaven's gate are a daydream,*" and confessed to Akello that he committed an unforgivable sin. Akello was frozen. His confession to Akello was not necessary, but Akello's questions were on the path of justice, and Eric believed his confession to Akello may allow him to sleep. He also allowed him to wear a tattoo of bravery, and he believes that Akello will become a fine leader someday. While the tattoo was engraved on Akello's shoulders, Gamba complimented the valor of Akello and his radium-eyed griffin. With a rough voice, he vocalized, "*I owe you one for the signature of griffin's claws in my chest.*" In seconds, Akello's shape was bathed in sweat, but the sudden laughter of Gamba clarified that it was a sarcastic joke. Eric called Figo 'steel wing.' He said that Figo's mentor recommended his name for the 'tattoo of self-possession.' Losing a family member is the pain that weighs 100-ton clouds, but even after losing his sister and brother-in-law, Figo was calm enough to analyze the situation and make clear-cut moves. He gave importance to his duty rather than personal emotion, it's rare to have this self-possession in teenage. The tattoo of self-possession was awarded only to a few. Now, Figo was added to the list. Like Akello and Figo, a few other Alaokan soldiers were also awarded with sticks and pokes. Gamba commented to Eric, "*These two brats are like ice and fire. The mountain brown lad has fire in his attitude, but Figo was just opposite to him, focused and perfect.*"

Eric thought, "*If I was not calm like Figo and behaved furiously like Akello, the reign of Varuonans would have ended before their alliance with pirates and most of Alaokans' life would be saved.*"

Everyone fears the no-moon sky, but these men sailing in the black sails have no fear buds. They are wanderers who are never lost in the blue. Their arms are strong like anchors and have bull eyes to slay any predator 'who crosses their way,' but to survive in the salt chunk, strength alone is not sufficient. The outlanders call them pirates. Pirates always travel in companies and seeing a single black sail is merely impossible. Nightfalls are their favorite and pirates cherish the long darkness with ale mugs by singing a song of stars in unison. They love stargazing and every pirate has a better knowledge of stars because they navigate and find a change in the winds with the help of star positions. They believe in one god; his name is Polaris. In troublesome times, when they chin up in the north, one can easily find the brightest light of Polaris, and it's a sign of hope.

Somewhere under the diamond-spread sky, a pack of 15 ships were sailing in the formation of crocodiles. The first ship sailing in the position of a crocodile head led to the formation. Waves gently caressed the lion's head figure on the ship, and the captain was gently lying on the top deck. His brown eyes were fixed on the shire of Polaris and his ale-smelling brown beard was a humiliation to his subordinates and captives. They never take baths or brush at regular intervals; they live like pigs in mud. At the speed of the sails, the captain noted their ships were moving far east from the Polaris. The man in the navigation bucket noted the flashing of fireworks at the end of his eye. The next moment, he howled in fear with mixed excitement, "*We are near home!*" After hearing his howl instead of heavy cheers, every face on the ship panicked and big whispers began. Captain gently walked to the bow of the ship and his ears were listening to the whispers about their failed coup against Alaokans and fear of facing the leader. Pirates tinted the flavor of red blood in Alaoka and looted many valuables from the cluster island, but at the same, they lost eight best captains and 100s of strong men. Beyond all, they also lost two of their warships. No pirate has enough guts to face the rage of a leader with this defeat. Captain's vision recalled Kayon's meeting with pirates and they were in a pact with Varuonans after the successful coup against Alaoka. Varuonans promised to give the cluster islands of the Alaokans to the pirates.

As ships headed further toward the east, tall standing masters with amber crowns welcomed them with their burst and leak of lava from crates. After seeing the fireworks of the volcano, ships lowered their sails and followed one another in a linear fashion. After crossing a dozen slow volcanoes, the captain of the first ship blew the bull horn to notify the harbor about their arrival, followed by him and other ship captains also blew their horns. Each and every horn reflects a unique sound; this unique noise helps in communication from a distance and identifies the ships. The sound of the horns reached the ears of the pirate lord and other living beings on the mainland. There is a custom for pirates; the leader's ship should be anchored at the entrance of the port.

The first light touched the head figure of every ship and slowly walked into the homeland of the pirate. The land of pirates was the favorite child of the sun. The sun stands here for 18 hours a day. Plants are leathery and grow with thorns and spikes. Hot sand, dry air and poisonous snakes are always ready to drain life. This land was cursed with sand dunes and endless hot summers!

In an aerial view, the mainland of pirates is located between the islands with active volcanoes with a scarcity of green. The mainland is a wild desert but in the wonders of nature it has a small repository of a freshwater lake in the middle and the lake never drained until this day. The freshwater lake and red meat made life possible on this land. The captain of the lion head figure ship was leading the camel herd, carrying big loot and Alaokan captives to meet the lord of pirates. Camel felt it hard to carry him because he resembled a beefy beast whom Akello had taken down. When the sun reached above the heads, camels crossed the broken old huts and marketplace and trekked in the dunes to reach the red-round hut of the leader with heavy sweat. Hot lands drained the water out of riders and a foul smell of sweat knocked on the doors of the red hut. Pirates waited outside the hut. Hours passed, but the sound of moaning in pleasure never dimmed out. Around the hut, strong crew members of the leader's ships always guard the leader and ensure his safety.

The sun moved further west. Finally, the lord of pirates showed up with a lighted cigar between his lips and a spear in his grip. He forgot to cover his sloppy body with outfits. The men waiting outside the hut moved their eyes out of nuts, and they were shocked to see the spear-picked (impaled) head of their leader. The sloppy man holding the spear was a crew member of the late leader, but now he is their new lord. The life of a pirate is hard. In the current solar calendar, this naked man is their fourth leader. Betrayal was mainstreamed in pirate culture. The leader change at this point of time was happy news for the raiders of Alaoka; their new lord, Adio, was one who was against the alliance of Varouanas and the war against Alaoka. Lord Adio cleared his throat to announce his presence. In response, the beefy pirate Druzo went down on his knees in acceptance of the new lord and the other captains following him to save their heads from failure. Pirate captains submitted loot and slaves on the new lord's foot. Adio's eyes scanned them. His eyes were attracted to the sack of white seeds and he grabbed the handful of seeds and inhaled its aroma. The aroma of it made Adio's peanut brain recall the taste of cooked white seeds. Alaokans call it 'rice.'

Chapter 3

Graveyard of White Sand

The day after the harvest season, Akello was simply lying in bed and staring at wide blues. Clues for the arrival of winter started all over Alaoka, winds started to blow toward the wide Shridhal range. The wind disturbed the fertile soil in agriculture fields and carried the red dust along with her toward the west. It is a sign that the density of wind has become thick and they can expect the start of the winter in a week or two. Hours passed by, but Akello had not moved his butt from the bed. The sun reached the top; he had no good purpose to move, other than filling his tummy, and all his friends were busy. Kino became close to handicapped Ekon. Though there were a lot of differences between their age, attitude, and grade in the Alaokan army, one common thing was they survived the war by sacrificing their griffins. Kino's pain was curable by the one who undergoes the same pain. Amara and her family traveled to a faraway village to celebrate the harvest festival with her maternal grandparents and her uncles. Figo was busy with his family rethatching the hut roof for winter. Typically, Akello has nothing on priority and no need to call Neo. After some time, the mother's love made Ava serve the food to her lovely son in bed, which made Akello more comfortable. With dull yellow light, the sun started to set. Akello's eyes got sight of the entire scene of sunrise to sunset, bright yellow to pale yellow. Later, a thick blanket of darkness covered the wide blues. Today, under the hood of the sun, Lord Akello of Ava's hut only stepped down from his bed four times just for urination.

The dark sky was clear and stars were clustered here and there and the crackling sound of the woods escaped from Akello's hut. Ava was preparing the dinner and Moona was helping her. In Alaoka, women are the best cooks and a 3,000-year-old civilization believed men had no good taste in cooking and remembering the ingredients and quantity of it was difficult for their brains. When the females of Akello's houses were busy, Akello was simply taking a nap in the gentle breeze. The aroma of cooking meat entered the nostrils of Akello and made him up with a growling stomach. He walked to the cooking bay in his small hut and prized her mom for the aroma of food. She acknowledged his compliment with a wide smile. It was about dinner time, but grandpa didn't reach the hut. Akello and others waited for him, but he didn't show up, so the family enjoyed the rabbit meat without grandpa. It's been an hour since dinner, but still, grandpa didn't show up. Akello and his family were puzzled. The old saying, "*Empty mind is the devil's heart.*"

Akello's mind was fresh from the morning, which made him overthink. His mind iterated the scenarios in which something would have happened to his 100-year-old man. He heard the sound of whispering outside the hut. He pushed his legs out of bed. It was grandpa and his apprentice. Akello sensed the excitement in their faces and voices. They were not empty-handed, and five of grandpa's men carried a giant fossil (bone) of some mysterious creature. Osseous white matter they carried reflected in the luminous moonlight. Akello and others presumed the fossil to be the rib cage bone of a mysterious beast. The fear factor is that a fossil was 2x the size of well-built Alaokan men. Grandpa confirmed that the fossil was definitely not the bone of an ancient dragon. Being centuries-old, many other fossils in the caves have completely vanished into white dust. Grandpa excitedly uttered, "*There were a lot of elephant tusks around the cave. Maybe this rib cage belongs to a giant elephant.*" But he got his words back within seconds. From his words, Akello understood something massive and cruel lived in the caves centuries ago. The cave was located next to the 'village of 15 huts.' For the very first time, it was discovered by the eyes of Neo. Later, investigations of inscriptions on the haunted hut walls made Davu find the route to the cave. He named it 'caves of 1,000 deaths.'

Akello was curious to know which animal species the fossil belongs to. All night, he was sleepless because he took a long nap in the evening, and that made him up all night. A sleepless night developed a curiosity. Being up all night around dawn, Akello fell asleep. He missed the chirping sound of birds and the morning fresh air but not breakfast. When the fireball reached the center of the blues, he had his breakfast. At the same time, his sister was having her lunch. She mocked him for his noodle hair. After having breakfast in the afternoon, Akello decided to surprise his grandpa in the 'caves of 1,000 deaths' and was also curious to see the fossil of tusks. After the bath, he trekked to Cov Mountains; a short trek on the steep mountain path made Akello reach the cliff. The cliff was wide and long. From the edge, his forwarded eyes could see tall vertical mountains standing in the wide southern ocean. The sunrays gazed at half of the mountains and sparkled the ocean water. There are 10 tall vertical mountains in total but not wider in breadth (pillar caves). All vertical mountains were dressed in green and a loud squall made the continuous waves hit the bottom of the rocky Cov Mountains. The Cov Mountains were only open to griffin riders. The bite scars of the griffins are the entry pass to the trek. The locals called the cliff in the Cov Mountains as 'summoning-paari.'

Bull-eyed champs can see the opening of the caves in the vertical mountains. Those openings are doors to hybrid eagles' nests. No one has plucked up the courage to visit the griffin's nest. There were many griffins flying around tall mountains, but after the pirate war, griffins were reduced in number.

The Alaokan griffin myth says, "*The coal-black griffins are doorkeepers of the nest, the nut-brown are the warrior class, iron gray are elders (decision-makers) of the nest, olive-green and peacock-blue griffins are offspring of the royal king. Royal griffin king eyes were gold plated and their feathers were blood-red."*

The red and gray feathers are unseen in the wide skies and long landscapes of Alaoka. Akello decided to summon Neo. With a loud tone, he shouted, "*Neo!*" The call for Neo echoed on the cliff. "*Neo! Neo!*"

Griffins are praised for their sharp eyes, ears, and good memory. Akello roared Neo's name again. It's much louder than the first call. In a few seconds, a loud screech, "*Krr...*" tore the sky in response to the call. He got sight of his majestic olive griffin flying toward him. The next moment, the strong claws of Neo scratched the ground of 'summoning-paari,' Akello ran and hugged the eagle head with a happy heart. He prepared himself to ride and directed Neo to the 'caves of 1,000 deaths.' It takes two hours to reach on hooves, but with wings, it won't be long. From the aerial view, Alaoka was beautiful. After crossing the haunted ruins, Akello identified the 'caves of 1,000 deaths' with the mares and mustangs standing outside the cave. The entrance of the cave was guarded by Alaokan soldiers. Akello understood that the cave is located in the middle of the deep forest to protect the horses and his companions. Grandpa requested hoplites for security.

Akello directed Neo to land near the cave. Half a dozen hoplites moved near Akello with swords and spears and asked him to evacuate the area. One of the hoplites noticed the tattoo on Akello's shoulder and recognized the tattoo of bravery. Hoplite whispered about the tattoo to fellow comrades. The next moment, Akello can feel the rise of respect in their words. Akello explained to them that he was the grandson of Davu; his respect increased much better than before. With the designation of 'Archaeology Legend Davu Grandson,' Akello convinced the hoplites to enter the cave. Akello patted Neo and asked him to stay silent. He walked toward the caves with the untouched marshal. The entrance of the cave was a small mouth, but a small entrance of the cave unfolded into a deep tube-shaped tunnel, moving deep down. The grace of the sunlight ended at a certain point and his barefoot felt the moisture of the cave. Suddenly, darkness made his vision worthless, but his coal-black lens caught the sight of a small flame at a distance. He carefully made his steps toward the distant fire to light his marshall. The moment he lit the marshal, he felt himself as an explorer and started to explore. Cave walls hold a series of inscriptions which were written with the help of stones, but Akello's average brain cannot decode the information on the walls of the cave. By scratching his head, he continued on his foot. A wide tube tunnel took him to the large empty hall, and the hall has three big openers to the next chambers. Akello was all stuck now. He didn't know which opener to choose, and his skin was eased by the moisture of the caves. Akello stood silently. Rounding his eyes, he noticed the white pigmentation in the walls of the hall and a small dripping sound of water disturbed his ears. The next moment, hope appeared in the faint echoes of Davu's voice.

Faded echoes of Davu's voice were leaking from the middle tunnel, Akello followed the echoes and stepped into the middle one. The center opening has fossil bones of dead animals; later, the path became steep and Akello got to work on his reflexes to proceed further. Echo of his grandpa's words was clear; the path he selected landed him in the place where everything was covered by semi-white color sand and he also got a sight of giant bones popping above the sand. The moisture in the caves no longer exists, and from the torched marshal, he saw glitters in the sand. He got a spark in his brain and found the truth about white sand. The white sand is not actual sand. All white around him were powdered bone fossils. These fossils were unexplored for centuries, thereby making calcium lose its definite shape. For a moment, Akello felt like he was walking in the graveyard of the ancients. He whispered, "*Lot and lot of bones! What sort of place is this?*" With astonishment and wonder, he continued ascending. Continuous conversation between grandpa and his apprentices made it easy for him to reach them.

The cave was enormous. From the chamber opening, grandpa was very happy to see his lovely Akello in his workspace, and grandpa was loud. "*Unexpected to see you here, my boy!*" The chamber in which grandpa and his apprentice were working in was also covered by white sand. Davu excitedly guided his grandson on a tour. Davu mentioned that this cave has many subdivisions and different levels. He mentioned the place where they were standing was the ridge part. He took Akello to the hall with three openings and walked to one on the very left. Davu advised Akello to keep an eye on the ground and asked him to follow his steps. After a few dozen steps, they reached a cliff inside the cave. On the downside of the cliff, Akello caught sight of a narrow horizontal path covered with stagnant water. Davu explained that yearly rainfall brings water inside the cave and creates a pond here. Akello was paralyzed to see the beauty of nature. Grandpa's fingers pointed to the pond. He mentioned this was the groove part of the cave; he also said that in case of heavy rain, the hallway that they walked in would be flooded. Akello recalled the moisture in the cave and the white pigmentation in the cave walls. The white pigmentation was caused by an increase in water level.

With a smile and happiness, Davu took Akello to the last opening in the hallway. The third opening was short and narrow. Akello's vision was colorless because of the darkness in the cave. Out of curiosity, he asked, "*Grandpa, what's special here?*" With laughter, he raised the torched marshall above. Small and big reflections from the roof glittered in Akello's eyes. It looks like a firefly, but it's a bright white light and immovable. Akello's face was filled with amusement. Grandpa took a white stone from his pocket and exhibited his legacy. In the light of the fire torch, a white stone reflected with all his powers; the reflection made Akello shrink his eyes. Grandpa put back the stone in his pocket and mentioned that the stone they found had high reflecting quality and this is the first time in history we have found one like this in Alaoka. At last, he also took him to the graveyard of white sand and Akello saw grandpa's apprentice digging white sand using shovels carefully.

Akello was not aware of why they were digging in the white sand. Cashew nut has a unique character; the seed of the fruit always grows outside. Akello has a similar character. Before the explanation of his grandpa, he started to speak about white sand, but this time he was right.

He asked his grandpa, "*These white sand are powdered bone fossils. Am I correct?*"

Grandpa replied, "*Excellent! My clever grandson found out the truth about white sand.*" He explained how bones were converted into white sand. Akello was very happy and started enjoying a one-day trip in 'the cave of 1,000 deaths' with his grandpa. Davu named this chamber as 'the grave of white sand.' He also said that this chamber was at a high altitude in the cave, so the remains were untouched by water and were safe for many centuries and awaiting gramps like him to explore. The tiredness of the cave tour reflected on Davu's face. He sat down on a big rock near the chamber entrance and rested his back on the cave wall.

All of a sudden, white sand diggers shouted in excitement, "*We found something here!*" Grandpa and Akello rushed to the site of the diggers. There were a total of seven members, including Akello. Davu can sense the light of success on his co-workers' faces; he also questioned them, "*Anything precious?*" A stout man replied, "*We have found the fossil of some weird creature covered completely in sand. We are trying to unearth the fossil without damage.*" Grandpa understood very well the difficulties in his job. Tired old Davu suddenly took the shovel and started digging with other young men in the caves. Akello was fascinated and puzzled to see his grandpa. A moment ago, he was fragile and rested down on a rock, but this very moment, without considering his age, he was pushing himself hard. Akello also had questions for himself, "*What is the source of grandpa's energy*?" He thought his passion for the profession was generating enough strength to work. A good-shaped hoplite guarding the cave entrance showed up in the graveyard of white sand. He was loud and clear.,"*The sun is about to go to the extreme end. It is not safe to be in the cave any longer*." Sunset is a problem, and it's not safe for horses to stand out. With sad faces, everyone decided to leave for the day. The worries on grandpa's face doubled; he is worried about tomorrow as winter begins. The grace of sunlight is less than expected, so they can't explore the entire cave before the next rainy season. Grandpa knows the consequences, but still, he is curious to know what is hidden in the white sand. Putting his trust in Akello's strength, he requested his grandson to guard the entrance of the cave. All the faces in the cave began to bloom after hearing Davu. Akello replied, "*Yes*," without a second thought. He had never seen his grandpa in the position of the requester. When Akello said yes, the happiness on Davu's face was priceless to Akello. He felt proud to do a favor for his grandpa. Everyone positively nodded their heads and started to resume the work with the same excitement. After an hour, Akello assured their safety and walked to the cave entrance to stop other wild animals from hunting. Akello signed the mission in the trust of Neo, and he sent a message through guards to his village and other apprentice villages that Davu's team would stay in the caves for the entire night so that their family could rest without worrying about them.

When Akello reached the cave entrance, he caught sight of his sleeping olive bird. The size of his belly clarified that he had a good hunt of rodents in the forest. He saw the bright sunlight and slowly it became pale orange and a gentle chilly breeze hugged Akello with pleasure. Akello approached his beast friend; he smoothly rubbed his forefinger against the yellow beak. Neo gently raised his back foot. After a lazy break, he stood erect and showed his affection by rubbing his face against Akello's chest. This happens every single time. Neo gave a head rub on Akello's heart.

Akello told Neo about the mission, *"We are on a mission to protect the cave entrance and horses so that grandpa and others can be safe inside. I am not afraid, Neo. You are there to armor and shield me."*

Akello's words made Neo scream in pride. The cave entrance was guarded by Akello and a half-quarter dozen of hoplites. Two of them were carrying the message of Akello to villagers, and the rest walked to gather greens for horses. There were eight horses in total. By the time the other hoplites returned to the entrance with enough grass and firewood, the forest became gloomy and the buzz of the insects rang in their ears. Akello believed Neo's furious war screams would dare anyone to come near the cave. In the darkness, Akello was fascinated to see Neo's semi-golden color lens contraction and expansion. The neigh of the horses brought the visitors to the cave entrance. Instead of fighting them, Akello directed his hybrid-eagle friend to make a war cry on a high pitch. The next moment, the sound of escaping paws with fear made

Alaokan soldiers laugh, but as an adverse effect, horses were frightened by Neo's scream. When the moon visited Alaoka with stars, she brought a new guest along with her, the cold breeze. But Ms. Cold Breeze's gentle breath was not bearable by fellow Alaokans. To fight her cold breath, the campfire was lit near the doorway of caves. To avoid incoming predators, Akello ordered Neo to scream at intervals to bring fear into the predator's heart. Luckily, his strategy worked well.

The sun, little by little, wiped the darkness of the night and created a morning-twilight in the sky, especially from the woods; it was a feast to Akello's eyes. The light beam of the sun made fog naked to the vision. By penetrating the fog, the sunlight touched the water droplets on the leaves. The comfort of light energy and the song of chirping birds and singing monkeys melted the soul to cherish nature. Akello walked into the cave with great hope of seeing the unearthed fossil. When he reached near the hallway, his nose sensed the delicious smell of a cooking fish. In the white graveyard, digging continued to get to the bottom of the fossil. In the corner, grandpa and his men were cooking delicious fish for everyone. The aroma of the BBQ fish tempted his taste buds, so he stepped toward his grandpa and grabbed the bite of fish from Davu's hands. Protein and fats of fish melted in his mouth. He felt he was well paid for last night's guard duty. After four fish settled in the tummy, his brain started to work. He understood that his grandpa managed to get fish from a pond inside the cave (groove part of caves). He walked to the digging ground to see the surprise. The fossil is the skull of some mysterious creature, but it was not fully unearthed.

The size of the skull was twice the height of an average Alaokan. No doubt that the owner of the fossil was a furious predator in the olden days. From the Marshall Fire, Davu can see more ancient inscriptions written on fossils and Akello too noticed the inscriptions.

Grandpa said, "*I am more eager to know the inscriptions written on the fossil.*"

Grandpa brought up an important point. Ancient people have a habit of writing valuable information on bones and cave walls; these are clues and teachings they left for their future. Fossils were proof of how the ancients led their lives. Information like a formula for curing the rain flu and brewing the first alcohol was written as an inscription in the fossil once. Davu asked Akello to keep the fossil private from outsiders and continued his path with a shovel. Akello left the cave with the information that grandpa gave and the crew will be back to their village at sundown. Akello reached the hut and explained to his mom and sister the necessary filters for keeping the fossil information private.

Akello's eyes were burning because of sleepless nights. He felt sorry for the hoplites because they own a responsibility to secure the cave and they can't rest like him. After having breakfast at home, he hugged the bed in tiredness and Neo occupied the cattle shed. Pity, the new cattle in the shed were afraid of Neo's snoring sound, and they froze in fear. Akello's dreams were full of fossils; he created shapes and color for the owner of the bone. When he woke up, it was nightfall again, and he had no memory of his dream. The eyes caught a glimpse of the sky and the radiance of the moon explained it was a full moon day. Akello purged some water from the pot to wet his throat and checked for his grandpa. He was fuzzy after seeing an empty cot. The next moment, he walked to check with mom but she was sleeping so he moved his foot out of the hut. He felt the chillness in the soil on his teeth. Cattle were fitted with two cows and an ox, and a large space of the cattle was occupied by Neo. He worries that his grandpa's horse has not reached home, which means grandpa is still in the cave. The song of the dire wolf added flavor to Akello's overthinking mind.

Akello grabbed his sword and wore a seven-hand tall cloak. Alaokans wore cloaks made of jute to fight against the breath of Ms. Cold Breeze. The full moon in the sky brightened the villages and terrains. Neo was carrying Akello to the graveyard of white sand again. While in the air, his hands were frozen. He wished to fly with Amara, and he wanted her warmth in this cold winter. After spending some time in the air, Akello's eyes caught sight of the cave. Logs were arranged in a zig-zag pattern and a bright campfire was lit to fight the winter. Escaping smoke and dancing flames were influenced by the cold breeze. While Akello was sleeping in the morning, the cave was occupied by new visitors. The size of horses and hoplites was exponentially increased by two, along with roaming tamed fangs and mountain bears. Tightened security and new visitors increased the suspicion of Akello. He asked Neo to land near the caves. When Neo's claws touched the gates of the cave, Akello was surrounded by his fellow Alaokans with pointed weapons. Akello moved his tattooed shoulder, undone the hoodie and introduced himself under the umbrella of his grandpa's reputation. He purposely showed the tattoo by relaxing his arms. He enjoys the way others talk about his tattoos. The lead of hoplites moved his eyeballs in yoyo fashion at Akello. His bravery tattoo and Davu's reputation made him pass the guards. He left his beast at the entrance and walked with a lighted touch toward the cave. A scary dire wolf was sleeping at the cave mouth with a loud snore. Akello was meeting the same dire wolf for the second time; it was Gamba's 'Blu.'

When Akello was walking, the clashing sound of swords clung to his ears when he ran into the hallway that looked like a marketplace. Elders and high-ranking Alaokans fitted in. Wooden barrels of ale added extra entertainment to the cave.

The roasted pork aroma made everyone drool, and it tasted heavenly. In the center, two elders were swinging their swords and dodging with their agility. The crowd enjoyed a fun fight with a wager. Grandpa Davu, leader Eric, and first-in-command Gamba were also carrying the ale mugs and enjoyed the clash of swords. Akello maintained himself low to avoid conflict. After some time, Davu noticed his grandson and welcomed him with a warm hug. He noticed the eye bags of his grandpa and he was worried about the two sleepless nights Davu had. The sad part is the crowd had plenty of ale and empty ale mugs, but no one offered a mug of ale to him. Humorless jokes and meaningless laughter made Akello feel he was getting old every minute. In the devil's hour, many dozed off and only eight were awake. Grandpa walked into the chamber where the unearthed skull was kept. First Alaokan Eric and other elders followed him. Gamba's defined eyebrows found the vigilant Akello, and he rounded his eyes to find anyone was up. Gamba called Akello and put his muscular hands on Akello's shoulder and accompanied him toward the fossil. At that moment, Akello was astonished to see 30+ scars and four tattoos of honors on Gamba's hunk body.

The unearthed skull is lengthier, 10 ft tall. It was uniquely defined. It has only one opening for the eyes and teeth were spiked and rodded. All over the skull, the small crooked horns were grown. There were 30 horns in total. All nine members, including Akello, were shocked to see the shape of the skull. Out of the nine, none were Davu's apprentices. Eric moved the lighted marshall near the skull. The inscriptions were done all over the skull. Higher officials commented, "*Holy shit! What animal does this skull belong to? What if such a beast was in existence today?*"

The archaeology legend of Alaoka was silent. He had no answers to posted questions. He is not simply called 'Archaeology legend of Alaoka.' His passion for archaeology made him explore plenty of caves in Alaoka. He unlocked the secret chambers of the sacred Alaokan caves of Mt. Shridhal. Davu looked at Akello; it was a pitiful look.

He breathed to Eric and other officials, "*My grandson Akello is not an elder or higher official in Alaoka. I see no great purpose for him to stand here along with the legends. If he is welcomed here because he is my grandson, I request Eric to banish him outside the chamber.*" Akello was shocked to hear Davu and his anger escape out of his nostrils. Gamba's eyes caught sight of Eric. Eric nodded his head with a smile, and his eyes were focused on Akello. Akello was tense at that moment. Once again, all eyes in the chamber were fixed on him. Eric smiled and boasted, "*Looks like brat's shoulder was decorated with a tattoo of bravery. Now, he has his own respect, and no longer needs to piggyback your name, Davu.*" Akello was happy to hear such a compliment from their leader. Instead of feeling proud of his grandson, the fear of losing him budded in Davu's mind.

Davu shook his head in affirmation and started, "*The skull was totally covered by powdered bones. Being skull was not exposed to moisture; it made the skull completely safe from the powdering process. There were a lot of inscriptions scripted in the fossil. The pictures of the animal engraved in the inscription were out of existence many years ago. The inscriptions in the left hemisphere of the skull talk about the prehistory of civilizations that emerged in the blue-green land. Knowledge of the fossil is not just limited to Alaoka! It speaks about the endless battle between Beku-neu, Alaoka, Draguva, and Yuvalle. The information imprinted in the fossil stands as the first proof of the existence of gorgeous Yali, Aalikai, and an invisible island guarded by strange tides. To my knowledge, I swear this giant skull is the oldest archaeological finding we have ever discovered.*"

When everyone began to whisper, Eric was silent, like the ocean before the storm. No one has ever heard the name Yali and Aalikai before. Alaoka is not the only civilization that emerged in the ancient world. Beyond the boundaries of Alaoka Beku-neu, Draguva and Yuvalle were leading their life in the defined borders with their own chaos. There was no sharing of cakes between these civilizations, but they shared blood, gore and skulls of fallen as offerings. Akello pronounced, "*Aalikai.*" He wondered what it was, and at the same time, Gamba was thinking about 'Draguva.' At that moment, his eyes were burning red. Davu bent his legs near the skull. In the vision of the dancing fire, his bagged eyes focused on inscriptions, and the mouth reciprocated his vision.

Davu started with a note, "*I am going to blow out our past beliefs and history that we knew till today. Facts that are decoded from the skull are really unbelievable.*" He continued, "*Once Alaoka, Beku-neu, Draguva, and Yuvalle shared bread and beer instead of blood. We all lived in peace and supported one another back in critical times. People of civilizations lived under the reign of their beloved leaders, who always cared for the happiness of their people as their priority. Every year on the first harvest week of the lunar calendar, leaders of all four civilizations used to meet on the central vast island. This meetup of leaders is not just a conference; it's a festival that happens for seven consecutive days. As per the inscription, the central island was located in the craggy oceans as a paradise with a tropical climate and various varieties of fauna and flora garnished across the vast landscape. The rulers of the island were born blind, but their extraordinary aura can read the happenings of the future. Not only Alaokans but all the other civilizations had a belief in their predictions.*"

"In these seven days, one of the biggest events was 'meeting of four,' where leaders discuss the wealth and welfare of the civilizations, and they talk about new problems to find resolutions. In the death of the night after rituals, blinds of the native lands read the future under the light of a million stars. The ultimate goal of all leaders is the same, to deliver a better lifestyle for the people under their hood. Knowledge sharing about herbs, shrubs, weeds, taming animals, hunting, agriculture, food recipes, and medical science was exhibited by representatives of civilization. It is a kind of reunion of friends from different civilizations, to spend time together doing their common interests and sometimes intra-civilizations marriages happen too. This skull is the standing evidence that fire created by rubbing of stones was exhibited by Yuvalle, ale was introduced to the world by Draguvans, techniques of hunting and taming the wild beasts were taught by Beku-neu and Alaokans shared the bags of seeds and taught agriculture to the world." While narrating the gift of Alaokans to the world, Davu's tone sounded proud and all patriots in the hall had blossoming smiles on their faces. Young Akello was surprised to hear all these at the same time. He also doubted his grandpa's words because grandpa was sleepless.

Davu started again, "*Years...*" But his old throat started to cough. The first man of Alaokan aided him with the jug of water and asked him to take some rest. Eric is a kind man, and he always trusted Davu without a droplet of doubt. Davu's discoveries of old palm leaves about agriculture and farming gave rebirth to Alaokan farming techniques. The whispers buzzed around the skull and the ripe man started to decode the information again. "*The blind rulers of the central island crafted similar swords and gifted them to rulers of four great civilizations as a sign of unity and prosperity. Swords were not made of steel or copper. It was crafted out of rocks fallen from the sky and its handle was made of the dark spinal cord of the Yali. For the festival, people used to bring their tamed animals to show off the world. The crowd cheers and welcomes the leaders to start the exhibition. Each and every land has its own unique pride, which other civilizations do not possess. Trades of rare roots, animal hides, and hunting gears were sold in exchange for other valuables. When everything was going well, that year, blind priests failed to predict the clash of shields and swords. Jealousy and vengeance slowly started to root in the minds of leaders and their people. In the beginning, this vengeance had no name. Later, vengeance got the shape of local gods, power, and pride. The first war was waged by Alaokans against Beku-neu in the 'meeting of four'.*"

After hearing Davu, Eric's face was doomed for a reason. Akello and others noted the change of seasons on Eric's face.

Within a decade, harmony and unity were shattered; they gathered on the central island to show off their powers. Instead of sharing new inventions, they share blood and vengeance. All party and marriage halls became murderers' godowns and armories. Decades rolled; all four civilizations were lost in never-ending vengeance. When the trust trembled, they had no belief in the alliance. They stood alongside their fellow bloodline and fought independently. The weeping part was vengeance, and power lust selected the central island as their stage.

Continuous bloodshed on the central islands changed the soil color to deep red. The serenity of blinds and their people was shaken; the armyless blind kings had no power to stop the war. The central island people came up with peace ideas, but their ideas to maintain law and order were ignored by lords of civilizations. The people under the blind kings found a way to stop the war on their tropical island. They found magic to tame the mythical animal Yali, the living monster on land, and Aalikai, the demons in the deepest ocean. The city and shore of blind kings were guarded by the Yali army. Yali tore flesh and crushed the bones of the intruders and weak boats do not have a chance against strong tides that are created by the demons of the ocean. These strong tides protected the central island from four civilizations. Tide and tall waves were fair enough to hide the central island from existence.

Gamba's loud laughter echoed in the chamber. The vocalization of Davu was stopped, and everyone's eyes fixed on Gamba. Gamba said, "*Ridiculous! So your imaginary island and these imaginary animals were guarded by tall waves!*" and continued his laughter. Gamba's joke was only a joke for him. Others made a smirking smile and moved their eyes to Davu.

Davu continued without reacting, "*As a result, all four troops were banished out of the central island with the note: 'If four leaders come up with their royal swords and peace, the tall tides of the central island open the door.' Local chaos made the civilizations give up the war, but it was not an end.*"

The atmosphere of Davu's eyes changed and pain leaked through his eyes. "*As we share our borders with Draguva, in my life I have seen two wars against them and we lost many lives in the burning fire. Wounds of the Draguvan war drank the life of my son too.*" Pain in his heart made him go down to his knees, and he wept. Akello was paralyzed to see his grandpa in such pain. His eyes were gloomy, but he managed not to shed tears. Gamba rushed to console the old man, comforted him with a warm hug, and showed empathy. There was huge silence in the cave, and as a failed leader, Eric's head was down in shame. The sound of wheezing winds started eating the eardrums. Davu's and Gamba's names, along with other Alaokan fathers who lost their sons and daughters, were engraved. Gamba underwent the same pain as Davu, and he took ale as a cure.

Eric started to walk out in silence with a downed head. His mind never failed to say, "*He is a failed Alaokan leader.*" He was not the one who waged the war; he used the Alaokan army as a shield to save the future of Alaoka! With his knowledge and strategies, he minimized casualties, but blamed himself for not predicting the outbreak of war! He is wise and clever enough to know that the power of the military is not the real solution! The hall was silent. The sound of the wind drilled into the ears. Before leaving the cave, Gamba asked Akello to stay with Davu and aid him. With all the help, he could decode the rest of the information about the skull.

Akello was excited about working with his grandpa, but all his excitement became sloppy in five days. He is tired of staring at the skull for long hours and the worst part of his job was after staring at the inscription for hours Davu still complains, "*I have not found anything.*" Even after all the disappointments, when Akello was preparing to leave the cave at sunset, grandpa offered him guard duty at the cave entrance! Akello has no time for his friends and Amara, but apart from all the bad things, his tummy was filled with the taste of cavefish. Days turned into months! Unluckily, Akello has no escape. He was waiting for the start of the rainy season, so the hollow part of the caves would be submerged in water and a graveyard of white sand was inaccessible. At the same time, grandpa was worried that the rainy season was not far.

One day, Akello was surprised by the visit of Amara and Figo to the cave. The smile on her face was priceless! Her eyes conveyed how much she misses him! When both of them were romancing in the eyes, Figo walked to check on Akello's grandpa. Davu was happy to see Akello's friend, and they called 'Akello' out loud. Akello took them for a cave tour and both of them wondered to see such an inhuman skull! Akello and his friends took their seats on a rock just opposite the skull. From there, they can see grandpa and his team staring at the skull. Hours passed, but there was no change in their staring positions.

Figo asked, "*What is your routine in the cave?*"

Akello started saying his misery, "*When these weirdos stare at the skull! I stare at them from the exact same position that we are seated now!*" After hearing Akello, laughter bloomed in Amara's dimple chin, and Figo banged his head on his palms for Akello's reply. But Akello was not done yet. He continued, "*After staring at them for hours, I will go fishing in the cave pond.*" He waved his hands. A fat man replied to him with a wave.

Akello bloomed, "*That fat man cooks good fish! And then with a filled tummy, I guard the cave entrance.*"

After hearing his misery, Figo and Amara can't hold their laughter! Loud laughter echoed in crooks and tunnels of caves. Grandpa's team yells at them, "*Get out!*"

Finally, the most awaited day of Davu arrived. He invited the nobles of Alaoka to the hall. When Akello heard of the invitation of nobles, he was wondering how he had spent the entire winter staring at the cave walls and people around the skull. Took a deep breath and murmured, "*Job done!*" He waited at the entrance of the caves. The nobles of Alaoka walked in! Akello was not invited to the meeting, and he was not bothered about it.

Davu spoke about the inscription on the right hemisphere of the skull. He claimed it was way older than the inscription in the left hemisphere. He confirmed both were scripted in different eras. Davu said, "*Engraved Information on the right was beyond our knowledge.*" The sun and moon on the skull confirm it is a cycle of occurrence. Davu believed it could be a prophecy noted in the fossil by ancestors. The engraving has a wide sky with flat clouds. It has a vertical dash below the clouds, but the weirdest part was it also has an engraving of a wide ocean and clouds under it. From the ocean clouds, vertical dashes were popping toward the sky. Still, there is room for our assumptions. Deep punch dots in the skulls refer to the formation of stars and he also clarified Alaoka has never seen such a weird star pattern in the sky. But something more strange in the inscription was that the ocean was raining upwards. Beyond all in between the sky and ocean, massive battles between the human race and overgrown creatures were well scripted. There were many symmetric stars behind the skull. Only known in these patterns was the formation of four stars that appear during harvest season. Eric never heard Davu's words with these many assumptions. Davu was scratching his head in confusion and was not able to discover what these inscriptions were trying to convey.

"*This prophecy on the skull is millennia old. Who are these giants? Why have we not seen them once in our forests or terrains? Star pattern is a cycle that will definitely decorate the dark sky again, maybe tomorrow or 1,000 years after death claims our souls. Do the vertical dashes mention anything other than the rain? Twelve similar star patterns refer to a period of time?*" These questions were posted to the table by Eric.

On top of Eric's questions, old man Davu placed a new set of questions. "*Either we or our future generation have to face a destiny? If there are no giants in existence today, who do we have to fight or our ancestors have already killed every giant on land?*"

After listening to a bunch of questions, Gamba's butt was pressed against the cave wall to stand erect. He wailed, "*Too much friction!*" He asked one valid question, "*A group of strange giants, an island guarded by high tides, meteor swords and strange star patterns in the sky. Do we have any proof of the existence of one of these? Then, is this skull information worth storming our brains?"*

Many in the hall inspired Gamba's questions and thought it was valid. Eric unsealed his long sword from the scabbard. It was pitch black but not shiny.

He flipped the sword to Gamba. When Gamba got hold of the sword, its length didn't match its weight. Gamba examined the sharp edges and valued the robustness by scratching against the cave walls. Its handle was not made of wood, but it reduced vibrations. Gamba witnessed the sword and agreed it was not a normal blade. When he handed over the sword to Eric, Eric said, *"I have seen the same sword in the hands of my father Gorath and my grandfather. My grandfather mentioned that this sword was a tradition and a long-running one in the hands of Alaokan leaders for centuries and more. Gamba, this sword is living proof of the information on the skull and more over fossil we found was not the human skull."*

Eric asked Davu to find more information about the inscriptions, and he asked everyone to keep this information a secret.

The sun and moon shifted their positions. A gust of wind changed its course on the cycle. Yearly rainfall and harvesting crops were better than decent. All these days, the Alaokans have spilled their sweat on rebuilding their fallen pride. Akello spends his own time on Neo's back, along with Amara and his friends. Their love is strong and tangled like roots; they have to wait for four more years to hold each other's hand in marriage. He also got a few chances to show his valor during escort missions into the deep forests. The whole year, Davu found nothing interesting, and the information in the skull was still a secret. In the dead of the night in the underground city of Alaoka, a man slowly walking with a lighted marshall stopped his foot near the medium size hut. The entrance of the house was decorated with the skull of a lion; he ignored it and knocked on the brown door of the hut. After a few knocks, the snoring sound inside the hut was stopped, and the door was opened slowly. A man expelled from the door had a chiseled body and an X-shaped scar on his chest. After seeing the man with a torch, he questioned in a serious voice, "*Chief! Any new problems to handle?*" Eric added, "*Nothing to worry about*," and asked Gamba to follow him. By peeping the head inside the hut, Gamba collected the pelt to cover his chiseled shape, and then he followed Eric.

Eric took Gamba to the treasure chamber in the deepest part of the cave. The leader was only allowed to enter into these chambers. No other higher officials of Alaoka have access to these chambers; the fact is, many are unaware of the existence of these chambers. When Gamba entered the chamber, 10 to 15 marshals were lit at long intervals and the vision of Gamba found the cave was a complete mess that looked like someone was searching for something. The treasure of Alaokan was not gold and diamond, it was full of clothes with inscriptions, centuries-old junk, and weapons. These junks are artifacts of tomorrow's world. The messy room created panic in Gamba. All of a sudden, he vocalized, "*Have anything stolen, Chief?*" Eric hanged marshall in the holder, and from the mess, he took a sword and released it in the air toward Gamba. Gamba got hold of it and unsealed the sword. He was holding it for a second time; it was the same unique sword as Eric's.

But all of a sudden, Gamba's defined eyebrows were shortened to recall that he saw Eric's sword hanging in his belt. He moved his eyes to confirm the same. After seeing the clone of the same sword in Eric's belt, he was amazed. His face melted in happiness and thanked Eric for giving one of the unique swords in the world as a gift for him. He spoke a paragraph of thanking notes. After hearing all this, Eric banged his palm on his forehead and said, "What? It's not a gift to you. It is our key for peace." After hearing the sword is not for him, Gamba's face expresses disappointment and also scratches his head without understanding the context of Eric's words.

With a hidden smile, Eric patted Gamba's shoulder and walked him deep inside the chamber. Treasure deep inside the chamber was covered by spider webs. Both are seated on a long horizontal rock. Eric told Gamba,"*the sword you are holding is one of the quadruple meteor swords. Today, Alaoka has two swords: one belongs to us and another one belongs to Beku-neu. Three centuries back, in the war between Alaoka and Beku-neu, we defeated them and looted the leader's sword from the battlefield. For the last three centuries, this sword was sleeping in the tunnels of sacred caves*", but Gamba's eyes were focused on the reflecting metal behind the spider webs. After listening to Eric, he changed his focus. He said, "Incredible! Over 300 years, there has been no sign of rust in the blade, but chief, you mentioned 'peace.' How is this sword going to bring peace?"

With a little devilish smile, Eric said, "*It's simple! We are going to return the looted sword back to them.*" Before completing his sentence, Gamba's eyes were wide-open, and he exclaimed, "*What?*"

Eric replied to him, "*Giving back their leader's sword is a sign of peace, and it will bring new friendship. The commander of the Alaokan ground units is the right one to carry my message to Beku-neu.*"

Again. Gamba breathed, "*What?*" He carried a weird expression on his face.

The day when Davu blew Eric's mind with information in the inscription, Eric's mind made a plan for eternal peace between the civilizations. As per the inscriptions, the Alaokans started the war. Again, the same Alaokans are in pursuit of bringing peace. Eric decided that he was going to talk about the idea of peace to the elders of Alaoka at tomorrow's meeting.

Nothing entered into Gamba's mind; his eyes were fixed on the reflecting iron under the dust. Eric noticed his vision and walked to find the reflecting metal. Finally, he purged out the reflecting metal. It was an axe, and he thought it was perfect for Gamba. After seeing the shark-teeth curved edges and strong jackfruit wooden handle of the brutal axe, stars twinkled in Gamba's eyes. Eric swung the axe twice and rated its amazing craftsmanship. While swinging it, Eric decided Gamba was the right owner for the axe, but he decided to play a trick with his best friend. With a smile on the corner of his lips, he commented, "*Shark-teeth axes should be a fine gift for a young Alaokan soldier*." At that very moment, Gamba's twinkling eyes turned to disappointment and felt bad for losing the chance to use the axe. The next moment, Eric made a sarcastic laugh and gave the axe to Gamba. With the happiness of receiving a new weapon, Gamba praised Eric with paragraphs of gratitude and left the chamber. Eric is not aware of anything about the shark-teeth axe. To find the history of the axe, he needs to do a lot of readings on the inscriptions buried under the spider webs.

In the discussion with the elders of the Alaoka, Eric spoke. "*Let this thirst for blood and vengeance end with us. I wish our future generation to hold the torch of peace and kindness to all lives in the world.*" His words reflected thoughts running through his mind, but the same words have no effect on the elders of Alaoka. Discussions with the elders of Alaoka hurt Eric's soul. No one agreed with his idea of peace. Elders had a point of rejecting Eric's idea that the previous war had made the Alaokan army vulnerable.

The elders and Eric knew very well that another war was not a place of triumph for Alaoka. Months passed by, the height of crops increased and seasons changed, but still, Eric didn't give up on his idea of peace. As an old saying, "*Soak the ant and rub the stone*," continuous discussion of ideal peace made the elders agree to his idea of sending the messenger to the lands of Beku-neu. Even though Eric won the majority, some elders were like rocks in the hurricane. Finally, Alaokan winds started sailing toward the north. Beku-neu is located in the north-west. In the near history, Alaokans visited Beku-neu three centuries ago. This voyage was going to be hard because the route they were going to sail was centuries-old and they may have to encounter pirates. The quest to return the sword and bring peace and brotherhood began.

Chapter 4

Friend or Foe

The news of Alaokans going to sail to Beku-neu with a peace request spread to every corner of Alaoka. By carrying the wishes of friends and family, Alaokan ships wide opened their sails toward the north. The beginning of the new quest started with excitement, cheers, and bashes of drums in the Alaokan ships. There was a total of 12 ships in the count because elders approved only those ships. Eric was happy with 12 ships in hand, but commander Gamba was unhappy with it until Eric explained his game plan. Eric believed a pack of seven ships was enough to handle the pirates on their way and reach Beku-neu. Eric wore a grin on his face and graced the ocean with a million of dreams, as he expected, even the weather favored the Alaokan ship by turning the winds toward the north. The push of the wind and the new voyage excited the crew. Eric was also excited to see his people enjoying the journey; he wished to sail back to Alaoka with the same headcount. For the safety of the crew, he made animal sacrifices in Alaoka. By staring at the sky, he begged for blessings from his ancestors for the success of the mission, but he was unaware of the upcoming and he dug the grave on his own.

Akello and Figo's valor in recent times welcomed them to the deck of medium-sized ships. Rather than adding experience and wisdom, Eric appended the ship with young champs on purpose. In fact, these blooming warriors are the main players in Eric's plan. Alaoka's best strategists knew that these brats were the future of his people, and he wanted them to carry his idea of eternal peace. Alaokans build ships, but their expertise is not to the level of pirates to build ships with giant decks and strong hulls. Alaokan ships are neither massive vessels nor small rowboats; they are medium in size and are functioning in the power of rowing with single pole sail. The ram of the ship was not strong, and the hull was a herculean enough to survive two to three strikes. Sails of Alaokans were made of cotton and do not fit for long journeys; therefore, they carry extra sails. Still, the Alaokan engineer's spark and effort resulted in building a large ship with three sails. Yet, it is not a match for a pirate ship. It has big rooms to carry the friendly beast. Eric summoned his animal friend Kamau to the Beku-neu. There were 750 Alaokans in total. Alaokan has no gender inequalities. Out of the 750 Alaokans, a quarter and more were Alaokan shield maidens, but Amara was not qualified. She never showed valor in her recent missions. Eric was clear: they are not going to wage war. He knew an effective way of achieving peace is by politeness and humble behavior. Sea travel is the first time for plenty of youngsters. Their excited roars certified that they were a group of amateurs. Most of them were enjoying their first sea voyage by filling their stomach with varieties of fish and singing the voyage song in unison. At the same time, some of them were affected by seasickness. As usual, Figo was silent and enjoyed the company of the moving clouds above the wide blues. Figo was weird. When other youngsters were enjoying the sun on the horizon, he loved to spend time with the stars and moon in silence.

"What *a pleasant night! The shadow of the pearl lighted the silky ocean along with the song of waves. I feel like I am into a fairytale that my grandpa created,*" said Figo.

Figo changed his bedroom to the upper deck. The soft dance of a floating ship made him feel like he was sleeping in the slowly moving swing. Akello was stuck inside his own memories. His lips expelled a short smile from the moment he boarded the ship. The smile he carried never diminished, even when he tasted a spicy recipe that burned his gut. He simply recalled a gift and pain given by Amara, and the pain he got was the outcome of her love.

"*When you fall in love, even the pain is sweet! Daydreams have a high precedence over daily chaos and ambitions. I am sure Akello is not alone a victim of this chronic love fever.*"

The gift he got was expensive. It was filled with love and care. Beyond all, it was not an object. It is a feeling of push and pull. Akello wanted to summon Neo and fly back to Amara, but he can't disobey the orders and already he became popular because of a terrible incident. This voyage is a chance to fix his mistakes and attain respect. In his daydreams, getting a new tattoo as a reward from Eric was also included.

The day before the start of the sail, in their favorite spot, both love birds met. Amara was not willing to allow Akello to sail, but she didn't want to chop his dreams. This time, the view of the falls is totally different. The falls of heaven were no more! It's a nature-made waterfall, but it only appears to be a waterfall in the period of the rainy season of the year. For the rest of the year, water stops pouring from the top, and the craggy rocks and caves behind the waterfall are naked. Akello was happy that he was selected to sail Beku-neu, and he told Amara that he was excited to feel the soil of Beku-neu underneath. Amara portrayed that she was happy too, but internally, she was in a ball of fear. She doesn't want to lose Akello; she can't either imagine a lifeless or handicapped Akello. All she wants is to live a decent life with him, along with their legacy. At some point, Akello's overthinking mind pops out and speaks of the various possibilities he feared. *"Amara! What if I didn't come back?"*

Amara's panic doubled and the atmosphere of her eyes changed to pink, but the idiot griffin rider didn't notice discomfort in her face and continued his nonsense scenarios. She can't hear his words. So, to stop his nonsense talk, Amara broke all her second thoughts and pulled him by his collar and got Akello's thick brown lips between her soft lips. The very next moment, she closed her eyes, but her fear escaped the stream of tears. Akello's idiotic mind stopped the flow of thoughts, but the only thing running between his eyes was Amara's dimple face. The small pleasure of pull and push between the lips added a flavor of lust and love. Akello also wanted to live with her, and he never wanted to leave her by his side. All of a sudden, her long finger pushed him back. On the other hand, she wiped away the tears, but the red-golden rays of the setting sun highlighted the track of wiping tears running down her cheeks.

"*Idiot! Hold your emotions and tongue in the new world! The most important thing is whatever it costs, come back to me. Remember, I am waiting here for you!*" Amara's mixed love imperatives touched Akello's heart. Akello felt he was lucky to get a girl like Amara. With love-carried eyes, he hugged her tight and apologized to her for being the reason for her tears. Unexpected anger rooted in her eyes. Her arms went back to a certain distance and moved forth with great speed. With spread palms, she slapped him with the force as punishment for hurting her heart and for talking negatively.

This fearsome slap would be more effective before a kiss, but Amara's love is different. First, she comforts him with a hug and then she breaks his bones. Not only us, but the setting sun, laughed at this cute and freakish couple before twilight. Idiots like Akello take more time to understand Amara and her feelings. After all, Amara is not from the warrior bloodline, but her father is the respected medic in the whole of Alaoka. He is also a victim of battle in the sleeping volcanoes.

Akello was still living the moments of Amara's kiss, but the sun and the moon shifted their sides twice. In the middle of the ocean, it was heaven for Akello and the other young warriors. Along with the taste of delicious fish BBQ, rookies of Alaoka flooded the top deck to enjoy the beauty of the ocean and the orchestra of seagulls added pleasure to the ears. When all was going well, the problems were rooted in the ships in the form of griffin. Hybrid birds are not like other beasts; their freedom is mandatory for them. If griffins lose their temper, it is a bad sign for other tamed beasts on the lower deck of a big Alaokan ship. To calm down the griffins temper, they unleashed griffins from lower decks in the evenings to relax and have a glide. Alaokans also used the claws of griffins to hunt the fish for dinner. Griffin drives from the air toward the target. When claws gently touch the surface of the water, it catches the prey and smoothly drops them on the deck of a big ship. While the twilight decorates the sky along with the beauty of nature, the dance of the griffin pack above the ships was a feast to the eyes. As expected, the next problem came in the form of pirates. It was a lucky evening when a pack of Alaokan ships crossed the three huge pirate vessels. After seeing a pack of Alaokan ships and furious griffins flying around the ships, it convinced the professional hunter of the ocean not to mess with the pack and their griffins. Gamba looked at the grin on the face of his leader and was puzzled about how this man predicted the event that had just happened. Eric also feared that pirates and Draguvans would attack Alaoka in his absence, so he left the huge army to guard the cluster islands of Alaoka and ordered the remaining ships to guard the Alaokan sea.

As the vessels moved closer toward the north, days became shorter and it looked like ships floated into the territory of Ms. Cold Breeze. To guard the oceans against intruders, she summoned the mist to cover the eyes of sailors, and it slowed down the ships. In the night, sails were set to low. Everyone was sleeping with their heads buried under the quilt, with the exception of a few archers who were on guard duty. The fire burning in Eric's heart did not let him sleep. The squeal of his majestic beast made Eric direct his foot toward the lower deck; it was unexpected for Eric to find Gamba on the lower deck. Gamba's green eyes were admiring the griffins, and he was also amazed to see Eric on the lower deck at this darkest hour. The Alaokans' leader patted Gamba's shoulder and walked to his beast, Kamau. Kamau means warrior. Kamau spends most of his time in the forest, and he is not fit to live along with human settlements. Whenever Eric needs Kamau's help, he treks deeper into the savanna. The call of his unique whistle summons Kamau. Eric patted the rough skin and sharp horns of Kamau and convinced his beast, "*Kamau! Apologies for putting you in a small shell. If your feet land in the Beku-neu, it will change the purpose of our visit. But if needed, let's pitch in to shake up the troops of Beku-neu.*" He also crossed his fingers and wished for a warless voyage.

Gamba commented, "*Chief! Covering mist is a sign that we are heading closer. None of us is aware of how Beku-neu will look. How strong they are?*"

Eric advised, "*Keep aside confusion.*" He asked Gamba if he had selected comrades who were going to accompany him. Gamba nodded his head and confidence reflected in his eyes. The eyeballs of Eric ran over the fine-standing Neo and whispered, "*Color of it says he is not ordinary. Time will give the answer.*" He walked Gamba to his chamber.

The sun and moon changed their positions twice, but still no sign of land. In the deepest of night, the cry of whales haunted the ships of Alaokans. In response to the whale cry, the lower deck was doomed in fearful howls. Ships were sailing in the formation of sparrows. The head of the sparrow (the first ship in the formation) maintains a distance from other ships, and its role is to act as a decoy. Ideally, other ships change their sails based on the message from the head of the sparrow. Alaokans use dire wolf loud bark and howls to commute messages. If the howl is long, it means danger. If they howl with short gaps, it means they are engaging in a duel. One bark for full sail, two for half sail, and long non-stop barking means to anchor the ships. Moreover, griffin riders fly over the head of the sparrow to carry important messages between vessels. Alaokans never use a blow horn because of its sound radius, due to the huge radius it sends invitations to pirates.

Gamba presented four companions who were going to accompany him to Beku-neu to his beloved Eric. A griffin rider flying over the sparrow's head carried the message of the existence of the land. With a clear plan, they forwarded their sails, and soon the Alaokans got the visibility of Beku-neu's shores from a long distance. There were no ships in the ports, but the wooden docks were built to tie the ships. As per the plan, out of 12 Alaokan ships, only one ship approached the dock to avoid panic in Beku-neu. All the other ships were anchored far away from the north-west. Gamba's mind was recalled by the words of Eric, "*Peace can't be achieved by military solution and anger.*" Eric also mentioned that if he didn't get a word from Gamba and his team by dawn, he would approach the land of Beku-neu, along with Kamau and the troops. Eric is not a fool to send his men and women without the idea of protecting them. By cutting the waves, the Alaokan ship docked at the shore. Three black griffins and one olive-green griffin walked out with their rider, followed by Gamba on his Blu. With the peace request and as a gesture of peace, Alaokan carried five bullock carts full of wheat and coconuts. Each cart was locked with two bulls. The man on the olive griffin was the holder of a valor tattoo, and his brown lips were broken at the center because of the coldness in the air. The day was dull, and the sky was covered by light pink and red clouds. The whereabouts of the sun were completely hidden inside the clouds. Akello's eyes graced everything, and underneath his feet, he experienced the chill of the beach. Gamba walked in front of everyone and turned around to check the face of his comrades and he shook his head at Neo, Rudo (Figo griffin) and other griffins. Today, a beast, who attacked Gamba in the village of Varuonans, bent his head to show his respect and was ready to take orders from him. It was strange for Akello and he wondered, "*What made Neo bow in front of Gamba?*"

The night before Eric walked to the lower deck, Gamba had a short talk with selected griffins. In light of the torch,

Gamba stood outside the griffin stable and pointed fingers at Neo, Rudo, and the other two griffins. He called them near him. At first, the griffins ignored him. The next moment, he called them by the name of their riders and fumed, "*I came here to save the lives of your rider.*" His words' worth summoned the griffins in front of him.

"*I selected your riders to accompany me on the mission, but I have not selected them based on their valor, wit, or fame. I selected them because of you, griffins! Among all those in the stable, you four griffins have incredible speed and agility to dodge the arrow shower. In the worst case, if I get arrested or executed by the leader of Beku-neu, without a second thought, spread your wings and evacuate the area with your riders. In the pursuit of escape, your wings should only stop at this big Alaokan ship. I don't expect any young Alaokans to die or be imprisoned along with me in Beku-neu.*" The expelled words of Gamba were out of bravery and selflessness; his words prepared the griffins for the rough day.

The valor and courage of Gamba were respected all over Alaoka for this reason. Without fear of griffins, he tapped his forefinger on the beak of an olive griffin. Olive-green griffin screamed in anger. Gamba moved his forefinger to his lips and said, "*Sh...sh,*" to stop screaming. His fearless angry eyes and confidence made Neo stay low, but anyway, the scream of Neo disturbed the sleeping Eric's Kamau. Gamba said to griffins: "*Your riders carry the Alaokan blood, and they will never agree to abandon me. I, the commander of Alaokan ground units. Griffins! Your priority for tomorrow is to safeguard your riders.*"

Pursuit of Peace

Paws, claws, and hooves continued their walk on the shore and reached the market. Market areas were empty, and they could not find any humans in the market area. The wide wooden stalls were horizontally built by wood, but the wood of the stalls was wet and broken. The moisture in the air made the Alaokans understand that the market area was recently attacked by cyclones. Mild whispers gained the interest of Gamba; he found an old man with an unshaved beard wearing a black non-cotton outfit. The fabric of the cloth is not familiar to Alaokans. Alaokan has no knowledge of dying clothes, and they wore only cotton outfits.

The old man was not in good shape. The foul smell of last night's ale around him clarified that he was in a hangover state. Gamba erected him up and made him open his eyes. Blurred visions of the drunk man graced Gamba's hunk body and the fangs of Blu. He froze in fear, and his eyes were wide-open. Gamba bribed him with coconut to reach their leader. He forcibly pushed the coconut into the hand of the drunken old man. Gamba's act caused the legs of the drunken man to tremble in fear. Out of fear, he pointed his trembling forefinger in the direction of the north and fainted in fear. Gamba laughed at the man and continued in the direction that the old man pointed. The direction they walked opened to a pine forest; tall trees with wide conical branches flooded all over the forest. The paws of Blu walked first. Griffins escorted the bullock carts they carried. In wintry weather, while moving deeper into the forest, pink clouds started to rain.

"Yes! It is a drizzle of snowflakes." Alaokans had never experienced snow, and this day was their first encounter with snow. Gamba's eyeballs noticed monkeys in the forest with fine fur. Snow pearls from clouds gently decorated the fur pelt of the Alaokans outfit. Akello and Figo raised their necks to scan the sky. Tall, conical trees and white dust from pink clouds made the teens move their hands to collect them. Griffins bend their beaks to check for the settled snow. The end of the forest unfolded to a wide landscape covered by a white blanket. Going deep in the blanket of snow, Akello felt a hot breath on his lips and nose, and he loves that hot breath.

Falling flakes were dense. While moving forward in the landscape, Figo leaned down his body from the griffin back and grabbed some snow in his hand. The chillness he felt on the palms gave him a new experience and he couldn't hold it for long, so he shot the snow at Akello. Akello shot at the other riders. All four started to play in the snow. Gamba was also experiencing snow for the first time, but he worried about the upcoming.

Gamba lampooned with a smile, *"Bunch of rookie!"* Gamba was very happy to see a big smile on the teen's face, and he prayed to the Alaokan sun god, *"For the long life of these rookies!"* He graced the sky, but he couldn't find the sun in the middle of a red and pink cloud.

Out of the cold, one of the oxen sneezed, but Alaokans never felt shortness of breath because of their daily routines, and the fresh air of Alaoka gifted them a robust lung tank. Gamba's brown-mixed-gray beard was decorated with snowflakes;

his light green eyeballs got sight of massive structures in the middle of the white desert. To get the attention of the brats, Gamba mocked them by calling them 'kids' and a funny part was all four of them responded to his call. After all, they were a bunch of teens. The kids were astonished to see the gigantic structure in the snow paradise, but falling flakes hid their vision. Moving closer, they understood these white showers showed no mercy and the massive structure was closer to their vision. They found that the structure was built with a stack of stones. A big stone-raising has an entrance with herculean doors made of pine wood.

Beku-neu is a land area covered with ice. To protect the people from cold and predators, they built huge outer walls around human settlements. The outer wall is 80 feet tall and located over a small mountain in the landscape. From the towers of the outer wall, they spotted the Alaokan from a mile away. News of the intruders marching toward the castle gate was carried to their beloved leader. The messengers of Alaoka walked to the entrance of the stacked wall. Gamba and other Alaokans got a full view of the stone castle and rolled their eyes to greet the magnificent wall.

Gamba noticed the archers standing in the crenellations of the fort wall, and he ordered griffin riders and carts to stop at 200 feet distance to the gate. However, Gamba thinks that he and his company were standing away from the vantage point, but the fact is they are already within the range of archers. Gamba underestimated the bowing range of Beku-neu's weapon by comparing them against their own. The arrows of the archers in the crenellations pointed at the Alaokans, but the arrows were not released. All alone, Gamba walked near the gate on his dire wolf, and as a calling bell, he directed his Blu to howl, but none of the archers dared to shoot the arrow at Blu and Gamba. Gamba wore a grin on his face and recalled Eric's plan. Eric's strategy started to play. Alaokans walked into the land of ice with a peace request and hands full of crops and coconuts as a gesture of peace, and as Eric directed, the Alaokans also emptied their scabbard and quivers before they stepped in. The day before the journey began when Gamba was polishing his new axe. Eric commented to Gamba, "*Gamba! Your new shark tooth axe has no work to do in Beku-neu.*"

Eric's Strategy

"Eric is not aware of how strong Beku-neuns can be. Above all, they are warriors. No pure lineage will dare to defame their own name by killing the unarmed Alaokans. By sending unarmed messengers, the probability of getting killed by arrows and spears was minimized. In the worst case, if they don't like the idea of peace, they may imprison the messengers, but they won't kill them. In such an unavoidable case, Eric decided to march with all his troops with a request to get back his fellow men and enforce peace."

Eric's wise move started to work. The message about an unarmed small team of griffin riders led by a wolf rider reached the ears of Beku-neu's leader, Azog. After hearing the words, "*Griffin riders*," Azog fumed, "*The Alaokans!*" But another question stormed his mind, "*Why are they here?*" Behind the other side of the pine doors, Azog assembled with troopers and issued an order to open the doors. Latches of the big doors were made of ivory to increase their strength. The sound of unlocking the latch made Gamba rejoin his fellow Alaokans. Wide pine doors opened. From the doors, woolly giant mammoths walked out in the formation of a 3x4 matrix with their mahout and copper armor added to protect the vital parts (elbows and heads) of the mammoth. Footsteps of the mammoths created a decent depression in the snow blanket. Giant beasts with long tusks and armors planted fear in the rookies' hearts, but Gamba was wondering why the people of Beku-neu wasted plenty of copper on forging the armor rather than the weapons. Mammoths formed two rows on either side by leaving the openings of the gate. Following the mammoths, two griffins walked out with their riders and a man on the white dire wolf walked in between the griffins. Gamba was paralyzed after seeing the black griffin in the armies of Beku-neu. In their whole life, Alaokans believed griffins were only living in Alaoka. After seeing the griffin, even the Alaokan griffin made short hoots.

The riders who marched on the black griffins were two women. Alaokan rookies were fascinated to see griffins of the north with breastplates, and they also wore nosebands and reins like horses. The weapons of riders looked very different from Alaokans; it was a tall spear with two swords at either edge made of robust, shiny metal. The man on a white dire wolf walked forward with a female griffin rider. The attire of the wolf rider and courageous sight explained to Gamba that he should be the chieftain of Beku-neu. The man on the white wolf wore a snow-colored fur cloak. His attire and color of his beast made people call him, "*The ghost of snow.*" He has an olive complexion with short brown hair and he chose a mutton chopper's beard. His muscular shape is covered inside the white outfit made of wool. Alaokans have never used wool in their life and they have no need for woollen outfits in the hot weather of Alaoka. Azog's words strike like thunder, "*Why are Alaokans in the north?*" With a warm, melting smile, Gamba directed Blu to approach the 'ghost of snow.'

The young woman in the blackbird raised her double-edged sword to stop forwarding Gamba. She shouted, "*Stop.*" By ignoring her words, Blu's paws forwarded. Alaokan troopers noted not only her sword but also her eyes were holding knives. Except for her eyes, all attributes of her face were enfolded behind the helmet. Gamba's courage was loved by Azog; he allowed Gamba to approach him. In perfect silence, the sound of white wind drilled into the ears. Gamba and Azog faced one another, and their wolf made a short growl. Azog noticed the green lens of Gamba has no sign of fear. Along with the sound of wheezing winds, Gamba bubbled, "*Peace,*" and trumpeted, "*I am the messenger of Alaoka. I walked into the white lands, carrying the will of our beloved leader, Eric. He is willing to meet the leader of Beku-neu to establish peace between Beku-neu and Alaoka. The initial meeting of peace will happen on our ship anchored near the sea of Beku-neu. During the meeting, the ship will be abandoned and the doors of the ship opened only for leaders of both civilizations. To strengthen the new friendship, Eric, the Leader of Alaoka, decided to return the leader's sword of Beku-neu, which was looted by our ancestors in the war, which happened 300 years ago. As of now, we bought five carts of coconuts and food crops as a gesture of peace.*" The words bloomed from Gamba created tension. Four griffins waited on high alert. In case of attack, griffins were ready to execute the orders given by Gamba. If Azog accepted the carts, then he agreed to the peace. If not, then what will come up? Even though in a high-tension situation, Gamba maintained a cool look like falling snowflakes. Alaokan rookies' faces expressed tension; in the freezing weather, Akello's forehead released a sweat. There were only a few minutes of silence, but the wheezing white winds had no full stop. Azog muttered, "Alaokans with a peace request!" and his eyes scanned the stacked walls and soldiers of Beku-neu.

Along with the sound of the wind, Azog said, "Peace," in a rough tone and directed his white beast to walk to carts. All eyeballs were fixed to the paws of a white wolf. Azog's hands took a tender coconut and voiced, "*For peace and unity, we take the bullock carts inside the fort and will meet your leader in your ship tomorrow at dawn.*" He asked four of his horsemen to accompany Alaokans to the shore. Griffins left the side of the carts and walked in reverse. The hoplites of Beku-neu slowly approached the carts, examined and walked carts into the castle. The sharp rays of the red sun escaped the pink clouds and warmed the hands of Gamba.

Happiness and smiles developed in the faces of the Alaokans, but the knife-eyed young warrior did not change any expression in her eyes and her companions too. While walking back to shore with horsemen, there was perfect silence for minutes. Akello casually started a conversation, and he praised the giant fort walls. Out of curiosity, he asked a question to the accompanying horsemen, "*How did you train massive tuskers?*" Figo asked Akello to stay low, but the horsemen answered him with a warm smile. "*We called the method of training massive elephants, Yanna.*" He added, "*We call these tuskers, mammoths and these four-legged giants are our pride.*" Gamba wondered. Another Horseman said, "*The idea of peace sounds interesting!*" He wished for this successful peace talk. Gamba and the team were happy with the positive words of the horse riders. When they walked back to shore, it was completely covered by a snow bed. In the dock, Alaokans walked into the ship and horsemen waited until the sail opened.

Inside the stacked walls (castle), guards were examining the edibles in the cart. At first, they thought the coconut was a seed, but one clever, armored woman found it had water inside it. Beku-neu has no coconut-giving fauna, and they have never tasted a tender coconut in their life. Inside the castle, the Azog's men were not aware of opening the tender coconut in the right way but still managed to collect the tender coconut water in the bowl and served it to Azog. When Azog purged a small ounce of coconut water from the bowl, his taste buds were delighted with the sweet and nutty taste, but he refused to purge the next sip. He ordered guards to send one of the carts to farmers for agriculture and asked for the rest of the tender counts to be shared with civilians and warrior ranks.

On the other hand, the safe return of Gamba and the company created big cheers in the Alaokan ranks. Gamba conveyed the news to Eric; he explained every bit and piece of his journey.

Eric was happy with the first step of success. Everyone is waiting for the next dawn for the first change of centuries and Eric asked everyone to be more cautious because this is a huge chance to change history. Eric was curious and sleepless. In Beku-neu, many elders doubted Alaokan may betray them, but Azog convinced them with his power because he believed that peace would bring change to Beku-neu. The sun rose from the horizon. The rays of the dawn lit the vision to grace the forwarding ships of Beku-neu. The architecture of their ship was complex, with strong sharp rams to cut the ice and sail. Slowly, the sailing ship anchored near the Alaokan ship. As mentioned, Eric ordered all soldiers to abandon the big ship. One of the soldiers of Beku-neu entered the Alaokan vessel and ensured the safety of their leader. After a moment, the Azog landed his feet on the Alaokan ship. The meeting between the two of them lasted for an hour. So, everyone was eagerly waiting for the fruits of the meeting. Another hour passed by. Finally, both of the leaders walked out with a smile. In addition, Azog's hands are decorated with the ruler's sword of Beku-neu.

Once the Beku-neun ship left, Eric called the important members to the meeting hall. The big hall was filled with higher officials, and Davu was also included in the meeting. Along with older adults, four rookies who accompanied Gamba were also invited. Everyone assembled for the meeting. Eric announced, "*We have reached our first milestone. Azog has agreed with the idea of peace. He conveyed that he also explained to Azog the information in the inscription. After knowing the knowledge behind the inscription, he was shocked but gave his strong words.*" He and his people will join the Alaokans in the quest for peace, and their archaeologists will join the hands of Davu to unravel the message in the skull. The message from Eric excited all the members in the meeting hall. Eric was loud to everyone. Beyond all, as a sign of gesture of the new alliance. Alaokans were invited for dinner inside the big stone-stacked walls. By looking at Gamba, Eric said, "*I gave my word to Azog that we are coming for dinner. Will stay there for a few days and plan our next moves with our new alliance.*" With a long smile, Eric asked everyone to spread the news to other Alaokan vessels. After hours, all Alaokan vessels got the news of peace and the idea of a new alliance. Gamba walked up to Eric with a puzzled face and speculated, "*How safe it is to trust them? Is it safe for us to stay in their place?*"

Eric replied, "*When we invited Azog for the first meeting of peace, he might also have had the same fears about Alaokans but he trusted us.*" He continued, "*We initiated the peace request, and it's our time to trust them.*" He also believed it is a good opportunity for us to understand their culture and people. In the evening, Alaokans ships reached the coastline of Beku-neu, 100s of Alaokans walked to the shore and 30% of the troops were ordered to wait on the ships. Akello and the company widespread their eyes to check if this is the same place that they visited yesterday.

Akello and company mentioned to their comrades that the place they walked yesterday was entirely different today. It looked like a big festival. People crowded on both sides and created a way to walk for Alaokans. Along with snowfall, the welcoming cheers of people excited the Alaokans. Many Alaokans liked their black outfits and the fur shoes that they wore to fight the snow. Alaokans are also willing to try the shoes and outfits. Azog's ministers and mammoth-tied chariots were waiting to welcome the outlanders to the big marketplace. Snow gently powdered the shoulders and heads of the Alaokans. Alaokans felt it was heaven, but they were unaware that the land of ice is a den of predators.

In the twilight of evening, elephant chariots, griffin, gray wolves, and horses marched toward the gates of the stone castle. After seeing the heaven-touching wall, the sound of whispers bloomed among the Alaokan crowd. In the crenellation of the fort wall, Archeress welcomed the Alaokans by holding fire torches. Curiosity to know what was behind the castle crooked in every Alaokan's mind.

Eric rode his mustang into the gate. The wide gates opened to 25 feet long tunnels. The flames from the torches lit the human vision. Eric looked up at the ceiling and found vertical falling gates. Eric's long-focused vision also found a similarly vertically falling gate at the extreme end of the tunnel. After seeing gates at either end of the tunnel, Eric murmured, "*It could be a trap.*" If the vertical gates were closed, entire troops would be imprisoned and hunted. A tunnel has its own purpose. In case the door breach, the tunnel will act as a murder house. "*After the door breach, enemy troops are open to access the long tunnel. Once a decent number of foes walked in, vertical gates would be closed manually. From above walls, fine archers will drill down the lives of the enemies.*"

Eric was astonished to see the engineering and defence of the castle. At the end of the tunnel, Azog waited on the giant woolly mammoth to welcome the Alaokans. Alaokans' eyes were on a feast to see the snow covered city behind tall walls. The chilliness of snow on their shape and underneath their feet expressed the mile-long smile on Alaokan faces. It was unexpected for them. When Akello and friends shared their experience of yesterday's snow with others, they thought they were exaggerating, but in their own eyes, they realized it was paradise. In the moonlight, fired torches brightened the city. Horns were blown as welcome music and Azog Bubbled to Eric, "*Welcome to the city of snow.*" The eyes of Akello and Neo twinkled to see the snow-covered roofs and huts. The city has large stables and cages for the tamed beast. The city also has enough civilian huts, medical halls, shops and storage houses of livestock and greens. All over the city, they have built archer towers, and they are always ready to tackle an attack. Next to the armory hall, there was a huge hollow metal inverted cup hanging from the 20 feet wooden tower. The pavement inside the city is spacious and covered by a thin snow layer.

People of snow walked the Alaokans to the tallest tower in the city. The tower was five-storey tall and located in the center of the fort walls and guarded by pine wood palisades. The tallest tower is called the 'great hall' by the snow people. The door of the tower is made of iron. In the case of war, future generations and valuables were guarded inside the tower. On the way to the great hall, Akello asked the griffin rider of Beku-neu accompanying him about 'the purpose of the hollow inverted cup hanging at a decent height.' She wore a hood and mask that covered her nose and lips. In the effulgence of the moon, her eyes looked sharp like a knife. Her body's curves were perfect, and the griffin she rode classified her as a fine warrior. She is the one who stopped Gamba when he forwarded to approach the 'ghost of the snow.' Her ears heard Akello's question, but she didn't give him an answer; instead, she graced him with attitude-filled eyes and walked forward. Her eyeballs were black. Akello gritted his teeth and fumed, "*Scary eyes!*" He complained to his comrades about her attitude. Alaokans widened their mouths at the astonishing beauty of Beku-neun men and women. Most of them have fair complexions, unlike Alaokans and Beku-neu's men had broad shoulders and were taller than average Alaokan and their women were lean. Most of them have welcoming smiles, except the one that Akello met.

Eric complimented Azog and the people of Snow City for their engineering and architecture. Azog walked the Alaokans to the dinner hall. It was a huge hall with 30 rows of big tables and each can fit 40 heads. The total hall capacity is 1,200 members. Once everyone had taken their seats for dinner, Azog introduced each of his ministers to Eric. Alaokans can't find fruits and greens for dinner. The dinner table was filled with fewer greens and more reds. It was just opposite to Alaoka. On either side of the table, pepper and salt bowls were placed. As per tradition, before starting dinner, both troopers were waiting for the ale toast, and most of the Alaokan were excited about drinking Beku-neu's Sura. Beku-neuns named their alcohol Sura. Eric stood up on top of the table for toast; Azog joined him with a jar of Sura.

Cheers for 'new peace' broke the serenity, and together both of them raised their Sura mugs for the toast. In unison, they both voiced: "*For eternal peace!*" Eric turned the mug down south and the Sura was absorbed by the ground. At the same time, Azog poured everything into his belly. Cheers of Beku-neu dimmed down and started to stare at Eric with fire in their eyes. In the tradition of Alaokan, the toasted mug of ale was poured into the ground as a gesture of thanks to mother earth but in Beku-neu's culture, wasting Sura is a sin. *Culture is always a head spin.* After finishing Sura, Azog was shocked to see the Sura poured on the floor! Azog and Eric explained each other's tradition to the troopers, but many Beku-neuns accepted it as their tradition, but still, some of the Beku-neuns were not consoled. After that incident, the cheers of Beku-neuns were downed by half. Eric was upset; he didn't want any crack in the new peace that was established after centuries by the name of fucking 'culture.'

Food was served on wooden plates, and the center of attraction was bison BBQ. The heat created by BBQ and finger-licking the taste of the juicy meat added pleasure to the body and helped them to fight the snowy breeze. Dinner ended with great laughter, fun, and gallons of odorless and strong Sura. After a great celebration and party, in the devil's hour Alaokans buried their heads in the fur quilt and snored like orcs, their snoring escaped from the towers and hit the ears of night guards, they exchanged laughter and loved the new friendship in the Beku-neu but not all. In the devil's hour, the scream of the owl made Azog wake up. With a frightened face, Azog moved his body near the window. All of a sudden, without bothering with the cold, freezing weather, he opened his chamber window. It was a wood color carrier owl. From the foot of the bird, he collected the palm leaf. When he was opening the message, he dropped a sweat, although it was freezing outside. After seeing the message, he was not afraid but laughed at it. At the same time, Eric's sleep was haunted by the events of dinner.

The next morning, Akello woke up on the fourth floor of the tower. His mind was running with a curious question of why, and the fourth-floor hall became a bedroom for 100s of Alaokans. Figo was not with him. As per Eric's order, Gamba and 100s of comrades decided to stay on the ship. When Akello woke up, the sun was not visible between the mountains, but the sun's fragrance slowly started to spread in the sky. He was tired of the snoring sound in the hall, so after a lazy break, he moved near the closed wooden window. The icy wind froze him and the dull sky made him understand it was not dawn yet. His mind started to find the answer to the big question.

"*Beku-neu has a better army. A big wall was built to defend their heads. Wooden vessels are good enough to cut the ice and sail. There is no doubt that they are stronger, but what could be the reason that stopped them for three centuries? Why didn't they wage war against Alaoka to find their leader's sword?*"

His hypothesis created so many answers, but none of them satisfied his mind. Akello decided to check with his wise old granddad. Senior and higher officials were provided with individual wooden chambers on the same floor. Akello searched for his grandpa in his allocated room, but he was unlucky to find Eric, along with his grandpa. Sometimes, what we feel unlucky is our real luck. Eric was discussing something important with Davu. Akello decided to walk out in silence, but Akello's footsteps pulled their eyes toward him. Davu bubbled, *"Akello! You woke up soon! Did Beku-neu do a miracle on my grandson?"* He started laughing and Eric joined.

Akello thought it was an unfunny joke, but these grown olds are expelling all teeth with giggles. To stop their laughter, Akello replied, "*I have a question for you, grandpa, but I believe you are busy now,*" and apologized to Eric for the disturbance that was created by him. But still, the laughter did not stop. Akello smiled out, but his mind murmured, "*Sick of old.*" Eric expressed his love to hear and address Akello's question. Without a second thought, Akello forwarded the question that was storming his brain. The laughter faded; Eric and Davu were silent for a minute. Their silence convinced Akello's mind that he had asked a quality question, but the fact is Davu was not aware of the answer, but Eric knew the answer and his hypothesis never failed till today. Eric's mind probes whether to briefly answer the teen. After a minute of silence, Eric acknowledged Akello for his presence of mind to bring up an excellent question and he briefed him.

"*The people of Beku-neu have great minds, but the geographic position of Beku-neu (land in the north-west) was not well suited for human life. They have only 35% of land for agriculture and human life. The rest was buried under snow. Most of the time, bright sunlight is rare. The north-west is always the apple eye for cyclones. 7 out of 12 months, cyclones will hunt the Beku-neu, and dark clouds will become a barrier to the sun. Troops of Beku-neu are the strongest. We can't deny the fact, but their troopers were completely busy in blood sports and guarding the fields and people from the deadly predators roaming in the white desert. Red meat is part of their regular diet because the greens they grow only satisfy 40% of their needs. Fighting in snow needs more stamina. The dull climate and falling white pearls reduced the efficiency of manpower. We need to applaud them for their engineering and survival strategies. Daily hurdles and a hard lifestyle evolved their brains in a better way. Heaven-touching walls reduced their troubles to half, but it took more time to build one."*

Eric was clever enough to map the point and understood threats in Beku-neu, but tradition is a complex subject. The tradition of one cannot be predicted with prior experience and knowledge unless you live in that community. Eric's explanation made Akello think and made him understand that *'when survival itself is a challenge, you can't do much.'* Akello was shocked to hear Eric's observations, but he was not done yet. A wise man with a long beard continued, "*People of snow made use of naturally opened deep caves in the northern ocean as shipyards and docked their ships to protect them from heavy cyclones. The place we docked on our ships is just camouflage for pirates and outlanders. Last night, all our ships moved to 'knörr caves' in the northern ocean of Beku-neu."*

All the higher rank members of both civilizations were assembled for the meeting before lunch. In the meantime, Akello looked at the sky. It was cloudy and mild daylight escaped from the clouds. Gamba walked to the meeting hall to join Eric. Snow City has three stables, and one in the right corner was allocated to Alaokans. When Akello was rinsing the feathers of Neo, Figo walked on the horse and praised the wonder of 'knorr caves,' and his words made Akello jealous. He regretted that he missed the ride to the deep cave. Akello's explanations about last night's yummy dinner, the strong Sura and the toast tradition of Beku-neu made Figo feel bad for missing the dinner. At the same time, all the higher ranks of both civilizations were assembled in the meeting hall. Many were happy about the peace, but still, Eric noticed the few unhappy and doubtful faces in the hall, but from last night's events, nothing less than Eric had expected. The wise leader of the Alaokans introduced his commander Gamba to the officials in the hall. Everyone complimented him for carrying the message of peace like a fearless saber. The man in the white garments praised Gamba. "*No need for the introduction! When I met him for the first time in front of the big door, a spark in his eyes and fearless smile conveyed that this man should be the vision of the Alaokan troops.*" Along with the compliment, Azog hugged to welcome him. Azog felt blue for not introducing his Commander Bora and reasoned, "*Bora and his army are busy on guard duty in agricultural fields.*"

Azog started the meeting with the word 'peace' and bloomed the minds of his minister with the inscriptions found in the skull of Alaoka. Very few of Azog's subordinates believed the information in the skull, but many Beku-neuns wore a doesn't-care mask on their faces. Eric understood the root that some of them gave their presence in the hall because of

Azog's power. Eric is wise enough to know they have trust issues with the Alaokans, but the people of Beku-neu can't be blamed. Archaeologists of Beku-neu walked forward, and she acknowledged, "*Information and prophecies from the ancestors were conveyed to the future in the form of inscriptions in the cave walls and fossils.*" She is a strong young lady, aged a quarter of the experience of Davu. Davu finds curiosity filled in her black eyeballs. Azog introduced the young lady as Frida.

Davu questioned Frida about the archaeological findings of Beku-neu.

Frida replied that they hadn't found anything interesting like a skull in Alaoka and wondered. "*Three years ago, we found a permafrost under the surface of the Folv mountains.*"

Davu hissed, "*What is permafrost?*"

Frida opened, "*Permafrost is a frozen layer, where every object is frozen and preserved in the ice. For instance, one can see frozen soil there. The permafrost we found in the Folv mountains is the oldest; the inscriptions in the cave walls are full of weird star patterns and the weirdest part is the same pattern was repeatedly scripted in the walls 11 times. As you mentioned, it may denote the occurrence of events in the sky. There is a chance to find more clues, in case the star pattern on the walls matches the pattern in the skull.*"

Words of Frida excited Davu, he muttered, "*Maybe.*" There was a spark in his eyes. Without hesitation, he beamed. "*Frida, shall we go and check the cave walls after this meeting?*"

Frida noticed the passion in the old man's eyes; she hung back and caught the eyeballs of Azog.

Azog answered, "*Most of the caves in Beku-neu are unexplored because they are buried under the snow. Beyond all, snow caves and white lands are conquered by deadly predators! And also thin air in the tall mountains became a barrier to mankind.*"

Frida apologized, "*Sir Davu! The Folv mountains are situated in the far north and these caves are not accessible in all the seasons! We can start our expedition when the wind changes towards the south.*"

Davu understood that the geographic position was a hindering factor. Eric noticed most of the ministers were youngsters rather than a bunch of gray grown adults like him. Azog asked Frida and her archaeologist crew to join team Davu to research and find out more.

Eric nods his head at Azog. As part of the alliance, all he expects is to 'work as a team.' Eric and Azog fixed their eyes on Draguva at the map table and announced that Draguva was our next member to join the alliance. Fearful muttering started in the hall. The whispering continued, "*Draguva... Draguva...*" The Darguva was the neighbor of Alaokans, and the sleeping volcanoes were the boundary that separates Alaoka from Draguva. Draguva covers the vast lands in the south and is the strongest of all. The land has its own tropical forest with a strong vegetation background. They own the copyright for bravery and the warriors of Draguva are cruel and fearless offspring of Grim. Wherever their troops walk, burnouts and black carbon remain as leftovers. Another name for Draguva is 'the land of dragons.'

Eric is conscious and discreet; he is aware that people and the Leader of Draguva are easily prone to fire. Draguvans are short-tempered and have enough power to convert both civilizations to the stone age. Azog's words not only reduced the whisper in the hall but also brought new hope to Eric's mind. Azog trilled, "*A spy of his has successfully infiltrated and leads a causal life in the land of dragons.*" Azog's words not only reduced the whisper in the hall but also brought new hope to Eric's mind. Eric's hands gave a big clap for the "*ghost of snow*" and also his conscious brain started to think from different angles.

Azog knows Beku-neu's strengths and sore points; he can't deny that he and his people are safe only until they're inside the stronghold. They are the weakest of all civilizations. For their safety, they should know what's upcoming. Azog had planted spies in all the green-brown corners of the map, including the Alaoka. After an hour of meeting, both Alaokans and courageous Beku-neuns agreed to send a "*messenger of peace*" to meet the witty spy to analyze the situation before approaching with a peace request and finding a way to add them to the alliance. More than inscriptions and fossils, both leaders were planning to give *peace* as a gift for future lineages. The next question that popped into everyone's head was, who was going to be a messenger of peace? Silently, Eric's eyeballs marked Gamba, Azog raised his forefinger, pointed at the young lady and announced her name loudly, "*Liya.*" She is around her twenties, her athletic curves are perfect and she has perfectly proportioned lips below a long narrow nose. Her eyebrows and eyes are as sharp as knives. Her skin complexion matched the shiny tusk of a mammoth. More than a woman with a shield, she is a beautiful princess, like the one in a fairy tale.

After hearing that, Liya was surprised and stepped forward. Azog mentioned, "*Griffins are the pride of Alaokans! She is one of the finest griffin riders of Beku-neu. I am appointing Liya as the 'messenger of peace.' From this moment, Liya coordinates all peace initiatives of Beku-neu and joins hands with Alaokan 'Messenger of peace' for the voyage to the south-east.*" When Azog selected Liya, there were many unhappy faces in the Alaokan race and it reflected like a mirror in their faces. Liya was the one who expected to be happy, but she was not. She has trust issues with Alaokans, but she can't defy the orders of her leader. On the same hand, Eric expected someone experienced to join Gamba; he never expected someone of the age of Gamba's granddaughter. Gamba is in his 70s now. The fact is, he is older than Eric, but Gamba's fine body portrayed his age as 60s. He knew very well that teaming up the 60s with the teenager was going to be the worst decision ever. Last night, Liya was the one who showed her attitude to Alaokan troops. There was perfect silence in the hall. Everyone waited for Eric to appoint a peace envoy for Alaoka. In the middle of the meeting, a sudden clashing sound of heavy metals dinged in the ears.

All of a sudden, Akello and Figo rode on hooves and claws to check the sound coming from the center of the city. Akello's eyes saw a man standing in the tallest tower and bashing the hollow inverted cup (bell) with a big iron rod. The vibration of the bell raised the small hairs of Figo and Akello. Troopers of Beku-neu rushed to stables and armories. Figo and Akello had no clues of what was happening in the city and where troops of Beku-neu were rushing. Immediately, officials of Beku-neu in the hall started to dismiss without orders from Azog. It was strange to the Alaokans. Azog grieved. "*Dinging sound is an alarm of emergency; it is a call to notify there is a problem in the nearby provinces of Beku-neu.*" He demanded the gentle excuse of Eric and other nobles, and he walked to save people and food crops in a nearby land.

The next moment, before the Azog left the meeting hall, a soldier interrupted the meeting. The wiener soldier barked at the message of 'the big white army approaching the fertile lands.' and he added, "*Commander Bora and troops need a backup!*" Azog said to Eric, "*Will resume the strategy meeting after the blood shower.*" Eric said that he and his people were ready to aid Beku-neu. Eric is clever; he knows helping Beku-neuns with local issues is a better way to win their trust. Azog exhaled with hesitation. "*It's a bloodspot! Your army is new to our geographic conditions.*" Eric convinced him by saying, "*Trust without a cost won't last longer.*" Azog acknowledged with a smirk on his lips. Eric whispered to Gamba to get the 200 best warriors out of them and asked him to add 70% with long-range combatants so that casualties can be minimized.

Eric believed, "*Trust that builds by paying blood as the cost is hard to unpair.*"

In the next 10 minutes, everyone suited up the armor and marched to the gates of the right wall. When Gamba marched with 200 Alaokans, whispers started in the troops of Beku-neu. In the stable of Beku-neu, when all warriors were suiting up their armors, a man walked to Liya. He was short, five feet five inches tall and had well-built arms and strong fingers that classified him as an archer, but in his left hand, the first three fingers were tied with tight cotton fabric and looked like he had an injury.

"*Hey, Kiba! Looks like your fingers are still not fit to fire arrows?*" Liya mocked.

The muscular man looked at his bandaged fingers and yelled, "*Medic advised two more weeks' rest.*" He ridiculed, "*I felt working with my big head old man is far better than doing nothing.*" Liya bubbled with laughter and asked, "*Any message for Ivar and your father?*"

"*I have no message for Commander Bora, but remind my brother Ivar about the gift for Arora's birthday. And I request you to get my brother home,*" Kiba answered.

Liya nodded her head with a warm smile and rushed to the gate on her griffin. She was surprised at the armored Alaokan ranks at the gate. Azog was sitting on his white wolf and Gamba rested on his big gray wolf and a pack of Alaokan riders were ready to follow them. Azog was leading three dozen wolf warriors, and he asked a few of his men to follow Gamba. Gamba was happy about finally getting a chance to test his new axe. Liya was the commander-in-chief of Beku-neu's griffin army because there were no big experienced riders in their griffin army. Gamba asked Alaokan air units to work under the command of Liya. Including Alaokan air units, there were a total of 40 griffins that led under Liya for today. Liya and another male griffin rider walked near Alaokan griffins. Akello was unhappy to work under the big attitude of Liya, but her armored griffin looked astonishing and his eyes were fixed on her griffin. The orders of Azog to Liya hit all warriors' ears, "*Fly two levels above the ground and escort the troops.*" He gave permission to launch an attack when the time was right. Liya approached Akello with a smile on her face and distributed goggles to him and other Alaokan riders. She said, "*They use the goggles to protect their eyes from low temperature.*" She also demonstrated to Akello the use of goggles and other features of goggles as well. Goggles have a rotator on the left to zoom-in and zoom-out the vision. She ordered the Alaokans to 'follow her lead in the air.' Akello expressed his thanks to Liya on behalf of all the Alaokans riders. Eric was on his piebald horse, and dozens of fine archers were under his command.

Liya wore her helmet; it covered both her beautiful cheeks and wide forehead. From the opening of the helmet, only her knife eyes and perfect lips were visible. She tied her long hair with a knot and an Alaokan comrade standing near Akello whispered to him, "The commander of the griffin army has a perfect figure and has strong hypnotic eyes." Akello ignored him, and he was ready for the ride. There were a total of 36 dozen soldiers, including Alaokans, waiting for the gates to open. After instruction, Azog blew the horn made of mammoth tusk. Everyone galloped the beast and directed them outside the wall through the right entrance. The sound of hooves and gallops of horses thundered the ears along with the scream of griffins. Beasts were at full speed on the white lands. Their speed disturbed the settled white dust and raised them above the ground. Griffin riders flying above ground level could see troops from the top view and escort them. After a few minutes, troopers crossed the human-made wide bridge to reach the next island. Around the bridge, everything was covered in snow; it looked like haunted white lands. The scream of Neo echoed throughout the surroundings. After hearing the scream, Liya was afraid that the echo could disturb the slack ice caps and ordered Akello to stay low. The bridge was long and also acted as a connector of two big land islands. With the speed of beasts, they crossed another bridge in a few minutes. Akello noticed staginess in the Alaokan fangs because of climate change.

Troops stepped into another big snowy region and far big mountains were covered by ice caps. From the sky, air units could see troops riding at top speed in the frozen ocean. Alaokans griffin riders were goose-bumped to view the frozen ocean and troops riding on them. At that very moment, they understood that the island was a frozen ocean. The ice was crystal clear; Akello could see underwater plants and even fish swimming in the ocean with zoomed goggles. Finally, after crossing the frozen blue, a mild sun warmed their skin. The snowfall converted to a slight drizzle, and a bunch of Alaokan griffin riders were astonished by the beauty of Beku-neu. One side of the mountain was covered by thick snow, but the other side of sloppy mountains was graced by the sun. In the grace of the sun, small villages and crop fields were feasts to the eyes. The moo sound of cattle melted the ears. On this day, Akello understood why the sun was the king of all gods. Suddenly, the trumping sounds of mammoths forced them to change their direction into the icy regions again. Liya shouted, "*The thumping sound is from Bora's mammoth armies.*" She added, "*Sound of the mammoths denotes, we are late for the party.*"

In a minute, Akello and Alaokan riders caught sight of an eight-foot-tall white monkey-faced beast, whose body was completely covered in white fur. It has powerful big feet and cooking pan-sized palms. Azog shouted, "*Kill the yetis!*" Akello's eyes did not get the sight of one yeti, but they were 20 in number forwarding toward Bora's mammoth army. Already, Bora and his men are already handling a few. In the mammoth troops, Eric can see a man on the mammoth bravely fighting with the yetis with a club in his hands. Eric's mind nudged, "*He must be the Bora.*" Liya loudly screamed, "*It's time for the takedown.*" She launches the first attack against yeti with a furious kick of griffin. The powerful kick of a griffin pushed the large yeti, but yeti managed to avoid falling down by kneeling down on one leg. In the meantime, Liya used her double-ended sharp sword as a javelin and targeted yeti's chest; the sword tore yeti's furry skin with the huge blood mesh. In the next moment, yeti was helpless against the attack and fell down like a corpse with wide-open eyes. Akello cannot believe his eyes, because she killed the big yeti in two blows.

In the meantime, Azog and troops joined Bora and the company. In the wild white land, the big feet of yetis stomped their feet on the snow bed and rushed at humans. Eric caught Azog's eyes and shook his head. The execution of the division started. Eric, on his piebald horse, attracted the interest of yetis fighting against Bora and his mammoth warriors. He released Alaokan wooden arrows at yetis, but the wooden arrows were needles of toothpicks against yeti. Again, to gain interest, he shot the arrows at the head of the beast. It didn't pierce the head but hurt them. With a furious roar, three yetis began to chase Eric and his dozens of horsemen. Eric and his men drove the yetis toward the left (west). The speed of mustangs favored them; they isolated big beasts far from Bora's Mammoths. At the same time, Azog asked Gamba and Alaokan fang riders to drive the forwarding 15 yetis to the east and ordered the griffin unit to hunt them once they reached the vantage point (in the east). A large army of wolves crossed the mammoths of Bora and ambushed the forwarding 15 tall yetis. Azog, Gamba and their best men used bite-and-run tactics and made the yetis run behind them toward the east. Strong mesh bites of wolves, axes, and spears created wounds on furry yetis, and their strategy worked. Eight yetis showed their interest in chasing the fangs riders, but a direct ambush of wolf riders on yetis dug their own grave under the big feet of yetis. Many men, women and wolves were crushed by pan-sized hands and smashed by big feet. The remaining yetis were occupied by a large mammoth army and dozens of Alaokan archers. The fact is the tuskers of Beku-neu are trained for this wild hunt. This icy afternoon was rare. After centuries, the two meteor swords were fighting on the same side.

East Battle Field (Azog and Wolves)

Initially, it was really a bad day for yetis. Wolves tore the flesh into pieces, ripped hands and faces. The deep red blood dripped onto the white lands. The rushing blood spread in the snow blanket. The arrows of griffin riders drilled the body of yetis. Azog's forwarded spear pierced the knees of yetis, and Gamba's shark tooth axe was more furious than he expected, creating deeper wounds on the white devils. From the air, the east battlefield (wolf fighting zone) looked red with corpses of wolf riders, smashed wolves and torn flesh of yetis. Yetis are beast warriors; they not only smashed the wolves but also griffins. When griffins tried to attack the yetis with cruel claws and strong beaks, yetis waited for the right time and caught the wings and claws of hybrid birds. To escape crushing hands, griffins executed the beak attack on the chest and face of yetis, but it doesn't loosen the grip of the stone-crushing hands. Yetis tore the wings of griffins, crushed their bones and kicked the remains of griffins like a footfall. Painful screams of wingless griffins in their last moments echoed in all three battlefields. The eight best warriors of the yetis reduced the wolf crowd to half and they are not done yet.

West Battle Field (Eric and Sharp Shooters)

Eric underestimated the rage and courage in the yetis' hearts. White furry beasts killed dozens of his men. There was humiliation in front of Eric's eyes. Humans were captured and squeezed in between yeti's rock hands. Troopers screamed in extreme pain and squeezed to death. The sound of their scream planted fear in the leftover men of their army. The squeezing pressure rushed the blood from all openings of their body. The eyes of the troopers were terrorized while watching their comrades being brutally killed by snow predators. Many horses were scared and started to slip away from the field. While yetis smashed both Alaokan and Beku-neu's troops, the remaining half locked their eyes on Eric and waited for his orders. Troopers' faces were thrilled, their courage melted down after seeing the brutality of the white monsters. Eric graced the troops and called out the remaining spearmen to follow him. To save his troops, Eric and his fearless men galloped their mustangs and mares against the hunting yetis. Eric took advantage of the horse's speed and ambushed the big legs of the beast with swords and spears. Weapons were targeted at the big feet of the snow monster. Spears pierced the giant toe and instep of the foot and made the white devil bleed and monsters screamed in pain. While approaching the smashing yeti, Eric's eyes locked on the target, and at the speed of the howling wind, he thrust his royal sword into the defined ankle of yeti and escaped from grabbing of crusher hands with the mustang's speed. He got away, but the meteor sword was stuck in yeti's ankle. The painful roar of the beast vibrated the hearts and drilled the ears. Along with Eric, only fearless mustangs and mares slipped away from smashing hands and others became prey.

Eric's plan worked; yetis have tall lower bodies when compared to the upper bodies. With the damaged legs of yetis, they are not fit to carry their huge shape. The white furry beings collapsed down in the snow.

While directing a horse, Eric turned their head to see the fallen yetis and shouted, "*Release the arrows*!" The moment his words hit the ears, the wooden arrow of Alaokans and the silver cupped pointy arrow of snow landers triggered on yetis. Immovable abominable snowmen are open to dispatch arrows. The silver arrows of Beku-neu have better speed and dealt a lot of damage to yetis. While wooden arrows created soft wounds on white monsters, silver arrows pierced out the thick fur of animals. One of the yetis raised his rocky hands to brace the incoming arrow targeting his head, but the silver arrow made a hole in its rocky palm and bored its forehead. All three yetis' heads reached the ground. The Alaokan leader's wit was praised by troopers. Eric wore a grin smile and directed his horse into the bloody river of fallen yetis to retrieve his meteor sword, but he was unaware that the fallen snowman was still alive. The gore of the abominable snowman was pungent and nauseated Eric. While he unplugged the sword from his ankle, the snowman screamed in pain and his soul was hugged by the god of death. There was perfect silence in the west battlefield, but howling white winds and falling-snow pearls showed no mercy. Fighting in the minus temperature drained the energy of the Alaokans. Two dozen and a half survived the furious attack.

Mammoth Battlefield

Mammoth units fought a big group. Tuskers and their riders blocked the beast with great confidence and strength. Snowland archers fired silver, cupped arrows and punctured the yeits' chest, biceps, and skull. Brutal death and anguish of abominable snowmen killed by Eric and Azog crews invited physically strong berserker yetis to the mammoth battlefield. From the moment they arrived, the situation went upside down. A group of yetis jumped in. Without a delay, they grouped into teams and started smashing the Beku-neun troops. Two muscled predators started the game of death with a furious roar and launched a heavy kick together at a mammoth's massive body. The power of the kick pushed the woolly mountain 400 meters away. The anguished cry of the mammoth touched heaven. A fallen big creature was not able to rise again. The merciless white beast smashed the skull of a mammoth rider with a heavy stomp and blood stain fixed to its big foot. With all strength, yetis rushed to the group of archers. The sound of a broken skull under the foot and blood footprints paralyzed the archers. Bora bawled, "*Fire arrows!*" The arrows triggered by the bowmen pierced the white fur, but they didn't kill the beast or slow their speed. Instead, the atmosphere of their eyes became red. Their next moves were arrogant and wild. Not only these two yetis, but other yeti teams also humiliated the mammoth's army. Their hands gained the strength of Thor's Hammer. Crushing hands and heavy tusks were in the duel. The woolly beast pushed all his physical strength into the tusks, but crushing hands blocked the tusks with the support of thrusting legs in the strong ice. It was a deadlock, but the rider seated above the woolly mountain had free hands to attack the white devil. The rider has a good elevation to attack, and they fired spears and arrows at yetis. The spears drilled the white fur, and life dripped out, but on the other side, yetis' hammer hands started to push back the woolly mountains, boiling rage and anger in their heart exponentially multiplied their strength and made them break the ivory tusks of the mammoth. The pain of the mammoths is expressed in the trunk. In the pain, the living mountain raised its front legs, which made riders fall down. Riders and mammoths whose backs touched the ground were ambushed by furry white beasts. Snow beasts used the broken tusks of mammoths as daggers and created blood fountains. The size of the mammoth army started to fall like dominos. The commander of Beku-neu and the chief of the mammoth army were paralyzed by such humiliation. In his life, he has never seen such terror and brutality of yetis.

The peer of Bora was tall and fighting, the yeti's from the dark brown mammoth. His spear and his mammoth tusks killed one of the two yetis they fought. He turned his shaved head to see the yetis marching toward archers. He ordered his brown devil to handle white evil and jumped down from his woolly mountain. He is seven feet and five inches tall and weighs around 110 kg. His muscular hands clutched heavy spears and his iron legs rushed toward the Yetis, marching toward the archers. He wore a black outfit; his bald head and welcoming lips don't suit his beefy muscular shape. He knows very well that archers were their only way to win this big yeti battle. People of Beku-neu call him 'man-mammoth' and his real name is Ivar. Man-mammoth is very strong in physique and his mental strength was built by trusting the physique. He decided to take down two berserker yetis on his own. In the Beku-neu, no one dares to mess with two white evils at once except Ivar. Yetis are rushing from the north and Ivar running from the east. Bora shouted, "*No! No! Ivar, stop!*" Ivar ignored him and rushed down his path. Anguish cries of friendly giants panicked the east and west battlefield. Azog shouted, "*We can handle the situation here,*" and ordered, "*Griffin riders to the mammoth battlefield.*" Liya withdrew her units from the east and rushed to support the mammoth brigade. Before reaching the mammoth war grounds from the air, their eyes witnessed the brutality and destruction. Liya could not believe her eyes; she had never seen these many dead mammoths at once and the red river. It's worse than the battlefield in the east.

Akello's eyes caught sight of Ivar's spear piercing the neck of the white berserker and blood rushed from the neck, but the beast was still alive. The wounded beast and its companion changed their direction to Ivar. So, archers are safe as of now. In the fast of howling winds, Ivar released one of his spears into the air against yeti, rushing him. Ivar's spear never missed the target, and it broke the knee ball of the white devil. With a painful roar, yeti collapsed down. Another companion of the fallen yeti rushed to the heavy man. Ivar's hands were empty, and the beast was forwarding to smash him. There was no fear in his eyes; he smiled at the target and prepared to duel the beast with his fist.

In the white dust, Ivar boxed with yeti. His strength and height were a little match for yeti, and his forceful punches worked against the white devil. Akello and the Alaokans were stunned to see Ivar and his courage. Ivar evaded the fist and kicks of yeti, but it didn't work for a long time. The scene of victory changed in flashing seconds. Yeti's kick hit the target and pushed Ivar 500 meters away. With a roar of victory, yeti forwarded at swooning Ivar. Without orders from Liya, Akello directed Neo to save the brave man. The scream of Neo gained the interest of yeti. With the speed of Neo's wings, Akello triggered the arrows in the eyes of yeti. He fired eight arrows in a row and luckily one arrow got the eyeball of the snow devil. With a wild roar and pain, yeti threw the corpses of the horses and dead comrades at Neo. No griffin in the world can stand against the agility of Akello's olive-green griffin; it dodged the corpses well. Akello has seen how the griffin wings were torn by yetis; he never wanted to put Neo in such pain. Wooden arrows are useless in the snow. He had fear, but he didn't exhibit them in his eyes. With a grin on his lips, he charged Neo against the white devil to save Ivar.

Neo's claws pulled out the vision of the yeti. The visionless yeti ran in the direction of the archers' crowd and started to smash. Fainted Ivar was backed up by his brown devil. Akello made Neo fly above the head of a yeti and waited for the right time to attack. When the time was right, Akello jumped down from Neo with his unsealed sword and landed his sword on yeti's skull. He balanced his shape by landing the legs on the shoulder of a snow beast. Alaokan steel pierced the skull and escaped its life out of the yeti's mouth. To save Ivar's life,

Akello charged the life of 20 archers. The yeti that was killed by Akello was stomped by a brown devil several times. Seeing unconscious Ivar increased the rage of his brown devil. Revenge for Ivar and fallen tuskers was executed by a barbaric elephant of Ivar. He carried the spear of Ivar in the trunk and walked into enemies. A mammoth became a nightmare for berserkers. Bones of yetis were crushed by the stomp of a brown devil. At sunset time, all berserker bogies were exterminated. Screams of half-smashed-alive comrades melted the eyes and also they asked good-shaped men to show mercy. With cold hearts and leaking eyes, mercy was shown at the tip of swords to badly injured comrades and beasts.

After the bloodbath, there was a heavy gasp and wheezing in everyone's breath. Clouds were influenced by the reddish-yellow light of the setting sun, and icy ranges reflected the yellow of the sun. The beauty of the setting sun calmed the restless troopers. Azog introduced his commander to Eric and Gamba. Commander Bora nodded his head and gifted an artifact made of ivory to Eric. The shape of Bora is similar to his son Kiba, with muscular hands and short in length, but in addition to him, Bora's head was bald. The glare of the reddish sun reflected on his bald head. Liya appreciated Akello for the attack on yetis and for saving Ivar's life, and that's how Akello came to know the man-mammoth's name was Ivar. Moments after the appreciation, she walked to Gamba and complained about Akello for acting on his own on the battlefield. Akello bashed his hands on the head and walked to the last row to hide his face from Gamba. More than half of the warriors were dead and in total 25 white monster heads were chopped down. Snow battles didn't favor Alaokans. Shortness of breath and snow reduced their efficiency, and many were hunted by the white beast. Eric was responsible for the brutal murders of Alaokans today, but he didn't feel bad about his decision to involve Alaokan ranks in the Beku-neu's internal warfare. He stood silent near Azog, but as expected, the people of snow began to trust the Alaokans. A man with a longbow whispered something in the ears of Bora. After catching the news from the bowman, Bora reported to Azog about the brave warriors who lost their lives in the battle against yetis. Bora's report comprises 190 lives departed in today's battle, which includes seven dozen warriors, 24 mammoths, four dozen horses, two dozen wolves and 10 griffins.

Azog mentioned, "*It was the massive yeti wave that we have ever fought in this lunar calendar.*"

Funeral rituals for dead warriors and beasts happened with the remains of their corpses. All faces were filled with sadness and many cried for fathers, sons, daughters, and comrades. Akello felt bad for his comrades and moaned about their afterlife journey. The wolf howled and respected the dead. In Beku-neu's culture, the howl of wolves invites the god of death to carry the fallen to the hall of death. The man-mammoth joined the funeral. Everyone patted his shoulders to congratulate his valor, but Bora carried an angry look at his son. Ivar bent his head down and showed his respect for the fallen. Liya walked near Ivar and whispered in his ears. The next moment, his eyes graced Akello, but Akello didn't notice it. Some humans lost their beast partners, some beasts failed in their mission to protect their humans. The faces of warriors who lost their beasts in the battle were grief-stricken, and the pain in the heart was expelled in the form of tears. Mammoths have one special quality, like humans; they shed tears for their human friend. Wolves expressed grief with long howls. In the griffins' case, none of the griffins let their humans die, but they sacrifice their own lives. Corpses of fallen comrades and friendly beasts were piled to form a mountain.

A middle-aged man wept loudly and said, "*In the last 40 years of my life, I never spent a day without my Kuntala (name of mammoth).*"

The middle-aged man showed his last respect to his mammoth by kissing it and cutting a small quarter of its tusk. That small quarter will remain with him in memory of his beast. Azog approached the mammoth rider and said, "*We are warriors! We know about our responsibilities and threats to our life. Be brave and face the future.*" Azog prayed for Kuntala's afterlife journey and consoled the comrade with a warm hug. One after another, everyone showed their respect for the fallen. They placed an arrow in the hands of each corpse. A Beku-neun standing next to Akello explained to him, "*An arrow kept in the hand gains respect for souls in the hall of death.*" After the bloodshed, the sun decided to take a break. The golden light of the sun dimmed and created twilight in the sky. With the help of dry woods and dried yak dung, Azog lit the fire to the corpses. The people of Beku-neu gave the same respect to fallen Alaokans and made a toast for the fallen Alaokans. This time Eric didn't let the Sura flow on the ground. In the tradition of Alaoka, they used to bury the corpse and plant a tree above the buried place, but in Beku-neu, being everything is covered by ice, they follow a different tradition to dispose of the corpses.

After the ritual, fragile troops were ordered to march to a safer place to spend the night. Hooves, pillar legs, paws, and claws hiked the steep mountains in the light of the fire torch. By dinner time, troopers reached the village behind the mountains. Villagers welcomed their saviors with excitement and treated the wounds of warriors. Azog walked Eric and Gamba to a special pond in the nearby forest, and Azog was 100 meters ahead. Eric was rubbing his hands to fight the cold weather. Around the pond, marshals were lit here and there. In the light of a fire torch, Gamba can see the mist around the pond. All of a sudden, Azog removed his clothes and dived into the pond without a word. While Eric and Gamba were rubbing their hands to fight the cold weather, the action of Azog made both Alaokans think, "*Is he mad?*" They exchanged weird looks but no words.

Eric noted that around the pond, snow was covered everywhere, but the surface of the water had neither snowflakes nor frozen. Moving closer to the pond, the weather became welcoming and warmness hugged him. Gamba bent on his knees to touch the water in the pond. The water was warm. Gamba wondered and invited Eric to check the pond. Azog pops his head outside the pond, "*Welcome to the Res-pan hot spring!*" He rejoiced, "*This warm healing water is one of the wonders of Beku-neu.*" Eric and Gamba joined Azog in the pond. Azog mentioned that there are plenty of hot springs around Beku-neu and this is the best of all. When warm water touches small cut wounds, they feel the chill instead of irritation. After the worst day, this temperate water comforts the heroes and eases their minds. Soon, most of the Beku-neun warriors took their Alaokan friends to the hot springs around the village, and the warm water became crowded. Gamba heckled. "*We should have come a little earlier.*" Eric and Azog bloomed in laughter. From three hot springs near the castle, Beku-neuns redirected the water into the castle for daily needs and also facilitated the castle with proper storage and sewage systems.

After a warm bath in the Beku-neu's Res-pan, Alaokans rested near the wheat fields of the village. The temperature was cold, but there was no sign of snowflakes and the icy wind. A big campfire was lit. In the influence of gentle wind, needle leaves of wheat plantation brushed one another to create a romantic whisper. The melody of crop fields, clear sky, and gritty soil made Alaokan miss their homes. They crossed three full moons after leaving Alaoka. Meanwhile, the nostrils of the warriors were knocked down by the aroma of the BBQ. Meat and green cooked by villagers put a full stop to the hunger of warriors and spices of Beku-neu, creating a water leak in Alaokan noses. While Akello was munching on the juicy meat, Ivar walked to him, expressed his thanks for saving his life, and introduced himself. After dinner, everyone walked to allocated huts to hug their beds, but most Alaokans preferred the wheat fields to rest their backs.

Azog invited Eric to his hut for Sura. All night, they discussed the threats and challenges they have faced in their lands. Eric's opinions on Beku-neu's problem were visionary. The door of the big hut was knocked; Azog walked to open the doors. He was very happy to see his pupils. There were two at the door, a man 7.5 feet tall and a young lady with knife eyes. He congratulated Ivar for his brave act in today's war and welcomed both of them inside the hut. Leader Azog served both Sura in a mug made of the tusk. Liya and Ivar gulped Sura. Azog happily introduced his students to Eric. Eric also congratulated Ivar for his valor and Liya for her new responsibilities as a peace envoy. Ivar said his thanks to Eric for the Alaokan troops and an Alaokan who saved his life. Azog mentioned to Eric, "*One of my students, Kiba, was not fit to participate in today's fight and his arrow is the fastest arrow in Beku-neu.*" When Azog introduced his pupils, Eric could see huge pride in his eyes. At the same time, Liya and Ivar can see the big trust in Azog's eyes about Alaokans. After Azog's party, everyone walked to their huts. The last moment pain of Alaokan warriors rang in Eric's ears and guilt in his heart didn't let him sleep, but he knew very well that the blood of Alaokans spilled in today's war changed the mind of Beku-neuns and strengthened their alliance. It rooted big trust in them.

Even though it was not snowy, the cold breeze and snoring sound rumbling in the hut made Akello roll on his bed. Akello was not feeling sleepy. He walked out of the hut and his coal-black lens graced the campfire and a charming young lady sitting near the warm fire with a bag of Sura. Akello recognized that she was the same knife-eyed lady who had ignored him yesterday and today complained about his act to Gamba. Liya waved her hands at Akello out of the blue; Akello never expected this change. Without delay, Akello waved his palm back, directed his foot toward her, and comforted himself near the campfire. The warmth of the fire was comfy; he applied a pig's fat to his parted dry lips and minor wounds. The cold breeze gently ceased Liya's hair and made the campfire dance with the crackling sound of wood.

Liya started a conversation with a question. "*Does the cold breeze disturb your head trip?*"

"*Yes, the chill breeze and moran snoring inside the hut disturbed my sleep,*" Akello answered.

Her smirk converted to laughter. Her large lower lip reflected the light of the flame.

She is beautiful if any other man around her in this darkest of nights would have started flirting, but Akello's loyalty to Amara is big!

Akello pushed a gentle question. "*Are you not feeling sleepy?*"

Liya sipped the drink and replied, "*I hardly sleep for four hours a day.*"

Liya's reply made Akello look at his fingers. He locked his fingers one after another, and finally, he said, "*I sleep for a minimum of 10 hours a day.*" Laughter bubbled in both faces.

The man inside the dark hut looked at the bubbling young lads.

Akello asked Liya how frequently these yeti attacks take place.

With a gasp, she began, "*Usually, yeti attacks once or twice a year, but this lunar calendar is the fourth wave. We have lost many of our skilled warriors, and the wave we fought today is huge, and those berserkers were merciless devils.*"

After taking up on today's battle, Akello understood what they had been through. At first, Akello hesitated, but his curiosity boomed out, "*Where are these creatures coming from?*"

Keeping aside her attitude, she answered that this predator hunts humans for red and they love to eat green in the fields. She also added that her grandma used to tell stories about the isolated regions of the yeti kingdom in the far north. Far north is the gate to hell; you won't feel the change in day and night. Everywhere, endless snow and falling snow from the mountains drain lives. Troops and previous leaders initiated the extermination of yetis in the length and breadth of Bekuneu, but no one succeeded in finding the kingdom of yeti, but in their journey, they found yetis' lifestyle. They live in families in deep frozen caves, where humans can't breathe. They sleep for months. Once they wake up, they come out in search of food. They hunt people and eat greens in the agricultural villages and go back to hidden caves in the ice. She was upset that she read more about Yetti's in the libraries, but no information is worthy.

When Akello opened his parted lips for the next question, Liya asked, "*How does Alaoka look?*"

Akello had never heard such a question in his life. He could have expressed it in a better way, but his thoughts and tongue were not in sync. Akello's mind flashed with the view of Alaoka from Neo's back. All he sees in his vision is vegetation, brown mountains, and the potential sunlight. The next moment, he compared Alaoka with Beku-neu. Liya waited for Akello's answer, but he was frozen in his own thoughts. To get his attention, she snapped his finger. The sound of a snap gets into their ears. By catching her eyes, he delighted, "*Paradise! Looks just opposite to Beku-neu!*"

With anger in her eyes, Liya replied, "*What?*"

Akello muttered, "*Oh! No! I am in a mess!*" But before the campfire fades out, he convinces her after a huge struggle.

The next morning, when the first light touched the fields, everyone mounted their beasts to the stronghold. Bora and a few decided to stay back to guard the village. Ivar also marched with other troops to the castle. He was sitting on his brown devil and holding a hunted elk on his shoulders. After two hours, all troopers reached the fort gates. After Azog blew the horn, doors split to welcome the troops. A huge crowd of family and friends were standing on the sides of the pavement to welcome their kin. Many were happy to see their men and women, along with the happiness, so many kisses changed at the gate. The very last mammoth of the troops marched inside the gate. Still, their eyes awaited the open gates for the return of their love. Azog personally addressed the family members of fallen warriors, consoled them, and also took part in their loss. This quality of Azog made Akello feel 'Azog is a great leader too and his views and actions were for the betterment of his people.'

Kiba, the fastest archer in the Beku-neu, was waiting with two kids at the entrance. The girl standing with him was around 10 years old and the boy he carried on his shoulder was around five. Kiba pointed his bandaid finger at Ivar seated on Akara (the brown devil of Ivar) and bubbled, "*Daddy's home!*" Excitement bubbled in the face of the kids, and Ivar's 10-year-old daughter's lips expanded in happiness. Ivar's brown devil was excited after seeing his little partner. Ivar's mammoth is Bora's own-breed, and Akara was once a playing partner for Ivar's daughter.

The bond between man and beast is complicated to explain. It's a feeling that everyone has to experience at least once in a lifetime.

She ran and hugged her pet mammoth. Akara's strong trunk became soft like a flower and gently lifted her up and gave her to Ivar. Ivar kissed her daughter on her forehead and rejoiced, "*Happy birthday, Arora!*" He continued, "*In the last six months, you have grown well!*" Rice bag legs and a giant head of mammoths danced in excitement. She giggled and hugged her dad with tears and beamed, "*Credits to grandmother and she asked about the welfare of her lovely grandpa Bora.*" It was a good family reunion. The kids met their dad, and the brothers hugged again after six months. Gates of the castle were experiencing both happy and sad memories, but it was not new.

After the great meal, everyone assembled in the big meeting hall. Azog appreciated the Alaokans for taking part in their fight and showed his respect for fallen comrades. Everyone was waiting for Eric to announce the *messenger of peace* for

Alaoka. Finally, he announced the messenger. He selected Akello over Gamba. There was big gossip that started in Alaokan rank. Gamba was holding a smile on his lips because his best friend and leader of Alaokans had already discussed it with him. Akello's name became gossip in the hall. Akello was unaware that he had been selected and was feeding his animal friend in the stable. Gamba ordered an Alaokan soldier to take Akello to the hall. Davu fears getting into perfect shape; he believes his grandson is not ready to take on such an S-rank mission. There was big anger and battle running through his head, but he decided to stay silent. Akello was summoned into the hall and Eric explained to Akello why he was summoned. After hearing the purpose, his face bloomed like a flower. He tried not to show his teeth, but his lips automatically expanded to a smile. The moment Akello heard he was going to join the mission with Liya, his expressing smile vanished. Azog talked about the secret way to meet his spy in Draguva. The tavern in the market is a place where Akello and Liya can find a Beku-neun spy. Spy provides cover for Akello and Liya and also supports them in the mission they seek. Azog suggested it is not advisable to fly to south-east lands (Draguva/The Dragon Land). If young champs get caught by dragon riders, it's definitely a free ticket to the afterlife, and it will break out of the war between lands once again. The words of Azog were clear and a fear factor to Akello, "If you get caught in Draguva, there is no possibility of coming back to homelands."

At first, there was a small shake in Akello's legs. His tutor Ekon's words rushed into his mind, "*Death is only once, but fame and success weigh everything you have in life.*" Azog's words clearly explained to Akello and Liya that they were going on a serious mission, "*If we fail in the mission, their lands will shower in the fire.*" Eric told about a secret cave that is located in Alaoka, which is hidden under the forest pond. This pond is located far east of Alaoka. In the rainy season, rainwater closes the doors of the cave and makes it unfit to pass through, but this year is predicted to be a dry summer in Alaoka. Dry summer made the pond lose all its water and the doors of the cave are open to pass. Eric advised to use the special hollows in Alaoka to intrude into the south-east lands. Every Alaokan in the hall was unaware of these hallows in their motherland. Even Gamba was hearing it for the very first time. After hearing from Eric and other Alaokans about wonders in Alaoka, it created excitement in the people of white land to visit the land of bamboo and greens (Alaoka).

The word 'but' from Eric made the heads focus on Eric. Eric continued, "*Being the south-east monsoon in Alaoka is one full moon away. We Alaokans have to open our sails soon to reach Alaoka or else mission Draguva needs to wait for another year*"

Hall was filled with perfect silence for a couple of minutes. Azog's mind was wheeling multiple questions, but he shook his head as a gesture of acceptance to Eric. After all, he didn't want to wait for another year to intrude on Draguva. In the darkness last night, Eric caught sight of relaxing Akello and Liya near the warm campfire; he believes teaming up youngsters will tangle the roots of grass and ice. On the other hand, the higher ranks of Alaokan thought it was foolish to send an amateur for an S-rank mission and they were valid. Eric can't deny Akello is an amateur, but his courage in today's battle is not amateur stuff.

Eric also loves to have Liya as the first resident of Alaoka from Beku-neu; he expects a charming love story along with the success of the mission, but none of the Alaokans is aware of the story known by the falls of heaven. At the conclusion of the meeting, Akello was invited to the birthday party of Ivar's daughter. Ivar asked Akello to join as a gesture of thanks for saving his life. Akello accepts the invitation of Ivar; he has never heard the word "birthday" because Alaokan never celebrates the tradition of birthdays. All they remember is the month of their birth. Beku-neu doesn't have a variety of festivals like Alaoka, but they celebrate birthdays as a special day. Every nightfall is a festival to cherish because they survived the sundown. So, they celebrate the date of their birth every year, along with the dearest people and the most-liked food. Beyond all, people who celebrate birthdays will get gifts from loved ones.

Akello was on cloud nine about the new mission, but when Liya appeared in his daydream, the angle of his wide, smiling lips bent down. He thought teaming up with Liya and collaborating was hard with her attitude. Akello expressed the happiness of his new role to Figo. Figo was happy for his friend Akello and added, "*When you are not around, I will help your family in rethatching the hut for winter.*" Because rethatching the hut is the hardest work and needs manpower and strength. Akello was happy for Figo's support and hugged him. Figo is also the perfect candidate for peace envoy, but Eric chose Akello over other youngsters. Eric believed, "*Justice and peace are conjoined twins, without one other couldn't survive.*" With wit and strategy, one can bring peace, but to maintain the established peace, one should not slip on the track of justice and be strong enough to question those who slip the justice. In his perception, more than wit and strategy, a peace envoy must have a pure heart and a strong will to question if someone slips the track of justice. Akello has a strong will to question the wrong.

The evening was pleasant inside the castle. The shops were bright in the light of marshals, and big campfires were lit in the city to fight the summoning of Ms. Cold Breeze. Before the arrival of the moon, Akello got the idea of 'birthday' from his Beku-neun friend. Time passed by the light of the luminous moon, along with snowflakes decorated the castle roofs, and Akello's foot started in the direction of Ivar's residence, but he has no navigation issue, everyone inside the wall knew the way to Ivar's house. When he reached Ivar's door, his shoulders were decorated by the snowflake. The hut's door was opened by Liya and she welcomed him with a warm smile. When Akello checked his shoulder, the white powder had melted down. Liya got a beautiful smile at the same time when she stared; she looked evil. Ivar welcomed Akello with many hugs; with a smile, he introduced him to Kiba and his legacies. Akello was not empty-handed; he came with a gift. He gave a bouquet made of griffin feathers to Aurora. She was excited to receive such a gorgeous gift that none of them had in Beku-neu. With the Sura mugs, dinner started and the sound of laughter and giggles escaped the chimney of the hut. Finger-licking taste of the Elk meat melted in Akello's mouth without hesitation; he raised the wooden plate for more meat. The conversation was healthy and funny. Liya gave the first griffin flight experience to Aurora, and she was excited, but at the same time, the stream of tears expelled out. Everyone around understood that Aurora missed her mom at this happiest moment. She lost her mother two years ago in the battle of the yeti wave. Her mother promised to take her griffin ride when she turns ten. The promise made by her mother was fulfilled by her aunt Liya. Aurora's tears were unstoppable and within seconds, giggles and laughter faded. No one noticed the drop of the tear that escaped from the man-mammoth's eye. Jokes cracked by Akello created rejoicing in Aurora's face. After some time, she was back to normal. The trumpet of her big pet made her walk to the elephant stable behind the hut. After emptying the barrel of drink, the party came to an end.

In the light of the moon, along with a gentle white shower, Akello and Liya walked to the tower. On their way, they both were battling without using swords and fists. It is a friendly debate regarding the beauty of Alaoka and the white land. Finally, when they reached the tower. The debate stopped but was not concluded. Liya asked a favor to Akello, and she asked him to meet her below the bell tower the next morning.

"*The beginning of a new friendship started out of debate; let's start a journey with them to know where it takes them.*"

Chapter 5

Bamboos and Ice Walks Over Fire!

Finally, the day arrived. On one hand, the Alaokans were happy that they were traveling back home. On the other hand, they were a bit sad that they were leaving Beku-neu and their new comrades. Ships of Alaokans started from knorr caves and reached the shores of Beku-neu. Along with the small golden rays and pink clouds, the people of Beku-neu flooded the shores to send off the Alaokans. New friend Ivar and his daughter were sitting on the brown devil and wishing luck for Akello and Liya. Along with Liya, 70 Beku-neuns, including Kiba, joined Eric's feet to travel to Alaoka. With farewell, the Alaokan fleets opened their sails toward the south. The wind was against them and the sail was kept low. In the rough weather, Liya and Kiba helped Akello and his friends in hardships. Events of rough weather changed Akello's views about Liya, but teamwork with her was still a big question for him. He didn't get much time to spend with Figo and others, but Liya and Akello discussed a lot about their common interests and about the mission. While Akello was standing near the rails of the ships, Liya walked near him and he casually got sight of her long fingers and palms. He was puzzled that Liya was a griffin rider, but her fingers didn't have any bite scar! With hesitation, Akello posted, "*Liya! Alaokan griffin bites the finger of its rider to sign the blood contract, but I wonder, your hands don't have any bite scars.*"

After hearing Akello, embarrassment decorated Liya's cheeks, and she wished to disappear right away but Akello was waiting for an answer, she said in a smoky voice, "*I believe griffins don't have any written rule to bite only on their rider forefinger!*" With a blush, she escaped by saying she has some unfinished work to be taken care of, but the wonder was she has two griffin bite scars on her shape and her father was a griffin rider too.

When no one was around, Davu questioned Eric with red eyes why he had chosen his grandson as a messenger of peace. Silence hit Eric's face; he had never expected such a question from the old, fragile friend. Anger in Davu's eyes busted out tears. With tears, he begged Eric to relieve his grandson from Alaokan duty and begged for Akello's well-being. Eric gave a warm hug to the old man to console him, and Eric whispered, "*With your sentiment, don't steal his limelight. There was no change in my decision.*" He started to walk out. Davu's pain increased the leak in the eye; he wanted his grandson to carry his legacy and name. Eric understood very well the pain of Davu; he paused for a moment and gave his words "*To protect the life of messenger, I will give 100 souls to Akello for a bargain and remember he is the rider of the olive-green beast.*"

Days passed by. The journey was longer than expected, but Alaokan vessels reached Alaoka before the first monsoon strike and people welcomed the Alaokans on the coast of the southern sea. At the same time, Eric and Gamba have a duty to console the families of those who did not return home. People of Beku-neu admired the golden rays of the sun on their skin and the hot sand underneath. Tender coconuts were served as welcome drinks to the outlanders. Amara was waiting for Akello. She never expected him to walk together with the Beku-neun girl. A million thoughts clouded her head. Without meeting him, she walked out. In the sea of people, Akello's eyes were searching for his mom, Moona, and Amara. All outlanders were allocated huts in the underground city of Alaoka. Crop fields, flying griffins and the sun kissing Alaoka created love in Beku-neun's eyes. Gamba called Akello and informed him that he and Liya had three more days to start the new journey. Other than Davu, everyone in Akello's family was happy about his success. No mother has the guts to send her son to a crocodile's mouth. Akello's mom hid all her pain inside her heart and wore a fake smile on her lips for her son. She knows if she cries, that will emotionally hurt Akello, so she never wants to shed tears in front of him. Alaokans' huts were filled with tales of snow showers and warm water.

When the heat under Akello's foot was reduced, he directed Neo to Akello-Amara's secret world (falls of heaven), but she was not there. He waited for a long time to see her dimpled face. Finally, when the sun started to set, she arrived. Akello was showing all his teeth and walked next to her, but her lips and eyes danced in confusion at hearing Akello's new position as a 'peace envoy.' She was worried. More than that, she was more possessive after seeing his new companion. Amara was not wise enough, like Akello's mom, to hide her emotions. She reciprocated all her fears in the form of anger at Akello. Finally, she asked him not to proceed with the mission. Usually, Akello is not clever enough to understand others' state of mind, but in Amara's case, he was not dumb. From her wet eyes, he can see her insecurities. He pulled her hands and buried her head inside his chest; it was a tight hug. When Akello's hug comforted her, the rays of the setting sun gazed at the pair. Akello expressed, "*I am all yours!*" He gently planted a kiss on her tomato cheeks and said, "*Decades will fly! Our kids and grandkids will run over huts! But my love for you is constant, like daylight and the moon! We may grow old and develop grays, but I will never forget to kiss your wrinkled cheeks in my mornings.*" Akello's words melted her insecurities and converted the tears into a welcoming smile and Akello promised, "*Will bring guests from all four lands for our wedding!*" Hope and trust in his words were rays of sun in the darkness and wiped the insecurities of Amara.

When Akello reached his hut, an Alaokan soldier was waiting near his crop field. He beamed. "*Leader of Alaoka has summoned you.*" While Akello was walking in the great

Alaokan caves, he felt new respect, and at the same time, many doubted looks added to his shoulder.

The doors of Eric's hut welcomed Akello. Eric called Akello 'Hope of Alaoka' and continued, "*Brat! Eternal peace between civilizations is wheeling in your hands. Remember, failure of the mission will drink the blood of my Alaokans.*" Akello's eyes caught sight of the dagger in Eric's hands; he never saw one like that; the dagger is curvy-cylindrical. The handle and pommel of the dagger were made of brass. Eric was having a conversation, but Akello's eyes were locked on the beauty of the dagger. Eric mentioned about the Alaokan spy in Draguva. "*It's been five years. We didn't get any message from the spy. I also believe he is no more.*" When Eric paused the words for a moment, Akello made his promise, "*Chief! Whatever it may cost, I will ensure peace between the civilizations. I am an Alaokan! I am not bothered, even if it takes my life.*"

Eric's eyebrows raised up and his lips made a sarcastic smile; he had a story to tell Akello before his mission. In the known pages of Alaokan history, it happened only once: the Alaokan-Draguvans alliance. The coast of the southern sea is a favorite for sharks. During that period, the attack of giant sharks made the southern sea get the name 'blood sea.' Ships, boats, and humans were crushed by the scary teeth. An undefeated hunter came out from the deepest ocean and it was 150 feet long silver shark. Many ships of Alaokans and Draguvans became debris of the ocean. The long southern sea was common for both civilizations, and a silver shark is a common threat to be handled. Finally, the general of both naval troops decided to take down the monster together. The united naval force had 35 ships in total to ensure peace in the ocean again. In the final war, rampaged shark turtled 10+ vessels of Draguva; many Draguvan soldiers were struggling for life on the surface of the ocean. Together with spears and arrows, we pierced the silver shark. The commander of the Alaokans ordered a few of his ships to save the lives of the dying Draguvans. On that day, with brotherhood, Alaokans saved the lives of 100 soldiers. Bearing heavy casualties, finally, the southern sea regained peace again. Defeated sharks had the eye size of an ostrich egg. Eric caught Akello eye to eye and beamed, "*For the lives of 100 men, we saved. The Draguvan commander gifted the dagger that was made of dragon-tooth.*" He gave his word, "*We owe you one hundred souls.*" Now, Akello understood what Eric was holding in his hands. Eric handed the dagger to Akello. The reflection of the brass handle twinkled in the eyes of Akello. The moment he accepted 'the dagger of 100 souls', Eric breathed, "*This dagger is worth 100 lives. Use it wisely and come alive.*" As Eric gave a word to Davu, he let Akello have the dagger.

Beyond Eric's words, Akello was puzzled by his own thoughts, "*Why dragons were not used to hunting the shark?*"

Three days flew by like a passing wind. Akello's hut was surrounded by 'good luck' cheers from friends and family. He didn't get the chance to meet Amara again alone, and the day of the journey has arrived. The night before the journey, when everyone was sleeping like a log in a hut, Akello's mom was sleepless and worried about Akello's mission. She pulled her up and walked to the stable. Tears wet the ground. She directed her legs toward the sleeping griffin and called Neo to come near her. Neo has a good bond with her because whenever she cooks a delicious meal with her hands, a small share goes to Neo's belly. Neo was confused to see tears in her eyes. She inhaled her dripping nose and gently touched Neo's head and mumbled, "*I trust you! Take care of my boy and bring him back to me.*" Neo made a soft scream as a promise to Ava. She walked back into the hut with a tear-filled smile. Neo heard the same words twice today. Ava's words were soft, but the moment before the sunset, old Davu walked to Neo and choked, "*You griffin! Never come home without my grandson.*" Now, Neo knows his responsibilities and his mission is to protect Akello.

The next morning, the cock was on time. With the blessing of the family, Akello walked to the great Alaokan caves. While Akello and Liya were listening to the advice of Eric, Gamba was having a conversation with Neo. Neo felt Davu was much better than Gamba. At noon, Eric and Gamba accompanied both to secret cave openings under the cover of a pond. It was unbelievable for Akello and Liya to find the cave there. The pond was dry because of the dry summer, and the cave entrance was naked. The opening of the caves does not fit for two, but it's enough for one griffin to pass at once. Akello and Liya bid farewell to Eric and Gamba and started their journey on griffin's back. They have not walked alone into caves; they carried the hope and courage of two civilizations along with them. The underground cave was totally deep and dark. In the darkness, Neo's eyes started to glow in gold and Liya's

Tuva eyes glowed in blue. It looked magical. The chillness in the caves gently rubbed Liya's milky skin, and both lit up the torch. The cave walls were filled with dark green patches. Algae on the walls maintained the moisture in the air. Every footstep inside the cave gets steeper more and more. After a few minutes, both reach the plain surface and their eyes can't find any algae on either side of the cave walls. The climate started to become normal. Now Liya recognized the steep path of the cave that acted as a barrier to stop flowing water and created a temporary water pond in Alaoka with the help of monsoon rain. Nature is more beautiful with its own idea of creativity. The steep part of the cave holds back pond water, and the other half is a normal cave with moisture in the sand. Along the way, the debate continues. Liya can't deny Alaoka is paradise but still stood against Akello on Beku-neu being more beautiful. Both of them finally reached the other end of the cave at the hour of sunset. The cave entrance in Draguva was covered with a huge bunch of climbing shrubs so that the existence of the caves was not visible to the eyes of Draguvans. Akello suggested to Liya that they can use the caves as their hideout. Liya affirmed Akello and added, "*Starting today, this nature cave is our home.*"

Both left the griffins inside the caves and ordered them strictly never to head out of the caves until they were summoned. Representatives of ice and grass headed outside the caves without disturbing more climbing shrubs. When they walked outside the caves, they were submerged inside the tall, overgrown grass. Liya delighted, "*Tall grass will act as second-level protection to hide the cave entrance from normal eyes.*"

Akello giggled, "*Our safe house has meadows.*" Moving further over the head, tall bamboo was covered, and the light of the setting sun shed the orange shade in the bamboo forest. As a double caution, both ensured safety around the caves. Both disguised themselves as peasants, wore hoodies to hide their faces, and started to walk in the direction of the marketplace. They decided to carry knuckles for their safety, but Akello broke the pact, also carried the dragon-tooth dagger (the dagger of 100 souls) along with him, and hid the dagger in his outfit. Akello decided to keep the dagger a secret for now.

While walking in the bamboo forest, the sun was almost down and darkness started to conquer the sky. Liya began, "*We need to go to a tavern located at the end of the town. As today is full moon day and it's the only day we got in the month to approach the spy.*" She added, "*The spy we are going to meet in the tavern got skilled fingers.*"

Akello guessed, "*Another archer,*" and giggled, but Liya's answer converted his giggle to a cough.

Liya's reply was, "*Not an archer, but a musician.*"

Akello complained, "*A musician? How could a musician be going to help with our mission*?"

Liya got knives in her eyes and smirked. "*It's not my fault!*" She explained to him how to connect with a musician.

"*We need to approach the musician with one large and two small ale mugs. One large mug holds the taste of caramel wine and the other mugs filled with venom-synthesized rum. Once a musician accepts the offerings, he will reply with the music again. The meaning of the music play is to wait for a spy behind the pothouse.*"

After hearing Liya, Akello's eyebrows raised and greeted them. "*Great idea to contact a spy!*" In the meantime, nightfall covered the sky, and both reached the entrance of the city of Draguva.

After crossing the bamboo forest, it opened onto the endless long road. Both of them noticed huts, wooden shops, and civilians. The shops were neither small nor big, but most of them were crowded. Dragon Land people have good physiques. Some of them wore shiny outfits, but most wore fine cotton outfits. It's very similar to the Alaokan cotton outfits and accurately matched the outfit they wore. Every shop and hut in the town glittered in the light of oil lamps. Eyes caught guards with throwing-knives and big axes all the way. Liya adjusted her hood and walked forward. The majority of the people have a dusky complexion and bald heads. Streets were wide and trees were planted on either side. Streets were filled with clusters of people, and eyes noticed one common thing in every civilian's face, i.e., 'the happiness.' It danced over their cheeks. Moving forward, the crowd became dense, so the shoulders of Akello and Liya battled to move forward. Finally, the long roads opened on either side, but the eyes of the heroes were stuck and the legs took a break. People wearing shiny outfits walked toward wide streets in the north and tight security was enforced, but the roads in the south were neither wide nor narrow, roads were loaded with a bald and cotton outfit crowd. Both south and north markets were brightened with oil lamps and the sound of laughter and fun hit the ears from both markets. Akello's eyes weren't locked in the beauty of the market, but his eyes scanned the black fort walls in front of him behind the walls.

Liya opened, "*Astonishing.*"

A sky-touching tower was built behind the walls; it has circular stairs leading to the top of the tower. The entire stairway was brightened by oil lamps. Akello's eyes witnessed the height of the engineering, the conical-shaped 'dragon tower.' The night view of the tower was elegant and beautiful in the oil lamps. Loud cheers in the market got them back to reality. At the very moment both recognized, they were standing in the middle of the street, and crowds were passing them cheered, "*Blue Daga...blue Daga!*" The cheers thrilled the ears. (Daga means rider of the dragon; for example, the blue Daga means rider of the blue dragon)

Akello raised his head up to check for the dragon. In an eye-flashing second, Akello and Liya were squeezed by the crowd. In between the thundering cheers, the doors of the castle opened. The eyes of Akello and Liya were fixed on the gates, but from the northern market, a dusky young man in a silvery outfit directed his ivory shade mustang into the castle. At the speed of the mustang, he vanished into the castle, but the love and cheers of Draguvans did not fade for minutes.

From the cheers, they understood. "*Man in the silver outfit is a rider of the blue beast!*"

Conflicts began! Both were not sure which road would lead them to the pothouse (tavern). They couldn't open their wide mouths and ask out because that would paste the flavor of outlanders in their faces. Akello suggested the north and Liya said the south. After a small quarrel, both decided to take the south. While walking in the south market, Liya ear dropped the conversation of ladies and found that on every full moon day, the blue Daga visits the big market, and it is a celebration. At the same time, on no-moon days, he visits the south streets.

After exploring the city, around night, both reached the tavern. They fell in love with the beauty of the wooden city and its bright oil lamps. They also carried red grams in *potli* bags to buy booze and for other expenses. Unlike Alaoka, Draguva uses red grams as a currency. For the two red grams, one can get three rice bags. After knowing certain varieties of ale are free in Dragon city, their happiness doubled. When they entered the tavern, they could see everyone enjoying the airag and rum with big chatters and dancing along with friends and family. Favorite drink of Draguvans is airag; it tastes sour but delicious. The pothouse in the dragon city was huge, and both occupied the table in the left corner. Wooden airag mugs reached their table for free and with a taste of airag; their eyes were searching for the musician with a fiddle. When booze kicked Liya, she asked Akello to join her for a dance. At first, Akello hesitated. Later, he joined the party. Ice and grass joined the dance floor. While dancing, they noticed a man sitting in the right corner with his friends. He got a fiddle in his hands. Liya's ears got to work. She walked toward the right and her ears fetched the discussion in the right corner.

The man with a fiddle was talking about his favorite food and fat cows. Meanwhile, Akello asked Liya about her favorite drink and dessert. Akello's favorite pineapple wine was Liya's favorite too. Pineapple wine costs one red gram per barrel. Akello invited Liya for a bet race on griffin's back tomorrow. The bet was that the loser had to pay for tomorrow's drink. Liya was confident, and she beamed, "*Get ready to spill grams from your potli bag.*" Every conversation strengthened their relationship, and they started trusting each other back.

An hour passed by, and both were waiting for a man with a fiddle to play the music, but he left the tavern with his friends before the end of the night. It's time for the heart of the night. The eyes roll in all directions to find the man with the fiddle. The doors of the pot opened. The entry of the young woman excited the boozehounds. Cheers and whispers rounded the pothouse. The owner stepped down from the red bean counter and offered the costliest cocktail. The owner's eyes were filled with lust. She took the large ale mug with long fingers and started walking toward the brewer's chamber. After seeing her beauty without bothering, the mission of Akello's eyes fixed on her. Not just Akello but every man's vision was pulled by the hot curves of the young woman.

Liya cursed herself for teaming up with Akello and grumbled, "*Vulnerable men!*"

With a rough tone, Akello retorted, "*We Alaokans are monogamists!*" He added, "*I told you about my Amara already.*"

With the arrival of the goddess, both lost their focus on the mission. In a few minutes, the sound of gentle music ruffled the ears, but it was coming outside the tavern. Both pushed themselves toward the sound. Akello never expected the same hot woman who was the owner of the fiddle. She was not alone; a few more musicians were also playing by her side and the whole crowd was attracted to her music. Liya waited in silence, and both were not ready to accept that she was a spy. At first, they expected an old man in his 40s and unpopular, but this woman with a fiddle is just the opposite of their thoughts. People's legs danced and cheered for her name. "*Zaya! Zaya!*" After the music party, she directed her foot to the table and took a seat in the corner. Liya and Akello stood a few meters away from her.

Liya beamed. "*It's the right time to approach her.*"

Akello whispered in anger, "*Crazy! She is popular, and definitely, she is not the one whom we are looking for. Let us wait!*"

Liya ranted, "*We can't live on the cover of the hood for longer!*" She walked to the pub table.

Now, Liya has started complaining about working with Akello. Finally, with a rasping heart, Akello and Liya approached Zaya with three ale mugs, as planned before. They both took their seats at the table where Zaya was seated, and they placed the offerings on the table. Liya greeted her, "*Skilled fingers!*" Liya spent six red grams for the venom-synthesized rum with the same amount they can buy a newborn colt in Draguva. Skilled finger called the worker by raising her hand with the sign of two fingers. Akello expected something like lime juice mixed with strong rum, but the worker brought two empty ale mugs to their table. She transfers large caramel beer into the two mugs and says, "*Enjoy the special drink!*" But within the next few seconds, she gulped both small mugs and held her head tight. Liya and Akello exhaled in unison, "*Wild!*" and sipped the beer! The savory taste of it was melting the tongue. With a shaky head, Zaya started to play the fiddle again. Peace envoys caught the eyes of one another and smiled in happiness.

The excitement in the crowd bloomed again. Team Akello was also happy with the music. The soft fiddle music was smooth to the ears. Both of them left the place and waited in the horse stable behind the tavern as per the plan.

While waiting in the stable, Akello grieved, "*Let's give up our bet.*" Liya's small lips expelled the teeth and her sharp eyebrows were raised up in laughter. Before they entered the pub, they placed a gamble between them for 20 grams. The gamble is about the look of the spy. Akello expected someone in their 40s, but Liya refused it and expected a fragile man in his 70s, which would let the spy live without raising alarms, but never expected one like Zaya, "*Sexy and wild!*"

After an hour, Zaya came to meet the duo at the horse stable. They introduced themselves and told her that they had left their beasts and weapons in the cave. Zaya was a little dancy in the kick of the strong shots but still conscious enough to bubble. "*This is not the right place to talk; she told both to follow her on the horse*" She bought horses from stables. Akello commented to Liya, "*Not just sexy and wild!*" and "*Wealthy too.*" Liya smiled and mounted the horse. Both followed her on hooves for an hour to reach the middle of the bamboo forest. In the deep dark, Zaya mumbled in a gassy voice, "*We are in the hunting zone*," and asked both of them to stay low. While moving forward, all of a sudden, they were forced to stop by three thieves. Akello's mind recommends, "*In total, there were three, and we were three. This is going to be a good fight.*" Thieves asked Zaya to hand over wealth and horses. In the camouflage of a peasant outfit, thieves underestimated the heroes of grass and ice.

In the vision of the fire torch held by the thief, Zaya's plump nose and bow lips reflected her beauty. Her green eyes signaled Liya and Akello to stand back and watch. The heroes caught the signal of the wild lady! Zaya opened her saddlebag and took out the crossbow. In the flashing second, she pointed the crossbow at the head of the one holding the fire torch. It was just one inch away. The other two thieves wailed and unsealed the dagger from the hip. Akello and Liya were empty-handed and for a moment, the duo was stunned by happenings around them but the most unexpected part was all of a sudden five unknown well-built men jumped from the trees and surrounded all of them. There was panic on the faces of thieves. Akello and Liya have no idea about who they are, and both were just spectators. In the light of the fire torch, Liya noticed the dragon figure in the sword's pommel held in the hands of well-built men. She felt a sudden race in her heartbeat, and she was clever enough to recognize they were rounded by soldiers of Draguva.

Akello noticed the same. They were frightened that their mission had come to an end. One of the thieves started running toward the east. Zaya aimed like a pro and shot the thief to stop him and other thieves were caught by night watchers of the Dragon Land. The words of the guards were friendly to Zaya; it was another shock to the peace envoys. Zaya asked the guards for the favor to hand over the thieves in the dragon tower in her name, and she told them that in the daylight she would come to collect her reward in the arena.

Finally, the expected questions were opened to Zaya. "*Who are these farmers and what are they doing here?*"

In a cool way, she handled the situation, and that explained she was a brilliant spy. Zaya informed, "*They are my new recruits from the Kall village of tall Dal mountains.*" With guts, she introduced them to guards and asked, "*Hey Lads! Follow me.*" She continued on track by ignoring the guards' words. Akello wondered how the musician got a bull's eye and became friendly with the guards of Draguva. She shot the thief like a pro and the weapon she used was a horizontal short bow and arrow with a trigger. Alaoka and Beku-neu have never seen such a weapon. Zaya helped both to get out of the situation. Everyone was silent and directed the horse and waited for Zaya to speak out.

Zaya began, "*Lads, I have traveled the length and breadth of this forest. I never came across any cave, as you mentioned?*" Liya took the lead and asked Zaya to follow her. Before entering the tall grass, Liya told Akello to check the surroundings. Zaya heard the prowling sound from the tall grass. She made her crossbow ready for hunting, but it was just a big jungle rat running between the grass. Once security was ensured, they walked Zaya inside the cave. When the torch was lit, all three pairs of eyes caught sight of the horrible romance of griffins. Akello fumed, "*Neo, we are in the middle of the mission!*" Neo ignored him. Liya yelled, "*Crazy!*" and stepped out. One after another turned their backs, left the cave, and waited outside the cave. Akello voiced, "*I never expected my green beast was planning a honeymoon in the cave.*" Zaya started to laugh first. All three started laughing. After a few seconds, Liya's laughter turned down, and her knife eyes targeted Akello. He expressed to Liya, "*Stop pointing your knife eyes at me. I swear it's not my fault.*" Zaya supported Akello. "*It was not his fault. He is not in a relationship with your griffin.*" She started laughing again at her poor joke, but a humping eagle scream made everyone laugh. The moment the eagle's scream stopped, they entered the cave. Akello walked near Neo and touched him gently and made an angry stare at him. His bird turned and looked at Tuva. Liya's eyes got huge bones of chinchilla (rodent) and she thought griffins managed to get dinner from the tall grass.

Zaya bubbled that she was a resident of the land of the dragon for the last 14 years and continued that she never knew there was a cave here. Akello explained the special features of the cave and excited. "*The other end of the cave connects to Alaoka.*" Zaya's widened eyebrows conveyed 'amazing.' Zaya was leaning back on the cave walls and asked Liya about the welfare of lord Deyu and his sons. With a sad face, Liya explained the demise of Deyu. After hearing Liya, a small smile bloomed on the spy's face. "*My old man was lucky enough to not get killed by his own brats.*" From the words of a spy, Liya understood she was the daughter of lord Deyu. *Deyu and his ancestors were serving as spies to Beku-neu for generations. The day Zaya was born, her head was assigned to the mission. Deyu trained her to influence people and sharpened her spying skills. As a result, she managed to survive in Dragon Land for a decade or more.* Akello was shocked that Zaya was laughing at her own father's demise. He whispered, "*Weird lady!*" inside his mouth. There was silence in the cave, but the crackling sound of firewood was pleasant to the ears. Zaya's eyes marked griffin riders and commented, "*The new alliance! I am happy about the alliance of ice and green, but Draguvans were not.*" She continued, "*Without a blood spill, you can't get the alliance of dragons.*"

With a thundered face, Liya asked, "*How did they come to know?*"

Akello guessed, "*The spies!*"

Zaya locked her eyes at Akello and expelled, "*Kid! When the news of the alliance spread all over the Dragon Land. With giggles and ugly comments, loud laughter broke out.*"

Zaya continued, "*The land of Draguvans is rich in valor and courage. They are the strongest of all the four civilizations and they can win the other three civilizations at once. The stronger never seek the help of a spy. In fact, the unique weapon I used was a crossbow, and it was the own invention of the Draguvans, but they didn't use it in the last Dragu-Alaokan war, because they didn't want to win the Alaokans easily.*"

The words of Zaya made a reflection of fire-woods burning in Akello's vision. After all, he lost his father because of the same war. Akello asked, "*If that is true, why did they use the dragon on the feeble men?*"

Zaya answers with laughter, "*Dragons were used against the griffin units of Alaoka but not on infantry and cavalry units. Draguva respects strength and courage in one. However, Draguvans feel other civilizations are inferior in courage and no match for them and the truth is that together we are no match for their strength and hard work of people in the land of dragons.*"

Liya was confused about whose side the spy was and came up with a strong question. "*Then how did Dragon Land come to know about the alliance?*"

"*The pirates!*"

"*The pirate ship was caught while infiltrating the borders of Dragon Land. After wholesome torture, they cried out that they saw ships of cotton sails anchored on white lands,*" said Zaya.

Akello bawled, "*Remember! Courage is not just copyrighted in the name of Draguvans!*"

Zaya walked near Akello, patted and praised him and his Alaokans for their triumph against the unexpected attack of pirates.

Akello muttered, "But *how?*" and banged his head with his own hands. Zaya winked her eyes at Akello and bubbled, "*Spy has their own ways to track and get information.*"

That night was sleepless for Akello and Liya. Griffins made mild romantic screams, and Zaya was sleeping like a log.

Her snoring was louder than Akello's grandpa's and echoed in the deep caves. The next morning, the sun rose between the tall grass and the yellow fragrance sneaked into the shrub-decorated cave entrance. It was a new day in the land of dragons. When they woke up, Zaya was not in the cave, but she left her crossbow behind. Liya took the unique weapon and her long fingers gently caressed the crossbow. Heroes bored inside the cave. The sun moved toward the extreme west and deep black covered the sky. To wipe away the darkness, the moon appeared. Finally, the spy arrived at the hideout. Zaya gave a warm smile to the griffin riders, but the riders' eyebrows were bent like bows and stared at Zaya. From their looks, she understood she had made them wait longer. As a sign of apology, she decided to take them both to the pothouse. In the deep dark, hooves started the journey towards the tavern. On their way, Liya asked about the beginning days of Zaya in the Dragon Land. Akello was also curious to know about her survival and how she acquired her fighting skills and the eagle eye.

"*Life is not easy for a spy. It's a rough ocean. A spy's first rule is to survive. When I was sent to Draguva, I was 14 years old with spying and musical skills, but only with these skills survival was a challenge. So, I mastered combat skills under the barbarians. Later, the barbarians stood against Draguvans for land and the throne. Barbarians are just brats against the large army, so they are disguised to cause trouble. Dragon Land's leader hired bounty hunters to end the barbarian rebels. I became one among them and started to hunt like a leopard in the wild. Against the efficient bounty hunters, rebels started to fall like dry leaves, and to gain the trust of Draguvan, I eliminated the commander of the rebels; he was the one who taught me how to hold the knife. The Draguvan leader put a full stop to rebels with the help of bounty hunters; the leader gave respect to the valor of bounty hunters. But not all the rebels were eliminated; some became thieves in the forest, like the one we faced yesterday."* Zaya held a smile on her lips.

Akello noticed zero regrets on her face and muttered, "*Heartless!*"

Liya was silent after hearing Zaya. Both exchanged a pathetic look. One thing was clear to Akello that she was stronger than expected. Lights in the marketplace welcomed the riders on the horses; they reached the entrance of the tower and there was a division on the roads. Zaya directed her mustang into the wide roads in the north. Being with Zaya, guards in the northern market smiled and welcomed her apprentices. Eyes captured the richness in the outfit of the civilians and the luxury in their hands. Instead of huts, they were able to find only luxury wooden cabins. Shops with good foundations were raised to a two-storey or more. Zaya delighted. "*Welcome to the market of the rich.*"

Similar to taverns in the southern streets, the market of the rich has a huge pothouse. The smell of airag excited the lung tanks. From the window view and balcony, the big arena was visible. Zaya mentioned in the daylight Draguvans start to practice like demons and their sweat wet the big oval arena till evening. Both were amazed to see such a big arena and its purpose. Zaya opened up about the geography of Draguva (the land in the southeast). Southeast lands are vast and covered by tropical rainforests. It's neither as hot as Alaoka nor as cold as Beku-neu. In the north, 25% of the land is a prohibited area for normal people and isolated for dragons and their soul riders. Trespassers will be fed to dragons without interrogation. There were a total of eight dragons alive today and they were deadly enough to convert bones to ashes. Punishment for spies and intruders was brutal, sentenced to death in dragon fire. Zaya added that she has seen a dragon once in a decade. It happened five years ago when the spy of Alaokan was caught and executed in the dragon fire in the arena in front of people. Feeding of dragons and medical assistance for dragons were under the governance of the dragon minister. The last 500 years of history say that dragons had never shed blood in wars. Another 40% of the land was used for vegetation and the remaining 35% of the land was towns and nearby villages. There is a rumor running around in Dragon Land that dragons will select their riders based on their will-power and physical strength. Dragons will train the selected riders, and riders' will-power train the dragon to obey their words, and above all, the most magical one is a dragon fire that does not hurt the chosen. It was interesting for the duo to hear Zaya's observations and myths.

The waiter in the tavern excused and placed a small airag barrel on the table. Akello's tongue danced in joy. When Akello purged the first mug into his belly, Zaya giggled and let them drink.

Akello asked, "*What's funny about me making you giggle?*"

Zaya said, "*Airag is special in Dragon Land. Do you know what it was made of?*"

Akello was puzzled and went for another round. From his action, she understood and briefed, "*It was made of fermented mare's milk.*"

Akello coughed out what he drank. Liya and Zaya were laughing at him.

From the windows of the tavern, giant brass doors inside the arena were visible. It pulled a vision of Liya and she questioned Zaya about the door.

Zaya opened, "*It is one of the entrances to the prohibited forest and from the guards I heard that giant doors open to Dragavan gardens. Draguvan gardens are training grounds for dragon riders!*"

Akello's attitude-filled eyes caught Liya and asked, "*Zaya, you are proficient! Tell me that you have trespassed on those brass doors.*"

Zaya giggled, "*Brat, you have underestimated the Draguvan security guard. Even the rat never escapes their eagle vision.*"

Words of Zaya praised the Draguvans and exaggerated their valor, their innovation, and their luxurious life.

At a certain point, Akello's rage busted out and asked, "*Whom you are working for?*"

Zaya smiled, and she lifted the remaining quarter barrel of airag in one hand, and her other hand held the ale mug.

Her hands danced like scales of the weighing machine, and finally, she lifted up the ale mug and downed the barrel and whispered, "*I like you both, and I am standing for Beku-neu!*"

Akello took a gasp and whispered to Liya. "*Can we trust her?*"

Liya commented, "*Do we have any other option?*" She continued purging the mare's fermented drink.

Sun and moon shifted positions and three months passed like a week or two. Under the cover of Zaya, both spent three months in wide streets and bars to find a way to approach the leader of the Draguvans, but unluckily, they didn't find any strategy to approach. One thing was clear to them: Draguvans were matching the exaggeration of Zaya. Wherever Akello goes, he hid and carried the dragon-tooth dagger with him. Griffin enjoyed their honeymoon inside the cave and cave meadows. Every night, they spend time in a pothouse of a rich market and they drink for free because of Zaya's popularity and her beauty. The tavern owner has a huge crush on Zaya; he used to treat her and her guests like VIPs. They used to sit in the next booze cabins of ministers to eavesdrop on the information spoken in the bar. Literally, every day, ministers drink airag and sing songs about Rizon and make fun of outlanders living in different corners of the map. Rizon is a dragon minister and is expected to be the next heir to the throne. In the kick of booze, the words of Draguvan increased Liya's anger. With a knife in her eyes, she walked out of the pothouse. Inside the hideout in the hangover, she complained about the attitude of the Draguvans. All three of them became closer, and the time they spent together made their roots stronger. They talked about their culture and personal information. When Liya opened the past event of her life, Akello's face was grief-stricken and felt relieved to be born as Alaokan. Most of the time, Akello talks of two things: one is his griffin, Neo and another one is his love, Amara. Zaya talks a lot about the varieties of alcoholic drinks and the adventures she took part in. Liya was a quiet listener with a mug of rum, and later, she used to go for another mug until the rum trips her head.

In the meantime, Zaya trained and helped Liya in mastering the crossbows and helped Akello in handling spears with high accuracy and causing deadly damage. In the evenings, in the Dragon Land, they used to watch the training session of the leader and ministers in the arena. It was the 90th day in the Draguva; they never missed a single day. The oval-shaped arena was too big. Zaya used to say all eight dragons can easily fit inside the arena. Till today, they have never seen the triumph of a leader. He is strong and would be the same age as Eric, but he has no gray in his head. He trains himself to fight against 60 of his men simultaneously; he can manage to fight till the sun comes down. During the training, they never touch weapons; they use fists and reflexes of their bodies as their weapon. The leader managed to dodge 45 palms without scratching his figure. These practice sessions look like devil fights. In the beginning days, the duo complained Zaya for singing the pride of Draguvan, but now the duo joined Zaya's side.

Akello and Liya can't deny their determination and will-power in their fight; it inspired them a lot and made Liya say, "*Dragon*

Land warriors are not human. With hard work, they evolved to gain the strength of demons."

Stars in the sky confirmed that a year has passed, and there was no progress made by the grass and ice duo, but they understood the culture and lifestyle of Draguvans better. In the last year of their life in Draguva, they have never heard the name of the Draguvan leader at least once. Every official and civilian calls him the 'Lord of Dragon.' Draguvans are loyal to their leader and obey his words without a second thought. Even with the hangover, they never spell out his name. One cloudy evening in the pothouse, Liya asked Zaya, "*Do you know the name of the Lord of Dragon?*" Zayas smiled at her and walked out of the tavern. She was not ready to accept her failure, so she evacuated the pothouse. She used all her sources to find his name, but no one knows his name. The management skills of the Draguvans were excellent, and they handled the slaves very well. Slaves do all the work for the rich, so the rich people focus on the development of the Draguva. Dragon Land's farmers work on farms to do the vegetation and they take a portion of the harvest and send the remaining to the tower of 1,000 lights (dragon tower). Being south-east has enough rainforests, Draguvans never faced any scarcity of food and water. The market in the south is called as 'market of slaves' and the farmers are slaves of the royal Draguvan; Farmers don't have any rights to stand against Draguvans or to touch weapons. Slaves' only work is to sow, yield, and service the rich. They have rituals called 'Motasa.' This ritual happens twice a year. During the Motasa feast, slaves are invited to the feast, and before the feast, males' heads will be cleanly shaved and slaves have no right to grow hair for a longer period of time.

A year passed by and the frustration of not being capable of doing anything cracked in the faces of Akello and Liya. Hanging out with Zaya converted them into boozehounds. The sky is clear. All were seated inside the cave, Zaya staring at Neo and Liya's griffin for a very long time. Akello noticed it and asked her, "*What made you turn toward the griffins?*" She trilled that color of Neo, and its magical eyes attracted her. She also recalled Akello's words. In Alaóka, the olive-green griffin was considered as the direct offspring of the griffin king, and she pushed a question to Akello, "*With such a prideful status, why Neo has selected a dumb like you as his rider?*" Akello was already tormented that they have not made any progress in winning the alliance of Draguvans. The words of Zaya changed the atmosphere of his eyes to deep red, and he fumed like a snake. He showed all his incapability and anger toward her and started to move out. Zaya was silent and accepted all his yelling, and Liya was a listener. Zaya stopped Akello with a question. "*Do you really have the determination to unite all four civilizations?*" Akello took a deep breath and trumpeted, "*Remember, I am not on a tour. I came with a purpose and to achieve it; I am ready to pay my life as a cost!*" He left the place angrily. Liya followed Akello to console him. Zaya took her fiddle and started to play the music for the evening. Zaya caught the passion and spark in Akello's eyes, but she didn't regret asking such a question.

The next morning, Akello woke up because of a scary dream. In his dream, he saw Alaoka burning. All night, he took a comfortable place at the branch of the Banyan. Akello's puffy eyes caught sight of dark clouds. He decided to take a hangover shot in the marketplace and walked on the spacious roads of the rich market. Zaya walked just opposite him, but the angry man continued his steps by ignoring her. Zaya convinced him and accompanied him to the pothouse. Once they reached the tavern, Zaya ordered venom-synthesized rum for her and didn't order anything for Akello. Akello was confused because she used to ask him in the first place what he would like to drink. Once their order was served on the table, she asked Akello, "*Do you still stand by your words?*"

With gritted teeth, Akello replied loudly, "*I stand on my word till my last breath.*" In a gassy voice, he whispered, "*That's our Alaokan way!*"

Zaya asked Akello to enjoy the new batch of venom-synthesized rum that she had ordered. Akello inhaled the odor of the drink and questioned her, "*What's wrong with you?*"

While Akello was having his drink, Zaya hissed, "*Without blood, there can be no alliance here!*" Akello noticed a change in the mode of her voice. The moment he completed the last sip, she started to shout in the tavern, "*Spy! Spy! Spy of Alaoka!*" Her cry was loud and audible all over the tavern and roads.

Akello was stunned and not able to recognize what was happening around in the kick of heavy ethanol. In no time, guards surrounded Akello and made him immovable. She showed the ink print on Akello's shoulder as proof that he was a spy. She also complained that Akello cheated her by saying he was an orphan from the village in the Dal mountains. Akello was locked between the wild, dusky hands and his way of escape was blocked. In the whispers of the crowd, Zaya left the place with a grin on her face.

One of the guard's fists delivered a strong punch to Akello's stomach. The power of the punch made him puke the rum, and they dragged him to the arena. The punch Akello received completely disabled him. On the way, the civilian crowd around him spit on his face and nasty comments circulated about the Alaokans as 'swines and cowards.' He wasn't able to listen to their words, his hands were tied, and he was not able to shut his ears. Finally, they threw him inside the dark prison of the arena. Akello had the precious dagger inside the shoes, and it was still safe with him. After an hour, he regained his strength to stand on his feet and puked the blood out. He remembered the curses and laughter of people around him in the market. The uncontrollable rage leaked the tears. At late noon, guards dragged him to their leader in the arena. There was a huge crowd waiting with great pleasure to see the death of the Alaokan spy. Akello felt he was a griffin and was ready to take down the lions. He remembered the lessons of Ekon, "*At the end of a rough day, either you live long with a new entitled name or you die and your name stays in the hearts forever.*" Every minute in the prison, he was in a hood of shame and muttered continuously, "*Alaokans are not cowards!*" The huge crowd, majestic figures of the Draguvan leader and their ministers saw the Alaokan as a pest. The thundering voice of the Lord of Dragon roared, "*Silence.*" In no time, rounding swears and whispers stopped in the arena and waited to hear more.

The Lord of Dragon ordered his guards to free the spy's hands, and he boasted, "*Draguva is not a place for spies and cowards.*"

Akello fumed at the Lord of Dragon that he was not a spy and introduced himself. "*A messenger of Alaoka with a peace request.*"

Leader choked, "*Your Alaokan valor is lower than our slaves; a spy has no permission to speak in my court.*"

Akello decided to bargain for peace by holding the *dagger of 100 souls* in his hands and began to bargain. After seeing the fine dagger, Lord of Dragon recalled the stories he heard from his old gramps.

Akello, instead of saving his life with a dagger, in exchange, requested the Lord of Dragon to meet the Alaokan leader once in the sleeping volcanoes. At that moment, Akello's mind had no fear of death. His heart failed to flash about his kins, even his mother disappeared from his heart. All he wished was to win the alliance of Draguvans and the success of the mission.

Lord of Dragon asked for a dagger. A guard came near and ordered the spy to hand over the dagger. Akello's stiff hands loosen the grip of the dagger with a short victory smile; he believes that he has won the bargain. The Lord of Dragon and his son examined the dagger and addressed the crowd, "*We never make a decision over the word of the spy.*" Cheers bloomed again! The leader boasted, "*He decided to send back the dagger to the Alaokan leader so that in the next war, it would be useful for him to beg his own life.*" Akello thundered, and his smile turned to anger. The shape of his eyebrow bent like a bow. The crowd cheered the leader's decision and shouted, "Kill the spy!" It echoed and reached the height of the sky. Two soldiers standing near Akello came closer. Suddenly, the arena heard the furious war cry of Neo. It was a wild scream. It punctured the eardrums of grandmas and grandpas in the arena. In an unexpected manner, Neo's foot touched the ground. His robust beak cut the throat of the guard, who stood right next to his rider. Dripping blood changed the color of its beak. As Zaya mentioned, blood began to wet the soil, and the events Akello saw in dreams were no longer a dream. It is a vision of the future. Clouds blocked the red giant, and its red fragrance from the clouds covered the arena. In a flashing second, the guard standing to the left of Akello marked his spear to charge Neo.

Without delaying a second, Akello fist-punched the vital part of the guard. Blood rushed from the guard's mouth. It was the same soldier who crashed Akello in the marketplace. Akello repaid the guard with interest. No one in the arena understood what was going on around them, but the Lord of Dragon enjoyed the valor of the olive-green beast and his brown Alaokan. To execute the bird and the spy, intermediate-level warriors stepped into the arena, but the furious war cry of Neo tumbled the hearts of forwarded guards. The Lord of Dragon muttered, "*The grass beast is not going easy on us!*" His attitude filled with laughter bloomed. Akello took the spear from the wounded guard and climbed on the back of Neo. From Neo's back, Akello roared at the Lord of Dragon after spitting blood mixed saliva on the ground. His valor created a new fan for him. Her name was Zaya. From the shadows of the big arena, she enjoyed the 'Akello's valor show.' She muttered, *"Akello is not just a bunch of words! He has really got some nuts."*

Akello expressed with great valor, "*Nameless Lord! How can I prove myself to you that I am not a spy?*" The leader's hand sign stopped the forwarding troops, and he ordered them to open the big door made of brass. Cheers doubled and between the flashes of eyes, echoes tripled. Cheers increased Neo's rage. Neo's wild war cry made the arena pause the cheers, but it was not the end. The roar of the dragon thrilled the arena.

As Akello expected from the big brass doors, the gigantic beast walked out. It had two devil horns on its head; its long neck from the belly connected to the killer face and red eyes carried blood lust. The aggressive growl of the black dragon outran the sound of a griffin cry. Neo was preparing himself with the scream, and it motivated Akello as well. Neo was just the size of a giant dragon's head. The skin of the dragon looks rough, and the wings are wide and long to lift the beast to the sky.

Civilians' excitement at seeing the dragon was reflected in their cheers. The thundering voice of the leader strikes the ears of Akello. "*I am impressed by the valor of the green bird. Let's spice it up!*" The Lord of Dragon addressed his people, "*Kins! Griffin and its rider have tasted the life of our fellow Draguvan; I am eager to see the cruel death of olive-green and his rider. I bet savages will turn to dust before sunset.*" Sweat escaped from Akello's forehead. He swallowed the fear of facing the dragon inside his heart and placed the negotiation before the Lord of Dragon. "*What if we survive this sunset?*" Laughter developed in the crowd, but the silence grounded in the leader's face. The leader pointed at Akello and challenged, "*If you manage to survive this sundown, then I will consider hearing out the message you carried!*" Akello was not in the position to deny or postpone; he was left with the only option 'to survive.' The clashing sound of metal objects began to cheer the dragon.

Lord of Dragon's gibberish words excited the black dragon and its loud roar tumbled the hearts in the arena. Akello directed his companion to fly over the clouds. Akello took advantage of the oversized dragon's body. The wings of dragons took time to lift up the beast to the sky. In the meantime, Neo was already flying above the clouds. In the sky, the red eyes of the dragon started to search for green feathers. Akello commanded Neo to fly inside the clouds to escape from the eyes of the dragon. It was a blender. Akello underestimated the dragon. The cloud that blocked the vision of the dragon made him angry. With boiling anger, it puked out the furious fire in the clouds. The power of flame it puked vanished the clouds from existence, but it was a lucky day for Akello. The fire was targeted at the wrong clouds. The power of the dragon flame made Akello clear that hiding inside the cotton rolls won't help for a long time. Akello was in a hurry to come up with some strategy.

Dragon fire has disappeared a few clouds out of existence. On its way, the dragon flew above the massive cloud where Akello and Neo were hiding. It was the right time for Akello to attack. Akello decided to execute the surprise attack from the gaseous clouds; he directed Neo toward the dragon and Neo's wild scream made the dragon search for its prey. From below the clouds, Neo popped out with a scream. Akello's spear ambushed the belly of the dragon. It was an unexpected attack, and he pushed the spear with enough power, but it didn't create any impact on the thorny dragon and applied pressure to break the spear into two halves. Akello wondered why the spear did not even land a scratch on the dragon. Within seconds, the dragon's vision caught sight of green feathers and it started chasing Neo. With a loud war cry, Neo cut the air with its speed and moved forward. With agility, Neo dodged the dragon flames, but Akello experienced the radiance of flame on his skin. All of a sudden, from the cluster of clouds, Akello heard the scream of the griffin; he suspected it could be Liya.

Akello decided to warn Liya, and the call of the other griffin distracted the heavy dragon for seconds. Meanwhile, Akello changed the course of flight toward the east and disappeared inside the clouds. From the distance, his eyes caught the sight of two rider-free griffins forwarding toward him and their feathers were gray. After seeing gray griffins, Akello was paralyzed. According to the Alaokan griffin myth, gray feathered griffins are elders and hard to find in Alaokan skies. Akello wondered whether they were responding to Neo's scream. After a moment, he was clever enough to recognize that these gray griffins were summoned by the scream of Neo. Neo's bloodline is not ordinary, and he also heard the myths that royal offspring have superpowers. He never expected this would be real, but today he witnessed the power of it with goosebumps. The special power of Neo comes in handy at the right time. Now, the battle between the triangle of griffins and the dragon begins.

Multiple questions flashed through Akello's mind. All of a sudden, he heard a wild griffin scream and the furious roar of the dragon from the west. He wailed, "*Oh bad! It must be Liya in the west.*" The scream of the dragon clarified the dragon got sight of Liya and the chase began. Akello needs to be quick to save Liya; he seeks Neo's help to communicate with his summoning. "*He asked the gray griffins to fly on the adjacent sides of the dragon. If a dragon fires at the left, the griffin must move under the thorny belly of a dragon to attack it with claws and beak.*" After hearing Akello, Neo reacted with a weird scream. Akello understood the scream and gently patted Neo and replied, "*Don't worry! We will save your Tuva! The dragon can't react faster with its heavy mass and firing under its own belly was hard, so the gray feather will be out of the dragon's firing range. When the griffin on the left side moves down to the belly, the work of the right-side griffin should start with a scream. Scream attracts the dragon to face the right-side griffin. When the dragon releases the fire, the griffin has to flip the flame and move under the belly of the black dragon. When the right griffin reaches the belly, the left griffin must move out to distract the dragon again. Ask them to repeat the same until we find a way.*"

Neo was at his maximum speed toward the west to save Liya and her Tuva (her black griffin). At the speed of flight, Akello and Neo's eyes caught sight of Tuva. Black griffin was escaping the attacks of the dragon very well with her agility. Gray griffins forwarded and executed the plan as Akello had communicated before. Because of the arrival of two new enemies, the focus of the dragon was diverted, and it made the dragon lose its interest in Liya's griffin. Akello told Neo to call Tuva. Liya's Tuva noted Neo's screams and rejoined team Akello. At the same time, Akello's idea of 'dodge and play' worked as expected. Gray griffins confused the dragon's eyes.

Liya was happy to find Akello alive. She came near Akello on her griffin and beamed, "*Zaya told that you got caught because of your Alaokan tattoo, and when I rushed to find you, the roar of the dragon took me here.*" She stacked the questions.

"*Akello, whose griffins were those? Are they backup units from Alaoka?*"

With anger in his eyes, Akello muttered, "*Zaya!*" He briefed, "*Those gray fighters are our ally...and the most important thing you need to know is to deliver the message we carry. We need to prove our worth by surviving the sundown!*"

Liya was already pissed off by Draguvans' attitude toward other civilizations and she decided to teach them a lesson. Her eye enabled the knife, and she insisted, "*Akello, do you think survival will kill the head weight of Draguvans?*" She recalled Zaya's words, "*Without blood spill, there can be no alliance!*"

Akello stormed, "*That bitch, Zaya! She tricked me and handover to guards!*" He exhaled, "*The blood of Draguvan guard already wet the soil, soon war will break.*"

Liya shouted back, "*Fool! The blood she was referring to is dragon's blood!*"

"*No one has ever seen a single droplet of dragon blood in the last 500 years!*"

The people of the dragon city need to see the bloodshed of the dragon. That's the only way they can break the head weight of these people, and it's the hardest way to win the respect of the Dragon Land. Akello agreed with Liya. "*Enough of our discussions! Our griffin friends can't hold much longer. We need to execute the powerful external attack on the dragon together. To do that, we need to find the weak spot of the dragon.*"

In the metal music of thunder, Liya's eyes emitted success! Her smiling lips were delighted that she had already found the weak spot of the dragon when she was dodging the attack. Soft tissue was found on the dragon's long neck, which allows dragons to turn their heads quicker. Akello was surprised to see Liya's analytical and sharp mind. With a plan, Akello was ready to face the dragon; they decided to launch an unexpected attack on the neck of the dragon. Being the skin of the dragon was thorny, Akello didn't believe in swords or spears to pierce the rough skin; instead, he trusted in the claws and beak of the griffin. After delivering the attack, Akello ordered Liya to fly toward the arena. On her way, he asked her to wait for Neo's wild cry until the last moment of sunset. If she didn't hear Neo's scream, Akello asked her to evacuate the land of dragons as quickly as possible. Before agreeing with Akello's plan, her thoughts made her silent. Maybe this could be their last day together. In the last one year, they both developed a strong bond. The atmosphere of her eyes changed, but she didn't let the tears escape.

She replied to Akello's plan, "*Once you come back, the party is mine.*"

With fake laughter, Akello beamed, "*Tonight! The tavern is going to run out of rum.*"

The sun started to go down the mountains. Liya directed her Tuva at its full speed. The scream of Neo, "*Krrrr,*" alerted the attack to the gray feathers and asked them to dismiss. With the speed of Tuva, Liya delivered the nitrous claw kick to the face of the dragon. This time, the force of the claws made a scratch on the beast's head. Moments after the attack, Liya directed her griffin toward the arena and followed Akello's instructions. The power of Tuva's kick made the dragon lose its balance, and it started falling a bit. With an angry growl, the dragon's eyes locked on Liya and its heavy mass tried to regain its balance. Akello motivated Neo, "*Green feathers! It's time to taste the dragon's blood.*" At that moment, Neo had no fear. He put all his trust in Akello and its wild cry ruled the sky. Perfect partners executed a surprise attack. Neo was flying down toward the dragon with its speed, and Akello tightened his grip. Neo's cruel claws grabbed the neck of the dragon. With the tightened grip of claws, the olive-green bird executed a continuous beak attack on the neck. After five centuries, Akello was the first person to see the blue blood of a dragon and Neo's yellow beak gets a strain of blue.

Neo's claws loosened the grip from the neck; Akello ordered Neo to 'fly fast to the arena.' Akello turned his head to check on the free-falling dragon. Things happened as Akello expected. The dragon managed to avoid descending down and started chasing Neo with a huge rage. If the dragon had fallen down from this height, the dragon would face severe injury or death.

The death of the dragon will definitely break out a war. Liya's heart trembled in fear of losing Akello; she was floating in the air and her ears were waiting for the 'call of Akello.'

Akello directed Neo to reach the arena as quickly as Neo could. There was a huge distance between Neo and the dragon. So, dragon fire attacks were useless. The sun walked inside the mountain but the radiance of yellow-red spread all over the sky. In the arena, a huge whisper rounded, but the Lord of Dragon was silent and put his focus on the red sky. Akello asked Neo to communicate with Liya's griffin to reach the arena at full speed. The sound of the griffin's scream expanded Liya's cheek to smile. With new energy, Liya directed Tuva toward the arena. Akello and Liya landed in the arena by cutting the air and the claws of the griffins scratching the ground. Everyone in the arena was shocked to see Akello alive and another griffin rider along with him.

The cheers began. "*Another griffin!*"

After hearing the furious war cry from the dragon, the leader stepped into the arena. He took his stand in front of the griffins to control the rage of the black dragon. The leader was loud, and he spoke a different language. The dragon landed in the arena without attacking Akello and Liya, but it expressed its rage in a heavy growl. The leader walked near the black and gently rubbed on the head to calm the beast and noted the scratches of claws. In the light of twilight, slowly a droplet of blue blood dripped down from the dragon's neck. After five centuries, dragon blood wet the ground. The leader and the crowd noticed it in silence. At that very moment, the leader of dragons adjusted his head to see the griffin riders and griffins. He caught sight of the bloodstains in the green beast's beak. His eyes rolled to see Liya. He saw a knife in her eyebrows and a spark in her eyeballs. There was dead silence in the arena, but the thunderclap of clouds cheered the duo.

The silence made the crowd hear the fast gasps of the dragon. One among the crowd broke the silence with cheer, "*True warrior…true warrior…*" The voice of one multiplied too many in unison. People cheer made Akello recall Ekon's words, "*At the end of a rough day, either you live long with a new entitled name or you die and your name stays in the hearts forever!*" Akello ignored the cheers and kept his focus on the Lord of Dragon's actions. He looked into the eyes of the Lord of Dragon and roared, "*Alaokans are not cowards! Dripping blue blood is living proof.*" Lord of Dragon's reply to Akello was a warm smile, and he gently approached the wound of the dragon. He applied pressure to stop the blood. Out of pain, the growl of the dragon expelled out, and it silenced the crowd once again. He climbed onto the dragon's back and made his seat comfortable. He waved a finger to open the big brass doors. Before disappearing into the doors, the most anticipated moment came; the leader greeted the success of young griffin riders and asked them to join for tonight's dinner in the dragon tower. It was unexpected for everyone in the arena. After hearing him, Akello's eyes marked Liya, and she nodded her head in acceptance. The leader summoned Ishiri to assist Akello and Liya, and he walked on dragon foot inside the doors. At that moment, the leader stepped out of the arena. The guards started to evacuate the crowd. A tall man with a long beard walked near the griffin riders. All of his body, from neck to toe, was covered inside the silk outfit, and each of his fingers was decorated with tattoos. He introduced himself as the medical minister of Draguvans.

Ishiri asked Akello and Liya to follow him to the medical chamber in the tower, but Akello refused to go and requested him back to take their giffin's to medical care immediately. Ishiri nodded his head with a blossoming smile, but his disastrous hairstyle and teeth stains made the blossoming smile totally uglier. Oil lamps started to brighten the city and blue blood created whispers in every corner of the streets. Deep clouds started to touch the ground. Rainfall slowly wiped out the strain of dragon blood from the soil. However, rainwater removed the strain of blue blood, but today, something is clear for Draguvans. "*No longer dragons were undefeatable*."

Chapter 6

Arrival of Legends

On a rainy evening, Ishiri accompanied Akello and Liya to the royal stable located inside the fort walls. When Akello stepped down from Neo, out of energy, his legs started to dance and suddenly he reached the floor in no time. Soon, he regained his balance and complained, "*I never want to live this day again!*" His words broke out in laughter in the stable. The veterinarian in the stable investigated griffins and treated minor fire burns caused by the radiance of flames. Ishiri asked them to leave the griffins in the stable. Akello gently wiped out the blood of the dragon from the sharp, long beak and praised Neo. "*You did a great job today.*" He hugged his beast tight. Once Akello freed his beast in the long stable, Liya gave a tight hug to

Akello and delightedly said, "*You too, did a great job today.*" Akello sensed the happiness in her tone, and he hugged her back with the same excitement. Akello replied, "*Remember! You owe me a treat,*" and he asked for the costliest rum in the pothouse which cost 15 grams, the same cost as weaving a hut. Akello explained to her what Zaya had done to him, but unexpectedly, it ended well. Finally, both reached the medical center for their treatment. Their small burns were packed with medicinal herbs.

After a long day, it was relaxing for Akello and Liya in the tower. 1,000 oil lamps were lit, and they never imagined a day like this would come. The window of the conical tower welcomed the cold breeze into it. Both were seated at a circle-shaped dining table for dinner with the Dragon Land leader and other ministers. The diameter of the table is huge, and it was occupied by 16. The dining hall was decorated with 100 oil lamps hanging in the ceiling of the hall. Liya compared the hanging light with the stars and her smile on chubby lips was perennial. Akello was amazed by the aroma of delicious steamed vegetables and strong wine. Except for Liya and Akello, everyone at the table wore shiny silk outfits. Akello recalled Zaya's explanation about these shiny outfits as 'murderous fabric.' The course of the dinner was started with a welcome note from the Lord of Dragon, "*Alaokan hurricane and Beku-neun frost, we Draguvan acknowledge your valor and courage.*" In the light of the oil lamps, the warm smiles of Draguvans comforted Akello and Liya. They introduced themselves as messengers of peace with a message. The toast was not with the ale mug or horn, but it was done with a medium-sized barrel. Steady hands of Rizon raised the wine barrel above his head and made a toast, "For the courage of Akello and Liya!"

He took a huge gulp from the barrel, and the barrel was circulated around the table. Everyone purged a lot, and finally, it reached Liya's hands. She was surprised to see the barrel was almost empty. After the toast, the leader addressed that they were the first ones to wound the dragon with bloodshed in the last 500 years and recognized their valor and gifted a pair of fine smooth silk outfits to them. Akello doesn't like to react to murderous fabric; his mind traversed the humiliation he faced in the marketplace. Luckily, he has Liya by his side; she accepted their gift and shrugged, "*We apologize for our actions. Bleeding the dragon is not our intention. The message we carry is peace and we seek unity.*" While she was delivering the message, Akello stared at her and recalled her words in today's battle. "*Let's bloodshed the dragon to slice their head weight.*" Liya is good at playing with words; Akello thought she was the better person to deliver the message that they carried.

Liya explained the discoveries of Alaokans and detailed the unknown figures mapped in the skull and voiced, "*Peace treaty between civilizations needed to be enforced.*" She also added that the archaeologists of both civilizations were currently working together to unravel markings on the skull. During the hot hour of the conversation, Liya politely asked, "*In the name of Beku-neu and Alaoka. I request for the alliance of Draguvans for a better future and to unearth the unknowns of our world.*" There was absolute silence in the hall after hearing Liya; the silence was not for the information she shared, but it was because of the alliance request. Liya gently kicked Akello's leg. The next moment, his eyes looked at her. She rolled her eyes toward the leader. Akello understood that she wanted him to address the ministers. He opened to break the silence, "*Along with peace, it would be a good chance to know the culture and understand the lifestyle of other civilizations.*" He beamed, "*With this peace, let us open our world for knowledge sharing.*" Liya thought Akello's words were sensible, but the fact was he copied the words uttered by Eric in the Beku-neu. Akello chuckled in pride because after hearing his words, the silence of the Lord of Dragon was broken.

The Lord of Dragon started, "*A year back, one of the members of our archaeologist crew came up with the discovery of giant dragon bones with inscriptions engraved on them. The archaeologist denoted that inscriptions on the fossil were hard to translate. Later, the lead archaeologist requested to allow the crew to investigate dragon caves in the north, but the lands and caves in the north were not open for normal humans, so we denied the request.*" With a pause, he continued, "*It's time to allow the archaeologist crew into the caves to investigate more and unearth the history about us.*"

Lord of Dragon called out Rizon to carry the message to Alaoka and Beku-neu on his behalf. "*The Lord of Dragon and Draguvans agreed to join an alliance with ice and grass.*" He was also interested in meeting the leaders of both civilizations with their ministers in Draguva. He invited them to celebrate the new friendship and peace. After hearing him, happiness doubled on Akello's and Liya's faces. As usual, whispers started in the dinner hall, but no one dared to speak against him. He also announced Akello and Liya as royal guests of the Draguvans and asked them to stay in the tower and gave permission to access all luxuries of the tower and north market.

After dinner, while walking to their allocated chambers, Liya congratulated Akello. "*You have accomplished our first milestone of the mission.*" Akello corrected her with 'WE.' He replied to her, "*However, we claim, we accomplished it! But the truth is we were just puppets of the whole plan. The brain of this mission was Zaya.*" Liya agreed with Akello and both have the same question running through their mind, "*Where is she?*"

They both decided to search for Zaya in the first light.

Liya was an insomniac and hardly slept for four hours a day, but the excitement of victory didn't let her sleep. In the middle of the night, she decided to knock on Akello's doors. Liya walked near his doors and knocked on them for more than a minute. She did not get any response from the doors, but she heard the deep snoring of Akello. Liya knew that Akello was exhausted because of the challenging day. So, she decided to walk back to her allocated chamber. In the deep dark of the night, while walking back, she was attracted by the interior beauty of the tower. The tower's interior works were gorgeous, and she had no words to express its artistry. Her shoe-free foot experienced the chilliness of the black marble, and her eyes caught sight of the mirror reflection of oil lamps on the marble floor. When the chilly breeze rubbed her petal skin and caressed her long hair, she heard the footsteps of someone walking near the stairs. Liya was curious to check who was up at this time and decided to follow the sounds. She thrust her toes in the marbles and forwarded to find who it was. The moment she reached the stairway, she could see a young man with an athletic body climbing the stairs. She could see his frame but not his face and was not sleepy, so she started tailing him.

Liya tailed him like a cat for four floors. When she reached fifth, a guard sitting on the steps stopped her. The guard sounded polite. "*Sorry, young lady, you don't have access beyond this floor.*" With a nod, she turned back to go down, but the lightning voice of the young man made her expel the teeth between her small lips. The young man's voice was neither scratchy nor rock. He ordered the guard, "*Allow the griffin warrior to pass the floor. She is our important guest.*" Also, he asked the guard to lend his shoes to her. The guard watched her up and down with attitude and lent him his shoes and let her pass. Liya was surprised that the young man was clever, and he already knew that she was tailing him and let her tail him from the beginning.

The shoe size was big for Liya. She can freely move her toes and fingers inside the shoes. With a stomp of oversized boots, she crossed the stairs, which opened to a wide space without roofs. It was the tallest balcony in the tower. Liya was very excited; she was standing on the top of the tower. She can see the young man standing to her left; she walked near to him and greeted him, "*Hello!*" She introduced herself as 'Liya.' He turned his face to reply to Liya, "*Greetings, young lady! I have seen your fight with our dragon. Your moves were fast, and attacking the neck of the dragon was an amazing strategy.*"

The young man's greeting made her feel proud that she has done amazing work today. Liya can see something different in his emerald eyeballs, but she doesn't have words to express that. She can see the cut scar below the left eye, which crosses his long nose and ends at the beginning of his right cheek. His scar and words made her clear that he belongs to the warrior class.

Liya acknowledged him, "*Thanks for your appreciation!*" He told Liya he used to come to the balcony to see the stars and the beauty of our Dragon Land. Liya's eyes were pulled to the gravity of him, and he explained, "*In the north, you can see sleeping dragons from here. In the west, sleepless glowing markets give it charm. East and south were spread with vast agricultural lands and all night we can see farmers guarding their crops against wilds.*" After hearing him, Liya's wide eyes experienced the beauty of Dragon Land from the tower, and she was mesmerized for a few minutes. When she came back to reality, Liya could feel the freezing fingers because of the chillness on the balcony. With excitement-mixed shivering, Liya rejoiced with a smile. She understood the cold wind was the reason that he asked the guard to lend her shoes. But still, Liya could not bear the moist air at the top of the tower. The young man noticed her tightened lips and closed palms to fight the summoning of Miss Cold Breeze. A man with a scar said briefly, "*The height of the tower was 290 meters tall. It was not easy to stand here wearing the cotton outfit."* Even though Liya was from Beku-neu, the altitude, soft outfit and strong winds trembled her shape. After seeing her suffer, the young man called out to one of the guards and told him to escort Liya to her room. Shivering, Liya's type-rating lips muttered, "*Thank you,*" and she left the balcony.

Once Liya reached her living room, she was looking for water. She took the water pot and purged till the last drop, and she needed more to burn her thirst. All of a sudden, she heard a knock on the door; she opened the door and found a maid at the door. The maid was holding a tray with a hot water kettle and tea leaves. Maid told Liya, "*She was ordered by the guards to deliver the hot water and tea leaves.*" Liya felt bad about herself; she did not ask the name of the smart guy she met on the balcony. Along with thanks, Liya asked the maid, "*May I know the name of the man with short hair with a horizontal scar on his face?*" With hesitation on her face, the maid replied that she had no permission to spell out the name of the warrior class and muttered sorry to Liya.

The next day, both Akello and Liya were searching for Zaya in all the places; they have not found any clues or the whereabouts of Zaya. Liya was puzzled and commented that Zaya was clever and didn't leave any trace of finding her. Akello praised Zaya, "*She is darkness at night and she is green in the forest. Without her wish, we can't meet or find her!*" In the evening, both walked to the stable to leave their griffins. Liya told Akello about a person she met on the tower top and view of the Dragon Land from the tower top with mandatory filters to not get mocked or trolled by Akello, but Akello noticed the excitement in her words and her bright eyes. Akello asked the name of the person that she met; Liya was silent for a second and told her that she forgot to ask with a sad expression. Akello giggled with mixed laughter. Akello notified Liya that tonight they were going to view the Dragon Land from the tower top and asked Liya to wake him up in the middle of the night. The moon started to smile in the dark sky. Dinner was yummy, and everyone hugged their beds. Liya was looking at the moon from her window and waiting for midnight to meet the same person at the tower top. In the deep of the night, Liya put on fur clothes and walked out to knock on the doors of Akello. The doors of Akello were knocked, but the snoring sound of Akello clearly says the dumb ass is not going to wake up tonight. Liya walked alone to the balcony, and no one was there, so she stood alone for an hour and enjoyed her own time in the melody of the wind. While standing, she turned her head several times to check the entrance of the balcony. Then, with a dull face, she walked to her bed.

It is a new Liya; she changed a lot after joining hands with Akello on a mission. In Beku-neu, she is an orphan with a dark past. She loves to spend alone time in her own thoughts. She has no friends, but Ivar and Kiba never let her be alone. They forced her to accompany them and tried to make her laugh and smile. The brothers struggled a lot to get her along with them and their families.

It was a hot day in Alaoka; Eric's heart was filled with fear about 'mission of peace.' The doors of his hut knocked hard.

He rushed and opened the doors. His eyes caught wheezing Gamba and from his body, the foul smell of sweat was leaking; Eric rubbed his nose with a weird face.

With a heavy gasp, Gamba barked, "*Dragons are flying in our boundaries.*"

In shock, Eric questioned, "*How many?*" Gamba's answer brought a smile to Eric's lips.

Gamba said, "Only one, and it was blue. A decade back, the same blue dragon hunted the griffin units like a hungry beast."

After hearing him, Eric blossomed with a smile. "*Being alone, he should be the messenger from Draguva.*" Eric rode his mustang along with his commanders to the valley of sleeping volcanoes. It was brown land with wide-legged mountains. The sides and land around the mountains were green and the volcanoes in the mountain were sleeping for millennium years and more. When Eric and his men arrived, blue Daga directed his beast to land on the ground. Blue jaws were wide and horns were made blunt and it has five horns in total. The moment dragon nails touched green, it roared to bring fear into the hearts. But Gamba's wolf, Eric mustang and the black griffin of the newly elected air unit commander made their fearless stand in front of a gigantic blue. A man in a white silk outfit jumped down from the blue dragon and walked toward Eric and his company. The man in the white silk was Rizon. Eric noted a welcoming smile on his face, and he responded with a warm smile. Rizon introduced himself as a minister of Draguva and delivered the message he carried on behalf of the Lord of Dragon. After hearing the message of Akello's valor and the invitation to Draguva, Eric's doubts converted into butterflies of happiness. Eric accepted the invitation of the Lord of Dragon. As a sign of acceptance, the Alaokan leader undid his tiger nail amulet and gave it to Rizon. Once Rizon evacuated the sleeping volcanoes, the first thing Eric did was he called Gamba and told him to convey the message of Akello's success to Akello's mother. He knew very well about mother's heart and her sufferings. Even though he is the best strategist of Alaokan, he still values the emotions of his people.

News of Akello's successful encounter with the dragon reached the huts and forest of the Alaokans. After hearing the news, Ava's right eye shed tears of happiness and a smile bloomed on her lips. More than mission success, she was happy that her son was alive and in good shape. When Figo watched the moving clouds, the sound of 'Akello's success' cheers hit his ear. After hearing the news, Figo was proud and happy for his kin and Amara was very happy too. A thousand stars glowed on her face. Apart from Alaokans, news of success even hit the ears of Davu in the Beku-neu. The message was carried by the rider of a dark brown dragon. When he visited Beku-neu, there was a heavy snowfall. Brown Daga helped Beku-neu clean the snow as a sign of friendship. News of Akello's success made Davu sing, "*Akello is my grandson*" to all his new friends in Beku-neu and in the excitement, he danced with others. Azog accepted the invitation. As a sign of acceptance, he gave his white cloak to brown Daga. The Azog's fort and mountain villages celebrated Liya's success. Ivar and Kiba walked to their master Azog's door for celebration. In Eric's green Alaoka,

Gamba conducted an ale party. On the other hand, both Akello and Liya were waiting to sail back home. It's been a long time and their lungs were waiting to feel the air of their homelands.

After two weeks, in the afternoon light, ships from Alaokan and Beku-neu civilizations reached the bay of dragons. Dragon Land ministers and people welcomed both civilization representatives with happy faces. In total, 150 members from both civilizations landed their foot in Dragon Land with their beasts. The people of Draguva opened their mouths wider after seeing the mammoths of Bora and griffins of Alaokans. After the duel between griffin and dragon, Draguvans gave a new name to griffins. They called the griffins 'Dragon Bleeder.'

In the same way, the outlanders were amazed to see such a beautiful, wide city. Both Akello and Liya waited along with the Lord of Dragon at the entrance of the tower. Gamba, Eric, Bora, Azog, and other people from both civilizations entered the gate of the giant tower. After seeing grandpa, Akello couldn't control his emotions; he ran toward him and hugged him tightly. Droplets of tears spelled down from both of their eyes. After watching Akello's action, Gamba commented to Eric, "*Still a kid!*" Eric smiled back at Gamba and walked forward. Liya used her eyes to make a sarcastic look. From her look, we can convey what she wanted to say, "*Poor brat finally reunited with grandpa.*" At the same time, she felt bad that she didn't have a family to cherish and support her like that. She controlled her emotions and welcomed Azog. There was another surprise waiting for Akello! In the crowd of Alaokans ranks, the scream of a griffin made Neo reply with an excited screech from the stable. The screech of Neo made Akello's coal-black eyes check the crowd, and he caught sight of two black griffins, and those griffins were very familiar to Akello and with a mile-long smile, he rolled his eyeballs to check the riders of griffin! He was delighted to find his girlfriend Amara on the griffin's back, a smile dancing on her dimple to see her Akello. At that moment, his five senses were paused for a minute and his vision magnified her apple face and green lens. Akello delighted, "*Amara!*" Without a shake in the eyeball, he rushed to the Alaokan ranks and hugged her and blossomed, "*Amara! Happy to see you here!*" A well-known voice hit Akello's ears, "*Idiot! I believe you remember me!*" Akello turned his head and bubbled, "*Figo!*" He gave a warm hug to his best buddy. He tapped on Figo's belly and commented, "*Hey, Figo! You have put on some weight!*" They laughed.

Figo scratched his head and voiced in pride, "*Not just weight and also added a new tattoo on my left shoulder.*" He showed his bravery tattoo (the claws of the tiger). Akello excited, "*Wow!*" He praised his fellow man. From the dancing ponytail and apple face, Liya guessed, "*She should be Amara.*" She was happy for Akello. At the same time, she rolled her eyes to find Ivar and Kiba, but she couldn't find either of them. With love in his eyes, in a soft voice, Akello asked about the welfare of his mother and little sister to his friends. Amara beamed, "*Figo goes once a week to check the welfare of your family.*" She added, "*I have a message for you from Moona.*"

Akello was delighted to hear that, but the sound of the trumpet started to eat the ears.

The sound of a trumpet disturbed the reunion of friends and the Lord of Dragon welcomed Azog, Eric, with a warm hug, and other Draguvans also welcomed the people of the other nations with great respect. After seeing the rain of respect from Draguvan, Akello caught the eyes of Liya, and both of their minds nudged the same. "*Is a single droplet of blood changed everything?*" Guards of the Dragon Land were assigned the responsible duty of taking care of the guests and their beasts. After hearing the sound of other griffins, Neo and Tuva replied to them back from their stable. Liya can see a lot of happy faces around her. Guards guided the guests to their respective rooms inside the tower and Akello walked his friends to the stable. On their way to the stable, Akello's lips carried his best smile and joy in his heart, not letting down his smile. Meeting Alaokan griffins made Neo's legs dance and all the griffins screeched in excitement. The screams echoed in all the crooks and corners of Draguva. In a reply to the scream, the wild roar of dragons paused the heartbeat of residents and guests for a second. Amara questioned, "*Did you really make a dragon shed blood?*" Akello scratched his head and briefed, "*Neo's scream summoned gray griffins to fight the dragon, and the blood of the dragon matched the color of the lighting.*"

After refreshment, the Lord of Dragon personally took Azog and Eric for a tour inside the fort walls and tower. Gamba congratulated Akello, "*Well done, kiddo! You proved to everyone that our leader has not selected the wrong person.*" Bora and Liya were involved in a long discussion, and Azog and Eric were amazed by the architecture and science of the tower. The lever mechanics of Draguvan impressed the outlanders; it solved their big question of how such a tall standing tower was constructed. The blanket of darkness started to cover the sky at its full speed and a no-moon night started. Oil lamps were lit in the market and tower. The tower's beauty with oil lamps twinkled in the eyes of outlanders. Akello took Amara and Figo to the market of the rich. In the crowd, Akello clutched Amara's hand and pushed his shoulders to move forward. Even in the crowded street, the Alaokan lovers' lips widened and all their teeth got the reflection of the oil lamp. Akello and Amara required some alone time for their hearts to speak in silence, but it was not hard when Figo was around. In the marketplace, Akello bought a doll made of jute for his little sister Moona, and he also paid for souvenirs bought by his friends.

After finishing the tower tour and market visit, the Lord of Dragon took Alaokan and Beku-neun crew to join for the dinner. The dinner was arranged in the tower. The dinner hall was occupied by 70 members of all three civilizations. The dinner hall looked great with black marble, and the light made the dining table look gorgeous. The reflection of oil lamps in the marble made outlanders feel like they were walking on the stars. The dining table was full of all special green, tropical fruits, and red eatables. Rizon started the dinner with a medium-sized barrel of airag and took it over the head and made a toast, "*For unity and peace!*" He purged a small position and passed the barrel to multiple hands. While the barrel was crossing hands, Eric and Azog made eye contact and recalled a day in Beku-neu. After crossing leaders, finally, the airag barrel reached the hands of Gamba. He purged the remains of the barrel and put a green signal for dinner. Most Beku-neuns tasted mango, jackfruit, and banana for the very first time in life. Dishes on the dining table were delicious and well-cooked in the stream. Everyone enjoyed the great dinner. Before the wine, the leader of Draguvan asked everyone to assemble in the meeting hall tomorrow by noon. When all three civilizations' members were enjoying the wine, the leaders of the three civilizations walked to the top of the tower to discuss more.

While having dinner, Akello was about to introduce Amara and Figo to Liya, but she paused him and opened, "*Smiling apple face, you must be Amara.*" She pointed her long fingers at Figo and added, "*Tall, lean man, I guess you are Figo. Akello used to talk about both of you a lot.*" From hearing Liya, both Alaokans were delighted to smile.

Liya complained to both, "*Share me some tips to handle knucklehead Akello. He is a troublemaker...*" Her list was long, along with clashing ale mugs. Laughter and fun decorated the dinner hall.

Dragon tower has another nickname, '1,000 door tower,' as its name stands tower has thousands of rooms. It has enough rooms to accommodate all guests, and each guest was allocated individual rooms. Even though everyone was allocated big rooms and it was time to snore, Figo and Amara heard legends of Akello in his chamber. The doors of Akello were open. The breeze entered the doors and caressed the skin of Amara. After explaining his legends, Akello asked Figo, "*How did you get a new tattoo? Have I missed any adventure in Alaoka?*"

With a sarcastic look, Figo replied, "*No, Alaokan adventure is bigger than bleeding a dragon. As usual, during last year's harvest season, the cluster island became an apple for the pirates. They started to hunt the residence and we griffin riders were a little late! Our team killed dozens and stopped forwarding pirates, but most of the harvested greens were still looted from the coastal village! Zina and I got a tattoo of bravery for our actions in the combat.*"

Akello coal lens marked at Amara. Without a delay, she nodded her head in negation. Akello wondered how Amara was aboard the ship without a tattoo. Tattoos are tickets for a rookie in Alaoka and earlier tattoos of Akello and Figo helped them in getting seats in the fleet for Beku-neun voyage.

Out of curiosity, Akello asked about a recent event that happened in Alaoka and the prophecy told about '*welcoming the dead festival.*' After hearing Akello, Figo muttered, "*Prophecy.*" Amara caught Figo's eyes.

Figo recalled the order. When the Alaokans boarded the ship to Draguva, the first order that hit the Alaokan ears was, "*Never share the prophecy with outlanders and our fellow Alaokan in Draguva!*"

Figo asked Amara, "*Check the doors and seal them!*" He knew very well how fast information could leak.

Figo began, "*Akello! This year's prophecy is a series of troubles! More than that, we got orders from our leader not to share the prophecy with the outlanders and the Alaokan peace envoy!*"

The smile on Akello's face was doomed, and Amara hesitated. "*We defy the orders for a reason! We want you to know the prophecy. On your mission, understand the situation and act wisely.*"

Akello fuzzed. "*Guys! Tell me the prophecy. Your words frighten me!*"

Amara voiced, "*Alaokan rain! Floods the Beku-neu!*

The smell of Airag hugs the Alaoka!

Ale, Sura, Airag and Rum! Stroms the ocean!

Souvenir! Black fleet's souvenir crawls the verdant and terrains!

Glaze and blaze! Sails the streams of hell! But the gale will halt and blow again!"

After hearing Amara, Akello tried to process the information, but it was hard for him! Akello mumbled, "*Black fleet delivers the souvenir!*" He giggled.

He scratched his head and beamed. "*Guys! Your words were far better than this prophecy.*"

Amara and Figo exhaled hot air. Figo continued, "*But you are right! It is confusing. So Kino, Amara, Zina and I seek the help of gramps and grannies to decode the prophecy. We heard weird answers. The most relevant is that a disaster is coming! War of Draguvan! Or friendship of Draguvans! Natural disasters! Alaokan will face less damage! But Draguva and Beku-neu will face heavy casualties.*"

Figo was puzzled and voiced, "*Beyond all these hypotheses! Akello, do you remember the granny with brown mangoes? She caught you red-handed while stealing her mangos.*"

Akello recalled the tastes of those mangoes and blossomed, "*It tastes great, right?*"

Figo muttered, "*Fool!*" and Amara fumed, "*Idiot! For stealing those mangoes, she made you work the whole day in her field as punishment! Does your peanut brain forget that?*"

Figo said, "*Guys, leave the taste of mangoes and punishments when Kino and I visited her to decipher the prophecy! She sees it in a different way, but Kino believes it doesn't make sense, but I feel her perception may be right. Glaze and blaze! Sails the streams of hell! But the gale will halt and blow again! She presumes glaze, blaze and gale as messengers of peace. Akello, you are a gale. Liya is glaze, and the Draguvan messenger of peace is a blaze. They both will die while seeking the mission to unite Yuvalle, but you will halt and win the peace.*"

After hearing Figo, Akello made a terrible face and beamed, "*Crazy!*"

Figo replied, "*Kino said the same thing. On your next mission, make wise decision and never share this with anyone.*"

Akello puzzled, "*Fantasies of mango granny are extraordinary! And she believes that I am going to win the alliance alone!*" He giggled.

Amara recalled Akello, "*Rookie confronts the superior, and that rookie is you! Don't underestimate the Alaokan prophecy.*"

Akello lamented, "*You guys clouded my mind with prophecy.*" He fumed at Figo, "*You recalled the taste of Alaokan brown mangoes, but your hands are empty.*"

Figo smiled at the corner of his lips and bubbled, "*Yes! I didn't get any mangoes from Alaoka, but I managed to get your lover to Draguva!*" He caught Amara's face.

Akello turned to find Amara's face. Amara opened, "*Figo knows about us!*" Akello's ears failed to parse the words of Amara and beamed, "*Figo! Nothing like it!*"

Amara voiced, "*Akello, listen, he knows what's going on between us! Zina was the one supposed to sail Draguva. She fell down from a small cliff, and that made her temporarily unfit for the journey. Being that I belong to the same team, I used that as a chance to sail to Draguva to see you. The brain behind this plan is Figo.*"

After hearing Amara, Akello turned his head to catch both of them. Within seconds, he hugged Figo in joy!

Figo beamed. "*I thought I was your best buddy! You will tell me first when you fall in love! But you failed my hopes!*"

Akello downed his head without a word and Figo continued, "*I am not like you! I am in love with Zina. If all goes well, I will tell her soon.*" Amara was surprised to hear him.

After hearing him, with a giggle, Akello said, "*Zina and you? Figo, I am sorry to hide about us, and I am happy for you and Zina.*"

Figo replied, "*I am leaving! Have some alone time and remember the Alaokan code of marriage.*" Finally, Akello gets some alone time to spend with Amara after a long year. The silence decorated the room and the sound of whooshing winds ate their ears. Without a word, their eyes were locked and their lips expressed the best smile. It was a long night for the Alaokans lovers.

After Amara left the chamber, Akello hugged his bed tight and traversed into deep sleep mode. Snore of him buzzed the ears of the wind that trespassed into his chamber. In the dead of night, Akello's room doors were knocked. At the same time, Liya was walking down the stairs. She found Alaokan at the doors of Akello; she walked to him with a funny giggle and bubbled. "*This door will never open at night.*" She asked him to keep his ears at the door. Knocking Alaokan did the same as she mentioned. All he heard were the deep, long Alaokan snores. Laughter bloomed at the closed doors, and then both walked in different directions.

The next morning before sunrise, Akello's room door was knocked on again with a great sound. Luckily, he opened his eyes and checked out the window and complained, "*Even the sun is not up.*" He cursed himself for waking up early. With gloom-bagged eyes, when Akello slides the door, he finds an Alaokan soldier with two tattoos. Alaokan at the door carried a message from their leader, "*Our leader has summoned you.*" He also grumbled, "*Looks too hard to wake you by knocking on the doors! Maybe, I will use the trumpet next time.*" Without wasting a minute, Akello rushed to the doors of Eric.

Eric welcomed Akello with a great smile. Akello bent on his knees and downed his head to show his respect. Eric beamed, "*Rise colt!*" The moment Akello stood on his feet, Eric recollected his words. "*Akello, you are no longer a colt. You are mustang now.*" He called him, "*Alaokan mustang!*" Akello's cheeks blushed with pride. Eric mentioned that he couldn't find time yesterday to talk with him in private, so he summoned Akello now.

Eric mentioned to Akello, "*The Lord of Dragon praised your brave act, and he also returned the dragon-tooth dagger to me in front of Azog as a gesture of new peace.*"

Eric applauded Akello for his great show in the arena and beamed, "*This alliance is because of you. I heard from Gamba that your mother is proud of you.*" Akello's heart was filled with joy mixed with sorrow, and he wished to see his mother and sister soon. Beyond all, Eric gifted the dragon-tooth dagger to Akello and asked him to 'keep the peace safe and nurture it to grow as a banyan.' Once the entire Alaoka thought Akello was savage, but today everyone in Alaoka praises him. One thing was clear to him when he was walking back to Alaoka he was no longer a brat in people's eyes.

Akello asked Eric about Dragon Land oil resources and engineering.

Eric said, "*Draguva was the wealthiest nation that we had heard of in literature and their lands were located in the perfect geographical plots. As mentioned by our ancestors, 'The land which has good rainforest, the big mountains as borders, clean water flowing rivers and rich agricultural lands are the qualities of strong and safe land.' The Draguva possess all these qualities, and their warriors are strong-willed. They push themselves an extra mile every day to get themselves stronger. They used their chemist brains in a better way than we expected. Dragon Land chemists found a way to filter out the oil from the dragon pee since it is quite a long process to convert them to oil. They have constructed a well in the Draguvan gardens to store the pee of dragons. Based on their needs, they will convert the pee into oil and use it. The tower we are standing on is the tallest tower we have ever known and the Draguvan lever mechanism helps them to uplift the heavy load. The Lord of Dragon mentioned it took two centuries for them to completely build the tower and the age of this tower is 40 years now. They constructed this tower based on the view of the future. This tower will act as a protective shield in case of natural calamities like storms, hurricanes, and earthquakes too."*

Out of curiosity, Akello paused Eric. He asked, "*How is this tower not vulnerable to earthquakes?*"

With a smile, Eric continued, "*The foundation of this tower was 160 meters deep and strong. They didn't have enemies and threats like Beku-neu to take care of, so their only focus was developing themselves stronger and building a better future for their offspring. The Draguvan leader handled the internal clash with barbarians in a better way! Rather than using the army solution, he hired the machinery from slaves and exterminated the barbarians without wetting his hands and bending his pride.*" Words from Eric about Draguvan gave goosebumps to

Akello. Every time, the Alaokan leader blew Akello's mind with his analytics and logical skills.

After meeting Eric in the early morning, he walked into his chamber. Morning daylight entered the window to wish good luck to the hero. The birds' chirping was very relaxing to Akello, so he decided to walk to the stable and spend some time with his friend. Once he reached the stable, his eye caught Liya, and she was gently rubbing her griffin's head. Neo makes an eagle scream, which made Liya notice that Akello was in the stable. She turned her head around to see Akello. Akello made a hand sign of good morning, but she didn't give any response. Instead, Akello got the sight of anger in her sharp eyes. Her eyes gave a clear sign to Akello that something was terribly wrong. He has two options. Either find the reason for her anger and convince her or run away and brace himself for her anger waves.

Akello gently walked near Neo and caressed his beak, and his beast was feeling comfortable. It rubbed his head on Akello's chest as usual. Akello politely asked Liya what was the reason for her anger. Akello got a response from Liya without context. "*No point in responding to the person who hides the information from his comrades*." She agonized. "*You are not worthy of my trust.*" Liya's eyes and gritted teeth reflected her anger, but in her voice, Akello sensed the pain. Akello was not dumb this time; he found the reason for her anger.

It was all about the dagger hanging in his belt, "*Dagger of 1,000 souls! or Dragon tooth dagger.*" Akello apologized for hiding the information about the dagger. He confessed to

Liya, "*I should have told you about the dagger beforehand.*" He let his fears flow. "*I thought in case you and Zaya came to know that we have a lifeline. I personally thought that could affect the seriousness of our mission, so I decided to keep it a secret close to my heart.*" With a shaky voice, he beamed, "*I kept the dagger as our last resort. Our duo's efforts matter more than the dagger.*" His words did not calm down Liya's anger, but they agitated her anger more. Hot air pumped out from her sharp nose, and she decided not to spill any words. His words made her feel what Akello thought of her. "*If she came to know that there is a lifeline, she would go easy on a mission.*" After a few moments of silence in the stable, Akello graced Neo and put his head down out of guilt. Neo made a pleasing cry for his rider's mistake. Still, Akello noted doubts and redness in her knife eyes. She ignored Neo and turned her back on Akello. He pulled out his dagger and graced the brass handle of it. Akello promised on his griffin and said, "*I trusted you like a rock, but out of my insecurities, I didn't reveal the dagger, but I never expected one sunset and droplets of blood could change everything. TRUST ME!*"

"*Starting today, this prideful dagger is mine. I got this as a reward for what we have accomplished. Moreover, you have equal rights to it. Keep this with you. It's my sign of comradeship, honor for you! TRUST ME! I need our friendship to be eternal.*" Liya's eyes fixed on his vision; Akello's words didn't console her head, but the truth in his eyes won her heart. His eyes expelled, "*Respect and care he has for Liya.*" For an orphan like Liya, this kind of friendship was unexpected. Her tight eyebrows got relaxed and the flavor of her eyes changed to pink, but her strong attitude didn't let it flow down. From that moment along with Kiba, Ivar and Akello were also added to her family. With emotions in her voice, Liya promised, "*Our friendship will sail more and for longer.*" She walked out to hide her feelings. She also felt Amara was lucky to have him as her partner. Regaining her trust reduced Akello's guilt, and at the same time, he flew on Neo's wings to grace the beauty of the morning.

At noon, the meeting hall was filled with officials of the three civilizations. They had their differences. Alaokans clothed in gray cotton. Beku-neu's dressed in wool, and Draguvans wore silk. Everyone was waiting in the meeting hall. Lord of Dragon accompanied Azog and Eric to the great hall. There was a big table in the hall. Draguvan called this hall a war hall. The strategies of the war will be discussed here. All three leaders placed their black meteor swords on the table. Swords looked like identical triplets. There was no inch of difference in their size, shape and quality; Akello thought, "*If someone jumbles the swords now, how will leaders find which one is theirs?*" He whispered the same in Liya's ears; her answer was she made an angry stare at him. The people in the hall graced the swords with curiosity. The Lord of Dragon welcomed members of grass, ice, and Draguvans. Azog asked Davu and Frida to address their new finding in the snow caves of Beku-neu.

Davu introduced himself to the crowd, but this time in a different way. "*I am Akello's grandpa and lead archaeologist of Alaokans.*" His words showed that he was proud of his grandson. After hearing him, Akello's teeth were expelled, and he could see deep happiness in his grandpa's eyes. Davu delivered an important finding that they unearthed in Beku-neu. In the last months of archaeological research conducted in the Beku-neu's permafrost caves and ancient temple, we found a pair of giant mammoth tusks with inscriptions in them. Inscriptions on the tusk show once people of Beku-neu and yetis were friends. One of the tusks had details of the yeti valley and the other one talks about the war between yeti and humans. We are in search of finding a way to reach the yeti valley and the language that communicates with yetis. Davu bloomed, "*There were myths that yetis live longer. We believe yeti valley will unfold the answer to a million questions.*" After hearing him, whispers started in the hall. Draguvans have never heard the word yetis. Later, Azog explained how it looks and the way it hunts. Gamba and Eric were waiting to hear about repeated star patterns in the cave wall. Davu cleared his throat and opened, "*At last, we examined repeated star patterns in permafrost walls; it was matching with the patterns in the skull. We are ascending to unlock mysteries.*" Gamba wore a smile and voiced, "*The fruit of alliance!*"

Lord of Dragon introduced Valon, the lead archaeologist of Draguvans. Valon said, "*Almost a year ago, Lord Rizon gave a fossil of a dragon nail with unknown symbols in it, and he asked me to decipher the information in it. It was very hard to decode the symbols. The inscription looks like the deep ocean is releasing the eggs to the surface of the water.*" Lord of Dragon requested Davu and Frida to investigate the nail which he was talking about and directed Valon to join a unified archaeological team to unlock the secrets in Beku-neu and other corners of the world.

From the beginning, Azog noted hesitation and uncertainty on Rizon's face in every conversation made in the war hall. With a smile on his lips, Azog asked Rizon's opinion of a unified archaeological team. With the relief of getting a chance to speak, Rizon opened, "*Great idea of joining forces to unravel the histories and artifacts.*" With a pause, his hesitation was expelled. "*But it's unbelievable to accept the facts in the fossil, especially the island guarded by the waves and Aalikai.*" In the moment of silence, Azog noted the same chaos of believing the odds in the fossil reflected in everyone's face, and he was smart enough to give clarity on Rizon's question, "*Cave arts and bone fossils with inscriptions are the keys gifted by our ancestors and till today most of them guided for a better future.*" By eliminating second thoughts aside, let's celebrate unity. When one more similar sword decorates the table, we will find more interesting facts to discuss.

Beyond the confusion, Azog boomed, "*The land of the dragon is not going to select the messenger of peace for now. They asked for a moon rotation to decide the right candidate.*"

Eric harpooned Liya and Akello, "*As we all know north-east lands (aka) Yuvalle is our next member to join the new peace and we leaders made the decision that peace envoys are not allowed to take the beasts along with them to Yuvalle.*" Akello and Liya were thundered and Eric was not done yet. He added, "*We have neither seen their sails in the wide blues nor their troopers in our territories. In the last 50 decades, we presume they are self-sufficient to live within their boundaries with such discipline and we suspect that Yuvalle should be a developed civilization. In this situation, walking into their land along with a beast may create the wrong interpretation in their mind that 'we are waging war.' So, this mission is going to be much harder. Peace envoys have to win the alliance of the north-eastern lands without a friendly beast."*

There was perfect silence in the hall. Liya and Akello were paralyzed by the decisions of the leaders. Azog added, "*When we seek alliance and peace, we need to go polite.*" Akello started, "*But chief!*" The Draguvan leader interrupted Akello and beamed, "*They are the strongest of all the civilizations.*" Everyone was shocked after hearing him. Till today, Alaokans and Beku-neuns, even most Draguvans, believed Draguva is the strongest of all, but the words of the Lord of Dragon created a large whisper. Azog and Eric caught the eyeball of the Draguvan leader. He nodded his head and continued, "*I am the grandson of commander Zion. In the history of Dragon Land, a few pages were erased. About 15 decades ago, after winning, both Alaoka and Beku-neu without spilling a single droplet of dragon blood, Zion led an army of 5,000 men and five dragons to the Yuvalle. We never knew it was commander Zion's last mission. The big army of mighty Zion did not return home. A Draguvan spy was sent to get information about the large army of Zion, but along with them, a skilled spy also vanished from existence."*

"*We don't know what beast it was? But they have a dragon killer on their side!*"

The land area of Yuvalle was completely covered in a blanket of dark clouds. Even griffin's eyes can't see what's behind those clouds. From the shaky voice of the Lord of Dragon, Akello and Liya read the fear, and they were clear that winning the dragon killer was nearly impossible. Eric gave his word to send the strongest ships of all three civilizations, the Kallan, and a crew of sailors along with the ship. He also promised the ship would soon reach the bay of Dragos. Azog mentioned, "*I will send the rough captain of Beku-neu to sail the rough seas and he will lead the crew*." The decision was made and the sail date marked two full moons from today. More than the words of the Draguvan leaders, Akello and Liya were literally broken to leave their griffins behind.

That night, Akello walked Amara to the tower top. More than astonished by the beauty of the tower, he was worried about the mission without Neo. Luckily Amara was near Akello, and when she clutched Akello's fingers, his wavy thoughts blasted and he noticed the love on her face. He rolled his eyes at the entrance. After finding no one around, he kissed her cotton cheeks and his nose sensed an attractive fragrance on her. Her fragrance crushed his confusion and made his fingers clutch her hands tight. Amara pointed her fingers at the twin stars in the sky and voiced, "*Akello! The arrival of these stars in the sky means you are 20 now! All we have to wait is one more year for our marriage*." Akello bubbled, "*As promised, will bring guests from all four civilizations for marriage*." He kissed her forehead. Amara was delighted and recalled, "*Remember the prophecy and make decisions. Come back to me in good shape. I am waiting for you in Alaoka*." Akello hugged her tightly and voiced, "*When I meet you next year! I am all yours.*" Both cherished the beauty of nightfall.

After a week, Alaokans and Beku-neuns decided to set back their sail for their native. Akello was sleepless because the next morning, Akello had to give a send-off to Neo and he was frightened to continue his mission without Neo. On the death of night, the doors of his chamber were knocked on. When Akello opened the door, he was surprised to see his grandpa Davu, but his face was covered with sadness. Akello understood the reason. He proudly voiced not to worry about him and boasted, "*As I won the alliance of Draguvans, I will successfully complete my next mission too.*" Davu can see the confidence in his grandson's voice, but still, he is not ready to send his grandson on another life-drinking mission.

Davu began, "*The mission you took on your shoulder was not child's play. We neither know any detailed information nor spy in north-east lands.*" Davu was fragile and old and he confessed his fear of losing his grandson, and he sobbed, "*If worse happened, I couldn't face your mother, Akello.*" He hugged his grandson and his emotion leaked from his eyes. Akello was speechless and Davu opened, "*I am out of choices, perhaps! I believe in you and wait for your homecoming!*"

Akello saw rolling tears running over his grandpa's cheeks. He gave his promise, "*Tell mom, everyone is talking about the bravery of her son and also tell her I am missing her and her recipes. Tell Moona that her brother loves her more! Will return home safe!*"

If Akello's mother had been here, she could have handled it in a better way.

Along with the mission, Akello holds the responsibility of reaching home safely. Beyond a warrior life, he is so important to his family and friends. He can't ever let them down. Davu gifted a wooden compass to him for his success. It has markings in all directions and a magnetic needle in the center that always points north. Davu beamed at Akello. "*When you're stuck in the unknown world, travel in the south to reach home.*" It was a precious gift for Akello and hoped it would help a lot on the sea voyage. Akello's excitement was reflected on his face, and he expressed his thanks.

That night, Akello's sleep was doomed by his grandpa's emotion and withdrawal of Neo. He recalled his routines and legends with Neo in the grass, ice, and fire. He was rolling in the clockwise and anti-clockwise direction, but the sleep failed to touch him. It was a tough time, so he decided to walk to the royal stable to check on his loyal friend. First, he walked down to the wine warehouse and unlocked the doors with lock-pins and stole two bottles of 100 years old expensive wines. Akello became a brilliant thief too, all credit to his friendship with Zaya. Without raising an alarm, he managed to escape the warehouse, and then he walked to the stable. In the moonlight, Akello can see Neo sleeping. He crawled near Neo and rested his head on the back of Akello. The contact of Akello's head on Neo made the griffin open his eyes. The golden color lens is exposed between the opening of the eyelids. Moment radium eyes of Neo graced Akello; it gently moved his head to Akello.

Akello inhaled the energetic smell of wine and caressed Neo. In a kick of booze, Akello's mind flashed the best moments with Neo as gently rubbed his thumb on the bite scar in the forefinger. Akello voiced, "*Adventures of Akello and Neo will resume soon...*" He sobbed and fell asleep in the royal stable.

A bucket of water helped to wake up Akello's sleep. When he opened his eyes, the sun rays graced the stable and a small girl standing opposite him with a bucket in her hands, due to yesterday's hangover his vision was blurry. The next moment, Akello heard voices from behind his back. "*Good job.*" Liya tossed a bean to the small girl. Akello turned back to see it was Liya, leaning back on the stable wall. Liya told Akello that she tried to wake him up, but finally, a bucket of water worked. Akello graced Neo and silence hit his face. Liya understood the pain of Akello, even though she underwent the same, but the tragedy of her life made her mature and strong. Liya broke the silence. "*The ships are going to unleash the sails in a few hours.*" Akello walked to the water tub and splashed cold water on his face. With dripping water, he walked near Neo. He gently rubbed his beak and mounted. Akello and Liya were on the griffins and forwarded toward the harbor. The harbor looked busy and soldiers were loading the ships and setting them ready for sail.

Legends were standing in groups. Chief Eric, leader Azog, the Lord of Dragon, Bora, Rizon, and Gamba were standing in the group and everyone was happy and laughter bloomed in the group. As a fruit of alliance, sharing of crops and valuables started between the civilizations, and ships on the shores were already filled with tropical fruits and oil barrels of Draguva. When Akello crossed the legends, he whispered low, "*The fruit of alliance!*" Both Liya and Akello walked into their respective ships to leave their griffins. The bottom deck of the ship was spacious, especially designed for the comfort of the beast. Akello bent down to collect one of the fallen feathers of Neo and hold it in his hands. He controlled his tears and gave a small piece of meat to his lovely friend with a smile. Neo wailed in the pain of leaving his companion. Akello moved his head near Neo's head and said, "*Wait for my call from the cliff. Will see you soon, my friend!*" He left the ship, but Neo's loud cry was not stopped. At the exit of the deck, Figo and Amara were standing in silence. Akello tapped Figo's shoulders and beamed, "*Take care!*" Figo nodded his head back. Akello wished to hug Amara and inhale her scent to stop the chaos in his mind, but the busy deck didn't allow him to do it. He caught her green eyes and started to move out.

Once he left the ship, the sea breeze froze the tears on his cheeks. Azog's ships planned to land in Alaoka for a few days and then decided to continue their sail to Beku-neu. He wiped away the tears and walked to meet his grandpa on Beku-neu's ship. Davu was sitting with Valon and Frida. Akello conveyed his wish, 'good luck,' to team Davu for their archaeological adventure. Before leaving, Eric shook his head and Akello replied with a nod. Gamba winked at his eyes and patted the shoulders of his Alaokan gem. Ships of both civilizations are set ready for sail, anchored up and opted for high sail, and ships started to move toward the east.

The scream of griffins which escaped from the ship rang in the ears of Akello and Liya.

Days fell like dried leaves from the trees after the dispatch of ships. Akello and Liya spent most of their daylight in the prohibited Draguvan forest. They were pulled into the Draguvan combat training and directly mentored by Rizon and the Lord of Dragon. Both spent their evenings in the pothouse of the rich and enjoyed the refreshing smell and taste of the new batch airag. Every time, they sat at their favorite table. They both recalled their memories with Zaya and they missed her a lot. The surprise was that Zaya had not left any message to even Azog. It's been one full moon down. Heroes' lives are stuck in a repetitive cycle: waking up early to train hard, booze and sleep. With just a few more days left to begin the journey, they managed to complete the hard training, but the Draguvan peace envoy was not decided and ships from Alaoka did not arrive. One fine evening before sunset, Liya and Akello were walking on the stone roads of Draguva. All of a sudden, the rush of people started to run in the opposite direction from the market. Liya rushed to the nearby tallest building. From the top, she noticed the crowd rushing to leave the marketplace; it had never happened before in Draguva. From the whispers she understood, the great Kallan ship had arrived at the bay of Dragos. Akello and Liya's shoulders pushed through the crowd to reach the shore.

When they reached the shore, the surface of the sea and waves were influenced by the color of the setting sun. Akello's eyes graced the sky, and he smiled at the bunch of cotton balls; it blindfolded the vision of the sun. The red setting sun cursed the clouds for blocking his sight from seeing the beauty of the 'giant Kallan ship.' From the edges of the clouds, the orange light of the sun escaped out to create a beautiful evening. Slowly, clouds moved by the influence of wind and the light rays of the sun smoothly rubbed the brass lion head figure of Kallan and made it sparkle. The ship had three tall poles with red-blue canvas sails that were suitable for the rough oceans. The deck is large enough to fit in 40 griffins. Above the captain's deck, wheels were made of rare black wood with brass linings to control the ship and the ram of ships was stronger like the hands of Thor. The beauty of the ship made Liya expand her pupils, and she commented, "*Kallan is majestic! Looks like the king of oceans!*"

Alaokans welcomed Akello into the giant ship with cheers and he was happy to see members of Alaokan naval units and Liya accompanied him. There was a surprise waiting for Liya and Akello on the ship. While speaking with sailors, they heard the captain from Beku-neu had still not arrived. When no one noticed from the navigation bucket, a man jumped down like a saber and reached the deck with bent knees. The sound of his shoes made the heroes turn their heads. They found a short man, and he voiced, "*Looks like no one is missing me!*"

The voice of a short man excited Liya. She shouted on cloud nine, "Kiba!" She then gave him a tight hug. Akello was also excited to see Kiba. When he stayed in Beku-neu, he created new friendships. Kiba is one of them. Kiba patted Akello and congratulated both for their success. Kiba mentioned, "*Success is the ordinary word to describe all your hardships and pain."* The setting sun puts its last light of the day on the 'reunion of friends.'

After Kiba met the Lord of Dragon, Akello and Liya took him to the market of the rich. After walking in the wide streets of the rich, the large tavern became a better place to relax. Kiba delighted in the beauty of the city and his eyes reflected the oil lamps. When Akello asked Kiba about the captain of the ship, Kiba grumbled, "The captain did not travel along with him" and added a message from Azog, Azog mentioned, "*The captain will reach the harbors of Draguva before the full moon.*" Liya shouted in frustration, "*Full moon is just two days away, the captain has not arrived and the Lord of Dragon is still looking for the peace envoy.*"

In the taste of rum, they recalled Zaya and discussed their new mission.

Liya beamed. "*Last night, I was sleepless! I walked into a big library in the tower to find out more about Draguva, and I found a blue dragon aggressive of all dragons.*" With a pause, she amazed Akello and Kiba. "*In the army of Zion, there were three blue dragons, and he was also the rider of one.*" From her words, it's clear the army of Zion was really stronger than they imagined. Liya bawled, "*If the Yuvalle's mystery defeated such a strong army, they should be the offspring of demons or devils.*"

Akello laughed, "*When we see Draguvans training for the first time, we are told the same. Whatever the Yuvalleans are, they are also made of flesh and bones!*" After hearing stories of the north-east, Akello's curiosity increases to bring the alliance to put a full stop to all these conspiracies.

Suddenly, at the doors of the rich tavern, excitement and cheers blasted! It was the arrival of the royal prince Rizon; the cheers of blue Daga pierced the ears of the heroes. With a great smile, Rizon noticed team Akello at the last table, and he waved his hands at them. Akello replied with the same excitement. Liya introduced the fellow Beku-neun to Rizon. Later, she told the legends of Rizon, the blue Daga, to Kiba. The owner of the tavern wanted Rizon to start the new batch of seasonal wine. He honored Rizon with the very first jar of 75-year-old apple wine. He gulped every ounce of the jar without a pause and toasted, "*For the people and welfare of Dragon Land.*" The taste of the wine melted in his mouth. The taste of it says it was finely fermented with care. After finishing the jar, the taste of it made Rizon go for another round. He complimented the brewer, and he ordered the owner to serve the same to Akello's table. A few people walked near Rizon and talked about the new difficulties they are facing in the country and other problems. Rizon promised them that he will consult with the Lord of Dragon and take the necessary action. He never let the head weight of the leader's son conquer his head; he was very friendly with ordinary people. With the men in the pothouse, he was involved in arm wrestling and won in all of them.

Akello and Liya cheered for Rizon. "*Haaa! Haa! Blue Daga...blue Daga...*"

Kiba commented, "*He wishes to see the duel of Ivar and Rizon on the table.*" He suspects, "*It is going to be a great fight.*"

Rizon was more concerned about the happy life of his people. Monthly once, he used to visit the tavern of rich and poor markets. The reason for the visit is to find out the condition of his people. He believed drunken men and women will let out their fears and open their difficulties for daily bread and problems in society. With these interactions, he can find resolutions and help them. These qualities of his were loved by the people of Dragon Land and also many believed he was the best fit candidate for the throne.

After a great night, Rizon walked to his father's chamber. Rizon's eyes noticed the confusion on the Lord of Dragon's face. Rizon walked near him and gently opened, "*Is there any new chaos?*"

The leader of Dragon Land exhaled. "*It was all about selecting a peace envoy.*"

Rizon inhaled the cold breeze and added, "*Father, I came to discuss the same. Based on my analysis of Akello and Liya's characteristics and fighting styles, we need to select the messenger of peace accordingly. Dragon Land's messenger of peace needs to be a backup for two. The messenger has to possess greater survival skills.*"

Rizon has already selected the person in mind. Rizon requested permission from the Lord of Dragon to spell his name. The Lord of Dragon nodded his head in affirmation.

Rizon was delighted. "*It's none other than my younger brother and second prince of the Dragon Land*."

The Lord of Dragon vocalized, "*Yuda!*" The huge silence covered his face, and after a minute, he broke his own silence, "*Yuda has a silent nature and makes strong decisions which no one expected. Till today, he never shared his feelings, even with us. At the same time, he listens to orders but never executes them.*"

Rizon interrupted with a smile, "*But father, my brother never failed a mission assigned on his head; beyond all, he ensured the safety of the comrades in the mission as well.*"

The Lord of Dragon was silent for a few seconds and voiced, "*But!*"

Rizon disclosed the secrets he found, "*As of my conversation with Gamba, Akello acts on his own! And as far as I can see, Liya's line of thinking is sharp and fast!*" With hesitation, he added, "*Orders given to Liya and Akello are to find a way to approach the leader of Draguvans with peace, but they acted on their own to prove their worth and won the alliance! So, we can't add the one who takes the orders to this duo.*"

"Father, I beg you. Yuda is the right person to fit in."

After a huge discussion, he convinced the Lord of Dragon to select Yuda and he was a rider of the brown beast. Along with the victory of choosing Yuda, Rizon was forced to take paternity leave. His wife is going to give birth to his legacy in the next 20 days. She is also a dragon rider and Yuda was eager to see his niece, but now the mission called him.

With a worrisome mind, the Lord of Dragon summoned the guard who was standing outside the doors and ordered the guard, "*Get Yuda here in double quick time.*"

The Lord of Dragon probed Rizon. "*Did you remember the words of Azog about Captain Shaw?*" With a smug face, Rizon boasted, "*Father! Our Yuda is the right choice to handle the temper of Shaw.*"

On the other end, Liya and Kiba were sleepless, so they decided to walk to the top of the tower. The moonlight and clouds created a mirror reflection in the marble; it looks gorgeous and Kiba was astonished by the mirror reflections, and after crossing seven floors, it opened to the big balcony of the Tower. From the top of the tower, a gentle breeze rubbed Liya's cheeks. Both the north and south market shops looked like a cluster of stars from the top. The flow of the river was tiny from the top, but the long flow of water was highlighted by the silvery light of the moon.

Then that miracle happened. Kiba was silent for almost 20 minutes. He was always hyper, but he gets silent when he is angry or hungry. The silence made Liya recall the man she met in the tower and remembered the way he showed the geography of Dragon Land.

Liya broke the silence with a question. "*Hey, Kiba! Are you in this world?*"

Then she voluntarily explained to Kiba the geographical plot and night beauty of the Dragon Land, just like a man with a horizontal scar explained to her. "*On the north, you can see sleeping dragons with fire breath. On the west, you can see a sleepless market like small light flies. On the east and south, you can see agricultural land and farmers guarding their lands against animals with their fire torches and spears."*

While Liya was explaining, her mind picturized her conversation with the smart guy she met in the same place and she wished to meet him once again. All of a sudden, she heard someone climbing the stairs. She turned around and rested her back on the rails of the terrace and kept her eyes on the entrance to the terrace. A real miracle happened! A well-built man entered the open terrace. With excitement, Liya's eyes graced his face, and a scar ran below from his left eye, then crossed a long nose and ended at the beginning of the right cheek. It was the same smart guy with a short haircut. After seeing him again, her pink lips gently expanded and a short, welcoming smile bloomed. The smart guy's emerald lens caught small pink lips and replied with a warm, charming smile on his face.

Kiba didn't recognize the guy standing behind his back. Now, Liya was not in this world, and she failed to listen to her favorite gusting winds. The smart guy's eyes were stuck on Liya's sharp eyes, and for him, her eyes looked like a fish. Their eyes locked on one another without any eyelash movements. The wind caressed Liya's hair and gave her a new hairstyle that made her more gorgeous. Moonlight poured her focus on Liya; she adjusted her hair, which was falling on her eyes and cheeks. Her black lens sparkled in the moonlight. Gusting wind touched her perfect curves and wished to touch once more. At the speed of the wind, her dangling clothes reflected her perfect curves to him. For Liya's eyes, he was perfect, more than attire; her inner heart prowled and whispered many things, but heavy stomps on the stairs disturbed their moments. This time, Kiba too noticed the sound and turned around. His eyes captured an unknown man with a scar standing behind him. Within a millisecond, a guard entered the veranda.

The Draguvan guard bowed and said, "*Sire, the leader has summoned you to his chamber.*" Kiba was unaware of what was going on around him.

The smart guy responded to the guard by nodding his head, but his lenses were stuck to Liya. He excused himself, "*Sorry. I need to catch up with the Lord of Dragon.*" He wished them on their new quest and he started to climb down the stairs.

Kiba noticed a short smile in Liya and asked with a weird look, "*Who is this man in a silk outfit?*"

Liya gave a shocking look at Kiba and said, "*Good question! Will find his name today.*"

She ran to the terrace entrance without a second thought. From there, she could see the smart guy going down. Without wasting a second, she voiced, "*Hey, wait!*" Her sparrow voice stopped the man in the silk outfit and he raised his head to check on Liya.

Liya asked, "*May I know who are you?*"

With a breath, he politely opened, "*I am Yuda from Dragon Land. I am the younger brother of Rizon and the second prince of the Draguva.*"

After hearing his name, Liya's lips poured a fantastic smile that no one had ever seen on her face before. Small movements in her petal-lips mumbled his name for the first time, "*Yuda!" and appreciated,"Thanks for the tea leaves and hot water.*" After hearing her thanks, he made a hand sign to acknowledge her thanks. He moved his legs to answer the summoning. Liya walked to Kiba to answer his questions.

While walking down the stairs, Yuda's heart was thinking about the beautiful woman he had met. His grain reminded her that she was not just beautiful but also skilled enough to slice heads off opponents. Along with a small smile, his heart was loud to him. "*She is a perfect match for you!*" However, his brain was practical. "*Liya is holding an important mission to take. She doesn't have time for this.*" All of a sudden, Yuda's heart sent an interruption. "*She is worth a wait!*" Yuda stopped all wavering thoughts and entered his father's chamber. The moment he entered, he noticed his big brother was also in the room. Yuda grabbed an apple from the fruit basket. With anger, he rasped at Rizon. "*It's late at night! Now you need to be with my sister-in-law.*" With a mouthful of apples, he reported to the summoning, "*Father!*"

The leader took a deep breath. "*Yuda! We called you here for an important mission.*"

Before he finished, Yuda recalled the news he heard about the attack of a goblin shark on the Draguvan sea and thought he was summoned to cut the head of the shark. The Lord of Dragon finished the sentence, "*We appoint you as a peace envoy for Draguvans.*" After hearing his words, Yuda's focus was turned to Rizon, and he munched the apple faster and louder. His father continued, "*In the upcoming days, you will work closely with peace messengers of Alaoka and Beku-neu.*" He was ordered to get ready for travel and adventure. The room was silent for a minute, and Rizon waited for him to finish the apple, and the munching was loud.

After Yuda finished the apple, Rizon patted his shoulders and voiced, "*Congrats, brother! Akello's stamina is at a whole new level! He is good at working on a fast strategy but has a bit of a cashew nut nature. Liya is a quick learner with knowledge of biological systems, and she is an insomniac and just a little like you and has a little attitude! We know you, Yuda! One similarity between all three of you is the nature of defying orders. We think you are the right fit for the team to be a backup and protect both of them. This is a headless team and you can help your team to win its mission. We are counting on you to get good credits for Draguva and our old man!*"

Rizon's words made Yuda think, "*Is it a punishment for defying orders?*" But he nodded his head with a happy smile! Beyond the new position and responsibilities, he is very excited to travel with Liya. Lord of Dragon was about to talk about Captain Shaw, but Rizon's eyeball stopped him. Rizon told Yuda, "*Brother, Captain Shaw of the Kallan crew is short-tempered, arrogant, and heartless. Beyond all, he has great knowledge to sail in a rough ocean, so handle him with care like we handle our maternal grandma.*" Yuda recalled the old memories and wore a smile on his lips and Rizon replied to him back with a grin. With happiness and excitement, Yuda started to walk out and Rizon asked Yuda to introduce himself to the team. After Yuda left, the Lord of Dragon yelled at Rizon, "*Did you see any seriousness in his face? Even he didn't ask any questions about the mission; I am cursed to have your brother and his fucking brainless dragon!*"

Dragon Prince's heart was filled with excitement and he decided to meet Liya again in the tower. With great strides, he reached the tower top to meet Liya and his new Beku-neun friend, but he could find only one. A gentle breeze pronounced her name as Liya. Prince inhaled moist air to calm down his rasping heart. He walked like a cat to stand next to Liya, looking at her and he bubbled, "*The world is too beautiful. Two eyes are not enough to sense her wonders.*" With the surprise of hearing the same new voice again, Liya turned her head. Her eyes smiled and sparkled to see him again. Yuda enquired about Kiba and asked for a pardon, saying that he couldn't introduce himself to Kiba. With a quirky face she replied, "*Probably, he would be snoring by now.*" Both of them bloomed in laughter. Yuda's emerald eyes found she was prettier when she laughed and he checked a small dimple on her left cheek.

Yuda trilled, "*I am an insomniac. I used to get short sleep, so I spend alone time here in the beauty of the dragon city.*"

Liya rejoiced, "*I am an insomniac too.*"

Yuda praised, "*Oh great, finally, I got company for late-night talks and midnight crunch.*"

Liya's sparrow tone changed to melancholy. "*I am leaving Dragon Land after two suns. If I am alive, I will be glad to meet you again.*"

Yuda giggled, and it made her confused. "*Hey, Liya. Don't worry! I will be on the Kallan ship to disturb you and will give you company on sleepless nights.*" Liya was curious to hear, but Yuda was not done yet. He opened, "*I am appointed as a messenger of peace for Draguva.*" He kept his hands on his chest and began, "*My main mission is to back up you and Akello.*" At the same time, his heart made a silent self-promise. "I will never let you die!" After hearing him, Liya's face glowed in joy, and she welcomed him to the team, and internally, every part of her body was dancing. Flying cotton balls understood her happiness. As a gesture, it started to drizzle. The night was beautiful for young hearts, inhaling the freshness of the rain and discussing the mission and the odds that they heard so far. In the devil's hour, after crossing the rough ocean, Shaw's ship arrived at the coast of Draguva.

The next morning, when the sun brightened the leaves, Akello's doors were knocked on by Liya and Kiba. After thundering through the door, Akello's snore dimmed and doors were opened by his lazy eyes. The moment the door opened, both barged in. Liya was delighted with the excitement. "*Yuda was appointed as the peace envoy for the Draguva.*"

Akello paused her and asked, "*Who is Yuda?*" She briefed about Yuda.

Kiba interpreted her and said to Akello, "*The captain of the Kallan ship had arrived on the shores.*" With a pensive face, he added, "*He did not get a chance to meet him.*"

Akello raised his hand for a lazy break and mewed, "*Well, each of you was working while I was asleep.*"

With red on her face and a knife in her eyes, Liya fumed, "*Alaokan! Luxury is over. Prepare yourself for the sail.*" She walked out and left a smash on the door.

Akello and Kiba exchanged a look, and at that very moment, Akello voiced, "*My stomach is growling.*" He asked Kiba to accompany him for breakfast.

The meeting between the blaze and gale happened in the dining hall. Akello and Yuda were happy to introduce each other with warm smiles. Yuda was taller and a little wider than Akello, and Kiba was the shortest of all three. After loading their bellies, Yuda invited them to the armory! With giggles and laughter, they ambled into the armory. It was a long, wide chamber; swords, spears, arrows, daggers and bows were stacked hugely in number. Kiba's mouth opened wide, "*Wow...*" Most of the weapons were crafted out of bronze and steel. A touch of the sun's rays emitted a golden reflection from shields and swords. All three of them made different stops at their favorite choice of weapon. Kiba's lighting fingers lifted the arrows and started examining them. When he gently caressed the steel top of the arrow, his face was grief-stricken. He is an expert in arrows and skilled enough to find the speed and impact of the arrow by checking the weight and quality of the steel. He is a predator hunter, and the arrows used by Bekuneuns were crafted well enough to handle the force of icy winds and dealt more damage. It's an unwritten fact that Bekuneu's engineering and weapons are the best in the world. Yuda took a double-handed sword of his choice and Akello's hand ran over the spear; it was sharp enough to pierce through flesh and bone.

When Kiba's coal eyes were stuck on the bow, Liya walked into the chamber. She smelled the metallic-garlic odor of steel and bronze, it was mesmerizing and made her nostril deeply inhale the odor twice. But none of them noticed her. She was surprised to see all three of them in the armory. She was at the top of her lungs. "*Kiba, Yuda, and Akello!*" The echoes in the armory pulled the attention of the guys. The man in the silk outfit wore his best smile on his lips for Liya. After hours of selecting their weapon, all four of them took the help of horses to reach the deck of Kallan.

Liya was still wondering why Azog had sent Kiba along with the crew. All five of them walked to the anchors of Kallan to meet the captain, but the crew mentioned that no one had seen him since morning and whispered that the captain was a boozehound. The crew noted that he boarded the ship with his pet chimpanzee and hound. With the disappointment of not meeting a captain, peace envoys and Kiba walked out. In the late evening, when others were packing their bags, Liya walked to meet Ishiri to gather the necessary medical supplies for the journey. The medical minister gave the aspirin portions, energy revival portions and also a small container of the ointment made of aloe vera and herbs like yarrow and goldenrod with a note, "*Small pinch is enough to heal the bloody wound.*" Medics of Ishiri's team guided Liya in explaining the rare roots and instructed her on when and how to use them. When Liya was in the medical chamber, she heard the sound of boots approaching the medics. In a minute, a tall man, along with 10 members of the Kallan crew, walked in.

A tall man in the cotton outfit was in his mid-thirties. His electro-blue eyes were bagged, and from his beard, the strong odor of ale escaped. He wore a crocodile leather jacket and looked like a muscled hunk. The odor of ale made everyone in the hall rub their nostrils. The minister of medicine excused Liya and walked to the tall man. The tall man, with an almond skin tone, introduced himself as 'Captain Shaw of Kallan crew.' He asked for 6 kg of Fas powder and 50 dozen of tender coconut to board the ship. Liya has never seen him in Beku-neu before, but her subconscious recalled him once in the old Beku-neun tavern. The official gave his approval for tender coconuts but for Fas powder, he enquired for an explanation from Capitan about the use of it. Shaw's eyes went shorter. He was not interested in answering Ishiri's question. He walked near the official. Ishiri rubbed his nose because of the foul smell. Shaw opened, "*I have no good reason to answer you, wiener. I am answerable only to your leader and he had given me enough permission to take the drugs and enough rum from the repository.*" The captain was rude. Liya sensed fuming arrogance from his dark lips. After hearing from him, Ishiri asked his subordinates to hand over the necessary supplies to the crew.

Shaw adjusted his wavy hair and wore a grin on his dark lips and ordered, "*Lads! Load the supplies in the ship,*" and ambled out. Liya sensed that if Akello had been here, it would have gone differently. She didn't want to mess with Captain Shaw at the first meeting. After satisfying the needs of Shaw, the official walked back to Liya. She feared that Shaw's behavior could break the peace. She apologized on behalf of the fellow Beku-neun captain. Ishiri accepted her apology with a smile and gave her a bag full of roots and leaves. In addition to drugs, he gave a bunch of palm leaves as a gift. Palm leaves have details of 'how to find the rare leaves and use them as medicine.' With the wishes of Ishiri, she was on cloud nine to receive such a precious gift.

The day before the sail, Rizon sent his best men to help the Kallan crew but soon soldiers came back to him with a message, "*Captain Shaw and the best men of the crew loaded their harpoons and went shark hunting.*" After hearing Rizon's face become dull, he was worried and muttered, "*The behavior of the captain was worse than I thought. Definitely, it is going to be a huge drag for Yuda and he thought Captain Shaw came on the journey to test Yuda's patience.*" It was a fine evening. The sunset gave color to the marble floors of the tower. Rizon received a message from Kallan's ship with a gift. It was a 700 kg goblin shark, and the message from Captain Shaw made Rizon laugh. "*Kallan ship is ready for the sail and the crew killed the great goblin shark, which was threatening the sailors and fishermen in the bay of dragons.*" Rizon strode down to check on the hunted shark. After seeing the blood wounds from harpoons on the shark's body, he was puzzled because it was hard to defeat such a huge shark with four harpoons shots.

When Rizon was puzzled by the shank wounds, the door of the chamber was knocked on by Yuda, and he entered the room. Kirana and Rizon welcomed him with a smile. Kirana is Rizon's wife. Currently, her big belly is the home of Rizon's brat, and they are expecting the little one soon. Everyone in the family expects the baby to be a boy, but uncle Yuda wants a girl out of Kirana's belly. The purpose of Yuda's visit was to see his sister-in-law before he leaves for the mission tomorrow.

Yuda complained to Kirana, "*Sorry! I have to leave for the mission, and your husband takes all the credit for sending me to the mission now.*" Laughter bloomed and Rizon scratched his head and wore a big smile on his face. Both Rizon and Kirana love Yuda, and his new mission concerns Kirana a lot. Kirana asked him to never let his guard down and wished him a safe return.

Yuda never forgets to leave a message for his niece. He tells her, "*Uncle Yuda loves her more and will bring a gift for her.*" Kirana nodded her head and promised that she would convey it to her baby.

Rizon walked him to the big balcony in the chamber. The darkness started to crawl through the sky. He warned him and recalled the strength of the commander of Zion's army that he led to Yuvalle. The discussion was long; it was dark outside, and the moon was totally blindfolded by clouds.

At last, Rizon gave a farewell to his brother. "*Be careful, brother! You are more important to us than the success of the mission.*" No one knows what kind of future is waiting for Yuda in the north-east and maybe this could be his last mission too, but his attitude of seeing the problem is hack and slash. Discussions with Rizon and thoughts of Liya over Yuvalle made him curious. With a wild grin on his lips, he decided to uncover the mysteries of Yuvalle.

Somewhere in Yuvalle

In the dark night, along with the howls of owls and wolves, music and laughter in the deep woods attracted the moon. In between the woods, there was a beautiful, lush green village and the biggest hut of the village was located at the center. The hut's doors were busy and a mesmerizing ale odor from the hut declared it the best happening place in town. Fog-covered walkways and crop-free farming land conveyed that winter had just begun in the Yuvalle. As a standing-proof celebration, the sound of partying people escaped the chimneys of the pothouse. In the devil's hour, a tall young man with a hood opened the doors of the pothouse and his foot was staggered and swinging a little. The fog-covered pavement and chilliness in nature ruffled his skin and soon lips vibrated, but he was not empty-handed. He sipped the mead and continued his steps, then he entered the streets of tall doors as its name indicates the doors were double taller than normal. A man in a hood caught a glimpse of the full moon in his bagged eyes. His eyes were not gentle, vengeance rolled out the tears, and his dark lips wore an evil grin. While he was staring at the full moon, his height started to melt down. His flat stomach became bubbly, and his facial hair started to grow wild. He turned himself into an ugly dwarf. Most of his body was covered with gray and black hair. On his way, on the streets of tall doors, the sound of snoring was loud at every door that he crossed. All of a sudden, he sneaked into a house. He was just a quarter the size of a door. He checked the hallway and entered the chamber. There were neither jewels nor art, but a 3-feet tall baby was sleeping with tight fingers. It was a baby girl. She was chubby and cute like a fur ball. She has wide ears, tiny fur covered all over the body, and a grip of the fingers confirming she will become a fine warrior in the future. While the ugly dwarf was staring at the cutie pie, all of a sudden, the baby sneezed on his long nose and a little pop of his tusk reflected the light of the moon.

"*Yes! It's a mammoth calf with hands and strong legs along with straight standing spinal cords.*" There was a shock and panic on the dwarf's face and sweat rushed because of the baby's sudden sneeze. But in the snoring of papa and mama mammoths next door, the sneezing sound of the baby ran out. The dwarf decided not to delay a minute, and partially, clouds started to cover the moon. He took out a butcher knife from the bag he carried. His palms started to get wet in sweat, but the nerves in his eyes were deep red. With vengeance, he started to stab the cutie pie brutally with the devil's grin.

With a wild blood rush, a man opened his wide eyes and, aroused from the bed, took a deep breath and wiped the sweat. His eyes were filled with fear, and he stared at the moon and banged his head on the walls. *"I have no cure for this curse!"*

Chapter 7

Between the Shark's Fangs

When the sun slowly rose over the horizon little by little, the song of seagulls reached the ears. Golden rays of rising fireball graced the lion figurehead, red deck and herculean ram of the Kallan. The ram of the ship is like a chest; the stronger ram has a big chance of winning the naval battles. Melodies of the seagull were trashed by the metal-crashing voice of Shaw, "*Rise the anchors and open the sails*." In a few minutes, the ram of the Kallan ship cuts the waves at the speed of the wind and ascends into the ocean. Soon, the wide shores of Draguva started disappearing from the eyes of Kallan. Kallan is not just a ship; it carries the hopes of millions. On the ship, everyone was submerged in their own dreams and thoughts.

Akello was determined about the mission and excited about the new quest. Liya's ears delighted with the music of waves and seagulls. Kiba took his place in the navigation bucket and kept his bull's eyes on the blues. Yuda was still focused in the direction of Draguva and the gentle breeze and first light gave him a warm hug. Captain Shaw was the coolest man on the ship by inhaling the freshness of the air; he raised his rum-filled coconut shell bottle to say cheers to the sun and his other hand was busy directing the vessel. When the sun was naked, Shaw ordered full sail and let the ship run freely in wide blue. Most of the crew were worried about working under a crazy, weird captain.

Ears hit the news from the sailor that the captain called everyone on the ship for a meeting. Liya ambled out of her room and waited for the guys to join the top deck. Kallan is big, with three stores and quarters allocated for heroes in the middle deck.

After a moment, Liya heard Akello's voice and others from the cooking chamber. The guys walked out from the cooking bay of the ship with a handful of eatables. After seeing Liya, Akello said, "*You missed the barbecue salmon. It was Yippee!*"

Yuda commented, "*Salmon is well-cooked with enough pepper and salt, which made it an awesome breakfast. You should have come with us. The taste of the fresh fish made me go for a second fish.*"

Liya's face became dull, and she opened, "*Yes, I could have joined you if either one of you called me.*" She started walking to the top deck.

Akello's coal-black eyes caught the emerald eyes of Yuda; in unison both belated, "*I thought you would have called her.*"

After ambling for a few steps, Liya turned back and exhaled. "*Guys, how long do I need to wait?*" Then all three strode to the deck and joined Kiba.

Each and every member of the crew was assembled on the top deck. The door below the steering area is the captain's chamber. When the chamber opened, Shaw came out wearing a cotton outfit and held a sword on his hip side and two daggers placed on either side of the shoe and had a tight grip on a rum bottle. He climbed up to the steering area to see every face in the crew. He addressed the crew with full energy and introduced himself, "*I am Captain Shaw and in charge of your journey to the north-east and savior of your life in the vast salt chunk. Indirectly, I am responsible for the mission's success as well.*" With a pause, he opened, "*I want each of you to put trust in me, a blind trust! Ha...ha...to survive the storm and pirates, follow my instructions without a second thought.*"

He introduced sub-captain Tandoor to the crew. In Shaw's absence, Tandoor will be a legal person to touch wheels. Suddenly, everyone in the crew was shocked and whispers started eating the ears. Tandoor was his pet chimpanzee. After the captain addressed the crew, there was murmuring. He sipped a few ounces of rum and walked down to his chamber, but before bashing the chamber doors, he opened, "*Ocean, you are watching now may look calm and easy, but remember, she never shows mercy.*" His words and the wheels in the monkey's hands frightened the crew. Akello felt his words were filled with attitude and Yuda recalled the Rizon words about Shaw. This time, Liya was not a silent listener. Liya decided to walk into the captain's chamber and question him. But Yuda stopped and convinced her, "*Wait! Let's give time for ourselves to understand him and his ways.*" By seeing Akello, he added, "*Keep calm! At least for seven suns!*" While walking back to their rooms, Akello saw a hound fall asleep in the corner of the top deck. He walked to the hound and gently ruffled the dog's head. The hound woke up, stretched his muscles, and walked into the captain's chamber. Everyone caught each other's eyes and continued on their way.

After filling the tummy in the moon's silver rays, crews flooded the deck to enjoy a scenic view of the ocean. Along with the music of the waves, Yuda took out his pan flute of seven pipes and started playing pleasant music. Music not only was a feast for the ears but also eased everyone's heart. Shaw peeped his head out to check who was the composer of the music. When all the heroes were standing on the rails of the top deck, Yuda questioned Kiba, "*What have you noticed from the navigation bucket?*"

Kiba puzzled, "*I can see two types of woods were used to build the Kallan ship. In the light of the sun, I observed both red and brown wood on the deck.*" Since Akello is an Alaokan and a great Kallan belongs to Alaoka, he asked Akello, "*Why are these variations on the wood?*"

Akello wore a grin on his lips before he blew their minds. Yuda commented, "*I heard about the ship from Rizon. Is that a myth?*"

With a grin again, Akello began, "*I used to hear about Kallan's ship as a bedtime story when I was young. Not just me, most Alaokan in my age group believed it's a myth, and I never imagined that I would travel on the same ship today.*"

He continued, "*Initially, the color of the ship was brown and the name Kallan means 'death.' Once it belonged to pirates. This ship was never defeated in the oceans until its sails touched the Alaokan sea. The redwood that Kiba noticed in the daylight was the blood strains of Alaokan troopers.*" After paying the heavy cost of 200 warriors and the loss of nine Alaokan vessels, commander Tibor captured Kallan 70 years back. In the recent coup in Alaoka, the legendary commander spared his last breath. Without rampaging Kallan, Alaokan captured it with minor damage, and there was a purpose behind it. This giant ship was made of 300 jackfruit trees, and I also heard that the bottom deck of the vessel was decorated with a lot of weapons and one of the rooms was filled with 100s of skulls. It looked like a graveyard.

Yuda added a supporting point, "*Maybe pirates do have a hobby of collecting skulls as a trophy.*"

After a moment of silence, Liya questioned, "*What is special about the jackfruit-wood?*" Akello explained, "*The jackfruit-wood was very strong and had a lot of fiber content. This wood absorbs the vibration, and ships made of this wood can't be easily turtled.*"

Kiba asked a valid question. "*It's been 70 years. Why do pirates show no interest in retrieving their jackfruit-wood ship back?*"

Akello scratched his head, and with hesitation, he agreed, "*I don't know! This ship was hidden inside some wonders of Alaoka and no Alaokan has seen this ship for the last 70 years.*"

Kiba smiled, and he loved the specialty of jackfruit-wood and its fruit. The fact is Kiba tasted jackfruit for the first time in his life, three days ago. On the same day, he tried mango and pineapple. He was delighted by the taste of tropical fruits.

All three of them were astonished to hear the history of Kallan. Liya opened, "*So, technically, we are sailing on a ship named death.*"

Yuda buzzed, "*Does this ship have ghost myths too?*"

The conversation went long. Giggles and laughter strengthened the new friendship. At a certain time, all three ambled to hug their beds, and Kiba reached for the navigation bucket. In the darkest of alone nights, Kallan's sail was set to half and Kiba was yawing big and wide. The sound of the wild call of whales hit Kiba's ears. His sleepy eyes were fear-stricken, and he stood up and checked the empty top deck. Kiba recalled the ghost stories that made him giggle before guard duty. Pulse calls (whale's cry) were intense, along with the snoring from the captain's chamber. All night, he was scared in fear! It took all night for him to figure out that it was a whale's cry.

The sun and the moon crossed the ship several times. It has been a week; their eyes got nothing but blue ocean and sky. It's like a sandwich. Between the sky and ocean; Kallan is a loaded yummy cheese. Liya got tired of tapping her fingers and watching the sail change, so she started to run over the medical science of Draguva in the palm leaves. Yuda was in the process of understanding Liya. The nights were, as usual, long for both insomniacs. Yuda was also interested in spending time with Akello and his crazy talks. At night, the crew sleeps to the music of the panpipe and the breeze. In the night sky, Shaw takes control of the wheels. He enjoys the nightfall and stars along with a kick of rum. Kiba's bull eyes love the navigation bucket and he alerts the crew about rocks, whales and pirate ships. It's been one full moon, and the journey was smooth and the ocean was calm, but it did not last long. A few members of the crew have fallen sick. The medic examined the sick crew members and assisted them with medical support. The Head of the Medical core reported to the captain of the ship regarding the flu spreading on the ship. There was a sudden change in the captain's face. It was all he feared. Shaw asked the medics once again to confirm the disease's spread. Medics confirmed that it was 'Sefu' which was caused by the contamination of water and food. In his life, he has seen more seas, and he has also fought against black flags. He knows very well what to do next to stop the spread.

In the course of action, first, Shaw walked to the kitchen and mixed rum in proportion ¼ to the barrel's storage and water. The rum will act as an anti-agent to stop the contamination of water and kill other gems. He ordered medics to add more tender coconut to the diet of infected people. The captain announced the meeting and invited every crew member to the deck. The captain addressed the crew in a loud voice, "*The ocean started to show her real face. We need to fight hard to survive in the upcoming rough ocean.*" A member of the crew queried the captain. He asked, "A *Rough ocean?*" but the blue sky is clear. Except for Shaw and the lead medics, no one knew about the flu. Captain Shaw sipped the ounce and said, "*The storm is not the only threat in the ocean. I know you guys have heard that a few crew members have fallen sick. It was not a normal illness. It was Sefu.*" Many were not aware of 'Sefu,' but Yuda knew more about flu fears. Once the captured pirate was infected by 'Sefu,' it spread into the borders of Draguva and it drank the lives of many Draguvans. From that incident, Draguvans discarded the habit of keeping prisoners in their own shells.

Shaw boasted, "*I have taken the necessary steps to neutralize the spreading of Sefu; there will be small changes in the water taste. Accept it, and we need to compensate for the workload of those who have fallen sick.*" In a rough vocal, Shaw thundered, "*From today, no one gets free food in the crew.*" When he spoke out, his bagged vision marked messengers of peace.

The next moment, hot air exhaled from Akello's nostrils. Liya clutched Akello's wrist to leash his anger, and the eyes of the dragon rider made Akello stand down. Captain Shaw handover the scroll to the medics and the scroll contains the ancient method of treating flu. He asked them to follow the inscriptions. When ambled back to his chamber, he whistled to fetch his hound's attention. With a wagging tail, the hound crossed the crew and walked into his chamber.

Over the next few days, Liya worked with the medical team to aid the sick. At certain times, Yuda pushed himself to the navigation bucket to help Kiba from sitting in it all day. Akello joined the kitchen, and he handled the ladle and spatula better than others. He also joined Yuda and the other lads to work on sail changes; it was one of their bad days. They were working directly under the command of the sub-captain. Liya and Kiba trolled both, and the guys were not in a position to troll them back; they accepted their destiny and continued to do the same. Yuda's eyes noted one thing. Since he has prior experience in sails, he noted that Tandoor was handling the wheel like a pro, and he heartily praised his skills. All he had was one big question: how did Shaw train Tandoor?

When Yuda was wiping off the sweat, he turned around to check on the others. His lips wore a short giggle after seeing boiling Akello and Kiba. Yuda's memories nudged those sweaty golden days of his training. He recalled that Akello was mentored by Rizon. With an enthusiastic smile, Yuda opened, "*Hey Akello! Does the hot day make you recall your Draguvan combat training?*"

With a blue face, Akello beamed. "*I sweat hard! Sweat again and again!*" He fumed, "*You know what? Your brother tried to kill me in the hands of bloody monkeys, not once, but twice.*"

With a chuckle, Yuda rounded his eyes to show Akello that Tandoor was here.

After realizing the same, Akello banged his head on the palm and turned to check Tandoor on the wheels.

With a gutsy voice, Tandoor wailed a sad howl and kept an innocent look on.

Akello felt bad and was convinced. "*You are a good cutie pie, but they are not like you!*"

The deck was filled with quiet laughter.

That night was a miracle. Usually, Liya and Yuda were sleepless. But today, in the darkest hour of the nightfall, Akello ears were listening to the sound of waves and his eyes were grief-stricken to stare at Neo's feather and all his thoughts popped out his mother's face and memories of his friends. The success of the Draguvan mission and fame did not convince him. Missing home made his heart heavy like an anchor and his eyes became an ocean, but he never spilled down a drop. He pushed himself to the top deck for some fresh air. Slowly, the wind ruffled the ripple muscles, and his grief-stricken eyes found Kiba and Yuda enjoying the breeze of the ocean. The clattering sound of Akello's shoes attracted the deck. Both couldn't believe their eyes that Akello was on deck at devil hour, and Akello was seeing an empty deck for the very first time in his life. The company of cosmopolitan friends made his heart light like a breeze, and laughter decorated the deck. Kiba was curious and questioned, "*Monkeys and Draguvan combat training?*"

Yuda started with a proud smile, "*Draguvan combat training is one of the eight training stages that dragon riders must undergo. The purpose of the training is to increase the agility to evade and counter-attack the foeman!*"

Kiba's eyes widened more and remarked, "*Interesting!*"

Akello continued, "*Monkey challenge is one of three phases in it. It is an agility test! The mission starts at noon and ends at sundown! The task is to kidnap the baby monkey from the herd of 100s and evade monkeys and Draguvan traps till sundown!"*

After hearing it, Kiba took a deep breath. "*Crazy! I am lucky that I have not been selected as a peace envoy instead of Liya!"*

Akello rejoiced. "*Liya went through a different set of training, not the same!"*

Kiba got Yuda's face and commented, "*You, Draguvans, are insane!"*

Yuda laughed, scratching his head. He added, "*Such hard training is mandatory! These hard training sessions shape us to control the rage of fire-breathing dragons.*"

In the morning, heroes sweat hard in the blazing sun, and at nightfall, they relax and giggle under a million stars.

On a sunny day, everyone was busy with their routines. In the navigation bucket, Yuda took a sweat bath. He wiped out the sweat from his forehead with his hand and put back focus on the wide sea. When the sun was at the center, with the help of Beku-neun goggles, he caught sight of two pirate ships. Yuda used Goggle zoom-in to find intel on fleets. Armed pirates made him clear that they were waiting for a hunt. He also found one fleet with a coal-black flag and another with a blood-red flag. The red flag ship was wide like a Kallan and it carried more than 50 pirates with spears and halberds in their hands. All the weapons the pirates carried were short-range, but in the navigation bucket, Yuda noticed a man with a longbow and a man on the wheel wearing a sleeveless cotton shirt. He is fair and has a bow hanging on his back and his tightened belt is full of throwing-knives. The accompanying black flag fleet was 2\4 the size of Kallan and it was filled with 20 pirates. Along with cruel scavengers, there were three female captives on the top deck. The captain of the ship was bald and fatso. After seeing fatso's action, Yuda's atmosphere of eyes changed to blood-red. Bloody fat captain and his men were humiliating the tied captives with cruel hands and fat legs. The weapon strength of the fleet was that almost everyone on the crew was the owner of long-range weapons.

Dragon Prince rushed to the captain's chamber and his eyes were surprised to see the liquor collection of Shaw and barrels of liquor. He inhaled the deep smell of ale and whispered in the air, "*Is it a warehouse?*" Shaw was sitting on his luxury chair and his eyes were waiting for Yuda to see him. Shaw cleared his throat to get Yuda's attention, and it worked. Yuda opened: "*I caught sight of two pirate ships.*" He barked the intel he gained about the fleets. After hearing the intel from Yuda, as usual, Shaw purged out some rum and walked out of his chamber without losing his cool. His attitude was like, "*Oh! Puny pirates.*" Shaw graced the sky to check the weather and his chin downed to give an order. "*Reduce the sail to half and below.*" While the speed of the ship was reducing, he climbed the navigation pole to watch the scavenger fleet with his own drunken eyes. He walked down and ordered the crew to anchor the ship in the middle of the ocean and he trudged to his chamber without a word to Yuda. The sound of the drowning anchor rushed the heroes to the top deck. Finally, after a month of the journey, the anchor reached the bottom of the ocean once again.

The whistle of the captain hit the ears. It was not only for his hound but also for a crew member. A lad ran to Shaw, and he ran back at the same speed to howl the message of the Captain. Shaw summoned Kiba, Akello, and Yuda to his chamber. The guys stepped in after seeing exotic collections of rum and wine. Akello's eyes were excited. Captain Shaw gulped the rum and beamed, "*Best man of Alaoka, Beku-neu and Draguva! From our current location, the pirate fleet can't find us. Luckily, they don't have Beku-neun made goggles to find us and we are safe here!*"

Yuda choked, "*We can't let the captives die in the hands of merciless.*"

After hearing Yuda, Shaw roared, "*Axe goon! The ocean is not a place to show humanitarianism!*" He broke the pot. "*We have already entered the pirates' playground! I can't risk the lives of 80 lads for the sake of your mercy.*"

Usually, Akello's actions were similar to cashew nuts, but this time he was sensible and stood by Shaw. Akello's line of thinking was clear: the Kallan crew was not in a position to take down two pirate ships at once. He always loves to hit hard missions, but now he has stepped back. Surprise for Yuda to see silent Akello, either because he felt boneless without a griffin or because his prior experience with pirates made him wise. Kiba was silent like a rock and his eyes toggled between the speakers. Shaw told Kiba to take a position in the navigation bucket and asked him to report if there was a change in the direction of pirate ships. As a precaution, he ordered Yuda and Akello to flood archers and pikemen on the top deck. To execute the orders, musketeers ambled out from the ale warehouse of Shaw.

In the course of action, the top deck was lit up with a war torch. The archers and pikemen separated into two and created a pavement in the middle. Yuda and Akello were in the position to lead the brigade, but the fact was that both of them were individual brigades. Kiba's bull eyes noted every action of pirate fleets and at a certain point, he lost his cool after seeing the humiliation of captives. The ship was on high alert. The flu started to drill the ship, and the bottom deck became a medical hall. Liya and the medics were treating the sick. The scrolls of Shaw and Liya's palm leaves were still holding the life of many. Liya's presence is much needed on the bottom deck there; she was not invited to combat. Akello said that the boozehound captain was correct. "*Ocean is merciless.*" Around the evening before the sun went to bed, Shaw stepped out to check arrangements. After a gulp of rum, he inhaled the air and sensed the change, but it was not about an ale whiff to fresh air. He sensed moisture in the air. He suspected the change of wind may bring misfortune and fear of cyclones occupying his face. A man from the kitchen ran to Shaw and added, "*We may run out of fresh water in a week or two.*" From the bottom deck, a medic rushed to inform the first casualty. After hearing the news, everyone's face was grief-stricken. Shaw gazed at the sky and took a large sip. He ordered medics to preserve the corpse of the fallen in the coffin. Hard times started in the lion figurehead ship. Crew strength started going down and on the north pirate fleets were anchored and from the east, the cyclone may hunt Kallan in a couple of days.

The sun started to set down by letting out its reddish-yellow light. Kiba rushed to the captain's chamber to report. He was amazed to see the captain in the new look. Shaw used his knife very well. He chopped down his messy chocolate color hair in half and shaved his overgrown beard that expelled his cleft chin. Now, Shaw was a handsome man and his age reduced in new looks. To the handsome captain, Kiba reported that the red flag pirate ship had started to sail in the direction of the north. He also mentioned that a large fleet opted for full sail. Only Shaw's look was changed, but not his character. Again, he purged the rum and kept the ears at Kiba. Kiba continued that the medium-sized ship has no backup to support it, and he confirmed the black flag fleet's anchor was not pulled out. Kiba's anger made him bark about all the humiliation he witnessed and describe more about a pirate captain. With a slow kick of rum, Shaw became a good listener. Kiba quoted the pirate captain as a 'psychopath' and added, "*Fatso was a master of humiliation. He brutally made cuts on the foreskin of a captive to bleed and downed the captive alive as food for sharks.*" His crew is evil too and Kiba exclaimed, "*Fatso captain needed to be punished for his actions.*" Finally, Shaw asked for weapon information on the foe ship. Kiba voiced all the intel he visualized. After hearing him, Shaw wore an evil smile and asked Kiba to get Akello and Yuda to his cabin. From his evil smile, one thing was clear. Shaw prepared for some kind of fun.

All three musketeers were summoned in front of the captain. Whispers circled about Shaw's new look. Captain Shaw opened, "*Black flagship has no backup!*" He continued that the pirate crew has sent one of the captives to the gates of heaven and Kiba wants to punish the fatso captain for his actions. After hearing Shaw, the eyes of heroes sparked hope. Akello started, "*Our archers and pikemen are ready to taste the blood of the bastards. We have decent numbers to triumph over the medium size pirate ship.*" Yuda and Kiba nodded their heads in support of Akello's plan.

Captain Shaw moved his forefinger to his chin and questioned, "*What about the collateral damage?" He also revealed the brutal truth, "In case, our fleet faced damage in combat that will reduce the speed of the sail and our next enemy, neither human nor animal, but the chaos in the ocean.*"

Kiba was not silent this time. He wailed, "*Captain, do you mean the cyclone?*" He quizzed, "*But the sky is clear?*"

After a sound gulp, Shaw opened, "*In the air, I can sense moisture and clouds from the east may reach us in two days or fewer.*" He also disclosed his strong decision, "*I didn't want to take any chances with Kallan.*" After hearing Shaw, all the heroes were confused. "*Then, why the heck the boozehound captain summoned us?*"

Unpredictable Captain Shaw broke the silence, "*Yuda! The rider of the brown dragon and prince of brave Draguvans, Akello! You have earned the title The Dragon Bleeder, along with your griffin. I also heard the rumor that you both were trained in the hands of The Legendary Rizon. Kiba, you carry the lineage of Commander Bora! I have heard stories of your valor and Bekuneu calls you The Nightmare of Yetis.*"

He added, "*Among the three, no one is ordinary. I never expected you guys to need my fleet and crew to triumph against 29 pirates and their fatso captain. You really made me doubt your skills. I am the captain of the Kallan. This fleet will never be involved in this battle. It's your call to show mercy to captives or let them die and dismissed the musketeers.*"

The new look not only made Shaw handsome but also called out a devil in him. The meaning of his evil smile was that he wanted to test the skills of musketeers.

There was no sign of a cyclone; it was a bright day, and at nightfall slowly covered the sky and stars started to decorate the sky. Before dinner time, three pillars knocked on the doors of Shaw. More than mercy to captives, all their hearts were on fire to get back their pride by triumphing against the pirates. Shaw expected their comeback. After all, he lit the fire. Yuda began, "*We came up with the strategy to take down the pirates. Visual appearance on the object always brings confidence or fear in our minds.*" He explained their plan to Shaw. After hearing the strategy, he enjoyed the plan along with rum. Everyone's lips expressed an evil smile. Guys requested Liya's involvement in the slaying of pirates, but Shaw denied it. He wants Liya to look after the sick in intensive care. Captain walked the guys to the weapon repository which is located on the second deck of the ship. The repository looks awesome, with all short and wide-range weapons and all three selected wide-range weapons, longbows and quivers full of arrows and Cetratus shields to stop incoming arrows. Apart from long-range weapons, they carried a single-handed sword, but Akello carried a spear instead of a sword. The captain named the mission 'Slay the Fatso.' After some time, Kiba rushed to his allocated chamber. Under the cot, he took a cloth-wrapped bag. He uncovered the wrapper to load the silver top arrow of Beku-neu in his quiver.

The guys suited up their armor, and as per the plan, a rowboat was ready to deploy, and it was filled with wheat and rice bags. Yuda decided to meet Liya before leaving for the mission. So, he walked with the suited armor to meet Liya in the intensive care unit. When he reached the bottom floor, it looked long-winded because of the serious spread of the flu. Yuda's eyes rolled to find Liya in the crowd. Finally, his eyes caught sight of Liya; she was busy treating the sick with her head facing down. He could not see her full face. Yuda decided to walk for the mission without meeting her, but he waited until she lifted up her beautiful face. Yuda's wait ended soon. His eyes graced the moonlight on Liya's face and his lips made a pleasant smile to express the joy in the inner heart. With smile-loaded lips, he walked out to the mission with positive vibes. The moment Yuda left the place, Liya's senses made her eyes check the place where Yuda was standing, but her eyes couldn't find anyone in that place. So, she continued her work without distracting herself. Yuda walked to the captain's room to meet others. All three were assembled in the captain's chamber and all of them wore a bronze armor suit, but Yuda wore black rough leather armor. The brigade of three stepped out to put an end to the merciless pirates.

The moon was bright, and a rowboat was rowing toward the pirate ship. After reaching the vantage point, mission 'Slay Fat So' phase one begins at 5,000 meters away from the pirate ship. Phase one was to attract prey and deploy confidence in the prey's mind. In the rowboat, fire torches were lit to show the whereabouts of the rowboat to pirates, and the light from the torch brightened the bags of wheat and rice. To gain the attention of the pirate ship, Akello and Yuda planned a small skit. They talked about how they were going to cook the food and expressed how delicious in a loud tone! They bumped the coconut shell bottles in their hands and cheered. In the silvery, calm ocean, their voices reached the ears of pirates on the starboard. As expected, the pirate crew got attracted to the food supplies in the rowboat. News of the treasure was reported to the pirate captain. Hearing a message from the low-rank pirate, fatso walked to confirm the intel about the rowboat with his short-range goggles. The excited captain sang to his crew, "*Get ready for the night party.*" The pirate captain took control of the wheels. In the darkness, the pirate fleet slowly moved toward the vantage point. The cunning skits of the musketeers ended well in success.

Yuda noticed the pirate ship moving toward them and cheered the brigade, and he wore a radiant smile on his lips. As part of the plan, Yuda's radiant smile is a sign of the start of phase two. Kiba's act begins here. He noticed the pirate ship moving toward them and he evacuated the boat after a deep breath.

Next, Yuda took a deep breath and dived in. Before the dive, Akello placed the torch in the touch holders of the rowboat and dived into the ocean. He did it purposefully to show the location of the rowboat. Pirate eyes were on fire after finding the riders in the boat evacuated. The pirate ship's captain ordered the arrow shower. Arrows pierced the surface of the ocean and entered the water world. The force of the arrows was reduced and the direction of the arrow changed inside the water. Our heroes swam to the deep of the ocean to escape the arrow shower. Almost six pirates dived into the ocean to reach the treasure (food) boat. The water world doesn't care about who is reaching her. She has a kind heart to allow everyone in her territory, but only the strong will survive. The brigade of three executed phase three. Every bastard in the pirate ship was focused on the treasure boat. The brigade used this golden opportunity to infiltrate the pirate ship by climbing through the starboard (right side of the ship).

Brigades climbed hard and halted their weight on the grip of their iron hands by holding the gunwale. Kiba put his courage to play; he is the first to push him inside the enemy ship and used his cat paws to climb to the navigation point without raising an alarm. In the excitement of treasure, the pirate crew let down their guard. Kiba decided to execute the Zap kill to eliminate the pirate in the navigation bucket; it is a perfect place from where he can free fire arrows in all directions. Zap killing is the method of taking down the foe by damaging vital organs. Kiba targeted the victim and attacked the throat at the very first level to disable the altering voice and executed the final blow by thrusting the dagger into the chest.

Blood flooded the bucket, and it slowly started dripping from the bucket. On the signal of Kiba, Akello moved to the rear side of the ship and infiltrated near the wheels. His bull eyes aimed the arrows at the fatso captain. Yuda entered the deck through the bow of the ship (front) and killed a pirate in the darkness. He moved to mid-ship and took cover behind the center pole. Still, pirates were cheering from left rails and bent their heads down to the sea. Yuda and the team took the position to pierce the skull of the pirates.

After a swim, pirates found they were fooled with sandbags. One of the pirates turned his head above to catch the eyes of the co-pirate in the navigation bucket. By that time, his mind recognized the man at the navigation point was dead. Kiba's arrow entered the eyes and pierced out the skull. All of a sudden, the entire pirate crew drew the attention of the intruders. Arrows released from the bows of Yuda and Akello drilled down the life of pirates into the underworld.

The speed of Akello's arrow killed the pirate and the force of it pushed the pirate into the ocean. Pirates too shot their arrows with bloodthirst. Many of their arrows rubbed the skin of musketeers and their armor. Kiba's arrows targeted whoever was charging at Yuda and allowed him to fight on his long sword. The exchange of arrows wet the deck in blood. In the next few minutes, Yuda was jarring his sword against the fatso captain. To save Yuda back and handle other pirates, Akello dropped his bow and rushed with his bloody spear. Akello was handling the three pirates at once; his spear was parrying their attacks. Unexpectedly, an arrow of a bull-eyed pirate pierced Kiba's arms, but he pulled out an arrow double quick.

Battle of Akello vs three pirates was rough and tough; he jumped a step behind and gave up his spear and decided to test the fistfight skills he acquired in Draguva. He evaded the swing of swords and spears and delivered a strong kick in the armpit of the pirate. The kick made the pirate lose the grip on the weapon and a rock punch on vital parts killed the pirate. He evaded the attacks of the remaining two and took them down with rock punches and log kicks. The fatso captain was twice as beefy as Akello encountered in the debut war.

Arrows fired at Yuda were stopped by Akello's Cetratus shields, but the shield was soon completely destroyed in the arrow shower. Pirates' arrows were triangle-shaped shark-teeth. The duel between Dragon Prince and the fatso captain was lighting up the sky. The sound of metal rubbing on one another rang in the ears. In the meantime, Kiba eliminated all the long-range units. Yuda's sword is not heavy enough to parry the fatso's axe. An unexpectedly powerful kick from the fatso pushed Yuda 15 meters away, and he fell on his back. The pirate captain was forwarding to finish Yuda. The arrows drawn from the quiver of Kiba and the spear of Akello disabled the elbows and legs of fatso, and he collapsed down. The moment the fat mountain fell down. There was a shake on the ship. The raging cries of the pirate captain hit the top deck of Kallan and broke the serenity of the night. Yuda was back on his feet and cursed Kiba and Akello for stealing the chance of good short-range combat.

Blood was dripping from Kiba's biceps, but he didn't care about it. After seeing the confidence and strength of Kiba, both Yuda and Akello were stunned. Pirates who jumped into the ocean are entered back into the ship via the bow (front of the ship) to die like real men. Yuda acquired the fallen axe of the pirate captain. He hacked and slashed all six of them in a flash of seconds. He walked with an axe to show mercy to the disabled captain. To rejoin, Kiba jumped down from the navigation point and landed on his knee. The moon was reflected in the deep red that spilled all over the deck. Akello and Kiba walked over the pierced heads and corpses of the pirates. Akello patched the bleeding on Kiba's biceps. The remaining was a three-man brigade with disabled fatso. Along with a gasp, the stubborn pirate captain was ready to accept his death with a mouthful of laughter. He also fumed, "*My fellow men will hunt you soon!*" The cold breeze of the ocean froze the spilled blood. After seeing the laughter on the bastard's face, Kiba's anger burst out and his mind recalled the humiliation executed by the pirate captain to the captive. Yuda stepped forward to finish, but after seeing Kiba's red eyes, he stepped down. Akello opened, "*He is not worthy of getting killed by the sword.*"

The pirate captain, painted in pain and with a gassy voice, checked, "*What do you call yourself?*"

Kiba replied to him, "*I am a reaper, and I came to humiliate and devour your life!*" After hearing Kiba, Fatso laughed hard. With anger in his eyes, Kiba kicked the pirate captain between the legs. In the pain of broken balls, fatso panted heavily. His cry broke the serenity of the ocean, and without delay, Kiba thrust his boot into the neck and stopped the pain of the captain. Along with the pain, his breath also stopped.

Kiba stayed on the top deck and released the fire arrow to announce the victory to the Kallan fleet. After freeing the captives on the top deck, Akello and Yuda walked down to the next lower deck to rescue the captives. They investigated every single room, but they couldn't find any captives. One of the doors was opened to the meeting hall. Rather than call it a meeting hall, it was a museum. The hall was decorated with hanging animal heads. The most recently stuffed head was a griffin head. Akello was angry enough to kill the captain once again in a different way. He yelled, "*Fucking trophies!*"

All stuffed heads indirectly refer to the pride of the fallen captain. Below the giant shark's jaw, the captain's name was engraved as Druso. The Kallan ship caught the signal and reached the pirate ship. Captain Shaw and crew reached the pirate ship with the help of ropes and hooked long ropes used to pull the fleet near Kallan. While Yuda was exploring, Akello and Kiba welcomed Shaw to the pirate fleet and showed what they had accomplished. In the middle of the blood-spilled deck, Shaw saw corpses and brutality. He was amazed to see the caliper of heroes but remained silent. He was also exceptional. Once all alone, he took down everyone on the pirate ship. Without a word, Akello, Kiba, and Shaw reached the bottom deck to support Yuda. All three and Shaw walked to the bottom deck in search of captives, and they found the captives as slaves in the prison. Fear of the captives increased after seeing the brigade, but in a few minutes, captives recognized they were in safe hands. Yuda and the crew checked the wellness of the captives.

While Yuda and crew were aiding the captives, Shaw walked to check the other chambers, and Akello and Kiba accompanied him. On the bottom deck, Shaw and his men found a treasure. It was two giant pots full of water. In the middle of the ocean, nothing is more precious than drinking water. Shaw is clever. By questioning the self-pride of heroes, he made them take down the pirate fleet, and he also found a resolution to the water crisis in the Kallan. They came across a big door; the outlook of the door confirmed it should be the captain's private chamber. Shaw kicked in the big doors and walked in. Suddenly, a woman in her late 20s delivered a powerful kick to his chest. Shaw lost his balance and reached the ground, and without applying force, she placed the tip of her sword gently on Shaw's neck. Kiba and Akello were stunned to see Shaw at knifepoint, and the woman standing in front of him was 5.8 feet tall. She had long black hair, but the heroes can see only her back poster. Shaw looked at her with a gasp, and his bagged blue eyes fixed on her hooded green eyes, and the kick he received classified her strength. In no time, she turned around to see the heads of men standing at the door. The next moment, a smile bloomed in Akello and Kiba noted the similar happiness on her wide lips and the anger in her eyes started to melt down. Smiles on both faces convey that they have known each other for a long time. She was a surprise package for Akello in the pirate fleet.

Akello rejoiced, "*Bitch, what are you doing here?*"

Kiba asked Akello, "*Who is this lady?*" He whispered in his ears, "*Dude, she knocked Shaw in with a single kick and arrested him at knifepoint.*"

Akello shook his head at Kiba and voiced, "Zaya." He asked Zaya to release Shaw and remarked, "*Shaw is the captain of our fleet anchored near. We uprooted every single pirate in the fleet.*"

Zaya dropped the sword, but still, Shaw's eyes didn't move from her. She grabbed the full-size rum mug from the table and finished it without a gasp. Gently, she took her place on a cotton mattress, and the silver light of the moon highlighted her silky body. Captain Shaw lost himself for a minute and started staring at her. His angry mind questioned, "*Who is this wild wind?*" After seeing her, Kiba thought, "*Competitor for Shaw has shown up.*" His eyes were marked at Shaw.

Zaya started to give her answer to Akello. "*Jackass! These black clowns took me as loot from the Draguvan ship that I was traveling.*" In Shaw's life, he has never heard of someone who called pirate as clowns. After hearing her attitude, Kiba and Shaw turned to Akello and asked in unison, "*What is she?*"

Akello revealed, "She was a Beku-neun spy who helped us in Draguva." Akello's words made Shaw understand that *she was not a wild wind but a hurricane.* She looked tired. The moonlight not only highlighted her beauty but also the wound on her left arm. Akello opened, "*We need to take her to the Kallan fleet for first aid.*"

Before walking out, Zaya winked her eyes and suggested, "*Guys! While disposing of the corpse, don't forget to take care of the wardrobe.*"

Kiba and Shaw rushed to the wardrobe. When they opened the doors, three dead pirates reached the ground. The lesions on the grounded corpse were perfect. She hunted like a lioness, and all her attacks were targeted at vital parts. Captain Shaw was attracted to Zaya by her actions. He turned his head to catch Zaya. She winked her eyes at him and walked to the Kallan ship with Akello. Shaw smiled back and remarked, "*She is not an ordinary woman but a perfectionist.*"

Shaw ordered the crew to loot all valuable things from the pirate ship. The rescued captives were taken to Kallan Medical Support. The musketeers and crew gathered all the dead bodies on the top deck. After looting all valuable resources from the ship, crew members of the Kallan ship evacuated the private ship. The powerful pirate crew defeated the glimpse of the moon, and the next dawn sunlight pierced the mist to check the pirate ship. The sun was shocked by a pile of corpses and eagles started rounding the pirate ship for morning breakfast. From the massive Kallan, Akello and Kiba aimed the fire arrows at the corpse. Bullseye warriors pyre the pirate ship with fire arrows. One brave eagle directed himself into the burning ship. When it escaped from the blaze; the bird's harpoon beak was not empty. It carried the ring finger of a pirate for breakfast. The fire started to spread all over the ship and smoke covered the sky with black clouds.

The celebration begins with the Kallan crew. Except for the medics, everyone enjoyed the old rum looted from the pirate fleet. The crew's loud excitement and victory cheers broke the serenity of the ocean, and the crew praised the three musketeers for their triumph against the pirates. In the evening, Shaw's thoughts were running through his first meeting with Zaya. His closed eyes recalled the courage in her hooded green eyes. A man walked to the captain's chamber to disturb his mood and barked a report of loot from the pirate vessel. After hearing the report, Shaw wore a grin because the Kallan fleet had enough fresh water and food to face the strong tides. Although the fleet was preparing for the cyclone, there were no clues in the sky about the arrival of the storm. Lad, who was reporting to Shaw, also gave him a unique pearl necklace. The necklace looked great with a big pearl in the center, and either side of the string was decorated with medium- and small-sized pearls. Shaw questioned, "*The pearl necklace?*"

Lad opened, "*The necklace was looted from the pirate's wardrobe.*" The reflection of pearls attracted Shaw, and he accepted the gift with great pleasure and decided to sell the necklace in exchange for expensive rum. At last, the lad reported that they had also looted eight turtles and cheered, "*Sire! At noon, we will have an exotic dinner!*" Until that very moment, Shaw was cool. After the hearing, turtles were sent to the kitchen. His calm was broken, and he shouted, "*Fools! Killing the turtles will bring us bad luck.*" He ordered them to release the turtles into the sea immediately. He also strives to ensure turtles are safe. Later, he summoned the three musketeers to his chamber; he also noticed Akello's tongue was craving to taste his rum collection. He walked near his collection, grabbed three bottles of exotic rum and gifted each a bottle of rum as a prize for their bravery. Getting a present from Shaw was something that needed to be chiseled in rock. He is a devil who never expresses his feelings. Although he gave his rum collection as a present, he never praised their valor in words. Holding the rarest rum bottle in his hand put Akello on cloud nine. He also waited for Yuda to walk out. After Yuda left the hall, he requested everyone not to reveal that Zaya was a spy, and she helped him and Liya in Dragon Land because he was afraid that if Yuda came to know about Zaya, his anger would break out. After all, Yuda is the prince of Draguva. Spy is the phrase that boils the blood of Draguvans. So, Akello decided to comfort his friend with cool lies rather than hot truth.

Under the hood of moonlight, the Kallan was happy, and music from Yuda's panpipe made everyone's heart melt. Many enjoyed the presence of alcohol in their veins. Akello and Kiba were especially under the influence of the 100-year-old rum gifted by Shaw. Liya applied the ointment to Kiba's wounds that she got from Ishiri. When she was working, Yuda's music attracted Liya to the top deck. Her wide-open eyes caught Yuda sitting on the floor by leaning his back on the wooden rails. She walked near Yuda and sat beside him, but Yuda's eyes were closed while he was playing the melody. Rizon always complains to his dear brother, "*Yuda, you are always letting your guard down when you play the melody!*" After he joined the team Kallan, he downed his guard on his new friends and Liya. When Yuda opened his eyes, he was surprised to see Liya sitting next to him; she waited for him to complete his music. When she was with Yuda, her eyes became welcoming and sweet. More than words, their eyes had a better conversation. Yuda asked about the condition of the captives they had rescued from the pirate ship. A small sadness rounded on Liya's lips.

Liya said, "*Everyone is fine, but the wounds on Zaya's shoulders were infected by microbes.*" She also added, "*As you know, medics were overworked in treating the flu. To heal Zaya, we needed a special antiseptic and the lead medic asked me to cook it! At first, I hesitated, but the lead medic said, 'You are ready for it!' and convinced me.*"

After hearing Liya, Yuda wondered, "*Wow! We also got a medic in the team of peace envoys.*"

Liya blushed, and a small smile blossomed on her face.

Moments later, Liya grieved. "*When Akello took Zaya to the medical chamber, at first, I was at the top of my lungs to see her back, but after examining her wound, my smile was doomed.*"

Liya boasted, "*Zaya is the strongest woman that I have ever met in my life.*" She informed Zaya had consumed rum as a painkiller and faced her battle against bloody pirates.

Her words made Yuda thought, "*Like peace envoys, there were outlanders who exist with the same bravery that Draguvans poses.*" He thought that Zaya would be a comrade of Liya from Beku-neu and questioned, "*Is Zaya a yeti hunter?*"

To avoid unnecessary conflict, as Akello mentioned, she decided to hide Zaya's color. As an affirmation, she shook her head. With a pitiful face, she agonized, "*I never expected to see Zaya in this condition! Zaya is a wild lioness. When her paws heal, she will become unstoppable once again!*"

Yuda patted Liya's shoulders and consoled her with his positiveness and comforting facts.

Liya congratulated Yuda,"*I am happy about your victory. When I was treating Kiba's minor wounds, he explained the 'Mission slay fatso.' I am disappointed at not being part of the mission and worried about spiking casualties of Sefu.*" Yuda complimented Liya, "*You are doing a great job. Saving a life is not easy, like killing one.*" She wore a short smile on the corner of her lips. As usual, his words comforted her. She bubbled to Yuda, "*Your words comfort me and fill my heart with joy.*" Yuda made a short smile as a reply again.

After a long talk under the moonlight, without Liya's knowledge, she fell asleep on Yuda's shoulders. Yuda's heart danced in joy. His eyes were locked on Liya's small lips. In the beauty of Liya, he became a poet and his heart didn't have words to explain the beautiful moment. After seeing her chubby cheeks, his heart crawled to plant a kiss on her moon cheeks, but his mind knew that was not right. He controlled his feelings and wore a great smile on his lips; it was an everlasting smile. Whenever his lips tried to shut the showing teeth, the joy in his heart expanded to the lips. After some time, his happy heart decided to take some rest by resting his head on the rails and he fell asleep. These hours of darkness that Yuda loves to recreate every nightfall. From the navigation point, Kiba's eyes got to the scene of Liya's head on Yuda's shoulder, and he was happy to see Liya. Kiba sipped a bottle of old rum and directed his focus on the wide oceans, and the same Akello's boozed-kicked brain made him overthink the prophecy. "*Glaze and blaze! Sails the streams of hell! But the gale will halt and blow again!*" The kick of rum created illusions of the corpse of Yuda and Liya in Pyre, and soon, he lost consciousness.

The wind breathed gently, and the sun was not up, but Liya's sleep was disturbed. When she opened her eyes, she found her head leaning on Yuda's shoulder. Their fingers were clutched tight. Her sweet eyes graced the face of a sleeping Yuda and she found a kid in him. After seeing him, her lips lost control and started showing all her teeth. Liya whispered to her heart, "*Whenever I think about my future with Yuda, my lips automatically smile.*" At this moment, Liya wants to lean on Yuda's shoulder for some more time, but her bladder can't hold much longer, so she cursed her bladder and undid their clutched fingers. When she loosened her hands, she could feel the shivering in Yuda's frame. Thus, she walked to her chamber and got her blankets for him. Blanket gave warmth to Yuda and Liya walked out with a half-mind.

The following day, when rays of the sun brightened the ship, Yuda opened his vision to see Liya. The disappointment hit his face that she was not there and his shape was wrapped in a blanket. He raised his frame to check the sun; he noticed partially scattered clouds started to assemble one after another and his nose could sense moisture in the air. Without a second thought, he murmured, "*Captain Shaw was correct. Before sunset, Kallan will sail in the gray.*" The wheels of the giant Kållan were already in Shaw's hands. Not only Yuda but also other heroes noticed the gray shadow conquering the ocean. Soon, musketeers reached the top deck to face the dark face of the ocean.

Shaw gave instructions from the wheel. Kiba was in the top bucket to navigate. Yuda and Akello worked on changing the sail. By noon, Kallan was all alone in between the gray and the rain, starting with a mild drizzle, and Mr. Wind started to sneeze. In the rough wind, Yuda's hands acted like tusks in sail changes and it was not easy; sail changes exhausted the crew but not the hands of Yuda. Kiba caught sight of the formation of twisters around Kallan; his throat beamed, "*Merciless ocean!*" The cough and sneeze of the wind raised the high tides. The ship started to jump along with waves and the ocean became unfit to sail. Even in the chaos, Shaw's hands never let down the grip of rum, and the smile on his face made the crew go crazy. By the influence of the strong wind, the drizzle became pointed needles. The merciless ocean cast a spell of flu on Kallan. Many fell sick overnight. To tackle the drizzle needles, members on the top deck used jute hoodies. In the evening, the wild wind converted into a cyclone. Kiba's bull eyes were hard to navigate in the spinning rain, but still, he maintained his focus on the wide ocean. Yuda and Akello had a heavy gasp in pouring down because the sail change drained their stamina. With courage in bagged eyes, Shaw enjoyed the scene of sunset and muttered, "*Chaos in the ocean has just begun.*"

When the sun was setting down, the color of the ocean turned gray in the reflection of clouds. The sound of thunder boomed. The heads and eyes on the ship couldn't find a single seagull. Gently, rubbing clouds created thunderbolts. It surfaced in the ocean here and there. Captain Shaw predicted a heavy storm in the next couple of hours; he made the necessary arrangements on the ship to face the storm. During the naval battle, the strong hull of the ship decides the victory. During the storm, the ship's bow receives most of the damage from high tides. More than a ship captain, Shaw was an excellent ship builder too, and it was one of the reasons for selecting him as a captain. More than pirates, storms are the biggest threat to the fleet. The bow of the ship cuts the wind and waves to push the ship forward, but during the high time of the ocean, the bow was exposed to strong wind and wild tides.

In most storm seasons, either herculean tides break the bow of the fleet with their force or storm-tossed arrogant waves turtle the fleet (the ship falls upside down). In both cases, the vessel became helpless in the middle of the ocean and sailors became prey. Experienced Shaw was a survivor of a turtling ship and he has a plan to handle this special case of storm waves. His idea is very simple. He ordered the crew members to increase the weight of the ship's bow in all three stories, which will reduce the speed of the ship but gives a high chance to escape the turtling of the ship. Beyond all, Kallan was made of strong jackfruit-wood, and it serves its purpose, which stops the vibration created by feral tides. It's merely impossible to smash the bow of the Kallan ship. The crew executed Shaw's orders like a repeating parrot. Liya and the medic were hopeless; the deadly flu started eating the lives of the crew.

Shaw examined arrangements made to tackle the coughing ocean. After checking the arrangements, he walked to the medical hall to enquire about the status of the sickness. He listened to medics without interruption. Finally, he asked about Zaya's condition. When he walked to the kitchen, he tasted the burning fish and greeted the chef. Chief complained, "*Captain! One of the hostages who we have saved is draining our rum barrels.*" After hearing him, he wore a smile on his beardless face and he walked out. The cool captain handed over the wheels to Tandoor and decided to take a rest before the storm. Yuda believed in the strong hands of a chimpanzee. The entire crew worked under the command of Tandoor, but this time, there was no trolling, and in their eyes, courage was reflected.

Clouds rubbed one another and blue thunderbolts grounded the sea. The ears on the top deck were tired of hearing thunderclaps and wheezing winds. Kiba has collected many stories on this voyage to tell his niece. In the long distance, Kiba's eyes sensed the danger, and he downed his goggles. His face was decorated with fear. He jumped down from the navigation point and ran fast into the captain's chamber. The sound of Shaw's snoring "*Kho...kho...*" rang in his ears. He called out "*Captain...captain*" in a loud tone to wake him up. After hearing the panicked voice, the captain's bagged eyes opened, and he erected his shape to listen to Kiba. When Kiba saw Shaw's topless body, his eyes were popping out to see a dozen more scars on Shaw's rippled frame. Kiba's eyes were locked on the bigger scar and his words failed to escape his throat. Shaw noticed the thunderstruck in Kiba, so he cleared his throat to draw his attention. The next moment, Kiba marked at the captain and he howled about the danger his eyes found. "*There are two big pirate ships coming toward us. If my calculations were correct, two big ships will meet Kallan in the darkest hour.*" He was not done yet; he also barked, "*With their weapons and manpower, they can take us down before sunrise.*" After hearing the news, Captain Shaw's reaction was cool, which Kiba was not expecting. Shaw replied, "*Come, let's have a look!*"

Shaw suited up, and he walked to the navigation point. He got the vision of the black flag fleets and found that those feet have good manpower and weapons. Since they are coming in two ships, they can attack Kallan in full force. The confusion and fear started ruling the heart of the captain, but his face still looked cool and his lips sipped his favorite old rum. After learning the intel of pirate fleets, Shaw walked inside his chamber with Kiba. He didn't reveal the fear, but he told Kiba to get ready for the battle. This situation was like being stuck in between a shark's fangs. If Kallan opts for direct combat against pirates, Kallan will face defeat for sure. In between the confusion, Liya knocked on the doors of Captain Shaw. With the force of a knocking sound, Shaw understood some other problems arose. He ordered a man outside the door to enter. It was Liya; she opened it with hesitation. "*Captain! The flu started to spread all over the ship. Our medicines were falling against fever and illness.*" With a downed head, she said, "*Almost 45% of the crew was affected.*" Captain Shaw was unhappy with the words that Liya spilled out; he sipped more and more rum and asked Liya to join the top deck. He knew the flu and fever were out of his control, and he put all his hope on saving Kallan from pirates. The tension developed on the ship was tremendous. No one can predict what will happen in the next few hours. Shaw wished for luck and asked the God of Storm not to abandon Kallan. He called his hound and gently rubbed its head with love. He wore a face tint of charcoal and loaded his swords and threw knives at the belt. When walked out, lightning and thunder welcomed the captain; he walked to wheels with a charming smile on his face. He took control of the wheel with strong will and courage. He ordered every member on the top deck to wait for his command and ordered them to hoist the red flag.

Captain Shaw did not show any tension in his mind to the crew; he was casual as usual. Kiba was inspired by the cool behavior of the captain. In the wild storm, Shaw's hands were like a log on the wheel. He tried to speed up the sail, but pressure and depression in the wind were not supported by a high sail. The interception time of the pirate fleets and the Kallan was not far; it was a bad day for Kallan. Needle rain droplets made holes in the sail. Even though they have an extra sail, it was not the right time to change one. The ship was on high alert. Arrows and spears were waiting for Shaw's orders. As predicted in the darkest hour, three big ships met one another and the pirate captains were attracted to the war torch and blood-red flag of the Kallan fleet. 'Blood-red flag' is a fearsome word in the pirate dictionary and the meaning of it was 'no mercy.' When the red flag was hoisted, it was an indication of other fleets. "*Whoever crosses their way, mercy will be shown in swords and spears.*" After seeing the fearsome look of the Kallan fleet, all eyes in the pirate fleet turned their heads to see the captain. Shaw wore a grin on his lips and his confident smile planted fear in the low-rank pirate's heart on the deck.

The best strategy was, "*Before quarrel, planting the fear in the foe's heart is an ideal success.*"

Shaw was a perfect match for terror pirates. Other than the concert of clouds and tide, there was perfect silence. All three ship crew members were waiting for the command of their captains to start the arrow shower. Heroes looked at each other's faces and waited for Shaw's howl. Slowly, the pirate ships forwarded to the adjacent side of the Kallan fleet. Kiba pulled the string of his bow to shoot the arrows. Hot air exhaled from his nose and warmed his forefinger in the string. Akello and Yuda were marked with their eyes on the ship crossing their left; Liya's eyes were locked on the ships crossing their right. Even at this high time, Shaw added an ounce of rum to his veins. Although all three fleets were at the attacking point; they haven't initiated the attack. In the next two minutes, pirate ships crossed the Kallan without attacking. Many in the Kallan crew thanked their favorite gods for the miracle. Heroes who believed in their skills had one question "*But, why? The pirates have the upper hand, but why didn't they launch the attack?*"

Captain Shaw has an answer, and he showed his gratitude to the storm by raising his rum bottle.

Akello and Kiba were followed by Yuda and Liya. A group of heroes assembled near the wheels to find the reason why the pirate ships did not attack the Kallan and moved away. Before they could ask the question, Shaw explained to them, "*If the pirate ships were involved in direct combat, they might easily defeat us, but they can't defend their fleets from collateral damage. Collateral damage reduces the speed of the sail and the vulnerable bow of the ship can't survive the storm. Pirates in the black sails were wise and did not want to attack us and get their ships damaged too.*" Akello was astonished. "*Strange, did the wild weather save the Kallan?*" Adding an ounce of rum, Shaw nodded his head. Kiba also noticed that crossed pirate ships were not made of ordinary wood. It was also special, like Kallan. From the actions of the pirates, it was clarified the storm was going to be crueler. Fixing the repairs was nearly impossible during the storm.

The long sail continued; the rays of the sun didn't rub their eyes for two full days and the flu found new hosts. Many members of the crew thought if the pirate had taken their lives, they would not be forced to live the next two days of the cruel storm. Zaya's wounds were treated with extras of the roots taken from Draguva; the wounds started to recover faster than expected. Soon, she will join the crew to share workloads. Medics reported apart from medicine and portions, Zaya's will-power helped her in her speedy recovery. With the iron hands of Captain Shaw and Tandoor, the great Kallan escaped the wild storm and the blazing sun gazed at the ship. After the storm, once again, the wind started to breathe slowly. Most of the crew were on the top deck to enjoy the warmth of the sun; Golden rays not only gave warmth and also planted new hope in the hearts of Kallan. Heroes supported their hands on the rails and enjoyed the light energy of the sun. The sound of thunder was replaced with seagull chirping, and the wetness in the wood started to dry.

Akello's eyes twinkled to see the scattered white, gray clouds, and between the hollows of the clouds, the glorious red giant escaped out. Not just Akello, everyone on deck opted for silence to heal their hearts and restored hope.

Liya cracked the silence and queried Yuda, "*What's special with the blue dragon?*"

The question of Liya moved Yuda's eyes from the sky to Liya and began, "*Usually, dragons are nonsense and angry; hunting is their favorite sport and they also practice cannibalism. If their stomach growls, they hunt, and if they don't feel hungry, then also dragon hunt! More than the color of the dragon, the number of horns it has decides the character of the dragon, but all blue dragons have at least four horns. Even dragon riders never wish for blue to hatch out. The leash of the dragon's anger is always in the hands of the rider, but in the case of the blue dragon, the story is different. Giant blue dragons are blood-devouring machines. In front of its red eyes and fire breath, nothing can withstand other than its own rider. The arrogant beast has a dominating nature, and it doesn't like other dragons in its den. They even show no interest in finding mates. So, they are isolated from others and set free on the independent island of the Draguvan coast. Working with a blue dragon is like a daily storm for blue Daga, but my brother Rizon found a way to calm it down and introduced a mate for his blue.*" With a light beaming face, Yuda opened, "*Luckily, I am a rider of brown!*"

Kiba opened, "*What about brown?*"

Unlike blue, brown is like a giant mountain. "*Easy, lazy! But once you lit the fire, they are a fine gem in the dragons!*"

Curiously, Akello nudged, "*The black?*"

Yuda laughed at Akello. "*Black is an underperforming student. When the black dragon works with a rider, you may expect the average result.*" The attitude in his voice and the fire in Yuda's eyes reflected like glass. "*Because you managed to make scratches on black, it doesn't mean you can defeat either blue or brown.*"

Liya was silent, but her knife eyes stabbed Yuda. Without spilling words, Yuda strode out! Kiba and Liya were frightened, but the act of Yuda didn't trigger Akello's veins. Instead, his line of thinking flashed the valor of Neo and his ability to fight back against the giant black dragon. Without reacting, he let the music of waves eat his ears. Under the roof, Yuda was worried. He never wanted to let the fire out. Unfortunately, the question of the dragon's nature had let the flame in his heart eat the brain. He felt bad for what he had done. The great brown rider's hands were trembling in the fear of losing a friendship and Liya's knife eye haunted him.

All of a sudden, eyes on the deck moved toward Shaw. He ordered for the low sail and heroes rushed on his order and soon he commanded to drown the anchor. Everyone on the deck was confused. Shaw addressed the crew, "*Let's take a day break!*" He noticed the tiredness in the crew and made a wise decision to pause the sail. The sound of howls and low sails invited Yuda to the deck, but Liya didn't look at him. Meanwhile, Akello and Kiba were losing their grip on the sails. Yuda wants to hide behind the doors, but he wishes to fix it soon. Except for the medics, everyone was happy. Liya knows her responsibilities. Along with the flu, many were infected by the common cold because of climatic changes. It was a hard time for medics to diagnose both. Shaw believed shark meat was a better cure for the crew suffering from the illness. In the sound of loud cheers, Shaw beamed, "*Deploy the boats for shark hunt,*" and graced the face of the heroes. The unhappy faces clarified to Shaw that something was wrong. The captain asked deep divers in the ships to collect medicinal plants to help the medics. Yuda's pride didn't allow him to speak to Akello, neither Liya nor Kiba. He dragged his feet to his chamber and shut the doors. After a few minutes, the door was knocked on. Akello and Kiba were at the doors. Their faces were carrying warm smiles as if nothing had happened before, and Yuda was speechless. Kiba began, "*We were waiting for you on deck.*" Akello voiced, "*Let's go and fill our tummies before the shark hunt begins.*" Yuda never expected, "*Akello will let down his pride for the sake of friendship.*" Yuda rejoiced with a great smile and joined, but Liya was a rough, cranky stone to convince.

Two rowboats were deployed into the ocean for hunting; Shaw ordered fresh livestock to be used as bait. Shaw and Kiba occupied one, and the remaining one was occupied by Yuda and Akello. Shaw loaded his harpoons with the Fas chemicals he gathered in Dragon Land. The light of the sun glittered on the surface of the ocean. Dolphin pods were playing in the east, and in the west, seabirds dived into the ocean to get their prey. When the blood-smelling bait was dropped, a big predator popped out by exposing its dorsal fins. Shaw connected a harpoon with a long rope, and the other end was knotted to the bow of the boat.

Shaw pulled back his arms and released the harpoons at the shark. His aim perfectly hit the target, but that shark was not easygoing. It started to drag the boat with its speed. Kiba was ready for his trial, but Shaw choked. "*It's my prey, Archer!*" However, Shaw didn't release the second harpoon to kill the shark. The speed of the shark started to slow down. Heroes understood that Fas powder used by Shaw made them unconscious. Kiba's eyes stared at Shaw. Shaw purged the ounce of airag and clarified, "*Fas power didn't affect humans.*" Kiba, Yuda, and Akello were silent watchers of blood sport. They dragged the fallen shark to their boat and punctured the shark's vital organs. The blood leak in the salt chunk invited the next dorsal fin to pop out. Shaw's lightning-fast harpoon pierced and hung between the fins. With rage, the shark jumped out of the water. Without delay, the spear of Kiba penetrated the eye of the beast and drilled out via another eye.

Akello and Yuda were stunned to see the action of the Bekuneuns.

After a decade, the speed of Kiba's throw made Shaw appreciate, "*Excellent throw Kiba.*" By late noon, the boats were back on the ship with four white sharks. One of which was hunted in an Alaokan and Draguvan combo.

The aroma of dinner cooking in the kitchen increased the appetite of the crew, and finally, dinner time arrived. Dinner started with shark liver soup. It was gray and creamy. Honestly, it tasted bad but Shaw suggested it was good for flu and cold. His presence in the dinner hall made everyone swallow the soup, even though it tasted like a rod. He also asked medics to forcefully feed the soup to the ill. Other than soup, the main course was topnotch and the finger-licking taste of the dishes filled the tummies. Lioness Zaya completely recovered and joined Akello and the company for dinner. Shaw walked to Akello's table and took his seat. With raised eyebrows, Shaw probed, "*Zaya, how did you end up in the hands of pirates?*" After hearing Shaw, a big lump in Akello's throat made him cough and Liya was stuck in hiccups because Yuda never knew the secrets of Zaya.

As Akello was afraid, Zaya beamed, "*After Akello wet the soil with dragon blood, I decided to surprise Akello and Liya on the shores of the north-east. I bribed the Draguvan fisherman with dozens of red grams, which I stole from the taverns of the rich, and I sailed the big boat named 'The Meg' in the direction of north-east.*"

Shaw muttered, "*Meg!*" With the wide smiling lips, Shaw was interested to hear the adventures of Zaya.

After hearing her, Yuda was puzzled and turned to get the face of Liya and Kiba, because he thought that Zaya was their fellow Beku-neun. Liya and Kiba turned their faces in different directions to escape direct eye contact with Yuda.

Akello decided to change the phase of the wind. "*Captain! Where did you learn to spearfish? The shark that you hunted today was delicious.*" But Shaw ignored it with a 'hmm' and kept his focus on Zaya.

Zaya continued by seeing Akello, "*After you bleed the dragon, in the cover of darkness, I roamed in the streets of the rich for a week to find the name of a Draguvan leader.*" With a pause, she added, "Bongyam is the name of a big attitude man!" Akello covered his face with his hands to hide from Yuda's eyes and Yuda's face was busting out mustard. But Zaya was not done yet. "*I am exhausted! I have been spying on Draguva for the last 15 years. I took this new peace between civilizations as a chance to free my hand from Beku-neu and to quit the Draguva.*" She inhaled the salty breeze and announced, "*I am a free beast now! I wish to live my life in the taste of ale and adrenaline rush in my veins.*" After hearing her, all three heroes were silent and downed their heads in the food.

Everyone in the dining hall was stunned after hearing legends of Zaya, but there was an exception. It was none other than Yuda. After knowing that Zaya was spying on his motherland, Yuda's rage doubled and started to explode. Akello can sense Yuda's gritted teeth and hot steam coming out of his nose and ears. It is expected to see such boiling anger in the face of the prince of Draguva. After all, Draguvans killed the spy on dragon fire, but Yuda saved the life of the spy from pirates. More than Zaya, he couldn't digest that his friends and Liya had lied to him. In boiling anger, Yuda punched the table hard with his fist, and he walked out. Akello was the first to follow him with a hand sign as he asked Kiba to stay back.

Yuda's walk-out didn't disturb the size of the audience and the narrator, Zaya, said, "*Her big boat was not found by pirates, but the boat approached the pirate fleet. Fucking Draguvan fishermen cheated me and they sold me to a pirate for five red grams. In my fight against Draguvans and pirates, I swooned with a wound! Later, when I woke up, I was stuck in the hands of pirates for a complete moon cycle, and they kept me aside as a prize for their newly elected pirate leader.*" The narration style of Zaya, her body language, and the ale mug dancing in her hands impressed Shaw.

Liya joined Akello on the deck. Yuda was standing alone by pressing his palms against the rails, and his focus was on the stars. Akello walked near him and put his hand on Yuda's shoulder and said, "*The reflection of the moon looks great today.*" Yuda turned his face and fixed his eyes on Akello, but soon without a word, he turned his focus back to waves. Akello and Liya were able to translate the silence of the Yuda.

Akello directly started a conversation with an apology and added, "*The truth is that without the help of Zaya, we were useless in Draguva.*"

Liya opened, "*I and Akello were cards drawn by Zaya to fight the dragon!*" She then stood silent.

Yuda fumed, "*I am the prince of Dragon Land. Like breathing, my pride is very important to me, but today I have purchased a defame for my Draguva by rescuing the spy from pirates.*"

At the top of his lungs, Yuda shouted, "*In the hall, a bloody spy was singing a song about how she had tricked the Draguvans, and she is daring enough to speak out the name of my father and leader of Draguvans!*"

Akello and Liya got sight of one another. Their quiver is out of words to console Yuda.

Liya grieved, "*Yuda! I have no excuses to console your anger.*"

There was silence. The sea breeze ate the ears. Yuda's eyes were staring at the stars. Kiba also joined the deck. After seeing the face of Akello and Liya, he understood nothing worked well to console the boiling Dragon Prince.

Yuda began, "*I will stay silent! I am bound by the laws of new alliances and new friendships. This environment of friendship with spies is new to me and something that I can't accept. I need time for this shit!*" With gritted teeth, Yuda warned, "*If she spills out the name of my father again! Her head will be tossed down and it will put a full stop to the new alliance and hardships that you have passed.*" He walked out in anger.

All three faces were filled with terror. Liya beamed, "*I will handle Zaya!*" Kiba grumbled, "*Storm and blood rush are far better than political affairs.*"

Apart from the spy, internally, Yuda was happy with the new friendships and Liya was already special to him. Even he started to go easy with Shaw's way. After Yuda left the deck, Akello and company walked to join the dinner. Liya thought that Zaya would join them, but she was busy clashing ale mugs with Shaw. Liya noticed Kiba's dull face and enquired about his well-being. He coughed and said, "*Exhausted because of the morning hunt.*" When she gently touched him, she felt the radiance of heat in the Kiba's shape. Symptoms of flu and normal fever were similar. It was hard for medics to diagnose the flu, especially since it was like finding a unicorn for an amateur like Liya. She suspected it would be a flu fever, and she took Kiba to the medical hall. Akello was all alone on deck with the company of wine.

After the dinner, Shaw walked near Zaya and started the conversation by gently pushing, "*Hello!*" The adventure of Zaya inspired Shaw. At the same time, Shaw's cool attitude made him an apple in Zaya's eyes. Yet she was not aware of Shaw's ale collection. If she knew about it, then she would be his biggest fan. Shaw was not aware of Zaya's brain behind winning the alliance of Draguvan. They both had hard lifestyles, and their chaotic past will never let them easily develop a friendship or love. Shaw is not expressive and Zaya is a don't-care type. Their conversation ended in a few seconds, but Shaw wants to know her more. With a chill smile, he sipped rum and walked to his ale dungeon.

In the gloomy moonlight, Yuda was dull and alone in his room. A gentle knock on the door hit his ears, and his eyes twinkled after seeing Liya at the door. Along with the ocean breeze, his heart whispered, "*The presence of Liya can fix his mood.*" However, his eyes were excited, but his words started to evaporate when he tried to express his thoughts.

Liya broke the silence and excused herself. "*Shall I walk in?*"

Yuda came back to reality and welcomed her with a mouthful of happiness. Once she entered the room, her eyeballs rounded. Her mind described all she saw in one word. "*Messy.*" Liya said in a funny tone that she will never share a room with him and smiled. Yuda got her joke and smiled at the tip of the tongue without exposing his teeth. He moved some scattered clothes and created some space for Liya to sit.

Liya said, "*I came to check how you are doing?*"

Yuda opened, "*I am fine,*" and apologized for his rude words on the deck.

Liya smiled back. "*No worries, your anger is meaningful.*"

After hearing from Liya that Kiba was infected by the flu.

Yuda bloomed, "*Look, it is a hard time for the flu!*" Both laughed hard.

After some time, they decided to knock on Akello's.

In Akello's chamber, he was puzzled about last night's weird bad dream! News of the prophecy affected Akello's subconscious, and unknowingly, it rooted fear in him. When Liya and Yuda reached Akello's chamber, they found the door was not locked. They just knocked on the door and entered the room. Liya can see a super messy room again and gets the emerald eyes of Yuda. Yuda exposed his teeth and said, "*It's a man thing!*" Akello welcomed them with great enthusiasm. Yuda and Liya found the circle-shaped wooden box with a needle in it, and they also could see a big olive-green feather on his mattress. Both walked near Akello and put their focus on the circle-shaped wooden box. Liya pointed her long finger and quizzed, "*What is this?*"

Akello mentioned, "*This cool gadget is my grandpa's gift for winning the alliance of Draguva. My grandpa called this gadget a compass.*" Yuda and Liya pronounced 'com-pass' in unison and their eyes were fixed on the compass and its needle.

Akello explained the application of the compass. "*With this gadget, we can easily find which direction we are sailing.*" Liya took the compass in her long fingers and looked at it with her wide-open eyes. Then she passed the compass to Yuda. Yuda looked into the compass and noticed directions and the needle was pointing north. Even though he turned in a different direction, the compass still managed to show north. Yuda was amazed and also puzzled that something was wrong with Akello's gadget. According to the reading of the compass, the Kallan was sailing toward the west direction instead of north-east direction, and Yuda decided not to complain about Akello's gadget and spoil his excitement. After all, this gift was from Akello's favorite person.

Liya confirmed, "*Kiba is infected with the flu! But he will be ok soon. Being Kiba is sick, Yuda decided to take up his work at the bucket.*"

Akello complimented, with a wink in her eyes. "*Our dragon rider is a backup of our squad.*"

With blossom on his lips, Yuda greeted, "*The direction gadget looks great,*" and gave it back to him, but Akello refused to take back the compass, saying, "*Yuda! You are going to be in the navigation bucket as a replacement for Kiba. May this direction gadget be more useful to you than me!*" Yuda agreed to keep the compass with him, and as a gesture of thanks, he hugged Akello. Akello's selfless nature gave him many friends across Alaoka and beyond!

Chapter 8

Shaw's Resolution

Nightfall covered the sky. All twinkling stars were naked to the eyes, and the sea breeze ruffled Yuda's hair. The flawless sky, pirate-free ocean and gentle breeze made Yuda feel the beauty and serenity of the ocean, which was restored. Music escaped from Yuda's panpipe and was a natural painkiller for the sick. It became routine as the Kallan fleet slept after the melody of Yuda. Dragon rider's eyes kept his focus on the wide ocean, but because of tiredness, he fell asleep on the navigation bucket. When Yuda woke up, he scolded himself for falling asleep at night, and his eyes caught the beautiful scene of the early sun popping out from the extreme end of the ocean and lifted up his hands to take a lazy break. When he was relaxing his reflexes from his pocket, Akello's compass fell down. Yuda noticed it and took the compass in his hands. When he casually opened it, he was shocked to find the direction of the rising sun that was accurate, but they were sailing in the direction of west instead of north. Yuda's head raised an alarm that they were sailing in the wrong direction. To make sure once again, he shook the compass box badly and turned in a different direction to check if the compass was working. The sound of the seagull made Yuda raise his head; he remembered his brother's words that in the morning, seagulls always fly in the direction of the sun, which is technically toward the east. He noticed the same behavior in the seagulls. With the readings on the compass, he confirmed the ship was sailing in the wrong direction.

Yuda came down from the navigation point and decided to raise the bell, to notify the captain that they were moving in the wrong direction and he found that Shaw was already standing at the wheel and directing the ship. Yuda's mind nudged, "*How could the experienced captain not be aware that we were sailing in the wrong direction? Apart from all that, he could have seen the same sun and flight of seagulls in the east that I have seen.*" He decided to investigate more before raising the alarm. He also doubted that Shaw was purposefully sailing the ship to the west. Since the sun did not fully come up, the top deck was almost empty and a few sailors on the deck were snoring loudly.

Shaw was at the wheel and Tandoor was at the bow of the ship, so Yuda decided to use this golden opportunity to infiltrate the captain's chamber to gain intel. Yuda found that the captain's hound was sleeping at the entrance of the deck. The distance between the hound and the captain's chamber was far. So, he made his move confidently and reached the doors of the captain's room without alerting Shaw, Tandoor, and the hound. He slowly pulled the latch of the door and infiltrated the captain's chamber successfully. The smell of the ale was mesmerizing in the chamber, but he put his focus on searching for the map table. He found the table behind the wooden wine shelf, walked near it, and looked at the map. He found that the location marked on the map was not Yuvalle. Instead, it was marked on some small island in the center of the northern sea. Suddenly, the creaking sound of the door panicked Yuda, and the door was slightly opened. It was the captain's hound. Yuda muttered, "*Damn!*" He decided to hide under the table, but within seconds, the hound sniffed the smell and traced Yuda. After seeing Yuda, the hound got excited and waved his tail. Yuda forgot the name of the hound; he told the hound to stay silent by making hand signs, but the hound made the calling bark to play with him. Yuda thought he was done, and he feared that he was going to get caught by the captain. He gently rubbed the dog's head to make the hound silent, and it worked well. The hound became silent and laid upside down by showing his belly.

Again, the doors of the room were opened. This time it was Captain Shaw. In the next few seconds, he found Yuda hiding with his hound. Yuda was speechless and stood up; he was caught red-handed by Shaw near the map table. Shaw called out, "*Simba,*" and the hound moved from Yuda and walked to his owner. It was a nightmare, and for the first time in Yuda's life, he was caught while infiltrating.

Yuda asked Shaw in a rough tone, "*Why are you directing the ship to a small island without notifying the crew?*"

Shaw smiled and said, "*Clever! You found that we're sailing in a different direction. Nothing less, I expect from Rizon's brother.*"

Yuda replied, "*Shaw! You are a responsible person. If there is a change in direction, you need to let everyone know on the ship. Apologize, I never expected this from you.*"

Shaw purged an ounce of rum and began, "*I noticed something strange. When we started our sail from Draguva, someone was tailing us.*" After hearing Shaw's sentence, Yuda's face became pale, and the captain walked near him. Shaw moved his ale-smelling mouth near Yuda and whispered, "*I suspected they were following us in the huge distance, and they thought that I would not find them. Later I found it was not a vessel, but a fully grown brown dragon following us approximately at the height of 164,042 feet.*" Finally, Shaw breathed, "*The dragon belongs to a rider named Yuda.*"

Yuda was shocked, and all his five senses were numbed. He had one question running through his mind. "*How did Captain Shaw come to know about his Asura (Yuda's dragon) tailing the ship?*"

Shaw choked Yuda, "*If you decided to share a word with the crew regarding the change in direction of sail, I will set back the sail to Beku-neu and call for a meeting with leaders to grumble that Draguvans broke the laws of the alliance.*"

Yuda recalled the amount of struggle and sacrifices made to bring this new peace. Shaw's words rushed the sweat in Yuda; he had no choice other than to listen to Shaw.

Shaw gloated with a smile. "*I hope Rizon's brother will make a wise decision.*" He put down his coconut ale bottle on the map table and added, "*I have some unfinished business to take care of.*" Yuda was silent, like a compass in his pocket.

Shaw ordered Yuda to get out of his chamber. When Yuda was about to leave the chamber, Shaw's dog walked along with him.

While Yuda was opening the doors, the captain made a short whistle! After hearing the whistle, his hound Simba bit Yuda with his furious scissors teeth. Blood rushed from his calf muscles.

Captain Shaw voiced, "*Dragon Prince, I apologize for my hound act and do not enter my chamber when I am not around.*" Yuda's eyes became red. Shaw has crossed the limits; he has to pay for it. Yuda was angry enough to summon his dragon to destroy the ship in a burning fire, but his eyes flashed the efforts of Liya and Akello. He calmed himself and caught sight of the hound. Simba was dull and made a pitiful face because of the bite it delivered to him. Yuda bent on his knees and gently rubbed the hound's head with a smile and breathed, "*It was not your fault,*" and strode out by bashing the doors.

In unavoidable circumstances, all of Yuda's strength and powers became useless; he tied his hands for the sake of unity, peace, and alliance. Once Yuda left the cabin, Shaw drank a bottle of rum and muttered, "*Draguvan brat underestimated me.*" He wore an evil grin on his lips. Yuda walked back to his chamber, washed the bite with water, took the strong rum gifted by Shaw, and poured the rum on the wound as an antiseptic. The ethanol in the rum was heavy. It created a burning sensation in the wound, and the blood rush has not stopped. Yuda remembered his brother's advice, "*Handle Shaw with care like handling our maternal grandma.*" He never expected this bastard to be five times worse than their grandma. He waited for the full sun to show up, and then he walked to Liya's chamber and knocked on the doors.

Liya slid through the doors, and she was surprised to find Yuda. After seeing Liya, even in the burning sensation, he made a warm smile on his lips. The unwashed morning face of Liya looked beautiful in Yuda's eyes. After seeing Yuda, Liya knew that he would never disturb her sleep unless there was some emergency. With her wide-open eyes, she questioned Yuda, "*What had happened? Any problem again?*"

Yuda answered, "*Kind of a problem! I accidentally landed my foot on the tail of Shaw's hound. In the pain, it bit me hard.*"

Liya's facial expression changed, and she asked him to walk inside the room to check the severity of the wound. Yuda entered the room and took a seat on Liya's bed; he rounded his eyes and muttered. "*Clean! Very clean room.*" It was just opposite his room, and there were some palm leaves on the corner of the bed. The palm leaves made Yuda conclude that she used to read in the room with the oil lamp. Beyond all, Liya's gravity pulled Yuda! She wore a semi-transparent outfit through which he could see the curves and belly button of Liya, which tempted Yuda, but still, the strong dragon rider controlled himself. When Liya bent herself down to examine the wound, he was more excited and got twinkling stars in his eyes to see her assets. She examined the wound and cleaned the wound with water and applied the patch to the wound with ointment. While patching the wound, Yuda complimented Liya on the clean room and reading habit. After Liya patched, she mentioned, "*The wound is deep. It takes at least three suns to heal and we need to re-patch the wound tomorrow also.*" Yuda muttered, "*Wow! Liya, I will come tomorrow at the same time to patch the wound.*"

Liya was puzzled. "*Why did Yuda want to come and patch at the start of the morning?*" Without thinking much, she said, "*Yes!*" After hearing yes, she can see the happiness on Yuda's face. When she stood up, again he encountered the inner beauty of Liya.

Yuda complimented, "*Thanks, princess!*" and walked out.

She was puzzled again. "*Why, princess?*" At the same time, she was happy to hear the compliments from her love. After Yuda left her chamber, casually, she noticed her outfit and gently banged her head with her hand and also a small naughty smile developed on her closed lips.

Apart from spending time with friends, the rest of the time, Yuda's brain was stuck in finding the answer to where the ship was heading to. Yuda's mind wasn't able to find a solution, so he decided to wait for Shaw's next move. While having breakfast and lunch, Yuda was trolled by Akello and Liya to get a bite from the hound. Yuda took the troll as the funny part, and he himself started to laugh, which made Akello and Liya lose interest in trolling him. Meanwhile, Kiba's sickness is getting better. Liya complimented, "*Kiba's immunity fought well against the flu while it took a week and more to recover for others.*" While all three were having their dinner, they noted Shaw was having a deep discussion with the lead medic. After the dinner, Shaw ambled near Yuda and enquired him, "*How are you feeling now?*"

Without exposing anger, Yuda politely answered, "*The bite wound is starting to heal.*"

Shaw suggested, "*Dragon Prince's well-being is important. Yuda, I am relieving you of all Kallan's duties for a week, wishing you a speedy recovery.*" Yuda understood Shaw's play, so he refused the offer. "*I am in good shape to continue my duties.*" Shaw noted the busting mustard in Yuda's eyes.

Shaw ordered, "*I, the captain of Kallan, am dismissing you of all Kallan's duties.*" He strode out with a grin on his lips.

Shaw knew very well both Kiba and Yuda will be a pain in his ass, so he appointed his puppet on the navigation point as a replacement. His puppet was neither intelligent nor brave. Without showing boiling anger, Yuda ambled out of his chamber and bashed the doors and fumed, "*Bastard Shaw! Where the hell is he heading the crew?*" The confusion ruined Yuda's sleep, but he is confident enough to face anything with the flame balls of Asura. Yuda knows very well that nothing can stand against his brown beast. Finally, he put a full stop to all his confusion and decided to hug his bed tight, but the moment he found Akello's compass in the bed again, the chaos started in Yuda's mind. Being it was not too late; he decided to return the compass to Akello to maintain his cool. When he walked to the doors of Akello, he was not around. Yuda decided to check for him on the upper deck. He found Akello standing alone, and his eyes were fixed on the waves. Yuda walked near him and gently put his hands over Akello's shoulders and beamed, "*Anything interesting in the waves*?" Akello smiled at Yuda and opened, "*I am tired of salt chunks and noisy waves! I'm looking for hot, gritty white sand to soak my feet and relax*." Akello's words made Yuda chuckle, and he can understand his eagerness to find the land. Since the three-moon cycle was completed, there was no sign of land and most of the crew were tired of the blue prison.

To make Akello comfortable, Yuda quizzed, "*How did you manage to escape monkey troops by kidnapping their baby?*" Yuda knew very well that to escape the deadly monkey gang of the Draguvan gardens, one must apply all the skills they acquired.

As Yuda expected, the question made a blossoming smile on Akello's face; he graced the bite scar of a griffin on his forefinger and gently rubbed it with his thumb. Akello melted in his own thoughts; the big Draguvan garden is a prohibited area in the north for civilians, and it is the home of dragons and a training ground for its riders. The vast area is filled with tall clusters of trees, deep hollow caves, waterfalls, and a dragon temple. Dragons love to eat their offspring once they hatch, but not all dragons are the same. Once the egg is laid, dragon riders collect it and keep it safe in the dragon temple. The dragon egg is bigger, like a rock, and they use a bullock cart to transport it to the dragon temple. Dragon temple is an incubator; fire lit in the chamber keeps the egg in warm condition and helps to hatch without hiccups from their mothers.

Yuda tapped Akello to bring him back to reality.

With a wide smile, Akello began, "*Proctor of the test is your brother, Rizon. I kidnapped the monkey baby in a jute sac and started to leap on the branches to escape the chasing monkey troops. I ran like a cheetah. The howls and angry growls of monkeys ate my ears. I was not in the position to turn my head and check on the monkeys. In the dripping sweat, I can successfully evade the hands and cruel teeth of monkeys, but it did not last long. Monkey troops aimed like a pro; they started throwing fruits and stones at me, gasping in my lung tanks clarified I can't run longer!*

I was left with no option to avoid the hit. I ran inside the nearby caves and the monkeys stopped following me. It was clear from the act of monkey troops; a big danger is waiting inside the caves. The wild roar of the lion stopped me. I was afraid to push my legs forward. At the same time, I was also frightened to go back to the monkey troops. I howled Rizon's name as loud as I could, but I saw no response, so I decided to fight the lion with the sword I carried."

Yuda laughed loudly, and he couldn't control it, and in the laugh, his stomach started to feel pain. He ridiculed, "*Idiot! The cave is home to the pride of lions, not just one.*"

Akello continued with sneering, "*I found more than 20 members of pride in the deep caves. A big lump in my throat blocked my breath, and my vest and briefs were wet in rushing sweat. A pack of three lionesses started to approach me; I put a prowling monkey sac on the floor and prepared to face my death. My left arm was holding a sword and my right was raised to counter the attack. My sword and I are just tooth-picking sticks in front of lionesses, but Neo's bite scar did magic. After seeing the scar, the lionesses stepped down and their fearful howl invited the leader of the pride. Neo's bite scar became a shield. The howls of lions and lionesses made Rizon and the guards rush inside the cave to collect my corpse, but Rizon took a huge gasp to see me alive. It was not done yet. We walked outside the cave and returned the baby to the monkey troop along with a whole 11 bunch of red bananas. The monkey troops' howl had not stopped yet, and they had never withdrawn their positions. Rizon told me that it was hard, but we have no other option. I was puzzled. What is hard to do?*

The next moment, Rizon asked me to stand nude in front of monkeys and to bend on my knees to seek an apology, but I was ashamed and refused to do that. Rizon and the guards left the place and told me to meet them at the temple. I showed the scar to frighten the monkeys, but a stone from a distance hit my chest. Scar did not work on monkeys, so I decided to follow Rizon's advice to save my life."

Yuda laughed loudly and opened, "*In my test, I reached the origin of the waterfall and threatened the monkey troops with a sac that I would drop if any of them tried to approach me. The deep howl of monkeys invited Rizon and guards with dozens of the banana bunch to calm them down, but it didn't work out, so I apologized to the monkey troops in the same way as you did."*

Both of them laughed hard at what they had done, and Yuda was relaxed after hearing the legends of Akello. He then gently handovers the compass back to Akello.

After the handover of the compass, Yuda kept all his confusion aside and got ready to sleep like a sloth, but there were many people on the ship to ruin his sleep. The doors of Yuda's chamber were knocked on. When he slid the door, he was surprised to see Akello. He also noted that Akello's face was painted with confusion. The moment he opened the door, Akello rattled into the chamber and screamed, "*We are sailing in the wrong direction!*" He showed his compass markings to Yuda. Yuda took a huge breath and his line of thinking was analyzing the multiple possibilities. At first, he was happy that Akello was clever enough to find the truth. At the same time, he couldn't appreciate Akello because if he stood against Shaw, Shaw would reveal the truth about Asura and the alliance would come to an end. Moreover, Yuda is not willing to reveal the presence of his Asura for now. He knew it was a weird situation that he must convince Akello before he reached out to other ears. Yuda fumed, "*What!*" He rolled his eyes to find something to create a makeup story to hide the truth, and he didn't know what to say. His troublesome eyes fixed on the windows and grieved. "*Akello, I am sorry! Grandpa's gift is malfunctioning, and I found it yesterday, but I don't want to hurt you by revealing it!*"

Akello choked, "*Crazy!*"

Yuda said, "*First, I was also confused.*" He pointed his fingers at random stars and breathed, "*I have knowledge of star routes. Can you see the three-star cluster that always appears in the north? Check your compass! It was showing south; that's how I am confirming it.*" Akello was not aware of star patterns; he scratched his head! Yuda used this opportunity and pointed to other stars and mentioned random shit. Akello was not easygoing. To evade Akello's question, Yuda stacked towers of random lies to convince Akello that his compass was malfunctioning. He also got the compass back from Akello by saying, "*Leave the compass with me. I will cross-check once again. It will take time.*" Akello is strong at making friends, but he blindly trusts them. At the same time, he easily falls for their traps.

Yuda was guilty of lying to Akello and his face was grief-stricken. He cursed himself, "*I am not aware of how I am going to convince Akello of what I have done.*" He fumed about Shaw, "*My reins are in the hand of a bloody fucking captain. Unknowingly, I became an ally of him.*" He was sleepless, and he hardly managed to sleep for a couple of hours.

When the sun's rays stuck on Yuda's face, he opened his eyes with great happiness that he was going to meet Liya. After washing his face, he was at the doors of Liya.

Liya opened the door. Her eyes were filled with sleep. Yuda was happy to see her morning face, but unlike yesterday, she didn't wear a semi-transparent outfit. It was a disappointment, but Yuda was not bothered about that he was still happy to see Liya in the morning, and he dreamed of planting a kiss on her large forehead. After seeing Yuda, Liya smiled and welcomed him inside the room. He took a seat on her unfolded bed. She examined the dog bite and said, "*Healing is in progress.*" She cleansed his wound and patched it with ointment. While patching, she downed her head and chuckled at the disappointed Yuda. After patching the wound, Yuda stood up with a smile and was about to walk out, but he was stopped by Liya.

She began, "*Why do you prefer patching the wound as a first job in the morning?*"

Yuda can't explicitly tell her, "*I wanna see your face in the morning.*" Thus, he created a story in the name of Rizon.

Yuda chuckled and opened, "*It is one of Rizon's lessons. To heal wounds quickly, one should start treating their wound at the first hour of sunrise.*"

Liya commented, "*Is it?*" and laughed sarcastically. He continued his way out with a hidden smile. Liya paused Yuda. When he turned to catch Liya's face, there was an inch gap between them.

With love-carried eyes, she whispered, "*I won't prefer semi-transparent clothes every day,*" and her teeth were expelled. Yuda was shocked that she had found it. He hissed, "*More than seeing you in that outfit, I love to see your morning face when the red giant wakes me up.*"

Both were silent for a minute, eyes never blinked, and Yuda's lips were just opposite her forehead. He was nervous and also he could feel the same hesitation on Liya's face.

Yuda cursed himself. "*Shit! I expressed my emotions out.*" The sound of rattling doors and footsteps disturbed their best moments. With hesitation, Yuda moved out. Liya locked the door, but the joy on her face never dimmed. She started her daily routines with an everlasting smile. Falling days started to give meaning to their relationship.

After three days on dinner night, Zaya joins team Akello for fun and food, but Yuda never makes any conversation with Zaya. He ignores her when she tries to make a conversation. Still, Yuda's shoes were stuck in the quicksand of pride and ego. Kiba was completely recovered, but he was sad that the navigation bucket was occupied. Liya began, "*Shall we share the interesting thing that happened in our life?*" She looked forward to hearing from Yuda, so her eyes were marked on Yuda. Zaya complained, "*My life is full of spider webs and rabbit holes,*" and made unamused lips, but Akello popped out to tell the story of his love and said, "*Amara!*" In unison, Liya and Zaya condemned, "*No, not again!*"

Yuda said, "*Wait, I never heard of it.*" Kiba was also eager to listen.

With excitement, Akello started, "*That night was different from usual!*"

Zaya completed the sentence, "*It was a special night.*"

Akello turned his focus to her and said, "*It was my special night.*" With laughter, Kiba and Yuda started to listen again.

Akello continued, "*Amara saved the life of my friend and comrade. With the help of her herbology skills, she ran out the venom, spreading in the veins of my friend Kino. I was attracted to her independent nature and strong decisions. After saving Kino's life, she walked to the doorway of the cave for a night watch. As a gesture of thanks, I walked out to accompany her. She was silent. Our eyes were focused on the woods, and our ears were listening to the thrilling insects.*

Then that special night began! The fragrance of darkness started to spread all over the sky. Along with the luminous pearl in the sky, I was amazed to see two dark moons moving right to left in her eyes. To fight the snowy breeze, we torched a warm campfire. I intentionally made jokes to make her feel comfortable. When she smiled, the enamel of her teeth reflected the flame yellow light and her dimple danced. In the melody of crackling wood and whooshing wind, her presence next to me lightened my soul to glow like a firefly. On that star-filled night, I decided to give the leash of my heart to her."

Zaya tapped the table and said, "*20.*"

Liya barked, "*30.*"

Akello acted like he never knew and asked, "*Are you counting multiples of 10?*" But the guys understood from Zaya's tone what she was referring to; she was hearing the same story of Akello's love for the 20th time.

Yuda's eyes were on and off on Liya, and Kiba was eager and asked, "*Hey, Akello! How did you propose to her?*"

Akello explained to Kiba like the first time he was narrating, Zaya and Liya giggled.

After hearing the love story of Akello and Amara, Liya and Yuda were delighted with smiles, and their twinkling eyes started a conversation. Tummies were filled. The melody of the sea breeze relaxed the young lovers. Every conversation is special, and it tangles their hearts. When they were gazing at the stars, Liya wondered, "*I sense something is wrong! Usually, a three-star cluster always appears in the north, but why do they appear in the south?*" Yuda's frame thundered, and he muttered, "*Why is everyone an explorer here?*" and he decided not to lie to Liya. When Liya was squishing her brain to find, "*What is going wrong?*" Yuda noticed a star with a white long tail falling from the sky. In excitement, he uttered, "*Liya.*" His rough fingers gently clutched Liya's wrist. The moment he clutched her hand, all her thoughts were shattered and her pearl eyes were locked on Yuda. Yuda excitedly said, "*A falling star!*"

Liya was numbed for a moment, and Yuda sensed the warmth of Liya; he rushed Liya to the bow of the ship! With a clutched hand, he bubbled, "*Make a wish! Draguvans believe the arrival of white tail stars will fulfill all your wishes.*"

Liya nodded her head and made her wish, but not loudly. "*I wish to keep my wrist inside Yuda's hands forever!*" She checked Yuda's face; his eyes reflected the falling star, and Yuda's subconscious mind made a wish. "*Let her be my Liya! He also wished for the success of the mission, Yuvalle.*" The shooting star disappeared from the sky, but Yuda didn't pull out his vision from it. Meanwhile, Liya graced the stars in Yuda's eyes. The night was long for the young hearts.

Captain Shaw's bagged eyes also witnessed the falling star, and he gulped ale and muttered, "*It is the perfect time to break the pot.*"

Yuda was happy that today Liya didn't find that the Kallan was sailing in the wrong direction, and he decided to hug his bed tight. In the darkness of the night, Yuda's chamber doors were tapped. Yuda was puzzled to find Shaw's puppet at the door. He barked, "*Captain has summoned you!*" Yuda shook his head, pulled his outfits, and ambled out. When Yuda was on his way to Shaw's chamber, under the moonlight, he heard a heavy snore in the navigation bucket. Yuda cursed himself for sailing in Kallan and entered the chamber. The smell of strong airag and ale drilled into Yuda's nose, and it conquered his lung tanks. Yuda's vision noted a dozen or more scars in Shaw's upper shape, and he rolled his eyes to find empty bottles of ale on the table.

Yuda asked, "*Why am I summoned to an ale warehouse?*" His words expelled the flame. Shaw caught the eye of the dragon rider and mocked, "*An ale warehouse would be a perfect synonym for my heaven,*" and smiled. Shaw directed his foot to the map table and Yuda tailed him; he put his finger on a small island and voiced, "*Before the next sunset our ship will be anchored on the shores of this island. This land has nothing wealthier. The shifting sands sing songs and the hot sun will give lesions in the foreskin!*"

Yuda posted a question. "*If nothing wealthier, why is Kallan heading there?*"

Shaw's reply did not give answers to Yuda's question, but after hearing Shaw, Yuda was paralyzed for a minute.

Shaw said, "*Instead of asking why, prepare to infiltrate into the land of pirates.*"

Till today, Yuda never knew of the existence of the land of pirates. He voiced interrogation, "*Land of pirates? Do pirates have their own land area?*"

After seeing the thunder in Yuda's face, Shaw doubted, "*I hope the leader of Draguvan has received the message from Azog! I was a pirate and former captain of the vessel named Killer. Once, the land of pirates was my home.*"

Yuda was stunned, like a log, to recall the scene that happened in his father's chamber. His father was about to speak about Shaw, but Rizon stopped him and advised him, "*Handle Shaw with care!*"

Shaw sipped an ounce of rum and waited for Yuda to react, but he was still stunned and locked in his own thoughts. By seeing Yuda, Shaw's line of thinking concluded, "*Probably, none of the peace envoys were aware of what I was,*" and continued purging the rum. Once Yuda came back to reality and Shaw began, "*I led the crew of 24 pirates.*" He took a long sip and gloated. "*I killed the crew in my own hands, as a reward for their betrayal.*

Till today, all pirates believe I spared my last breath in the ocean pit, but I survived!"

A moment of silence continued and the touch of the breeze created goosebumps in Yuda's frame. Yuda began, "*Captain, it was not time for revenge or personal vengeance.*" This time, his tone was polite, and the fragrance of respect was sprinkled.

Shaw muttered "Revenge!" and laughed, "*Revenge! I am on this mission because of my loyalty to Azog. Kid, I have lost interest in vengeance! I am not a member of the peace messengers, but still, as a captain of the Kallan crew, I am concerned about the success of the mission. Signing on a mission without intel is like suicide. I know a coward who traveled to Yuvalle and returned home and is still breathing. He was the only survivor in his crew. So, here is the plan: we are heading to my old home to abduct the pirate to gain some intel about Yuvalle.*"

Yuda was silent, and his silence was taken as acceptance by Shaw. Shaw gave a bottle of rare airag to Yuda. He said, "*Enjoy it, dragon rider! Maybe tomorrow is our last day,*" and wore a grin on his lips.

The killer fleet captain has another name, "*Fang of the Meg,*" but the pirates were wrong. They underestimated their kin. Shaw was not just a fang; he was a whole megalodon.

The tapping sound of Shaw's doors made Yuda turn his head around to find who was at the door.

Yuda was surprised when a bull-eyed archer walked in. Following him, a woman who lives in shadows entered, and then The Dragon Bleeder and knife-eyed yeti hunter assembled in Shaw's chamber. Yuda was happy to see his friends. Zaya filled her lungs with the smell of airag, and her eyes fixed on scars in Shaw's frame. Akello noticed Shaw's rare collection in the hands of Yuda. Akello borrowed it, had a huge gulp, and passed the bottle to Zaya's hand. Zaya had a big sip and her face melted in the taste of fine airag and purged a little more. She handed over the bottle to Kiba, and later Kiba to Liya. Liya drained every last sip of airag. When Liya placed the empty rum bottle on the table, Yuda's eyes were about to leak. Poor dragon rider didn't get an opportunity to taste a single drop of airag. Shaw showed his pitiful face at Yuda and addressed the cosmopolitan team. "*Signing on a mission without intel is like suicide.*" Shaw's words were not a question but a statement that can't be denied. Shaws added, "*I found some information from my old friend about a pirate who has toured Yuvalle and is still breathing.*"

Shaw's words surprised the team. Zaya doubted, "*But how to find him?*"

With a grin Shaw briefed, "*Days back, I changed the direction of sail to the land of pirates and Kallan will be reaching the shores of it before the next sunset.*"

After hearing Shaw for a minute, Akello and others were puzzled.

Zaya posted her doubts to Shaw. "*Is there something like a homeland for pirates really in existence?*"

Akello was loud with busting anger. "*The pirates!*" Akello's coal-black vision recalled Yuda complaining about his compass. He stared at Yuda, but Yuda downed his head without reaction.

Liya was silent like hell, and there was a reason behind it. Kiba put his hands around Liya's shoulder to comfort her.

Shaw began again, "*Yes! Pirates do have a homeland, and it is a perfect hideout. We need to reach the tavern in the center of the marketplace to find the pirate name 'Irie' and abduct him to gain intel about the Yuvalle. As we are not legitimate guests, we can't anchor in the royal harbor. The geography of the land of pirates is not welcoming; it was located in between a bunch of active volcanic islands and craggy oceans were perfect places to test the potential of the fleet captains. The craziest sea route I have ever heard of is sailing to the abandoned northern shores of the pirate island, and it is the only safest spot to anchor the Kallan fleet. From there, the quest 'Irie' begins.*"

After hearing his plan, Akello and Kiba were excited about their new mission, but there was a small shake in Liya. Zaya was sensible and proficient. If a person knew this much detailed information, he should be an insider and Shaw's love toward the ale and airag made Zaya suspect Shaw was a pirate too. Other than Zaya, no one has any suspicions about Shaw because he was selected for the mission by Lord Azog of Beku-neu.

Zaya posted an interesting question. "*Captain, have you already been to the land of pirates?*"

With a gasp, he said, "*Once my mission landed me there,*" but his words didn't put a full stop to Zaya's suspects. Yuda and Shaw decided to hide each other's secrets from the crew.

Quest 'Irie' was not easy, like baiting salmon; everyone in the crew knew that very well. Shaw promoted Kiba to take over his job when he was not around. The team was puzzled after hearing Shaw's words. Tons of questions were forwarded to Shaw; his answer was a sip of rum and the word 'dismiss.' Even though they did not have answers to their question, all agreed in unison to find Irie because it is much more important to gain intel rather than taking a suicide mission. While stepping out from Shaw's chamber, Yuda walked to console the mustard-busting Akello, and Akello's angry stare was dimmed a little. Yuda opened, "*Akello, your compass is working fine. Look, I need to brush up on my stargazing skills.*" Akello shook his head and ambled out without a word. Yuda expected the worst, but Akello's attitude toward friends made him calm. Yuda was inspired and decided to copy Akello's easygoing attitude with kins, and he gently turned his head to grace Zaya.

After a few minutes, the doors of Shaw's chamber were knocked on once again; it was our proficient spy.

Zaya asked Shaw with hesitation. "*Life is uncertain, and we are not sure about surviving tomorrow. I wish to taste your rarest collections stacked in the racks.*"

Shaw smiled at her and commented, "*I love your way of asking for my collection.*" He pointed the fingers at four-storey racks on either side and began, "*On the left, the first two racks were decorated with century-old port wines, and the rest of them were finely brewed airag. The right racks were allocated for ale, rum, and Sura."* He offered Zaya to take one from either side and enjoy this nightfall.

Zaya took the unique, and she invited Shaw to join her to celebrate this darkness. Shaw will never get a better opportunity than this to get to know more about her. Without sipping the rum, he said, "*Well!*" He accompanied her to the top deck. Apart from having dark days and survival struggles, it was the night that needed to be cherished for the proficient spy and the pirate captain. The sea breeze ruffled their hair and circled them to listen to the conversation.

Since they both had a lot of common interests, like blood sports and clashing ale mugs, the ounce of ethanol blend will allow them to open up their minds and hearts. Shaw has never seen a lady like Zaya and unknowingly he fell in love, but he does not recognize it. Zaya suspects that Shaw could be a pirate; she has seen his bravery and wit in handling the Kallan crew. She wants to explore his character more. Under the luminous pearl in the silence of the night, the light of the moon decorated the waves with her silver linings. A spy and a pirate were standing near the rails of a big ship and enjoying the breeze along with the airag in their veins. One hand carried the coconut shell bottle, and the other was hesitating to hold each other's hands.

Maybe Zaya was arrogant and hard. Beyond all, she is a woman. Captain Shaw needs to show his love and compassion to win her heart. She is a priceless pearl, like one decorating the sky; she can't be taken easily. She has seen more flirting men and heard poems that were written about her beauty. It was a surprise for Zaya. She was done with half of airag, but still, Shaw did not even open his mouth to ask how his rare airag tastes. So, she decided to start a conversation; she turned her neck toward Shaw and bubbled, "*Airag tastes heaven!*"

He accepted the greeting with a short smile on his lips and continued on his airag. Well, Zaya expected words from Shaw, but his reply to her was a smile.

Disappointed, Zaya expressed, "*Life is uncertain! If you get slaughtered by pirates tomorrow, shall I take care of your ale collection?*"

Shaw was shocked to hear her, but still, he maintained cool on his lips and began, "*Funny! But I will not die tomorrow.*"

In Zaya's life, men talk. She acknowledges them with a smile and sips her mugs. but today, karma hit her back. After some time, Shaw excused himself and walked to his doors. After a soft gulp, Zaya muttered, "*He is a weird jackfruit!*" Captain Shaw doesn't even know the meaning of empathy and affection, but that was not his mistake. Shaw spent all his 35 years around hustles and the art of survival. He has no one to love or to get loved. Beyond all, he spent half a decade with the chimpanzee and his hound. He doesn't have any special bond with humans; from humans, he has seen only betrayals. At the same time, Zaya is good at placing bait and makes everyone easily fall for her traps.

In the middle deck, Yuda knocked on Liya's door when Shaw was describing the land of pirates. Yuda noticed chaos in Liya's face, so he decided to enquire before it was too late. When Liya answered the knock, her lips were not smiling at Yuda. Yuda noticed the odd and ratted into her chamber and took his seat without her permission.

He gently opened, "*What happened? Why does the charming face of Beku-neun lady look dull?*"

She was silent and hesitant. Yuda understood she was not interested in answering him. A cocktail of confusion and anger started to brew in him. The moment of silence continued. Yuda swallowed his words, but they echoed in his heart, "*I thought I was close to Liya and I believed she would open up her hesitation. Maybe I was wrong! Did she consider me just as a comrade?*" He was worried.

Silence conquered the hearts without an excuse. With clouded thoughts, Yuda decided to walk out. When Yuda stood up, Liya's small lips opened her sorrow. "*When I was seven, Beku-neu was forced to counter the brutality of 10 black fleets and its three hundred and more pirates. We are not ready for that attack; our soldiers were hunted like elks. They entered the castle through the damaged walls that were hit by the lighting last night. In the middle of the night, they executed brutality. They have shown no mercy and killed everyone stuck in their eyes. Bell was rung to raise an alarm because the big army of Beku-neu marched to slaughter the scattered yeti families. During that period, my father was the leader of Beku-neu; he was wise enough to understand they can't win this battle. He analyzed the situation and ordered the evacuation of kids and tweens. It was a nightmare. I walked over to the blood and corpses of Beku-neuns. My father helped me and my elder brother to saddle up on his griffin and ordered his griffin to 'evacuate.' My mom kissed my forehead and told my elder brother to take care of me. At that moment, I was not aware that it would be the last time I would see my mom and dad alive."*

While Liya was telling about the tragedy in the north-west, her eyes stormed and dwelled in tears. As she was facing the wooden walls, Yuda couldn't find the river in her eyes until dripping tears started to wet the Kallan floors.

Liya continued, "*While our griffin was flocking to fly high, a bastard pirate shot a griffin hunting arrow and his target missed hitting the griffin, but it purged the life of my brother. The sound of alarm rushed the reinforcements and nearby villagers to the castle before dawn, but nothing was left alive. After checking the safe environment in the castle, griffin took me back to the castle and handed me to the Azog, the leader of the nearby village. When I reached the castle back, I saw tormented faces and stacked corpses. In the pile of corpses, I found my family.*"

She wept hard and grieved. "*In three odd hours, pirates took everything away from my life.*"

Yuda was out of words to console her; he hugged her tight to console her. Liya's head was resting on Yuda's chest. At that very moment, she never knew he was the man who was going to keep her smile forever.

Before the arrival of the red giant, Shaw summons Kiba to his chamber. Kiba reported, "*Aye, captain!*" Shaw questioned Kiba, "*Do you know why I selected you as captain when I am not around?*"

Kiba was silent and worried that he was not going to be a part of the mission. Shaw broke the silence and beamed, "*I expect you to make strong decisions in hard times. In case, Zaya, peace messengers, and I did not return to the fleet before the next sunrise.*" He ordered Kiba to consider as 'we stay behind' and set back the sail to Beku-neun. Shaw also gave his word, "*In my absence, the wheel of the Kallan fleet and Tandoor will wait for orders from you, Kiba.*" In the beginning, Kiba hesitated. "*No! I can't do it,*" but later, Shaw made Kiba give his word. When Kiba walked from Shaw's chamber, he saw the sun start to pop out from the horizon and the red-orange rays of it touched his sight. The seagull's morning song is an orchestra to ears. Kiba asked, "The sun for a good day." The ancient belief was praying to the sun during sunrise will make all wishes come true. Shaw knows his responsibility and the importance of the mission; it's been almost a decade since he visited his home. Shaw took the pearl necklace and put it in his pocket and he decided to exchange the necklace for the exchange of exotic rum.

Chapter 9

The Call of Dunes

After sunrise, Kiba bashed the bell to assemble every member of the crew. Within a few minutes, the crew assembled. Shaw addressed the crew and conveyed where he and the messengers of peace were heading. On one side, the crew was happy about reaching the shore after seeing 95 suns. Meanwhile, the fear of pirates was exhibited in the eyes of crew members. Shaw motivated, "*We faced pirates, storm, Sefu, and we are undefeatable. The place where we are going to dock our Kallan is safe. I gave instructions to Kiba to take care of the crew in my absence, and I strongly believe none of us is going to spare their lives in the land of pirates.*" Shaw's positive words gave confidence to the crew. At the same time, small fears murmured in their hearts. Shaw summoned Liya and briefed, "*We are going to the den of pirates and there is a high possibility of crossing the same face again. Keep aside your wheezing thoughts. Princess Liya, we can't change the past and we shouldn't kill the future with emotions of the bad days.*" Shaw explained her responsibility and wished her luck.

The sail was adjusted to the northern shore; Shaw stood near Tandoor and guided him into the craggy ocean. Shaw is preparing Tandoor's hands to handle the horrors. The ocean winds were eager to visit the land of pirates; they blew faster than usual and directed the ship to reach the northern shores. When the crew reached the northern shores of the land of pirates, their eyes could see huge sand mountains beyond the shore, which will block the vision of the pirates to find Kallan. After seeing the sloppy sand mountains, the messengers of peace, Zaya understood they needed to work their reflexes to find Irie.

Kallan was docked on the northern shores of the island; the crew was excited to land their feet on the sandy beach and their toes danced. Shaw purged an ounce of ale and inhaled the air! Flashing thoughts recalled the days of Shaw in the land of pirates. The most awaited order from Shaw hit the ears of the crew. "*Deploy the rowboats! These shores are home to hatchlings of olive ridley. Watch your legs to avoid bad luck!*" When Shaw ordered two rowboats to be deployed, one of them carried all preserved corpses and coffins to shore and another boat carried 20 more crew members to shore. The moment the feet of the crew members touched the yellow gritty sand, their mouths widened with a smile, and the heat underneath excited the brain. Feel-good feelings mirrored on their faces. Akello kicked his boots away and buried his foot under the sand. With closed eyes, he breathed, "*Wow!*" After months, the toes of sailors felt the touch of smooth, sticky small particles of sand, and Liya pressed her fingers inside the sand to pleasure her toes. Land and wind relaxed the minds of the crew, and the sea breeze ruffled the skin of the heroes. When everyone was relaxing, Shaw was collecting the pebbles from the shore, and it puzzled Zaya.

The crew's eyes caught sight of hatched shells, eggs, and young hatchings of olive ridleys. The sun made the sandy beach sparkle. The finger-sized hatchlings crawled and flapped their flippers to reach the heart of the ocean. The beginning of a new life and the passion of the turtle to reach the ocean lit new hope in the crew. Liya and Zaya took their seats on the sandy beach and enjoyed the race of turtles, and it eased the chaos in Liya's heart. At the same time, Zaya understood, "*Why do pirates abandon the shores of the north?*" Pirates never harm turtles, and turtles were sacred in pirate culture when northern shores were captured by the hatching of olive ridleys. Pirates abandoned the shore. Kiba and others started digging in the sand to bury the corpse. Team Akello and Shaw preserved their energy for the long day. After a few minutes, they showed their last respect to the corpses and conducted rituals for their afterlife. After rituals, corpses were placed in the dug spaces and covered with sand.

The lifespan of living beings is very small. According to the cosmic calendar, the age of the universe is 13.7 million years. One second out of 13.7 million years is 438 years. The human lifespan was less than 150 years. All achievements that every single human made were just in 250 milliseconds, according to the cosmic calendar.

After showing their last respect to death, Shaw and four others decided to drain their energy in hot deserts. Before leaving, Shaw made eye contact with Kiba and started trekking the tall, sloppy mountains. Their heads and weapons were hidden under the hooded cloak, and each of them carried a bag of water to consume. The hooded cloaks they wore were thick enough to protect the skin from sunburns. When Shaw's small brigade reached the top of the sloppy mountains, their eyes widened. Zaya commented, "*Shit!*"

Shaw laughed at her and commented, "*Hall of sand dunes welcomes you!*" He recalled his memories of camel races on sand dunes. To the edge of their vision, they found wavy sand dunes of different sizes. Yuda turned his back to check on Kallan. It looked tiny from the height of the mountain. They purged some water and commanded their legs to walk further. The heat of the desert created a leak in the skin and dripping sweat evaporated before reaching the hot sand. Shaw asked his comrades to follow his lead. Shaw's plan consists of Yuda and Shaw will lead the team from the front lines. He asked Akello and Liya to follow them at five feet distance, and Zaya was the tail of the formation; she followed Liya with a three-foot gap. Shaw trusted, "*Zaya! I am counting on you. Make sure not to leave behind anyone.*" Being new to the desert environment, the prince of tropical land was soon dehydrated and his water consumption rate was high. Their eyes caught poisonous creatures living all around the sand dunes. All their way into the dunes, thorny and leathery plants pulled their attention.

Shaw's eagle eyes were looking for the quicksand; it's a very dangerous threat in the deserts. The idea behind his formation was not to fall as a whole into quicksands. At some point, he found one and ordered, "*Halt.*" Shaw took out pebbles stone from the pocket, threw them at a certain distance and quicksand absorbed the stone inside it within no time. The crew thundered to see the condition of the pebbles. He threw the pebbles at increasing distances to find the dimension of the quicksand zone. Based on his test with pebbles, he found a new path to move further. His expertise in finding quicksand confirmed Zaya's doubts that he should be an insider, as the same act of Shaw sparked the doubts in Akello. After crossing, sneezing hot winds and sand dunes, all their eyes found a small town in the heart of the desert. All the water bags were empty and all the water they drank was sucked out by the burning fire. After a few minutes of walking, the red sun started to go down, but it was not evening. The sun stays longer in the land of pirates. Shaw and the team continued their walk toward the desert town. When the team reached the town, the yellow light of the sun vanished and nightfall covered the sky and slowly the temperature started to fall down. The town was small and glowed well in the light of insect jars. Pirates found a way to breed fireflies and put them inside the jar to use them as a source of light. Brutality was that fireflies were gaoled inside the jar until death, and food was fed once a day. Before entering the marketplace, Shaw's brigade covered their heads with hoodies and scarves to avoid trouble. The market was not busy and everyone in the streets covered their faces with shawls and wore a hooded cloak to stay anonymous. There is no common outfit for pirates, they are scavengers. Their last recent loot was in Alaoka, which resulted in most of the pirates being dressed in cotton.

Playing kids in the streets wore torn outfits, and some were holding daggers in their belts. An undisciplinary act of the kids spotlighted that they are orphans. After the arrival of the luminous moon, the town became a happening place, and everyone in the moving crowd had swords and threw knives under their cloaks. From the gap in Shaw's cloak, Zaya noted Shaw carried a long rope with him, and she was not sure whether it was a rope. At one point, there was a split in the road. Shaw opened, "*These both roads will end at the lake. The lake is the only source of water for people living here.*" To avoid the spotlight of being in a group, they decided to split into two teams and walked on either road. Shaw caught the eye of Yuda, and Yuda replied by nodding his head.

Shaw began, "*We divide as two teams here and will reunite on the roads that lead to the tavern, and he advised them to be on their guard and stay low.*"

Shaw asked Zaya to follow him and commanded Akello and Liya to follow the lead of Yuda. All three messengers of peace walked in the narrow street and Shaw walked on the adjacent road. Akello checked his compass and said, "*We are walking in the east.*" Liya and Yuda made angry stares at him. Their anger conveyed, "*Shut the compass! Stay low!*"

The streets were not broad, and small shops were on either side. Most of the shops looked like tents. With the support of four pillars like wooden sticks, the torn canvas of the sails was connected to the corners of the sticks. More than shops, brothels were found all over the town. In the center, there was a stage, and an auction was opened for slaves and women. Red beans, giant water pots, and paddy were used in exchange for slaves. Shops were providing rum as a welcome drink, and pirates were dancing and partying in the streets. On the other side, suddenly, men in the hoods started to fight, looking like two gangs were clashing their swords. After winning the fight, the winners cut down the heads of the losers as trophies and left the remains. The walking crowd did not care about the corpses; they overstepped and walked for their purpose. Playing kids looted the valuables from the headless corpse.

After seeing the events on the road, Liya commented, "*Brutality and cultureless rats!*" Yuda and Akello caught each other's eyes and continued on their feet.

Zaya and Shaw walked in the adjacent street; their eyes caught a small cattle farm with camels and a few life stocks. Zaya rolled her eyes and was astonished to find brothels, brewing shops, and people involved in friendly fights to test their skills. Zaya praised the market. "*This pirate world is a hall of strong survivors; from my vision, no rules, no integrity, and no dramas. It's all about looting and having a party. My tongue is tempted enough to taste the rum.*"

Shaw listened to Zaya and answered, "*Law and order of pirates is very simple. Everything is legal in the world, but taverns and brothels are not a place for blood and vengeance. I am well aware that you are proficient in your job! I know by now you would have found out who I am.*"

After hearing him, Zaya stopped in her footsteps. After a few seconds, with chaos in mind, she followed Shaw without a word.

The roads became narrow and the number of shops made up of wood increased. The smell of alcohol conquered her lungs, eyes caught that all shops had countless bags and vessels of rum, wine, ale, and airag. It took a few seconds for Zaya to recognize that she was in the alcohol market of pirate land. The excitement in her twinkled in her eyes, and the smell of blending ethanol made her take a deep breath with closed eyes.

Shaw whispered in Zaya's ears, "*This is the place where you can buy the best rum and ale in all civilizations.*"

Shaw walked into one of the shops. The shop he landed in was well-built in bamboo and it has one storey. Shaw gave 10 red grams from his pocket to the man at the doors and accompanied Zaya. Ale, rum, and port wines in the shop made her mouth wide open inside the shawls.

Shaw whispered in Zaya's ears again, "*Give me a word that you will be on your limits. This place is a paradise for alcohol lovers. Here you can taste the rarest flavors of ethanol blend and they charge five grams per head to taste them all.*"

After hearing Shaw, Zaya replied, "*Expensive! With five grams, one can feed his colts with grass for the whole year.*" She was rude in her voice, but her legs danced with the happiness of going to taste the rares.

Shaw wore a smile and was delighted. "*It is my gift for your bravery in the pirate ship!*"

Zaya smiled. "*Thanks, jackfruit!*"

Shaw muttered, "*Jackfruit!*" Without his knowledge, Shaw started to conquer the heart of Zaya.

As they both walked deeper into the shop, Shaw called the worker and asked him to assist her. Shaw moved his head near Zaya. The fragrance of Zaya was changed, and it attracted him. Shaw took a deep inhale of her fragrance and still managed to whisper, "*Be in control, Zaya. The mission is more important than alcohol lust.*" Zaya's fragrance changes are a sign that she started to love Shaw.

We humans evolved from animals. Females attract males with a special fragrance (it's a multi-cast signal). Male fights to beat other males to mate with females, but in the case of human beings, it evolved much better. The moment a woman feels her love for his man, a unique fragrance escapes from her and attracts her man (it's a unicast signal).

While tasting wine and rum, she found a black drink on the shelf. She asked a worker about a black drink. The worker boy replied, "*It's vodka! No one has permission to taste that vodka. This was specially brewed by the owner of the shop for the special person.*"

When Zaya rolled her eyes to find Shaw, he was not around, and he walked deep inside the shop and happiness jumped in his eyes; he walked to the billing counter, and no visitors were around. He placed a pearl necklace on the table and asked for a favor.

The shopkeeper was tall and had a sharp nose. All his fingers were decorated with 10 rings. He looked into Shaw's eyes and laughed at him. He said, "*Sorry, I am not taking missions now!*"

"*Oh! is it?*" Shaw again checked the surroundings and showed the big scar on his chest.

The shopkeeper was numb to see the scar. His eyes were stuck at Shaw's scar for a minute and pronounced 'Fang of the Meg' in excitement. Shaw asked him to lower his tone.

In a fraction of the time, he punched Shaw in the face. Shaw lost his balance and reached the floor. Being that the shop is big; the sound did not escape. With a warm smile, he helped Shaw regain his balance and walked him upstairs. While walking down the staircase, Shaw uncovered his face to see red, and he softly touched the scratches on his face created by the shopkeeper's ring.

Shaw smiled. "*Nothing less than I expected from you, Morgan.*"

Morgan bubbled, "*It is a small punishment for what you have done and for not contacting me for a decade and more.*"

With a neutral face, Shaw accepted. "*Totally, I deserve it!*"

Both reached the chamber upstairs. Morgan hugged tight and said, "*It has been 12 years. I thought you were dead.*"

Shaw's eyes were locked on the eagle in the corner of the room. He called, "*Nora?*" and placed a hand to summon the bird.

Morgan replied, "*Nora died three years ago. This is the offspring of Nora; it inherited Nora's colors and majestic nature.*"

Shaw said, "*Yes, I can see that white strong head, long brown body and bright yellow bill and cruel claws too.*" Morgan raised his hand and voiced, "*Sukra.*"

At the next moment, Sukra took his place in Morgan's hand. Shaw moved to touch Sukra's head. Sukra bit Shaw's fingers hard. Shaw screams in pain and holds his fingers tight.

Morgan added, "*Sorry, I forgot to say Sukra is not as sweet as Nora. Punishment for leaving me alone is for years.*"

Shaw shouted, "*Fuck! It hurts a lot! I have a mission to take in a few hours.*"

Morgan exclaimed, "*Mission! If others see you, it's a threat to your life.*" He helped to patch the wound on his finger. Morgan called out to the worker and told him to bring his special recipe. A worker walked down the stairs and filled the liquor bag with vodka. Zaya was not dumb; she understood that the special one was Shaw.

Morgan said, "*Do you remember I was involved in creating a bacon drink?*"

"*Almost six years back, I created this drink out of bacon, but I didn't find anyone close to my heart other than you to gift this vodka.*"

With a proud smile, Morgan voiced, "*This is my masterpiece. Taste it.*"

Shaw wore a great smile on his face, and he gulped new flavored bacon vodka. The taste of Morgan's masterpiece makes Shaw feel like heaven on his tongue, and Shaw closed his eyes to feel every ounce of it.

Shaw appreciated Morgan. "*The taste of bacon and the odor of ale made it flawless; it is a perfect masterpiece. You are the best brewer in all civilizations.*" He gave him a hug.

Shaw's comments on the bacon drink filled Morgan's heart with happiness.

"Innovators' needs are simple. A small token of appreciation excites them. They are like kids with badass brains."

Morgan opened the wardrobe and took out the torn piece of cloth and placed it in front of Shaw and began, "*These are the remains of your outfit that Nora brought back. That sunset changed my clock. The pain of your execution changed my life a lot. You left me alone; I had no one to share my emotion with.*"

In anger, Morgan slapped Shaw again and wailed, "*You're a stone. You never consider me either a comrade or a brother. You have not even tried to contact me once in the last 12 years.*"

After getting hit again, Shaw downed his face without expression, and his tongue had no answers to console him.

He hugged Morgan and grieved, "*I am sorry. I don't wanna show myself here again, but now, the mission took me here.*"

Morgan replied, "*Anyway, you're alive. Tell me how you escaped from 100s of ruthless fangs.*" Shaw explained how he survived.

After hearing all that, Morgan's eyes watered with a smile on his face.

"*I am proud, Shaw! You are the first pirate to escape from the ocean pit.*"

Shaw gloated 'pirate' and continued, "*I decided not to have that surname anymore. You have no idea how we dragged others' lives. If you go out of this desert, you can experience the pain, and that makes you regret what we have done.*"

Morgan's anger broke out. "*I have no idea what you are talking about, but it is not our mistake. We are bastard sons; we lived all our childhood in the ship of our sadist father and we never knew our mother's name. At the age of 12 years, we are forced to swim and escape the sharks as part of training to become pirates. This is our life. We are just roaming beasts. Our goal is just to survive the sundown.*" Shaw nodded his head as a sign of acceptance. Usually, the doors of Morgan's room have no ears, but Zaya was a shadow in the darkness. For a spy like Zaya, it is like eating an apple; she distracts the worker and eavesdrops from the doors. Her moves are like a wildcat, slow, steady and focused, not easy for even pirates like Shaw or Morgan to detect her presence. She knew that she would be caught if she stood at the doors longer. When both were talking about mission Irie, the doors were knocked on. Shaw got the message from the worker, "*Sire, a woman accompanied by you was searching for you!*" The word 'woman' made Morgan think that she would be Shaw's wife. Shaw sends back the worker with a message to her that he will be back soon.

Morgan quizzed, "*A woman?*"

Shaw pronounced, "*Zaya...*"

Morgan excitedly asked, "*Who is Zaya?*" Shaw beamed. "*No, she is just a crew member.*" After gaining intel, Shaw hugged Morgan and said, "*Send Sukra to me when the moon is at center. Since it bit me, he can easily track my blood scent. I will leave a message to Sukra about our next meeting.*" He grabbed the bacon vodka bag and left the chamber with a hand sign. "*See you soon brother!*"

Once Shaw walked down, he found Zaya at the billing counter. Zaya was leaning back on the wall, and she waved her hands at Shaw. He responded. Zaya said to Shaw, "*We need to walk soon to reach the tavern. If we come back alive, lend me red grams; I have to pay for the selected rum and airag.*" Shaw wondered, "*Interesting!*"

While walking down to the tavern, Zaya asked Shaw about his friendship with the shopkeeper. Shaw answered, "*He was an old friend. I walked in, to gain intel about Irie.*"

Shaw's words made Zaya laugh, and she beamed, "*We both have a dark past, but I am happy for you. At least you have a trustable brother!*"

Shaw questioned, "*Brother! Wait, have you eavesdropped on the conversation?*" Zaya winked her eyes and hands and asked for a vodka bag.

Shaw cursed, "*You damn spy!*" he gave her a bag of bacon vodka to taste and added, "*It was a gift from my brother!*"

Zaya said, "*I knew! Your brother mentioned that it was his masterpiece.*"

She sipped vodka, and her eyes sparkled at the taste. She praised the brewer. "*Such a sexy recipe!*" Without a second thought, she opened, "*I wish to marry him.*" Shaw laughed at Zaya; she laughed back.

The marketplace ended and again the dry desert began, but this time few people walked along the path and their legs crossed the lake and continued further.

The Kallan crew was enjoying the nightfall on the northern shores. They filled their stomachs with fresh barbecued fish. One thing they missed was Yuda's melody and their eyes were entertained by the slow action of small volcanic islands around them. From the shore, they can see the leak of lava on four islands. Kiba, the temporary captain of the ship, rested his back on the shore and waited for the safe return of Shaw and his friends.

Yuda and two others walked on the long road market. Akello's nostrils picked up the scent of food and his appetite increased. He can't control his temptation over the sweets made of fish and prawns. He walked into the sweet shop, and Yuda tried to stop him, but it was merely impossible. So, they walked into the shop. The recipes in the shop were made of fish, whale milk, prawn, and some edible fauna grown on the seabed. The food in the shop had a delicious flavor and a variety of shapes. Yuda whispered, "*Not to spend more than three grams, if we spend more that could alert the homelanders.*" He purchased all attractive food items and made Yuda pay for four grams; Yuda had a shrink in lips and paid for it. They walked outside the shop and took some safe places. They tasted the recipes they brought from the shop.

The food melted in Akello's mouth and his face looked brighter in taste, but others had the opposite expression on their face. Both Liya and Yuda make weird facial expressions, and they want to spit down the piece that they crunched. After seeing Akello on cloud nine, they didn't want to disappoint him. So, they manage to swallow the piece that they bite, but both are not ready to go for another bite. Even Akello's taste buds are not ready to share with his friend. Fish samosa, prawn pakora, and whale milk Kova, all these items filled Akello's tummy. Liya advised Akello, "*Be on your limit.*" However, Akello's ears ignored Liya's words and crunched the food items. The munching sound of Akello made Yuda mutter, "*Alaokan has bad taste buds.*" After munching and crunching over, they started their walk. They directed their legs forward and found a lake. All three of them collected the water from the pond and purged it to burn their thirst. Water content in the body increases stamina and makes the legs move faster. Hot desert now started to snow partially here and there. Shaw explained to Zaya that the temperature in the desert changes drastically from day to night because of dry air.

After crossing a lake, Shaw and Zaya reached the tall monolith erected in the middle of the desert. Shaw called it an 'entrance pillar.' The sound of music and party hit their ears, and their vision caught the light at a distance, which looked like stars in the darkness. Shaw and Zaya decided to wait for others near the pillar.

While waiting, Zaya questioned, "*We spent more time in the liquor market; I think they would have overtaken us.*"

Shaw answered, "*The way which we came is a shortcut to the entrance pillar, but they are coming through a long road; it will take some more time for them to reach here.*"

Shaw and Zaya leaned back on the adjacent side of the pillar; Shaw took the cigar from his pocket and gave one to Zaya. The cigar produces heat in their body, which makes them feel warmer. After devouring three cigars, Zaya probed Shaw, "*I doubted something could have happened to them.*" After releasing smoke into the air, Shaw choked with an unamused face, "*They are not kids and I asked Yuda to blow the panpipes in case of trouble.*"

They were standing inside the smoke of cigars; the bright moon put down the shadow of them on the opposite side.

Zaya began, "*Are you planning to reveal your true color to peace envoys?*"

Shaw exhaled the smoke ring and laughed, "*Is the spy's brain becoming blunt in the effect of rum?*" Shaw's words stirred Zaya's anger, but inhaled smoke with closed eyes and waited for Shaw's explanation.

Shaw briefed, "*Revealing my true colors is trivial for the mission. At the same, it starts a cold war! It is always enough to tell them what they need to hear instead of revealing everything.*"

Zaya crooked her lips to exhale the smoke and chucked, "*Looks like you have underestimated the dragon rider! Last night in your chamber, I noticed a shake in his frame and chaos on his face. He should have figured out who you are by now!*"

Shaw beamed. "*Yuda, he was clever! He found the change in the direction of the sails and dared enough to infiltrate my chamber. I was impressed, and I revealed who I was!*"

Zaya's lips smiled in pride, and her line of thinking echoed, "*As usual, Draguvans are exceptional.*"

Finally, peace envoys arrived at the show. With the lighted cigar between Zaya's fingers, she moved her fingers near the forehead and greeted Akello and others. Shaw gave cigars to all of them. Everyone lit a cigar and smoke rounded the pillar. After devouring a dozen cigars, the cosmopolitan crew walked out of the smoke to abduct Irie.

While walking to the tavern, Shaw addressed the team about the intel he gained. "*Target is 4.5 feet tall with a long beard. As per the intel, he used to spend more time in the tavern. In addition, he is an expert in using daggers.*"

Shaw briefed about the plan, "*After finding him, Zaya will approach Irie to start a conversation. With her words, she lays traps and gets him outside the tavern. When she starts the conversation, we will walk outside the tavern and wait near big palm trees.*"

Akello beamed, "*Tree?*"

Shaw purged an ounce and opened, "*Yes, there are 30 trees in total on this island and two of them are near the tavern.*"

Akello's doubts about Shaw started to grow. Yuda interrupted, "*Let's come to a plan.*"

Shaw purged again and continued, "*Once Irie comes near the palm tree, we will use tranquilizer darts (sleep darts) to abduct him. Liya will steal the horses from the nearby stables to escape.*" Finally, he added, "*Remember, before sunrise, we need to escape the island with him.*"

Yuda and Akello asked in unison, "*What am I supposed to do?*"

With an unamused face, Shaw commanded, "*Stand with me when the time comes. Let's spare our life to win the mission.*"

With the grace of the full moon, they can see all the objects nearby, and all five pairs of legs reached the best happening place in the world. Shaw doubted someone was following them; he turned around to check but he couldn't find any. A wide tavern in the middle of the desert was standing tall, along with two stables. The tavern is the place for pirate captains to show off their loot and exhibit the new slaves to the community. When the cosmopolitan crew entered the tavern, as Shaw asked, they separated into two. Shaw and Liya made themselves comfortable at one table and the other three occupied the adjacent table. Beyond all that, it's a safe house according to pirate laws. No one cares when the cosmopolitan team walks in. Shaw recalled one of the simplest rules of pirate land, "*Important rule of pirates: no fights in taverns and brothels.*" Most of them in the tavern put down their shawls and hoods and clashed the ale cups. A music band of 20 members with instruments is a feast for the ears. Yuda wondered and appreciated that pirates have a good taste in music. Shaw's eyes turn the pages of memories and recall the music band of 'Magic Moon,' and his lips dwell in a smile inside the shawl. "*They are 20 in the head count and the best music men of Pirate King. These Magic Moons play music with closed eyes. Once they start to play the music, they forget everything and play the music for hours. In history, one of the pirate kings, once cut the head musician to stop the music.*" Shaw has doubts. "*These bands play music only on two occasions, either to share good news or to mourn the death.*"

Liya and Zaya walked to check the surroundings, and their eyes looked for a short man with a long beard. Most of the pirates had unshaven beards, and their vision captured a few women pirates as well. Zaya made eye contact with Liya, which conveyed her 'negative.' Shaw and Liya turn on eagle vision at the entrance of the tavern. They were looking for a short man with a long beard. Yuda walked with Akello to the first storey of the wide tavern, but they could not find Irie. So, they returned to the table, and Akello opened, "*Negative!*" Zaya rolled her eyeballs at Shaw to notify him that the man was not inside the tavern.

After a few minutes, rum mugs were placed on both tables. The waiter collected the red grams placed in the corner of the tables. Each cup holds a different colored liquor and each of them denotes different flavored rums. Yuda and Akello are interested in light gray colored rum, but there was only one mug containing light gray rum. Yuda's hands moved to take the mug, but Akello's hands were fast enough to take the mug first. At the same time, when the light gray drink was placed at Shaw's table, Liya was about to take the mug. Shaw paused her with a note, "*Light gray drink is tuna rum. It tastes good, but not everyone's gut has a tolerance for it!*"

When Liya turned her head to warn Akello's table, all three of them were sipping their mugs.

The first sip of the rum melted in Akello's mouth, and he understood that it was made out of tuna fish and tasted creamy and tender. Zaya took a deep green ale and now Yuda was left out of choice, so he took the remaining one. It was colorless but smelled pungent. Yuda tasted it; it was the worst rum he ever tasted. Yuda cursed himself for teaming with them and placed the mug back on the table and focused on the left entrance of the tavern. After seeing tuna rum, Shaw was not happy because tuna rum has another name in the land of pirates "*A condolence drink.*" As Shaw was afraid, from the main entrance of the tavern man entered with his brown eagle. He wore a black outfit of Beku-neun; his face had a wide-open smile and his teeth were covered with black patches. After seeing him, Shaw recognized and muttered, "*Is this puny bastard a king?*" But he looked majestic and taller than Shaw. As per tavern rules, only a pirate leader is eligible to bring his beast inside the tavern.

The leader of the pirates was accompanied by two men. One of them was brown and dusky, the other one was a white bald head. Shaw purged a tuna rum and muttered, "*Individual pieces of shit are grouped now.*" He turned to check on Liya;

he noticed boiling anger in Liya's eyes and sweat from her forehead going down to mix with rum.

Shaw whispered to Liya, "*Liya! Stay calm.*"

Liya fumed, "*That white bald guy's fate is to die in my hand. If the fight breaks out, he is mine.*"

Shaw wore a grin on his lips and bubbled, "*If your throwing-knives miss the target, I swear I will kill him.*" Both eyes exchanged smiles. At the same time, Shaw's heart wished, "*Fight less abduct!*"

Shaw knows the customs of pirates. Pirates give free rum to share good news and bad news. The irony was that they provide free rum for both occasions, but the flavor differs. Alaokan cluster islands were apple eyes for pirates to loot pineapples. The rum made out of pineapples was served to share the good news and rum made out of tuna for the bad news, and on both occasions, the tavern will be flooded with pirate crews and their captains. Shaw was worried that it could make their mission complex. He and his weapons buried under the cloak were ready to face even a megalodon. So, he put his ears on the music of the Magic Moon band.

After a few minutes, a large crew of pirates and captains entered the tavern. One among them was Luka. He wore an Alaokan outfit. He had a dagger scar on his left eyebrow to cheek. He walked to the man with an eagle to ensure his presence.

After seeing him, Akello muttered, "*That man with a dagger scar turned his sail to save his life in the Alaokan coup.*"

Shaw knew Luka very well! Luka can't hide the dagger scar gifted by Shaw.

Music of different instruments, people chatting, and brotherhood made the tavern a paradise for pirates. Shaw waited for the announcement from the Pirate King. The wait was over. The king of pirates blew the horn, and the stubborn eagle sitting on his shoulders didn't even move his head and was not disturbed by the sound of the horn. Shaw was surprised to see the eagle and muttered, "*Not bad! But how did such a brave eagle get into the hands of this shit?*"

The tavern is silent and pirates wide open their ears to listen to the king's words. Still, the music was not stopped. A man walked to stop the musician, and the melody was paused. In perfect silence, the king addressed the crew about the demise of captain Druzo and his crew. The faces of Akello and Yuda were thundered; it was the same ship captain who was defeated by three musketeers of the Kallan crew. When the thundered faces of Akello and Yuda caught Zaya, she wore a don't-care look and sipped the rum. The king talked about the valor of Druzo and the crew. After hearing Pirate King's words, the team understood that they had eliminated the wild elephant, not a boar. Yuda's mind remembered the smile on Druso's face before spilling his last breath. The Pirate King raised his ale mug to give a toast to a dead friend and poured the rum for their souls on the ground, and the festival of rum began. A man served the three mugs of tuna rum on Yuda's table, but they did not order any. Yuda noticed other tables were also served with tuna rum. Before devouring the ale mugs, everyone in the tavern raised their rum mugs for the toast. Shaw and the team copied the moves of other pirates. Yuda and Akello made eye contact and raised their mugs. After the toast, sad melancholic music started to play by Magic Moon. In the crowd, the Kallan crew's eagle eyes were looking for a short man with a long beard.

Suddenly, Akello could feel the pressure and sound in a low tone. He buzzed. "*They are breaking out.*"

Yuda moved his face near Akello and asked, "*Who?*"

With a worried face, Akello said, "*I can't hold much!*" He leaked a fart. He excused Zaya and Yuda, and he ran to hit the restroom. With an angry face, Yuda complained to him about having sweets and snacks that he munched, but it was the effect of tuna rum he purged. Then, what else can we expect?

Akello tried to open the doors of the restroom but his bad, someone occupied it. Luckily, the next room was unoccupied, and he pushed himself inside to settle down the problem with his stomach.

The king moved around to random tables to enquire about the wellness of their ship and crew. When they were talking to the Pirate King, everyone lowered their hoods and shawls. Slowly, the music changed to hard metal music. The music was strong, and the musicians melted inside the music.

Unexpected begins! Pirate King moved to Yuda's table and asked about his welfare. After seeing Pirate King at Yuda's table, Shaw was shocked and motionless. Yuda and Zaya have no other choice; they need to remove their hoodie to answer the king. They downed the hoodies and shawls, and after seeing Yuda's face, a bird on the shoulder of the king started to scream at Yuda. When the Pirate King tried to calm down, his beast called the name of the eagle in an angry tone. "Pirro *stop!*" In the meantime, Shaw made eye contact with Zaya and Yuda. The eagle entered his head inside the big pocket of Pirate King and pulled out the ring from the pocket and placed it on the table. The king didn't notice; he turned around to call the muscular man. The muscular man came near and took away the eagle from the Pirate King.

Pirate King questioned Yuda again, "*You belong to which crew?*" The king was already puzzled by the sudden scream of Pirro.

When the Pirate King looked down, he found the ring on the table. He took the ring on his big fingers and said, "*Pirro brought it back from burning Druzo's ship; it belongs to my late friend.*" He closed his eyes. With closed eyes, the king's mind recalled and related Pirro's scream, plus the ring and the man opposite him. He related the connections between all three and found that the man sitting opposite him was involved in the assassination of Druzo and the crew. The sweat rushed down Yuda's foot, and Zaya's hands were inside the cloak to pull out the weapon.

When the Pirate King opened his eyes, the atmosphere of his eyes turned red. He forcibly tapped the table in anger and the ale mugs rolled down. In anger, the Pirate King roared, "*You bastard!*" The sound of the metal music outran his roar, but nearby tables got the attention of his roar. Shaw's hands pulled out the long rope and dagger from his belt. The long rope was black, and it had a handle; it was a whip. Shaw's hands were fast, like lightning. He slapped the whip on the ground, and in force of it, he waved the whip at the neck to Pirate King. In the fast of the wind, a black rope rolled over the neck and locked itself. If Shaw pulled the whip, it would break the collarbone of Pirate King. When Pirate King moved his hands to undo the rope around his neck, a knife thrown from Yuda's pocket punctured the back of his hand. It was just an inch above the knuckle and the knife pierced out. In the fast blow of the wind, Shaw ascended toward Pirate King, thrusted the dagger into the joint of another shoulder, and temporarily disabled his hand. The scream of the eagle outran metal music and drew the attention of partying pirates. At the same time, the whip in Shaw's hand was ready to purge the life of the Pirate King. The crowd in the pothouse was stunned to see Pirate King with a leash on his neck, and their eyes were rolled to check the hooded man holding the handler of the whip. Pirates were stunned to see the blood and use of weapons inside the pothouse, and it was a violation of their law.

After seeing the dripping blood on the Pirate King, the loyal pet Pirro's anger doubled. Suddenly, Pirro flapped his wings to devour Shaw. Yuda unsealed his sword against the claws of the eagle and took a position in front of Shaw. In no time, a white-headed eagle entered the tavern through open doors and started a duel with the foe's eagle. Shaw muttered, "*Sukra!*" Shaw found that Morgan had sent his eagle to spy on him and protect him. The eagles flew away and decided to take their fight above ground level.

After seeing the Pirate King hacked by a hooded man. Without a second thought, a muscular man defied the rules and released the throwing knife to save the king. His knife cut the wind with its speed and hit Shaw's upper chest. Shaw's will-power is so strong; he is not a cow to get easily slaughtered. Shaw downed his hoodie and shawl with a grin on his lips. Everyone thundered and recalled him. Before whispers began, in a fraction of a second, Shaw uprooted the thrusted-dagger from the king's shoulder. In the unbearable pain of the uprooted dagger, the king's throat expelled the loud anguish. The whispers of "*Fang of Meg is still alive...*" were loud. In no time, Zaya's knife pierced the skull of the muscular man when he tried to spell out the name of Shaw. His words collapsed inside the throat, and his lifeless body reached the ground. Blood started to leak on both sides, and other pirates waited for orders from Luka to begin the attack in the tavern. Luka is the right-hand of the Pirate King, and the Pirate king's left-hand man was already killed by the throwing-knives of Zaya. Zaya, Yuda, and Liya started their assault and drank the life of ruthless pirates at the entrance. Liya took her revenge on a white bald man with her sharp knives. Everyone was silent, but musicians were still playing without recognizing what was happening around them. Pirate King is a selfish man; he cared for his own life and stood silent without giving orders to execute Shaw and his company. Luka rushed to the front to reconfirm whether it was Shaw. Shaw's attitude-filled eyes and grin confirmed the same, and he also stood silent to save the

Pirate King. Pirate King and Luka share the same father, so he is not ready to take chances.

In the flashing seconds, Liya and Zaya walked on horses to flee. Shaw walked outside the tavern with the leashed king. Yuda was clever for a reason; he knew very well Luka was going to be a pain in the ass. From the horse, he released thrown knives to purge his life. Luka is not easygoing; he used the pirate next to him as a body shield to escape the throwing-knives. After seeing Yuda, Liya used tranquilizers on Luka, but he dodged well. Luka fumed and ordered, "*Get camels for the chase,*" but Liya threw fire marshals on the stables. In the fear of burning alive, the horses and camels fled away. After hearing the news of fleeing camels and horses, within seconds, pirates vanished from the tavern and started running behind Shaw to save their puny king. Before the king meets Yuda, the waiter walks in to get another barrel of rum. When he walked out with the barrel, the large tavern was empty, and of 20 musicians, four were killed by throwing-knives in an attempt to stop their music from playing.

Liya and Zaya noticed the knife that hit Shaw a few inches above the chest. The knife is stuck between the muscles of the chest and shoulder.

Liya questioned Shaw, "*Are we going to leave behind Akello?*"

Yuda said, "*He is brave and clever enough to find a way to reach us.*"

While running, pirates found scattered horses and camels here and there. A tall brown man rushed to Luka with a camel.

Luka thought, "*If someone has to reach the land of pirates, they have to win hurdles created by the god of thunder and storm.*" He suspects Shaw's fleet must be anchored near the northern shore.

Luka ordered his fellow men, "*Find and eliminate the newly intruded ship on the northern shores.*"

The man hesitated because it was turtle breeding season, but his fear of Luka made him say, "*Yes!*"

Pirates gallop the gathered horses and camels in different directions. Luka leads the team to save the king and a brown tall man named 'Darragh' leads the remaining to the northern shore. Darragh asked some of his men to get ships to the northern shore to destroy them if they found any vessels. The restroom was located at the rear end of the tavern. Akello had no clue what was going on. The music was not stopped. Shaw and the team rode their horses at maximum speed to escape, and Shaw decided to speak about a deal with a newly leashed pet.

In the tavern, Akello settled down issues with his stomach and walked out to get some fresh air; his eyes were shocked to see no one in the tavern and puzzled by whom these bunch of musicians were playing music. Musicians melted down in the music. They are physically present but mentally absent. All of a sudden, after seeing the corpses of fallen musicians, Akello realized that his comrades may have been caught red-handed by the pirates and his line of thinking related to the happenings with the prophecy, "*Gale will pause but blow again.*" His overthinking mind flashed, "*Pirates took his team as captives.*" In blinking seconds, a pirate walked in, instead of getting involved in a duel with Akello. He ran to the musician and damaged the musician's instruments to stop the music. The music was stopped and all 17 men noticed Akello's presence. Akello unsealed his sword and undone the hoodie. He recalled his training days with Rizon; the fruit of Draguvan combat training is that one can predict the enemy's moves. It is an art of dodging attacks and counter-attacks on vital parts. Draguvan's combat training made him spill more sweat in Dragon Land than in Alaoka. In no time, all 17 pirates began to attack Akello at once. They carried a variety of weapons, but Akello did not give them time to fetch the long-range weapons.

Akello's one hand was equipped with the blade and the other hand was holding the dagger to tear the skin of pirates. Blades clashed and dragged the blood of musicians. He parried the blades that were forced to attack him, and whenever he got a chance, he stabbed the dagger into the vital part of the pirates. Akello's training made it possible to predict the next moves of the enemies and gave him the ability to dodge and parry the slashes of blades and halberds. Akello found it hard to parry the attack of halberds, but he managed to dodge it. He put a full stop to the halberd user by throwing his dagger at his chest. Three of them forwarded to Akello with swords, and one of them was three feet tall, but Akello failed to predict his attack. Suddenly, they increased the speed of their foot and charged him. He dodged their blades and launched a furious kick. The power of the kick pushed him a few feet away, and Akello rolled on his feet to get back his dagger. Once the dagger reached his hand, he became unstoppable. But an unexpected jump of the pirate made Akello fall down; he stabbed Akello on his back. He took down all 17 with a new wound on his back. Akello underestimated musicians, but their fighting skills amazed Akello. The hand which holds the dagger became wet in the blood of the pirates.

Blood on his hands and dagger made him feel uncomfortable to proceed to the next battle. Thus, he decided to hit the restroom to wash his hands. He knew very well that every minute he was wasting would take the lives of his comrades. He rushed to the restroom, and a man walked out of the restroom. Akello made his dagger ready for a takedown. After seeing a man with a long beard and short length, Akello thought it would be Irie. Akello locked his red hand behind his back, and the short man raised his neck hard to get Akello's face. Before the short man walks back into the tavern, Akello decides to call his name to confirm.

"*Hello, Irie, nice to meet you!*" Akello's words were outstretched to the ears of Irie.

"*Hello, young man. How did you know my name? Have we met before?*" With his bagged eyes, he scanned Akello and continued, "*Young man! Move aside, I need to make a toast to my dead friend, Druzo.*"

Since the pavement was narrow, Akello moved aside and let him walk in front. In the fast of the wind, Akello used the pommel of the dagger and launched a surprise attack on Irie's neck. The next moment, Irie lost consciousness and swooned. Akello tore the cloth from the musician's corpse and tied the hands and legs of Irie with a constrictor knot, which is very hard to undo. Then he lifted the four-foot man on his shoulders. Irie's weight doesn't feel heavy, but his ale-smelling beard was humiliating. With a weary face, Akello walked outside of the tavern. On his way out, Alaokan brat found the corpses of the pirate and scanned the wounds created by throwing-knives at Liya and others.

Through corpses, Akello visualized his comrades' valor against bloody pirates. Once Akello's legs stepped outside the pothouse doors, his eyes caught a piebald mustang. Akello offered a free ride to the unconscious Irie. He decided to reach the Kallan, took out the compass to find the north direction, and galloped the horse with a neigh. It started to push his legs. He was amazed by the speed of the horse; it was faster than an Alaokan breed. He understood the heat of the desert evolved the hooves of the horses well. On his way, by seeing a series of corpses, he understood, "*His team is running for life in the west.*" It is a hard time for Akello, and he needs to select whom to save either the mission or his comrades. He stopped his horse and recalled the prophecy, "*Glaze and blaze will sail the streams of hell, the gale will halt but blow again.*" With a hard heart, he decided to proceed north. When Luka was chasing Shaw and the team, out of option, they rushed west. Akello galloped the mustang and the neighing of the piebald horse gained the attention of the pirate heading towards the northern shores. So, pirates forced their camels in the direction of the neighing sound of the horse.

In the north, Akello was alone with Irie. In the west, Shaw and company were rushing horses for their life. The full moon not only lit the desert; it also witnessed nightmares of a cosmopolitan crew. Akello's heart was filled with pain for not helping their friends and running like a coward to the Kallan fleet, but he was not a coward. Without Irie, their mission is suicide. At the same time, the hooves of 50 camels were chasing the mustangs of Shaw's company. Slow-moving, dense clouds crossed the vision of a luminous moon. The moon cursed clouds, and she sought the help of Ms. Cold Breeze to move clouds faster.

In the North

The cavalry of pirates started to run, along with Akello and his piebald horse on either side. Akello turned his head and found a mile-long smile on their faces. Akello escaped the few spears thrown by the cavalry units. The enemy cavalry was strong in number. They also had a long two-handed poled weapon with pointed edges. Some had axes on their edges, and most of them were halberds. Halberd has an advantage. With halberds, pirates can attack a foe from a safer range by sitting on the camel. Enemy cavalry was led by a tall brown man named 'Darragh.' He was the one who was sent by Luka to wreck the ship on the northern shore. There are almost 15 in total and have all varieties of weapons. Above all, they are sitting on the camel, and they have a good elevation to attack. Within the chase of two minutes, Akello was surrounded by the cavalry of Darragh. Akello never considered his life worthier than the mission. After all, he decided to fight alone with the dragon, and he created bloodshed. The pirates were rounding Akello. Having long-range weapons was their choice; he could expect an attack from all directions. Pirate decided to devour inch by inch. One of the pirates pushed his sharp halberd into the lungs of the horse. The horse crashed down along with Akello in no time, and its anguished cry touched the ear in the west. The horse had severe blood leaks from the wounds, nose, and mouth. Akello rolled on his feet and stood up. The next moment, rounding cavalry ended the misery of the horse in a pointed halberd.

Almost 15 cavalries of warriors began to attack Akello without notice. Akello dodged them, but still, some halberd created deep wounds in his shape. Still, he never lost hope and fought like a devil. A dagger in Akello's belt and a dagger in the sides of his shoes stopped the breath of three pirates. He threw the knife like a pro, but his enemies were not outrun in numbers. Valor of Akello's long sword parried the attack of more and more halberds, but he couldn't hold much longer. Leaks from previous wounds wet the desert, and he looked at the slaughtered horse and took an oath. "*They can't slaughter me like you.*" He stood in a defensive position. Enemies' long-range weapons made it hard for Akello to plunder weapons from fallen bastards. A few minutes after his stand against cavalry, halberds caused heavy damage and cracked his bones. Still, Alaokan was not ready to give up, and he knew that his end was near. A man without a horse and long-range weapons killed half a dozen pirates seated on their camels. It was not easy. One of the pirates praised Akello as 'tiger.' Wounded,

Akello's legs trembled his entire shape; the legs couldn't support Akello for a longer stand. He bent down on one leg and swung his sword. Camel rider with lance put final blows on Akello's back; the lance penetrated the flesh and popped out. The last blow rushed the blood puke from Akello's jaws, and he crashed next to the slaughtered horse. His reflexes failed to cooperate with his brain, and he added 13 new wounds to his body.

In Alaoka, Neo felt a bad omen in the middle of his sleep, which made him wake up. Neo is not the only one who lost his sleep. A bad dream made Neo scream; his scream disturbed the serenity of the griffin caves and all residents of griffin cave lost their sleep because of the wild scream of an olive griffin. But they have no option but to register their complaints about the superior. After all, he proved his strength in recent times. No griffin is ready to mess with Neo. Neo was restless, and he got hit on his head by a rock. He screamed again; it was anguish. In response to his scream, other griffins cried loudly. The loud cry from the griffin cave touched heaven and reached the forest, terrains, and huts of sleeping villagers. Jackals in the forest and birds in the trees chirped and howled in fear. The sound of crying animals panicked the villagers to wake up. The screaming of the griffin increased the blood flow in their hearts. The sweat rushed all over their bodies, which made Akello's mother wake up with wide-open eyes. Her heart felt hard; she took a water jug and gulped some water. Hearing a bad omen made Figo and Amara wake up, but they trusted the prophecy and believed Akello will be fine, but they were wrong. Maybe they didn't decode the prophecy in the right way.

In the West

The wail of the horse in the north disturbed the ears of Liya, but they had no time to even turn their heads and check. Luka galloped the camels and chased down Shaw and the team. Pirates trust their camels that never own out. It was clear to Shaw that pirates have bred the camels well in the last decade. In a few minutes, Shaw and the crew were surrounded by an army of pirates. Shaw's team has one trump card to escape. It is *'The Pirate King.'* After looking at the pirate army led by his brother Luka, the king laughed out loud, and it increased Shaw's anger. So, he trusted back the anger that he had uplifted him in the tavern. Pirate King's pain was a cry of anguish.

"*When I showed my last respect to you, I felt blue in my heart to lose a rival like you, but you proved to me once again that you are the best,*" said Luka. Liya was puzzled by his words.

"*Hey, Luka, instead of garbage like your brother, you should have taken the lead,*" Shaw sneered. After hearing Shaw insulting their king, the pirates shouted in anger. Luka made a hand sign to stop the howl.

Luka advised Shaw, "*Free the king and leave the land with your crew. I will avenge you in the wide ocean.*" Shaw's eyes rolled to check for Irie in the crowd, but as far as he saw, Shortman was not in the crowd. He laughed with great valor and pushed the king from the horse, but his hands never loosened the grip of the whip and he also jumped down. The tight grip of the whip made the king cough hard. Liya, Zaya, and Yuda unmounted their horses and took their stand near Shaw. With a gasp, Yuda's head turned to check Liya. Shaw fumed, "*I am not dumb to believe in your words*," and tapped the head of the king. He thundered, "*Yuda, summon the army!*"

After Shaw thundered the very next moment, Yuda took out his panpipe and started to blow hard. The high pitch of the panpipe hit the north, and the sound buzzed like a war horn. The horn sound from the panpipe of the Yuda not only disturbed the ear of punk humans but also hit the ears of Asura, which is flying 33,000 ft above ground level. Once the sound struck the dragon, the big beast's mind understood his companion's life was at risk. The beast took a free fall from the 33,000 ft toward the direction of the sound. The free fall of the giant dragon created a depression in the wind.

The mass and speed of the dragon split the air in the atmosphere and increased the free fall momentum. Pirates who surrounded Shaw and his company turned their heads and looked for the army but found no one. In the same way, Liya and Zaya have no idea of what's going around. The sparrow brains of pirates thought he was calling the rest of the crew for backup. At the height of the foolishness, the pirate herd laughed louder. All the pirates, including the king, laughed loudly, but there was an exception. It was Luka who remained silent because he took Shaw's grin as a serious threat and jumped down from his camel. After seeing Luka in action, the other pirates stopped their laughter and unmounted their horses and camels. At the same moment, Shaw's grin turned to big laughter, and it increased the temper of the pirates. Anger made the pirates, who were still seated on the camels, fire the arrow at Yuda. They are clever enough not to release an arrow at Shaw because he will use their king as a human shield. An arrow from the surrounding pirates slit the foreskin of Yuda, and his strong black armor stopped the arrow. Another arrow from the pirate crowds bolted the rippled arm of Yuda, but he never stopped the blow of the mouth organ.

Finally, the clouds moved aside and the light of luminous pearls showered the dry desert of the land of pirates. Moon focused her vision on the west to check on Shaw and the company. The dripping blood from the dragon's rider and the laughter on Shaw's face made her silent. Meanwhile, Akello's struggling breath gained the moon's attention. Wounds in Akello's shape and blood leaking from the mouth made the moon's eyes red. Sudden changes in the moon's color gave a red fragrance to the desert.

Akello's red lips muttered a few words, but his words died on a very short wavelength. "*Apologize, chief, I failed the mission, and I abandoned my friends to save the mission*." Out of guilt, his eyes leaked. "*Neo, if you were here, this victory of ours would be written in history too.*" The last word he spared was 'Mom,' and his lips lost the strength of muttering.

Akello's last seconds in the desert were hell. The pain of failure and guilt of leaving behind friends numbed the physical pain. His eyes windowed the gloomy moon. The vision slowly started to lose the moon's position, and then the eyes blacked out. The world has no replacement for a brave soul; Akello, the breeder of dragons. The short man Irie didn't regain his consciousness, but he was surrounded by fellow pirates and will be saved.

With howls and cheers, pirate cavalry began to celebrate the victory of the defeated Akello. A man who launched the last attack will get a new record for '60 kills' after slicing Akello's head. All of a sudden, the moon stopped to put her gaze on the desert. The sudden darkness spread all over the island. Within an eye-blinking moment, darkness was erased and bright moonlight gazed at the dry lands again. The brown man, Darragh, now landed his shoes on the sand to put an end to Akello. The fucking tradition of pirates needed a head from the corpse of a fallen warrior to celebrate. Bloodthirst in human eyes is the refined form of pure evil. He walked toward Akello and put his shoes on Akello's chest. Akello's body and eyes did not respond to the pirate. Akello's blood and dead horse wet the tan colored sand with red blood. Again, moonlight lost its rain over the dry desert, but this time, everyone gazed at the sky. Suddenly, darkness did not give them a better vision, but the roar of the Asura haunted the pirates' hearts.

In a few seconds, darkness was wiped out. When the big blocker moved aside, the big frame, the wide wings, and the long neck of Asura were naked to the pirates' eyes. It explained that blocker is one of the rumors that they have heard since young. The eyeballs of the pirates got paralyzed after seeing the dragon. At the very end of the dragon's roar from the wide-open mouth, fire breath escaped for a shorter distance. Stunned eyes of pirates sent a signal to brains, "*Run for life.*" Brown man and his comrade started to flee without cutting Akello's head. The war cry of the dragon stung Akello's ear and brought his consciousness back. It made him wide open his eyes in terror. But his body failed to cooperate with his wish because of deeper wounds in his legs and right arm. His eyes windowed the flee of pirate cavalry and wore an evil smile on his lips.

Pirates who stood against Shaw and company in the west were also thundered in the angry roar of Asura. Many pirates and camels started to flee, but Luka and his brave men took their last stand. Luka is a fearless freak and his quick unexpected moves brought lots of victories to pirates. He knew very well. "*Fire spray of the beast will also eliminate Shaw and company.*" He believed Shaw wouldn't be foolish enough to command a fire shower. Shaw whispered in the king's ears, "*Keelan! Say my hello to my old man.*" He undid the dagger from the shoulder of the king, thrust the dagger into the throat, and pushed him aside. Luka's eyes boiled in anger; he unsealed his sword and ran forward to slice Shaw's head. Zaya took the position in front of Shaw to protect him, and Liya joined her. All of Zaya's thrown knives were blocked by Luka's unsealed sword.

All of a sudden, Yuda's hands grabbed Liya's waist and pulled her toward him. She had no clues about what he was doing, but her head took the safest place on earth, Yuda's chest. Liya's long fingers marked her signature on the rippled, muscular shoulder of Yuda. Yuda's rough hands embarrassed Liya's lower back, but she loved her head on Yuda's chest and his hands around her body. With a puzzled face, Liya caught Yuda's eyes. His eyes carefully monitored Zaya's and Luka's moves. Yuda called out the name of Zaya and roared, "*Fetch it. You know what to do...*" He released the stone in the air toward Zaya. The lava-shaded, semi-transparent stone looked gloomy in the moonlight. Zaya's hands clutched the stone. Her eyes gazed at the stone and remembered the rumors of the stone. Yuda had a similar stone to him.

Luka's blades were about to reach Zaya. She turned around and jumped toward Shaw with the magical stone in her hand. Meanwhile, Luka swung his blade to kill Zaya. Blade slit the upper skin of Zaya's back. With a long cut, Zaya jumped on Shaw and hugged him tightly. Because of the pressure in his upper chest, the pain increased. Shaw lost his balance, and he rested his back on the ground with Zaya on top of him. In the blink of an eye, Yuda lifted his hands above. Asura responded to the signal with a fire shower on Yuda and his comrades. Shaw's eyes caught the big fireball coming toward them and screamed louder. The fireball wiped the nightfall and produced light equivalent to the sun for a short diameter. Shaw hugged Zaya tight in fear, and unknowingly, he pressed hard on Zaya's cut. Pressure increased the blood to leak more than usual and the pain increased drastically, which made her scream along with Shaw. Dragon's flame thrower covers a wide range. It melted the weapons and the armor of Luka and his men. Dragon fire emits the power of the burning sun. In no time, enemies' flesh and bones powdered down to ashes. A wildfire shower stopped and the Asura's cruel feet scratched the sands of the hot desert. Dusted ashes of the enemies mixed with sand and wind. There was no proof of the existence of Luka and his men. It looked horror. Within a minute, a gang of 50 bastards and their leader disappeared from the desert. The red moon wished for clouds to block her vision.

Asura's roar embarrassed Yuda because he found his hands around Liya's lower waist. All of a sudden, Liya moved a step away from Yuda. Yuda moved his hands from her waist. Both exchanged odd looks. Roar not only embarrassed them but also Zaya and Shaw. In pain, Zaya shouted at Shaw, "*Bastard, your tight press made me bleed more.*" Yuda fumed, "*Guys, stop complaining like kids.*" He moved his legs towards his three horned brown dragon. He appreciated, "*Ausra, you're on time to save our lives.*" Yuda's hands ruffled the stone skin of Asura. While ruffling the hard skin, Yuda closed his soft eyelids. After seeing Yuda, the dragon's thick eyelid covered its red-golden pupil. Yuda's ears still hear the noise of Shaw and Zaya yelling. Zaya was still yelling in pain. Shaw lost his patience and started yelling back at her. Loud and harsh words disturbed Yuda's concentration. He yelled at both of them, "*Are you going to stop now, or should I order my Asura to make some human barbecue*?" Asura roared in response; it looked like saying yes to Yuda's statement. Asura's roar made them silent and Yuda fumed, "*Allow me to concentrate!*" When Yuda was trying to concentrate, Liya cried, "*Where is Akello? I feel like something odd has happened in the north, especially the anguish of the horse.*"

Yuda fumed, "*I am trying to find the same. For that, I need to MING with my dragon.*" Shaw and Liya pronounced 'MING' in unison. Zaya began, "*Dragon allows his human friend to read his visual observation stored in the memory. To enable this brain connection, both human and beast need more concentration and understanding between them.*" Zaya was surprised, "*I thought the dragon stone that protects the rider and the concept of MING were rumors circulated among civilians.*" Yuda fumed again, "*Let me concentrate.*"

Eyelids covered the vision of Yuda and Asura. Yuda started reading the visual memory of Asura. After a minute of silence, his ears started to eat the sound of wind and at a certain point, he heard no noise. Yuda visualized the ship heading to the northern shore, but after seeing the fire rain of Asura, ships started to flee in terror. He also visualized the fleeing of cavalry in the north and a bunch of corpses in the far north. He doubted the fallen corpses could be Akello's triumph, but he was not able to find Akello around. Unlike the griffins, the dragon's eyesight was not great. When Yuda opened his emerald eyes, his face was grief-stricken. Like Liya, he also felt a heavy heart.

Yuda briefed, "*Kallan is safe! I saw pirate ships fleeing in terror. I can't find Akello's presence in the vision of Asura.*" With a moment of silence, he added, "*But in the direction of the north, I can see the bunch of corpses resting in the sand bed and fleeing pirate cavalry. I doubt. I am afraid that we may find Akello in the sand bed!*"

The breeze stopped, the moon was completely covered by clouds, and the droplets of tears escaped from Liya's eyes. Yuda's eyes stuck to Liya.

Zaya fumed, "*Watch your words, dragon rider!*"

A moment ago, Shaw was happy that the Kallan crew was safe.

Shaw beamed, "*Remember, we are on the battleground. Yuda, can you reconfirm?*"

Yuda opened, "*In the vision of the dragon, I can't find faces! I am heading north to find Akello!*" Shaw shook his head in affirmation. After a long time, Yuda took his seat on Asura's back and directed his beast to the north. With a wild roar, the beast disappeared into the clouds. While flying in the air, he pulled an arrow out of his biceps.

The moment Yuda left, the sound of the eagle scream scratched the ears. Shaw recalled it was Sukra's scream and turned his head to find an eagle. A surprise hit him. Shaw's lips expressed joy and happiness at finding Morgan with reinforcements. Shaw understood with his blood scent; Morgan used Sukra to backtrack him. With a warm hug, Shaw seized an ale bag from Morgan, and without a delay, Shaw purged the rum and it kicked his brain again. Shaw sought Morgan's help and his men to find Irie. At the same time, he borrowed horses and a camel from Morgan and rushed north.

When Yuda reached the corpses in the north, he spoke gibberish. The very next moment, Asura spit fire saliva on the sand bed. Yuda jumped down and in the light of fire saliva. Yuda started to check the surroundings. At first, he found a package. A long beard and short in length clarified Yuda; it was Irie. The very next moment, his reflexes rushed to examine the corpse, and he found a lifeless Akello next to the slaughtered horse. He was paralyzed for a second to find him in the blood river, and his mantle was soaked in the rushing blood. After seeing the grief on Yuda's face, his dragon roared. A sudden roar made Akello's eyes respond to the sound, and Yuda noticed the shake in Akello's eyeball. He bent near Akello and tapped him. He called his name to get a response. In no time, Shaw and company reached Akello! Liya started to treat Akello! Shaw was surprised to see the package and complimented, *"Alaokan brat accomplished the mission."* He caught the face of Yuda. Yuda reported, "*Irie is alive.*" The gentle wind touched Shaw, and he ordered the dragon rider, "*Take the package to Kallan and get the lead medic of the Kallan crew to the tavern.*" Shaw took Akello and rushed west to treat the Alaokan. At the same time, Yuda took Irie and flew to reach Kallan.

Yuda reached the shores of the north in no time. The giant legs of the dragon crushed the hundreds of eggs and hatchlings of turtles and landed on the shore. Kiba and the crew were surprised to see the giant dragon. Yuda asked Kiba to get the medics. The medic in the Kallan crew was the first outlander to get a ride on the dragon's back. Soon, Kiba directed the rowboats with medics. The red giant is an early visitor to the land of pirates. When the sun noted the shores of the north with crushed eggs and lifeless hatchlings, his smile turned upside down. The moment the sun graced the big turtle shells between the wide jaws of the dragon, his heart started to rasp and the crashing sound of the shell made the lips of the sun tremble.

The sin of killing the turtle and hatchling is an incurable curse! The dragon rider has to suffer for what his dragon has done!

Chapter 10

The Quest Begins

Giant Kallan is docked in the royal harbor of the land of pirates. Along with Kallan, two empty big ships were also docked. Both ships looked majestic, with shiny head figures and long decks. The ship with the goat's head figure belongs to late Luka, and the other one with the eagle head figure belongs to the late king of pirates. News of Akello's condition hit the ears of the crew. Other than praying to the so-called gods, they were left with no other choice. Alaokans in the crew recalled the day when Akello raised his voice against their leader, the entire Alaokan race was yelling at Akello at the top of their lungs, and a few were boiling in anger to slaughter him. But today, the same Alaokans on the ship asked a favor from the goddess of wind to save Akello. Yuda worked with Kiba to ensure the safety of the ship. As Captain Shaw ordered, two rowboats were deployed on the nearby coasts for surveillance. Hearing news of Akello's struggle to breathe and the hopeless face of Yuda tormented Kiba. He remembered the selfless nature of Akello. Although Akello was an outlander, he acted on his own and put his life on the line to save Ivar from rampaging yetis. When Akello saved Ivar, he was not even aware of his name. More than courage, one must have good intentions and a pure heart to do such acts. Except for Liya, no one is aware that one night is strong enough to change the poles upside down. Beyond all, the mission to find Irie is accomplished, and Irie is safe inside the locked doors of Kallan because of Akello. Kiba and a few other members volunteered to guard the ship and Yuda's gibberish commands withdrew the dragon from the eyesight of humans. Along with the remaining members of the Kallan crew, Yuda stretched his legs toward the pirate town. When the sun reached high, the crew marked their footprints in the pirate town with dripping sweat. The crew was excited to see the shops in the middle of the desert, but most of the shops were empty because of last night's chaos.

Shaw rides on horseback to welcome the Kallan crew. His wounds were treated and covered by a big roll of cotton cloth. He walked down from his horse, addressed crew members, and assigned a place to stay. At last, his focus turned to find Yuda. Both moved away from the eavesdropping point of the crew. Shaw asked for the status of Kallan. Yuda reported, "*Anchored position of their ship and two other ships in the harbor*." He also briefed that new safety arrangements have been made on Kallan and Irie's condition. Yuda stood silent, and he hesitated to ask about Akello's condition. Captain Shaw took a deep breath and opened, "*I summoned a few local medics to the tavern to treat Akello, but still I don't have high hopes.*" Yuda's face was grief-stricken and flashing thoughts recalled a big smile on the lips of Akello and his welcoming attitude. Shaw does not have any personal emotions toward Akello, but when he examined the corpses that were found in the tavern and north, they made him doubt, "*Do the griffin riders possess the ability of griffin*?"

Along with dripping sweat, a huge rush of horseshoes from the north stuck in the ears of Yuda and Shaw; their eyes waiting for forth-coming danger. Two dozen pirates approached them. Yuda unsealed his sword and prepared to create a blood river. Shaw's sharp eyes found a child pillion riding on the horse along with the pirate. Shaw raised his hands to stop Yuda; the horses stopped with the neighing. The pirates took their stand and bowed in front of Shaw. The crew was surprised to see the pirates bow in front of Shaw, and a pirate made the five-year-old boy bow in front of him. Yuda and the Kallan crew were confused by the weird behavior of the pirates. Yuda saw a smile on the kid and the kid's hands were busy playing with a clay toy. A man who wore a brown hoodie raised his posture and briefed, "*Lord Shaw, these men and their subordinates accept you as a new leader. As per rituals, a new leader has to execute the family of the defeated leader. To show their support to you, these men already executed three wives of the late Pirate King, Keelan. We are here to present to you the legacies of the late Pirate King. We wanted our new leader to execute the lineage of Keelan and address other fellow pirates in the hall of 18 pillars.*" Brown hoodie man's words stirred Yuda's anger.

Yuda yelled at them, "*Blood worms, how dare you come up with the request to kill the kid by the name of tradition!*" He unsealed his sword to cut off the head of the brown hoodie man. Shaw stopped him and voiced, "*I will handle it dragon rider.*" He dismissed him. In boiling anger, Yuda shouted at pirate rituals and strode out with a red face. Shaw replied to the native people of the desert, "*Glad to hear from you, brother.*" He asked the remaining civilians in the land of pirates to assemble in the hall of 18 pillars by midnight. Shaw took the boy along with him and marched his horse toward Morgan's shop. The pirate crowd caught the faces of one another and exchanged weird looks.

Yuda walked to the tavern to check on Akello. From the windows, he found a team of five medics, including Liya, who were treating Akello. From the window, Yuda could see deep wounds and noted there was no movement in Akello's shape. Zaya walked near Yuda and opened, "*Dragon Prince! Have it back.*" as she carried the magical dragon stone in her hands. Yuda graced her hands without looking into her eyes; he collected the magical stone from her, but no words were exchanged, and he decided to take a horse ride to Kallan. While mounting the horse, Yuda recalled Akello's forgiving nature and his blind trust in friends. Yuda mounted a horse and voiced, "*Zaya!*" Zaya turned her head in response to Yuda's call and she waited to listen more, but without a word, he threw a dragon stone back at her. She caught the stone and was puzzled to see Yuda. With trust in his eyes, he smiled at Zaya for the very first time and galloped the horse. Zaya never expected it and also she noted the new trust in Yuda's eyeballs.

It was a different night. The crew members' feet rested on the land, but no happiness filled their hearts. Liya, Zaya, Kiba, and Yuda had not joined the dinner table. Usually, Akello's stomach raised a hunger alarm first, and he called others to join him for dinner. Later, it became a routine on the Kallan ship, but today, Akello was not there to unite the cosmopolitan crew. After having dinner alone, Yuda rested his back on the sand bed of the desert and gazed at the stars in the sky. Like the forest, there was no thrilling sound of insects in the desert. In the deadly silence, Yuda took out his panpipe and expressed his feelings of melancholy. Music ruffled the ears in huts, taverns, and the Kallan ship. Yuda expected the music to touch Akello's ears.

The moon reached its maximum height, and pirates started to walk one after another like ants with a fire torch toward the hall of 18 pillars. The invitation was only for pirates, but a proficient spy eavesdropped on the information from locals and decided to voluntarily join the inauguration of the new king. The hall of 18 pillars was a roofless hall with tall standing 18 pillars erected in the shape of an oval located in the middle of the desert. This roofless hall was a war room for pirates, and all important decisions were made here. Zaya mingled with the crowd, and guards around the pillar were nobody for Zaya's expertise level in infiltration. The crowd was waiting for the arrival of the new king. Shaw purged an ounce of rum and entered the hall, and he was accompanied by Morgan by his side. Shaw also carried a kid on his shoulder and in his belt had a medium-sized *potli* bag that danced.

Gatherings in the hall welcomed their new leader with a pleasing smile. He took a position in the center of the hall and addressed the pirates. "*Fellow men and women! Sorry for the last night. My comrade's dragon killed 100s of our brothers.*" Hearing sorry from their leader is new for pirates. Whispers started in the crowd. Shaw cleared his throat to announce his presence and continued his speech. "*As a new king, I have decided to adopt this kid as my son from today,*" and lifted the boy with one hand. Muttering started again!

"*Listen, I wish to bring a change, and I am starting the change with my own name!*

I survived the ocean pit, and I encountered scary teeth closer than others!

Each of us has the desire to dirt our hands and legs in fertile lands!

Most of us dreamed of sweating hard to sow and eat our own food!

I have discovered an island in the west for us, which is not claimed by any human race. The land is full of green with sources of pure water. I had a dream of growing old in that heaven by inhaling the scent of rain wetting the fertile soil. Join me and let us sow our own food; we don't want to loot like scavengers anymore. We have spilled enough blood; it's time to migrate to the west and let us begin a new life."

His words created gossip in the crowd. In the middle of the gossip, Shaw tilted the *potli* bag hanging from his belt. Gritty red soil escaped from the *potli* bag and started to settle over the yellow sand bed of the desert. Gossip was loud; gossip changed to happy howls and cheers.

After the meeting got over, everyone started to leave the hall, but not everyone's face carried the same excitement. When Shaw was having a conversation with Morgan, suddenly, Shaw's vision glanced at the face of someone very familiar to him. So, he excused himself and moved for a while. The next moment, he walked near Zaya and made his attitude-filled look at her by lifting one eyebrow up. Zaya waved at him with a fake smile. She said, "*I was just excited to hear the new king's note to his people!*" In the meantime, everyone left the hall. Shaw called Morgan and introduced Zaya. Morgan giggled by fantasizing. "*Shaw and Zaya as couples.*" The conversation between all three went smoothly and sweetly.

Already, the moon had reached its maximum height; so, Morgan carried the sleeping kid on his shoulders and decided to walk home. Shaw accompanied Zaya while walking down toward their huts. He said, "*Whatever you have heard in the hall is the dream of these people. I want this meeting to be a secret.*"

By seeing his electric eyes, Zaya promised, "*I swear I won't leak the secret to anyone. I am impressed by your words and actions in the meeting. Maybe for others in the Kallan crew, you may look rough, but to my eyes, you are a good-hearted jackfruit."*

Shaw made a rough face at Zaya. In the moonlight, his face shone. Zaya laughed at him for that facial expression and said, "*Not again...*" Shaw experienced it for the first time, and his heart whispered, "*She is more beautiful with a mouth full of laughter.*" After seeing her laugh, his rough face developed a short smile, which faded in seconds, but Zaya noticed that very short smile.

Shaw briefed, "*I never expected that I would come here again, but I came. I killed the king and his bunch of clowns. By killing a king, I became a king. Being a former pirate, I know, the difficulties and I decided to do something better for my people.*"

Zaya asked for justification for letting the kid live instead of killing him.

Shaw briefed, "*In a decade I changed a lot. I was once cold-hearted to slaughter anything on my way, but today, I don't have the courage to stab a five-year-old kid.*"

Shaw's words were genuine, but still, Zaya queried, "*Adopting a child is a big decision. In history, I have never heard someone adopt his enemy's son. Moreover, you live in an ale godown and your life is always bound with adventure and voyages. How are you going to take care of the kid? Beyond all, your rough face and your ale-smelling outfit would scare a kid.*"

Shaw laughed and answered, "*My brother and I were raised by one with all the scary attributes that you have described.*

Moreover, I still remember when I was seven or eight years old, I was a troublemaker in my father's fleet. As a punishment, he used to push me into the sea, and then a rope was dropped from other sailors in the fleet to save my life." He laughed. At that very moment, Zaya thought her father was far better, and she maintained a silence.

"*My brother Morgan takes care of the kid until I come back home. I don't have other choices if I let the kid free from my hands. There is a high chance of the kid getting killed by one of his late father's foes.*"

With expanded pupils in her eyes, Zaya questioned Shaw, "*Do you think someone will marry you with your adopted son?*" Shaw was silent for a while. Zaya put a statement. "*I think you are not too old to marry a woman?*" Shaw tried to retort to such a weird question, but he replied, "*Maybe...*" With a doubtful face, he graced the stars in the sky.

Zaya opened, "*Definitely someone will marry you! I wish...*" *with a pause she continued after a deep breath, "let me come to the point, let us raise that boy without hardships. I have decided to marry you, and I wish to live the rest of my life with you.*" Shaw turned his head with a pathetic look. Zaya turned toward him with a great smile on his face and began, "*Yes, I decided to marry you! I will always be with you in the process of converting your dreams into reality! Morgan and your adopted son are a part of our family.*"

Shaw's body was paralyzed after hearing Zaya's words, but his heart was unknowingly smiling in joy. Zaya buzzed,

"*Captain, take your time!*" She winked her eyes and walked to her hut with his rum bottle. Without a word, he took his seat in the same spot and doubted, "*Did she either propose to me or inform me that she will marry me?*" At the same time, his brain raises an alert, "*Zaya is super amazing, but we two are highly independent, which may screw our marriage life.*" Beyond all, his heart developed a special feeling for her. His mouth whistled a melody, and he put all his doubts and fears on time. Because he knows very well that time has the power to change all dreams into reality. He rested his back on a sand bed and decided to get some sleep.

Early sun rays kissed Yuda. When he opened his eyes, he saw a scorpion crawling next to him. He was frightened and raised his body up. He muttered, "*After a long sleep, the day started with grazing scorpions.*" He directed his legs toward the hut. On his way, he found a dead man in a sand bed. From a distance, he couldn't find who he was. He rushed near the body and found it was Shaw, the captain of the Kallan crew. Sudden panic in Yuda melted down after hearing a long snoring Shaw and it confirmed that he was still fine. In no time, Shaw's sleep was disturbed by the sunlight. He gazed at Yuda's face and asked, "*Why are you staring at me?*" Yuda replied, "*Nothing,*" and started moving on his way. Shaw passed him and asked, "*Hey, come, let's go to Kallan for morning breakfast.*" Yuda replied with a short smile, and they both directed their legs toward the ship.

While walking, Shaw puzzled Yuda. "*What do you think about marrying a girl and starting a family?*" Yuda never expected such a weird question from Shaw. Yuda thought something was wrong with his ears and asked Shaw to repeat the question. Shaw replied, "*Nevermind!*" By that time, they had almost reached the Kallan ship. From the dock, Yuda noted, the glassy ocean inherited the color of red and yellow light. Bright sunlight warmed the body and mild wind ruffled the hair. Seagulls chirping in the east developed positivity in the mind, and bright light made Kallan's head figure glow.

When they walked near Kallan, they gained the interest of the crew. The crew waved their hands and welcomed the captain. Tandoor and Shaw's hound were happy to see Shaw again. The excited hound jumped around him to show his happiness. His chimpanzee hugged him and welcomed him back to the ship. Shaw enquired about the wellness of crew members, and finally, Kiba jumped down from the navigation bucket. Kiba, Yuda, and Shaw walked to the dining hall. Breakfast was served, and Yuda sipped the fish soup. His throat was thankful for the warm soup. Shaw asked Kiba about the wellness of the prisoner. Kiba wailed, "*Keeping Irie in prison is a pain. He shouts, shouts, and he shouts again. I wonder where he stores enough energy for shouting all day.*" Yuda had a pitiful smile at Kiba. Shaw sucked the soup into his belly and added, "*Don't worry! I will take care of him.*" Kiba asked about Akello's condition. Shaw exhaled and looked at Yuda and Kiba. Kiba eagerly waited for his response. "*Maybe my words look harsh, but in my experience, I have not seen one who escaped from such great wounds. In case he survives, it won't be easy for him to lift the spear again.*" Shaw's words made Kiba paralyzed, and Yuda was already aware of it very well. Yuda patted Kiba's shoulder to console him. Shaw continued, "*Losing a comrade is not easy, but remember, not all warriors are returning home alive. Akello did his part very well; he completed his mission to unite long icy lands and the land of dragons. There is no doubt in his valor.*"

Shaw beamed, "*Boys, come let's go and grab some information about the Yuvalle from that shouting bastard!*" Dungeon doors opened. Once again, his shouting noise disturbed the crew's ears. A small line of sunlight enters the windows of Dungeons. Irie paused his scratchy throat, and he put his focus on doors to check on the visitor. After seeing Shaw's face, Irie's eyeballs stuck, but his lips expanded to say, "*But how? I believe my eyes are not lying. Is there no escape in the ocean pit?*" Kiba is confused about what the ocean pit was.

Shaw replied, "*Hey, Irie, after a long time. A decade has changed us a lot. I am standing in front of you, which means there is a way to escape. Escape is an art, which requires bravery and a sound mind. You have no idea about either of them. You left your comrades behind, in the Yuvalle, for the sake of saving your puny life.*"

"*Shaw, it's easy to speak. You are not part of the journey and you have no clue what happened in the land of north-east,*" said Irie.

Shaw asked, "*Oh, is it? I would like to hear about your journey. It may change my opinion of you.*"

Irie laughed loudly and voiced, "*Looks like you got plenty of time to hear stories. If you don't mind, I will recommend you for babysitting jobs.*"

Kiba was puzzled. From the words, he understood they knew each other and caught Yuda's face, but Yuda's vision was locked at Irie.

Anger bubbled in Shaw's eye, but he remained silent. "*Am I looking like a fool? Tell me why you need information about those Yuvalle?. Why do you need it?*" Irie fumed.

Shaw wore a grin and replied, "*Clever! Within a decade, you have developed some brain. I am the captain of the ship where you are prisoners. My crew and I decided to go on an expedition to Yuvalle. Before proceeding, I need to know more information about it, which you have already toured.*"

Irie laughed again. Now Yuda and Kiba looked at one another. Their eye contact conveys the same meaning. "*What sort of bullshit inquiry is this?*"

Irie continued, "*So the captain and his crew decided to go to the 'gate of misery'? One suggestion: this is your second life, Shaw. You escaped from the ocean pit. Better reconsider this expedition idea. Shaw, I am considering knowing this information as your last wish because you will never come alive. I give you intel I know, but before that, free my hands and get me some rum.*"

Shaw sets his hands free, and Kiba fetches a mini barrel. Irie's shaky hands grabbed the barrel and devoured every drop in the barrel and beamed, "*Yuvalle is cursed land! Like other pirates, we lived our life with rum, voyage and fun. While looting the defeated ship, we found a man with yellow eyeballs and his pet turtle behind the bars of a prison. He looked weird with those yellow eyeballs. Our captain Helron took him into custody and started enquiring about him. Shaw, you won't believe it, but he survived the humiliation of Helron for a week and left only a little information. He also threatened Helron and the crew. On the full moon, he will execute everyone and take over the ship."*

Shaw was thundered to hear Irie's statement. Helron is the most notorious one out of all pirates, and he is a master of humiliation and torture. As far as Shaw knows, no one survived Helron's humiliation more than two suns.

Irie continued, "*In the pain of torture, the prisoner started to vomit information about him. In his statement, he bannered himself as a traveler from the Yuvalle. According to the rules of his land, traveling outside the lands of Yuvalle is a crime. If they find anyone trying to escape, they will be sentenced to death. The prisoner briefed that he wanted to explore other parts of the world; we found a map in his pants. The map has information about rivers flowing in the Yuvalle and streams which connect to the ocean. When asked about the map, he said the boundaries of the land were guarded by the spell, which allows no one to enter and exit the Yuvalle. He claimed that he worked for five years to find the escape route via rivers and streams. Threatening words of the prisoner created panic in the crew, but because of the blood leak and pain, he died before the full moon."*

"*The Yuvallen prisoner was dead, but his words planted curiosity in Helron to explore the Yuvalle. Sailing to Yuvalle is via icy-craggy oceans. Like other oceans, it can't be sailed in all seasons. After a tough sail, we anchored on the shores of Yuvalle before the disappearance of the beak from the sky (four-star pattern to form the beak of the bird). No ships were anchored on the shore other than ours, and the crew walked on coastlines. The black coast of Yuvalle opened to a nearby forest, but we have not found any life in the forest."* Irie coughed hard, and Yuda rushed to get the water.

Irie ignored the cough and briefed with sweat and fear in his voice. "*Yuvalle is cursed! The forest on the coastline of Yuvalle is deep and never-ending. One can trek all day into the forest, and when trekking backwards to the coast, you will reach the coastline in an hour. Captain Helron and crew realized that the prisoner's words were true; we cannot enter the mainland through coastlines, but on the day of the no-moon sky, streams of the rivers take you to the mainland. River streams open to the forest where sunlight is rare, and sunlight never touches the ground. In the cursed lands, principles of life are broken. Elephants carried the long spear and rode on other elephants! Humans are short, but eight-foot-tall elephants bend on their knees to three-foot-tall humans. The sound of thrilling insects breaks the head, and every nightfall is a nightmare. The ghost of the forest hunted the crew. Even a bee sting is powerful enough to kill stronger like Helron. That cursed land shook the roots of Helron! I beg you, please! Give up on the idea of exploring Yuvalle!*" He fainted. Yuda rushed to check on him and laughed, "*Captain, rum kicked his head, so nothing to worry about.*"

Kiba giggled and said, "*I believe he said everything in the kick of rum and exaggerated about his fucking captain and crew. Has anyone ever heard of a man who died because of a bee sting? May that Helron must be puny like him!*"

Shaw turned his head with an attitude look and fumed, "*That fucking captain is a notorious pirate outlaw and once his two sons were involved in a duel to eliminate him but he defeated both of them without shedding a droplet of blood, and let them live.*" with a short pause he continued, "*and My last name is Helron!*" He strode out by bashing doors.

Yuda was thundered for a moment, but after seeing Kiba's expression, he giggled at him.

Kiba was stunned, and his eyes popped out to hear that. Yuda walked to him with a giggle. He put his hands gently on Kiba's shoulder and briefed, "*Who is Shaw?*" *and finally added,* "*He is the new king of pirates.*"

When the evening twilight decorated the sky, Shaw checked Irie. He was in good shape to answer Shaw's question. Shaw bent on his knees and took a seat next to him and asked, "*Irie! I know you are loyal to my father and now tell me everything about what has happened in Yuvalle?*"

The whooshing winds rubbed the Kallan fleet, and it eavesdropped. "*Turtles and boats!*"

Then a rat ran into the chamber where Irie was imprisoned, and it headed, "*Cry of a full moon and cigars!*"

Finally, an eagle flapped down its wings and its claws clutched the rail of the ships. Ears of the eagle heard, "*Captain Shaw, those dark forests are houses of ghosts! Please give up on the idea of touring Yuvalle.*"

From the windows of the chamber, the smoke of cigars escaped out. Shaw voiced, "*I am happy that you're joining the crew of Kallan as a tour guide!*"

With a loud cry, Irie wailed, "*Shaw! No! I never said that!*"

Shaw voiced, "*Yes, but don't you dare to defy the decision of your new king!*"

Irie screamed and begged for pardon,.and the sound of his cry made the eagle scream.

Shaw opened, "*Once I had a dream in which I saw you were removing the weeds from your big farm. So, once we come back, as a payment, I will give green fertile lands.*"

Irie begged, "*This idea is great! But for that, we need to come back alive. Lord Shaw, please relieve me. I will spend the rest of the years of my life in the tavern!*" After hearing him, Shaw rubbed his ears and ambled out. His eyes rolled in search of a beak in the sky and found the beak in the far east. He muttered, "*Need to open the sails soon!*" Once Shaw reached his chamber, he purged an ounce of rum and his eyes graced the cigar on the table. Took cigars in hand and his eyes scanned them in all directions. *"Did he do the wonder with this five-inch tall cigar?"* He wore a proud smile. He summoned the sailor and ordered him to get Yuda and Kiba. When Kiba and Yuda walked inside, their eyes felt the burning sensation, and they found Shaw in the smoke of a cigar. Shaw voiced, "*You both heard the words of Irie in the morning about a beak in the dark sky!*" Shaw waited for them to nod their heads. The moment they nod, Shaw's words harpooned, "*We are starting out sails three suns from today!*" Yuda was a silent listener this time, but Kiba broke the silence with a shaky voice, "*But Akello!*" Shaw exhaled smoke from his nose opening twice; his line of thinking flashed Akello's face and thundered, "*We are running out of time. The sails of Kallan will open to the shore of Yuvalle, with or without Akello in seven suns from tomorrow.*" Shaw asked both of them to feed the news to the other member crew and dismissed both.

Somewhere in the Northern Sea

Four full moons rolled down. Kallan was just a couple of suns away to reach the shores of Yuvalle. In the moonlight, Shaw was sipping his favorite rum in his chamber and Zaya was sitting next to him and a bottle of port wine danced in her hand. Shaw delighted, "*Zaya, I would like to hear the name given by your parents!*"

Zaya muttered, "*Clever.*" With a chuckle, she added, "*Zaya is my name.*"

Shaw bubbled, "*I believe Zaya is a camouflage you wear in Draguvan. Moreover, it doesn't sound like Beku-neun's name.*"

Zaya voiced, "*Enough, Pirate King! Kyra is the name given by my birth father!*"

Shaw pronounced, "*Ky-ra!*" and locked his electric eyes on her. Zaya's line of thinking recalled when she heard her name last time. "*Kyra, I am counting on you.*" These are the last words that she heard from her father, Deyu.

Zaya cheered, "*I am hearing my real name after 15 years. You know what? You made me feel amazing, jackfruit.*" Shaw grumbled, "*Jackfruit!*"

Slowly, with hesitation, Shaw beamed, "*It's time to summon the peace messengers; I believe we are near!*"

After hearing him, she devoured every inch of wine. She opened, "*I have to finish sharpening my weapons soon,*" and directed her dancing feet to call the peace envoys.

Shaw's words paused her dancing feet, "*This quest of uniting the Yuvalle is not yours; better be a silent guest!*"

Zaya turned to him and fumed, "*My hands are free now and I will never take orders from anyone,*" and directed her foot towards the door.

Shaw's tight fingers loosen his grip and let the rum bottle down! He rushed his legs. With a hard bash, he closed doors and stood between Zaya and her way out. The sound of a hard bash hit the ears at the navigation point.

Zaya's almond eyes burned in anger; she lifted her chin up to stare at the tall captain!

She fumed, "*Shaw, stand by your limit!*" With soft eyes, Shaw bubbled, "*Kyra! Pirate King needs a queen and I wish not to lose my queen; give up this adventure!*" Zaya was stunned, and her almond eyes expanded. Shaw's brown lips gently caressed Zaya's petal lips. In no time, Shaw got a response from her lips. Their eyelids were closed, and they let their lips communicate their feelings. Moving wind paused at Shaw's chamber to cherish the new love!

Yuvalle is cursed! Cursed land has broken the principle of life!

Black shores never open to the mainland!

Dark forests and talking trees are the residences of ghosts!

Long rain and floating cotton balls never let sun rays touch the land!

The journey has just begun! Gale will halt and blow again!

Characters' Names

- Tibor: Commander of Alaokan naval units
- Zaka: Leader of Varuonans
- Akello: Young Alaokan warrior
- Figo: Young Alaokan warrior
- Neo: Akello's griffin
- Rudo: Figo's griffin
- Blu: Gamba's direwolf
- Amara: Love of Akello

- Zina: Akello's friend
- Kayon: Son of Zaya and commander of Varuonans
- Kino: Akello's friend
- Ekon: Commander of Alaokan air units
- Hibo: Griffin of Ekon
- Eric: Leader of Alaokans
- Gamba: Commander of Akello
- Davu: Grandfather of Akello
- Aro: Amara's griffin
- Moona: Sister of Akello
- Ava: Mother of Akello
- Gorath: Father of Eric
- Adio: Pirate lord
- Druzo: Captain of the pirate ship
- Kamau: Eric's beast
- Azog: Leader of Beku-neu
- Bora: Commander of Beku-neu
- Frida: Lead archaeologist of Beku-neu
- Liya: Messenger of peace (Beku-neu)
- Ivar: Strong man in the Azog's Beku-neu

- Kiba: Fastest archer in the Beku-neu
- Aurora: Daughter of Ivar
- Kuntala: Dead mammoth of Beku-neun troop
- Akara: Mammoth of Ivar
- Zaya: Beku-neun spy in Draguva
- Deyu: Late father of Zaya
- Tuva: Liya's griffin
- Ishiri: Medical minister of Draguva
- Rizon: Minister of dragons
- Valon: Lead archaeologist of the Dragon Land
- Yuda: Brother of Rizon
- Zion: Great grandfather of Draguvan leader
- Kirana: Wife of Rizon
- Shaw: Captain of the Kallan fleet
- Tandoor: Sub-captain of Kallan
- Simba: Hound of Shaw
- Irie: One who knows intel about Yuvalle
- Morgan: Brother of Shaw
- Nora: Shaw's late pet
- Sukra: Morgan's eagle

- Pirro: Royal eagle of Pirate King Keelan
- Luka: Half-brother of Keelan
- Darragh: Ally of Luka
- Keelan: King of pirates
- Helron - Notorious pirate outlaw

www.ingramcontent.com/pod-product-compliance
Lightning Source LLC
LaVergne TN
LVHW041139150826
845673LV00001B/47

9798888054239